Going Places

Billy Hopkins

headline

First published in 2003
by HEADLINE BOOK PUBLISHING

First published in paperback in 2004
by HEADLINE BOOK PUBLISHING

3

ISBN 0 7553 0220 6

Typeset in Plantin by Avon DataSet Ltd,
Bidford-on-Avon, Warwickshire

Printed and bound in Great Britain by
Clays Ltd, St Ives plc

Papers and cover board used by Headline are natural, recyclable products made from wood grown in sustainable forests. The manufacturing processes conform to the environmental regulations of the country of origin.

HEADLINE BOOK PUBLISHING
A division of Hodder Headline Limited
338 Euston Road
London NW1 3BH

www.headline.co.uk
www.hodderheadline.com

For my family

Foreword

Going Places is a work of fiction based on my experiences at home in England and abroad in East Africa. The incidents described in the book actually happened, though I admit to a certain amount of poetic licence in the telling. Apart from the famous names, however, the characters that appear in these pages are fictitious, created from the many people I met and worked with in Britain and Africa. I owe them all a debt of gratitude.

I should like to acknowledge the help of various people I consulted in writing this book. In particular, I wish to extend my thanks to those members of the Society of Medical Writers who advised me on medical matters; to Alan Domville, Motoring Correspondent of the *Warrington Guardian*; to my son Laurence and his wife Nichola, for reading and giving their reactions to an early draft; to the staff at Headline, especially Marion Donaldson and Sherise Hobbs, for their never-failing support and encouragement; to Justinia Baird-Murray and Andrew Wadsworth, for the design of the wonderful covers on all four of my books; and to Lynn Curtis, for her judicious observations in editing the finished manuscript.

Finally, my thanks go to my daughter Catherine, for her witty and imaginative comments along the way, and to my wife Clare, for her help, constructive criticism and patience in listening to my ramblings as I tried to arrange my chaotic thoughts into some kind of order.

If you derive as much enjoyment from reading the book as I did writing it, then my efforts have been worthwhile.

Billy Hopkins,
June 2003

Introduction

By 1950, the war had been over for five years and yet austerity and government controls were still the order of the day. There was a desperate shortage of houses in both the public and private sectors, the average time on the waiting list for council accommodation being between seven and eight years. The British people were suffering greater food shortages than any other Western nation, including the defeated Germans. Restrictions and rationing were even tighter than they had been during the war, particularly of meat. At Christmas the bacon ration had been cut to three ounces a week, barely half of what it had been in 1949. The Chancellor of the Exchequer, Sir Stafford Cripps, exhorted the country to further sacrifice, reminding the nation that there would be no jam today and none tomorrow either unless they had first earned it. 'We're up against it!' the posters announced. 'We must tighten our belts!'

'Easy for Cripps,' people said. 'He's a vegetarian.'

'A strange monastic-looking man,' said Harold Macmillan, 'emaciated and said to live off watercress grown off the blotting paper on his desk.'

Nevertheless the start of the year saw a change of mood as the cautious hopes of the early post-war years gave way to a new optimism. The second half of the twentieth century had begun and it was time for the nation to put the war behind it, roll up its sleeves and get down to the job of building a new Britain.

Towards the middle of the year, a number of notable events took place in the country. Soap and petrol rationing came to an end; Frank Sinatra made his London debut; and Princess Elizabeth gave birth to her second child, Anne. Denis Compton, the nation's handsome hero who not only played cricket for England but football for Arsenal, signed up to do the advertisement for Brylcreem and became forever associated with that product. Roger Bannister gave early indications that he would soon break the four-minute mile when, running against strong wind, he missed his target by only 14.8 seconds. In the FA Cup Final, Arsenal beat Liverpool 2–0, and prodigy Lester Pigott had already ridden fifty-nine winners before reaching his fifteenth birthday.

It was an exciting time to be alive, but for two young people at least these developments made little impact for they'd had other concerns on their mind. Billy Hopkins had been in a dream-like state ever since the day that Laura Mackenzie had agreed to become his wife, while Laura herself had been too preoccupied making final wedding plans to take note of what was happening on the world stage. Now all the hard work was behind them.

Chapter One

Billy and Laura sat opposite each other in a first-class compartment on the Manchester–Exeter express. It was the first time that either of them had travelled first-class and they revelled in the sumptuous wide seats, the deep cushions and padded arm rests.

'This I could get used to,' Billy said happily, gazing across at his bride.

'Me too,' she said. 'And, Billy, just think! A whole fortnight of bliss ahead of us. No school, no pupils, no time-tables and no bells ringing in our ears.'

'Only wedding bells,' he laughed. 'I think I can still hear them. Anyway, the ceremony seemed to go without a hitch. It shot by so quickly it's hard to take in that we're actually married and on honeymoon.'

'Billy,' she said, reaching across to take his hand, 'this is the happiest day of my life and one I shall treasure as long as I live.'

'Same goes for me, Laura, but I must admit it's a relief to have all the formalities over and done with.'

'Exactly the way I feel. Though one or two of our guests thought we'd left the party rather early.'

'Blame me for that. I felt our families might enjoy celebrating in their own particular ways: your lot having one of their posh musical evenings and mine having a knees-up down at the pub. Somehow I couldn't see mine listening to Schubert and nocturnes by Chopin. Apart from that, it's a long train journey to Devon, so we had to get away smartly. That's my excuse and I'm sticking to it.'

The guard's whistle interrupted their conversation, there was the waving of a green flag, and the train slid smoothly out of the station.

The luxury of the plush seats didn't last long. At Stockport the train became so crowded they had to give up one of their seats and share by raising the arm-rest. Billy moved across and they cuddled up to each other for the rest of the six-hour journey.

'I hope you don't mind?' a portly business traveller smiled, noticing the traces of confetti strewn about the compartment. 'I'm sure it'll be no hardship for you two young 'uns.'

Billy grinned as he held Laura close. 'We could complain to British Rail that we paid an exorbitant price for two seats and had to make do with one. Somehow I don't think we'll bother. Besides, it's the glorious twelfth and it may be dangerous to grumble too much with all those trigger-happy grouse shooters wandering about the place.'

The train wound its way through the western English counties, taking in the cathedral cities of Worcester, Cheltenham and Gloucester, but there was no respite from the overcrowding as more and more people boarded the train. Laura dozed off with her head on Billy's shoulder while he, lost in thought, continued to gaze out at the ever-changing prospect of cows and sheep, farms and fields, little towns and villages.

It was like a dream from which he might wake at any

moment. He recalled how he'd met Laura in the staff-room of St Anselm's School on his very first day of teaching and fallen for her the moment he clapped eyes on her. But their courtship had been far from easy. First, he'd had to woo her away from that prig Hamish Dinwoody, her long-standing boyfriend and the favourite contender with her father because of Hamish's glittering career prospects. Her dad had always hoped his eldest daughter would marry a man in one of the top professions, like medicine, law or accountancy, and Billy, a lowly teacher in a secondary modern school, hardly fitted the bill. Funny how things had turned out because Hamish was now engaged to Laura's younger sister, Jenny.

Then there had been Billy's own dad who'd objected to the match for exactly the opposite reasons.

'Listen to me, Billy lad,' he'd said. 'We're ordinary working-class folk while your girl belongs to the higher-ups. Mark my words, that can only lead to trouble. Best to stick to your own kind.'

The daft ha'porth, Billy said to himself now.

'A penny for them,' Laura said suddenly, opening her eyes.

'I was thinking how lucky I am to have you as my wife,' he said, hugging her tightly.

Late in the evening they arrived at Exeter's Rougemont Hotel, where bed and breakfast cost as much as Billy was paid in a week.

'I hope you don't imagine this will be our usual life style, Laura,' he said as they tucked into a five-course meal in the plush restaurant.

She took a sip of Beaujolais and laughed. 'You mean, you've been leading me up the garden path all this time?

You're not a millionaire and you've married me under false pretences?'

'Exactly, so that I could have my wicked way with you. After this feast, we'll be on basic rations. So better make the most of it.'

'Perhaps we should have brought a paper bag.'

After numerous jokes in this vein, it was time to retire to their room to spend their first night together and they were both nervous about the prospect. Apart from that, they were feeling drained, what with the excitement of the day, the long journey, the heavy meal and the wine. They wondered if their first night would be a success. Would they know what to do? And, crucially, would they be *able* to do it?

In sexual matters they were both naïve. At school they had learned about the birds and the bees, and in the sixth form had even reached reproduction in higher mammals – though never quite attaining that of human beings.

Much of Billy's knowledge had been gathered in the Fifth Form Smoking Club at lunch-times when members had puffed furtively on their fags in the alleyway behind the school and given each other the low-down. He was doubtful about much that he had learned: like the claim that all prostitutes advertised their profession by wearing a gold chain round the right ankle, or that the way to make a girl go mad with desire was to get your tongue down her right ear at the same time as caressing her left breast. These nuggets of information had never been confirmed as no one in the club had managed to get near enough to a girl to check them out.

On the other hand, Laura had been given dire warnings

at her convent school about boys and their licentious behaviour. The Reverend Mother had issued clear instructions on how to behave in their dealings with the opposite sex.

'First, as to periods. It will happen every month, and remember, it happened to the Blessed Virgin so don't worry about it.

'Second, if you're at a party and someone turns off the lights, go into the corner and announce in a clear voice: "I am a Catholic."

'Thirdly, if a boy invites you to sit on his knee, it is permissible so long as there's a book at least the thickness of the telephone directory between you and his lap.

'Finally, girls, whatever you do, never lose your mystery.'

Billy and Laura had laughed it off and taken it with a pinch of salt. But that had been at school, years ago. To fill the gaps in their knowledge they had read a Catholic Truth Society booklet entitled: *Before you Marry. What Every Catholic Couple Should Know*. Interesting though the booklet was, it didn't get down to specifics which, it stated, 'could be left to Mother Nature'. All very well but now they were faced with the real thing – sharing a room for the first time.

It didn't help matters when they found that the bridal suite consisted of two single beds.

'Didn't you book a double bed?' Laura asked.

'I booked a double *room*,' Billy said, flopping down on the bed nearest the window. 'I assumed that would mean a double bed. Where I come from, it's not the done thing for married couples to sleep in single beds.'

'I think you're supposed to specify a double bed.'

'Sorry. I'm not used to booking honeymoon accommodation. It's my first time. I'll try to get it right next time.'

'You could go down to the registration desk and complain,' Laura chuckled as she clicked open one of the suitcases.

'OK,' Billy said, arms behind his head, 'I'll do it provided you come with me. Can you imagine us marching through a crowded foyer and demanding a room with a double bed? Apart from that, look at the confetti we've already scattered about the place.'

'We could try moving the beds together.'

'No sooner said than done,' he replied, taking a firm grip on his bed and yanking it for all he was worth.

The bed didn't move. Not an inch.

'Wait a minute,' he said, getting down on all fours and looking under the bed. 'Laura, you're not going to believe this! The bed's bolted to the floor. It would take an engineer with a set of spanners and a fork-lift truck to move it.'

'Maybe single beds for married couples is the norm in this part of the world?'

'If that's so, no wonder there's a population crisis. Anyway it's been such an exciting day, I don't think I shall sleep well. You see, as a rule I'm not a sound sleeper. What I mean is: if I *were* a sound sleeper, I wouldn't sleep well.'

Laure giggled.

'You're mad. When I'm with you, I feel as if I'm in idiots' heaven.'

'Welcome to the club,' he said.

Billy remembered the advice his eldest brother had given him. Sam was an experienced married man with three kids and he, if anyone, ought to know.

'On your first night, Billy,' he'd said, 'don't make any demands and don't try anything adventurous. In other words, take it easy because you'll both be tired after a full day and a long train journey. Take my tip and do nothing. Get a good night's sleep.'

Sound advice and so they relaxed together, snuggling up close – not that there was much choice given the narrowness of a single bed.

'It's a strange thing, Laura, but I think fate is trying to tell us something. First we have to give up our seats and squash up. Now it looks as if we'll have to do the same in bed. It's a good job we're both Skinny Lizzies.'

'You speak for yourself,' she said, digging him playfully in the ribs.

That first night together, Billy provided the entertainment by going through his repertoire of imitative noises: bacon sizzling in a pan, eggs sputtering in a frying pan, bacon plus eggs sizzling and sputtering together in the same pan. To the romantic sound of these culinary impersonations Laura was lulled into slumber. Soon they were both in a deep sleep, their arms wrapped around each other.

Next morning they were up bright and early, and after a full English breakfast they re-packed their cases leaving behind a heap of confetti and a generous tip for the chambermaid. Then it was a wild dash for the morning train to Ilfracombe and from there a slow bus along labyrinthine roads to the small town of Combe Martin, their final destination. A taxi to the Marine View Hotel and then a fortnight of heaven.

They spent the rest of the day walking along the shore beneath the spectacular towering cliffs and exploring the little town with its steep, narrow streets where donkey-drawn carts were the only traffic. They discovered a thatched cottage-café and had their first taste of a Devonshire cream tea. It was a beautiful evening and the weather was mild. In the sheltered harbour they found a bench and, looking out to sea, sat there quietly in deep contentment, his arm around her and her head on his shoulder. Far out to sea they could see the lights of passing ships and the intermittent flashes of a distant lighthouse. They lingered overlong at the scene, both a little nervous about retiring to their room.

As dusk descended they returned to their hotel, and after a light evening meal went into their bedroom together. They undressed modestly as their Penny Catechism had instructed them to all those years ago, Billy in the bathroom, Laura in the bedroom.

'No looking!' he called from the bathroom.

'So, who's looking?' she laughed. 'Besides, what's there to hide? Have you forgotten that I have a brother? Not much is hidden in a family.'

The day had gone well: the journeys by train and by bus, the evening stroll to the harbour, and the walk through the town. Gradually, the village grew quiet. They lay together in the darkness, two young lovers in a new world, knowing each other for the first time. They could hear the murmur of the sea and far off the plaintive sound of a ship's siren.

'Listen to that,' she said. 'Have you ever heard anything so sad and sorrowful?'

They listened in silence for a while. Then Billy kissed her and they forgot all about the sea and the mournful sound of the ships. And they discovered that all their worries had been for nothing.

The fortnight which followed was euphoric. Every day they visited a place of interest: the Pack of Cards Inn, Appledore with its Maritime Museum; Great Torrington and its ancient market and glass-blowing works; the remains of the twelfth-century abbey at Hartland. In the final week they made the journey to the Elizabethan port of Bideford and gazed in awe at the statue of Charles Kingsley and the house where he had written *Westward Ho!* From there, they sailed across to Lundy Island – the puffin island with its grey seals, deer, wild goats and soaring cliffs.

'This place,' Billy said, as they made the return boat journey, 'would knock Blackpool Tower and its Golden Mile into a cocked hat. Somehow, the Pleasure Beach will never seem the same again.'

Too soon, the honeymoon came to an end and it was time to return to Manchester and reality.

Chapter Two

The taxi pulled up outside a large semi-detached house in Regina Park.

Billy said, 'Well, Laura, here we are. Home! I hope you're not expecting me to carry you over the threshold.'

'Why not? I think it's my right.'

'OK. As long as you don't mind being hoisted over my shoulder in a fireman's lift.'

'I think we'll forgo that pleasure and postpone it till we have our own house. Anyway you'd never manage to carry me up those stairs.'

Their rented flat was nothing to write home about, consisting as it did of a large lounge, bedroom, small kitchen and shared bathroom. Mrs Dobson, the owner, had had the first floor converted into a furnished flat for her son and his wife but his job had taken him to the south of England leaving the flat vacant – a stroke of luck for Billy and Laura. And on top of that Mrs Dobson, a nurse at Withington Hospital, was out on duty most of the time and so they had free run of the place. To add to their joy, they found they had £40 left in their joint bank account.

'You don't know how lucky we were to get this place, Billy,' said Laura, as they unpacked their cases. 'Flats like this are scarce as hen's teeth.'

'Don't I know it! Many couples have to start off living with the in-laws. Disaster all round. Our families are great but I wouldn't fancy living with either of them.'

'True. At the same time it *is* handy having my own family living close by in case we need them.'

'And we're also people of property now,' he laughed. 'See the things we own – two fireside chairs and a coffee table.'

'Bought second-hand from the Miscellaneous Sales columns,' she added. 'Perhaps the previous owners hadn't kept up with the HP payments. We can expect a visit from the bailiffs any time.'

'Maybe so but they can't touch our wedding presents. We acquired them legitimately. We have enough things to open a shop. Look at all the cutlery, crockery, table and bed linen, and I don't know how many assorted toasters, not forgetting the biscuit barrel from the school staff.'

They fell into a happy routine. Laura finished teaching at 3.30 and was home first while Billy was usually delayed by one thing or another and did not get back until around 5 p.m. They soon discovered each other's hidden talents and took up their specialised marital roles as if they had been trained for them since childhood – which they had. Laura conjured up the most delightful meals, baked her scones, pies, and the Mackenzie speciality – nutty nibbles. Billy revealed an unsuspected enthusiasm for DIY, tackling household chores and repairs: wiring up appliances, fixing sash windows, and putting up shelves.

'Billy,' Laura said one day, after he had successfully replaced the washer on a dripping tap, 'your talents in painting and decorating are legendary but I never knew you had plumbing abilities as well.'

'As a matter of fact, neither did I. Obviously you had not plumbed my depths.'

'Did anyone ever tell you that you're corny?' she asked.

'Not until now.'

A few days later, Billy was nailing down their new carpet, an off-cut spotted in a furniture shop on Stockport Road. He hit a carpet tack into place, and there was a satisfying, solid crunch as he hammered it home.

'There, that ought to do it,' he said, standing up. 'Another good job done.'

'Is there anything you can't do or wouldn't tackle?' she asked admiringly.

'We working-class types can turn our hand to most things. Chopping firewood, making fires . . . you name it, we'll have a go. It's called versatility.'

'What's that funny hissing noise?' Laura asked.

'Sounds like running water,' he said, peeling back a corner of the carpet.

Billy levered a floorboard back with his claw hammer and discovered the source of the sound. He had put a nail neatly into the cold water pipe. A small but steady stream of water was leaking through the ceiling of the room below.

There followed a madcap search to find the stopcock which Billy claimed had been deliberately hidden away by some malicious architect.

The next-door neighbour came to their rescue and showed them how to switch off the water supply.

'OK, I admit, there's a limit to my plumbing talents after all,' Billy said. 'I should have remembered the rhyme that claims it is the duty of the wealthy man to employ the services of the artisan.'

'Except we're not exactly wealthy,' Laura added, 'but now I think we'd better call Bob Parkinson. He's a real plumber. He has a sign on the side of his van which says: "We repair what your husband fixed".'

Pride of place in their possessions was given to the Sobel radiogram which Billy had bought on hire purchase from Campbell's on Market Street. A pound a month or five shillings a week, it hadn't seemed much at the time. Their collection of records was limited to the few Billy's brother Les had been willing to lend them. There were selections from *The White Horse Inn*, 'The Entry of the Boyars', Charles Kullman singing 'Angel's Serenade', and Ravel's 'Pavan for a Dead Infanta'. They played them over and over again until the vinyl was paper-thin.

Sometimes in the evenings they listened to the radio, made love, and listened to the radio again. Sometimes they did both at the same time. On Saturday nights it was Armchair Theatre and the voice of Conrad Black or Edgar Lustgarten.

One evening towards the end of October Billy came home from school a little later than usual, and as he opened the front door caught the aroma of apple pie baking in the oven. Laura had got home around four o'clock and it hadn't taken her long to get busy. He could hear her singing happily in the kitchen.

His mind went back to the Gardenia Court tenement where he had lived for many years with his parents and brother Les. There, the stairwell had reeked of pickled cabbage and rancid cooking oil, and the chief sound had been the strident bickering of the couple in the apartment below. Thank God I never have to go back to that dump again, he thought.

In the kitchen, Laura had dinner ready.

'Laura,' he said, 'I never thought I could be so happy. Every day when I get home, there you are. The simple fact that you are there takes my breath away. I have only to reach out to hold you and take you in my arms.'

'The same goes for me, Billy. I've come to recognise your footsteps long before you've turned the key in the door. I'm getting to know you so well: how you're feeling and what kind of mood you're in even before you speak.'

'This is the happiest time of my life,' he murmured. 'I can't get used to the idea that you are my wife. I'm so grateful to you for everything. And you look so happy, too. Radiantly happy.'

'I should hope so,' she laughed. 'After all, the motto of the Mackenzie clan is: I Shine, Not Burn.'

'Except, that is, when you forget the bacon under the grill. And whoever heard of a Scottish clan without Burns?'

'Very funny, I'm sure,' she replied. 'But I shine because I'm happy. I not only have a wonderful husband and home, but today I heard a wonderful piece of news. I was at the doctor's and it's confirmed – we're going to have a baby.'

Billy could hardly believe it.

'No! How did that happen? Is it anything I've done?' he exclaimed, holding her closely.

'I believe so. I couldn't have done it without you.'

'So that's how babies are made! That's where they come from! This is the secret my mam's been hiding from me all these years!'

'Billy, sometimes I think you're stark staring. Anyway the baby's due on the twelfth of May. Exactly nine months to the day from our wedding!'

'How about that for timing? Talk about a man of action! Now we must sit down and decide what we're going to call him.'

'You're sure it's a boy, then?'

'Of course. Why else would you be baking apple pie? Hasn't my mam told you that it's well known in Lancashire? Apple pie means boy; and cherry pie, girl.'

They laughed and joked the evening away.

A few weeks later Billy returned from school to find Laura crying quietly in the kitchen.

'What on earth has happened?' he asked, taking her in his arms.

'Mrs Dobson has been to see me,' she wept. 'Her son is returning to Manchester with his wife and their young baby and she needs the flat back. She's given us a week's notice.'

Billy was aghast.

'I don't understand. I thought we had this flat for a year at least. What happened?'

'Her son's taken a new job here. She was sorry and all that but there it was. She had to think of her own family first.'

'But a week's notice! That's just before Christmas. What are we going to do? Where can we go?'

'I'm sure my parents will put us up until we find something,' said Laura through her tears. 'Old Auntie Agnes can move out of her room and share with Gran'ma.'

'No, no, I'm grateful but I don't want to stay with your parents and maybe cause friction between Auntie and Gran'ma. Apart from that, your dad was so disappointed when we wed before we'd raised the five hundred pounds he reckoned was the minimum required for a sound start, I can just hear him saying "Told you so".'

'I'm sure Daddy would never say such a thing.'

'Maybe not, but he'd certainly think it. I'd rather stay with my own folks. Gardenia Court is no Garden of Eden but it shouldn't be for long. We'll soon find our own place.'

In the week before Christmas, they packed up their possessions – Sobel radiogram included – and loaded them on to the second-hand pram which they had bought from a junk shop in anticipation of the new baby. While Billy struggled with the two heavy suitcases, Laura pushed the pram. They trudged along Laindon Road which led to the Mackenzies' home where they were to store their things. To add to their misery, it started to snow.

'If I'd read a scene like this in a novel, even a Dickens one,' said Billy, 'I'd have dismissed it as melodramatic codswallop.'

'This year, instead of *watching* the Nativity play,' Laura said ruefully, 'we're *in* it.'

'Not merely *in* it. We *are* the Nativity play.'

'All we need now is a stable and an ass to complete the picture,' she added.

As they turned into Kedelston Avenue, they met Billy's friend Titch. How glad they were to see him!

Titch gave them a friendly wave.

'At least *he* looks happy,' Billy said.

'He doesn't look happy to me,' Laura remarked. 'He looks downright miserable.'

'That *is* Titch looking happy.'

As he approached, Billy said, 'Titch! We were just talking about you. How good of you to come!'

'I thought you might need an extra pair of hands,' he said.

'Sure thing,' Billy replied, handing him one of the cases – the heavier one. 'Here, you can be one of the three Wise Men. When we've dropped this stuff off, we can go back for the fireside chairs.'

For the holiday period, they went to live with Billy's folk in Gardenia Court.

'I'm sorry to put you to all this trouble, Mam,' he said. 'We hope we don't spoil your Christmas.'

'Nonsense,' she said. 'You're always welcome – it's still your home and we're here whenever you need us. You can have your old room back. And, remember, it's always darkest before sundown.'

Chapter Three

Billy had been dreading going back to Gardenia Court and hoped their enforced stay would not be a long one. The smell of the place was unforgettable. When he'd departed in August, he'd thought he'd left the malodorous place behind for good but it was not to be for here he was, back with his young wife, and nothing had changed. The same old graffiti-decorated stairwell with its stale food stench, the same nosy neighbours, the same old Mrs Mulligan from next door borrowing cups of sugar 'till Paddy gets his dole money', the same old Pittses in the apartment below shrieking abuse at each other in their never-to-be-resolved wrangling match.

Billy and Laura had considered the idea of renting a house but there was none to be had, not even a pre-fab. As for applying for a place on the Corporation housing list, it was pointless unless you had a house full of kids and were prepared to wait forever. All the same, they were determined to make their stay with Billy's family as short as possible. So, from the moment Mrs Dobson gave them notice, they had begun scouring the Houses for Sale columns in the *Manchester Evening News* for likely-looking properties. It had not looked too hopeful as most of the houses within reasonable distance of school were out of their price league.

Meanwhile they tried to spend as much time as they could out of Billy's parents' flat and out of the way. On their first weekend back in Cheetham Hill, they took the bus to Heaton Park where they'd spent many happy courting days, but the weather was miserable, the sky heavy with clouds that threatened more snow. It was bitterly cold and as the lake was frozen over, hiring a boat was out of the question. Even visits to Fletcher Moss were no longer enjoyable. Instead, they spent their evenings at the cinema and saw some of the great classic films of the day: *The Third Man, Brighton Rock, Sunset Boulevard.* It gave Billy the chance to introduce Laura to some of the district cinemas with pretentious names like the Riviera, the Temple, the Premier, the Shakespeare.

Mam was no problem and welcomed the newlyweds with open arms. She and Laura got on well together and it wasn't long before they were swapping recipes in the tiny kitchen. Laura shared the secret of the Mackenzie family's 'nutty nibbles', and as for Mam, when it came to the subtleties of Lancashire hot-pot, or 'tater-ash' as she called it, no one could hold a candle to her. And although she had spent twenty-two years ministering to Billy's needs – feeding him, seeing to the washing of his clothes, and in earlier days the back of his neck – now Mam tactfully left matters like this to his new wife.

No, Dad was the worry. He didn't take kindly to having 'visitors' staying in the house. Billy remembered only too well the time during the war when his sister Flo had brought her husband Barry home on leave. Dad had spent much of his time then muttering to himself and making disapproving snorting noises. Billy needn't have worried, though, for if anything his dad went out of his way to make a good impression on Laura. He even tried to crack a few jokes, like the time he remarked on some soprano on the Home Service singing a song about the merry pipes of Pan.

'Listen to that, Billy,' he said. 'Why, your mother can sing as good as that.' Then he added with a grin, 'Horrible, isn't it?'

And, wonder of wonders, he invited Billy to join him in the Milan, his local pub on Rochdale Road, the first time he had ever asked him out 'for a gill'. Billy felt highly privileged for Dad had always regarded his pub as sacred, his sanctuary and his one escape from family responsibilities. Once ensconced in his corner seat with his cards or his dominoes in his hand, he could cast off the roles of father and husband and become Tommy, one of the lads, laughing and joking like the rest of them, an altogether different person from the one they knew at home. 'He hangs his fiddle in the hall as he walks in through the door,' Mam used to say. In the pub, however, there was a different hierarchy and a different set of rules and Tommy's status was high, not only as a crib player but as one 'who always got his round in', though on this special occasion it was Billy who did the honours and bought two pints of best mild. He had often wondered what would happen if he asked for two pints of worst mild. Would it have been cheaper or stronger? He'd never put it to the test.

There was something special about a pub atmosphere – the sweet smell of ale, the tobacco smoke, and twenty men talking excitedly all at once – that brought out this other Dad, this happy laughing man they rarely saw at home. Whatever it was, it set him off talking much more than usual. Billy bought the beers and set them down on the table. His dad took out his Player's Weights and offered Billy one. Another first. Billy took it happily and was quick to light the match. They puffed on their fags and took a good sup of their ale. Dad leaned forward and adopted a confidential tone.

'I want to give you a piece of advice,' he said.

Hello, Billy thought. What's coming? What kind of advice? How to live a full life? How to achieve happiness in marriage? The 'advice' turned out to be more mundane.

'I'm glad to see, Billy, that you got your round like you did. Never be a man with short arms and deep pockets. Whenever you visit a pub with your mates, always, always pay your whack. You'll never be told when it's your turn to get 'em in and your mates will never let on if you fail to put your hand in your pocket. But make no mistake, it'll be noticed and remarked on as soon as you leave the room. The scandal will stick and it'll never go away. Your reputation as a "welcher" will follow you to the grave, and even after that it will attach to your kids. And, who knows, maybe *their* kids as well. Why, it may even become a permanent family nickname, like "the skinflints" or "the tight-arses", and you'll never shake it off.'

'Thanks, Dad. I'll remember.'

His father took a long pull at his pint and Billy watched, fascinated, the rise and fall of his Adam's apple as the ale glugged down his throat.

'The first drink of the evening is always the best,' he said finally. 'But, you know, Billy, drinking's a mug's game. I've never liked the stuff. Wouldn't give you a penny a bucket for it.'

I think I may have heard you say that before, Dad, Billy thought. At least a thousand times.

'You see, lad, it's the market. We work bloody hard from four in the morning till dinnertime and it puts a terrible thirst on a man. Market-men are hard drinkers. Every day I've put in eight hours pulling that handcart, slaving my guts out, and many's the time I've felt like jacking it all in. But there was always one thing that kept me going. Know what that was?'

Billy was tempted to suggest 'five pints of Tetley's bitter' but he already knew the answer that was coming. It was one of Dad's stock speeches.

'What was that, Dad?'

'The knowledge that one day you would make good. I always believed in a sound education and encouraged you to make the best of yourself.'

You bloody liar, Billy thought. How can you go through life fibbing to yourself like this? If it had been left to you, I'd have been working as your assistant porter, pulling the cart back when you went downhill and pushing like crazy when you were going up.

It was time for the second part of Dad's speech, though.

'You've got your brains from me. So have the rest of the family. They could all have gone to the top, but the others never had the chances you've had. You've got me to thank for that. Your mother was never keen on you going to that posh Damian Grammar School or that London college, but I saw where it could lead to. And now you've joined the higher-ups. A teacher married to another teacher from Regina Park. You've got it made, lad.'

Billy couldn't take much more of this. He had to escape, even if just for a moment. Dad had been the one who had opposed further education for Billy all along the line; it had been his mam who had done the pushing despite the obstacles Dad had put in the way.

'I'll just go to the back,' Billy said, adopting the local jargon.

'You mean, for a Jimmy Riddle.'

Billy left his pint and went to the urinal in the yard. When he came back, his glass was empty.

'What's up? Aren't you drinking?' his dad said, looking at the empty glass.

'I must be a faster drinker than I thought,' Billy answered.

'A chip off the old block,' his dad said proudly.

Tommy went to the bar to get his round in. While he was there, Billy could see him boasting to his cronies about his son, the teacher. Like a Jewish mother crowing, except that the position of teacher was not something any self-respecting Jewish mother would boast about. He caught bursts of Dad's conversation as he waited for the pints to be pulled.

'That's my son Billy . . . Father-in-law an Inspector of Taxes. Lives in Regina Park . . . Studied in London . . . Speaks French, knows algebra, does the *Telegraph* crossword . . .'

His fellow drinkers looked across at Billy as if he were a Martian and nodded in his direction. He returned the nods and tried to look like Einstein.

On the Thursday before Christmas Billy and Laura had a stroke of luck. They were poring over the *Manchester Evening News* as usual and had found only three likely-looking houses in the ads column. They read a little more closely and saw that one of them, located on the edge of Regina Park, had possibilities. The estate agent's description read:

Period terraced house of character with great potential in select, secluded, sought-after part of Regina Park. Three commodious bedrooms, attic and cellar. Dining room with unique traditional fireplace and unusual lounge. Compact convenient kitchen. Neat bathroom with separate WC. Sound plumbing and electric wiring. Ideal property for a DIY enthusiast keen on modernisation. Mature gardens. £1500. The road is maintained by the Regina Park Trust.

Billy declared, 'It's four and a half times my annual salary and that means it's out of our price range. Besides, where are we going to find the huge deposit that'll be needed?'

'It won't do any harm to take a look,' said Laura. 'At least it'll give us an idea of what's on offer.'

Though still unsure, Billy phoned the estate agent's from the local call box and made an appointment to inspect the house immediately after Christmas.

'You'll have to move quickly,' the agent told him. 'There's considerable interest in that particular property.'

On Boxing Day there was the annual Hopkins family get-together in the little Gardenia Court flat. Billy's two older sisters were there with their husbands and children. Flo and Barry brought their three youngsters, Polly and Steve their four, and with Les, Billy and Laura too there was hardly room to move. Only Billy's eldest brother and his family were missing.

'It's a good job our Sam has decided to stay in Belfast with his wife and kids this year,' said Dad, 'or it'd be like Maine Road football ground in here.'

Mam and Laura had prepared a magnificent buffet while Dad had used his influence at the Milan to organise a firkin of beer. That had caused a certain amount of amusement in the pub when he'd spoken to the landlord about it.

'Joe,' he'd said, 'I'd like to order a firkin.'

'A firkin what?' the landlord had replied, quick as a flash.

Good for a laugh amongst the regulars.

After the food and beer were seen off, the flat was filled with cigarette smoke and loud renditions of the popular numbers of the day, like 'I've Got a Lovely Bunch of Coconuts', 'Buttons and Bows', and sentimental ditties like 'Now Is the Hour', while Les gave his lively imitation of Josef Locke's 'Goodbye', the whole company waving their hankies in tearful farewell. Mam supplied an appropriate finale with her rendition of 'Keep Right On to the End of the Road' with everyone joining in the final chorus. Lastly, Dad gave his annual speech on how proud he was of his family and how he had always tried to bring them up properly, put a trade in their hands, taught them to be friendly and never get above themselves. Mam did the usual sniping from the sidelines.

'You've worked your fingers to the bone,' she said, 'and what have you got to show for it?'

'Bony fingers!' Billy said quickly before his brother Les could get it in, as he did every year.

'It wouldn't be Christmas without all this,' Billy's brother-in-law Steve Keenan observed. He took Billy and Laura to one side for a little chat.

'So, how are you finding married life?' he asked.

'Should we tell them the news?' Billy said, looking at Laura inquisitively. She approved with a smile and a nod.

'We're going to have a baby,' he announced to the company.

His brother Les was the first to react. 'I don't believe it. My kid brother, a father! The mind boggles.'

'Another grandchild!' Mam exclaimed. 'I am glad to hear that but if we have any more, we'll have to get a bigger flat for these here family dos.'

'A baby already!' his older sister Polly remarked. 'That was quick. Why, you've only just got married. When's it due?'

'May the twelfth,' Billy answered. 'And before you ask, we were married on August the twelfth.'

There was a brief silence while the family took it in. His eldest sister Flo consulted her diary and began calculating. Mam counted off the months on her chin.

Finally Polly said, 'Why, you must have started a baby almost on day one! Talk about fast workers!'

'Speedy Gonzales isn't in it!' Les cried, unable to keep the admiration out of his voice. 'There's this joke about Speedy Gonzales and an actress . . .'

'We'll have none of them smutty jokes, thank you very much,' Mam said. 'Remember, it's Christmas.'

'It's like a Victorian melodrama,' Flo's husband Barry commented. 'A baby on the way and no home to go to. We only need a cruel mustachioed landlord with a name like Jasper Hawkins ordering them out into the snow.'

'We've already played that scene,' Laura said, smiling. 'As for having no home, that matter is in hand. At least, we've begun looking. We've an appointment to view a house next week. Show them the *Evening News* ad, Billy.'

He passed the ad around the company. As he'd expected, it brought forth a succession of feeble jokes from the family who all fancied themselves comedians.

Les read out the estate agent's euphemistic descriptions

of the 'desirable residence' and Steve started the ball rolling.

'Estate agents are well known for laying it on with a trowel,' he said. 'Even the term "estate agent" suggests rolling acres of parkland dotted with trees around a big country house. They've invented their own vocabulary. For example, 'period terraced house' is shorthand for old and dilapidated hovel.'

'As for "great potential",' Barry laughed, 'that's estate agent speak for practically falling down and needs a lot doing to it to make it habitable, while "secluded" translates to "five miles from the shops" and suitable for hermits.'

Les, who had recently joined the Labour Party, couldn't be left out of the exchange. 'I see you're planning to live in the leafy suburbs among the Tories,' he remarked. 'But I'm sure that "compact and convenient kitchen" means it's just right for a couple of Tom Thumb characters who can reach all the cupboards without moving. At least you won't need to employ domestic servants.'

And Dad had to put in his two cents' worth.

'I don't know what traditional fireplace means,' he chortled, 'it could be a couple of stones in the middle of the room.'

'OK, OK,' Billy said, 'you've had your fun. It's academic anyway since we can't afford a house like this. Not with our tiny bank balance.'

'On a more serious note, Billy,' Les said, 'if ever you do find a house to your liking, let me know. The firm I work for has been using the services of a good financial and insurance consultant by the name of William Steele. He can advise you and even fix you up with a mortgage.'

'Thanks for that, Les,' said Billy. 'I'll remember it if we ever need one.'

At nine o'clock the party broke up when family members departed to put the kids to bed, Les went out to meet his girl friend Annette, and Dad, despite the availability of his firkin, could not resist the nightly pull of his local. At last, peace and quiet were restored.

'What a marvellous family you've raised, Mrs Hopkins,' Laura said warmly. 'All great characters.'

'You never met my brother Jim,' Billy said. 'He was killed in the war but he was my hero.'

'What was it about him that you admired?' Laura asked.

'Oh, I dunno. Maybe it was his free and easy approach to life, his sense of adventure and love of travel. He was a man after my own heart.'

'And look where it got him in the end,' Mam said quietly. 'No, our Billy, you're better off like you are. Learn to appreciate what you've got without always wanting to see what's round the next corner. And about that house you were talking about . . .' she continued. 'I've got a bob or two in the Co-op Bank, and I want you to know it's yours whenever you need it. You've only to ask.'

That bob or two she's talking about, Billy thought, has taken her forty years to accumulate by scrimping and scraping, saving a penny here and a penny there.

'Thanks, Mam,' he said. 'It's good to know that you're always there, ready to lend a hand when it's needed. But I think this house is going to cost more than a bob or two.'

Later in the week they caught the 53 bus and went to see the house which was situated some considerable distance from Stockport Road. There were twelve similar terraced houses in the street – six on each side. Like the rest of Regina Park, the surface of the road consisted of pot-holes filled in with mud and cinders.

'So much for the "maintained by Regina Park Trust" bit,' Billy said as they approached the place.

The owner of the property, Mr Jack Morgan, proudly showed them around the house and its amenities. He told them that he would soon be retiring with his wife Minnie to a cottage in North Wales, and how much he was going to miss this house's modern plumbing and electrics. Billy and Laura smiled, nodded politely, and made approving noises as the owner pointed out the most interesting features: the lavatory in the cellar with the light switch in the kitchen, the 'unique' fireplace which belched smoke into the room, the L-shaped lounge, the bathroom with its giant-sized cistern, its pygmy-sized bath and flatulent pipes, the Heath-Robinson hot water system, and the numerous cupboards and bedroom fittings which he had built himself.

'Talk about the house Jack built,' Laura exclaimed as they caught the bus back.

'Plumbing and electricity designed by Picasso and installed by Thomas Edison,' Billy said.

'As for that "compact convenient kitchen",' Laura laughed, 'I think that meant "big enough to swing a small kitten around". I can't see us buying it.'

'I'm sure you're right,' Billy sighed. 'But there are so few properties on the market that beggars can't be choosers.'

'We'd have to be desperate to go for a place like that.'

'We *are* desperate, Laura. I'd rather move into that house than go on staying with my folks, as nice as they are. But why are we talking like this? There's no way we can afford it. We have just a hundred pounds in the bank and we'd need to find a deposit of around three hundred. Then there's solicitor's and surveyor's fees on top of that.'

'And we have no furniture to speak of, remember.'

'Mam has offered to help us out but I think the sums involved are way beyond her "bob or two". Maybe we'd better forget the whole thing.'

'I never liked the house anyway,' she said.

'Sour grapes,' Billy replied.

Chapter Four

New Year's Day was spent at the Mackenzies. Everyone was there except Laura's brother Hughie who was still doing his National Service in Malaya. Apart from family members Jenny had brought her fiancé Hamish. And, of course, there was Duncan, Laura's father. To Billy, he was Big Dunk, an awesome figure who ruled his family with a firm hand and whose every word was law. An enlightened despot perhaps, but a despot nevertheless. Before dinner Duncan gave everyone a careful measure of Bristol Cream in correct schooner-shaped sherry glasses. A toast was drunk to George VI and to New Year 1951, and then glasses were raised in a strange pledge:

Here's tae us, wha's like us?
Gey few, and they're a' deid.

Billy made a mental note to ask Laura its meaning when they got back to Gardenia Court.

Everyone sat down to dinner and Duncan carved the leg of pork which had used up the family's weekly meat ration and been 'specially bought from Goldstone's the butcher in Manchester's Shambles. In allocating portions Duncan applied the same studied care he had demonstrated with the sherry. His wife Louise and their three daughters, Laura, Jenny and Katie, brought on the rest of the meal – the gravy, apple sauce, roast potatoes and wide selection of vegetables.

'I always said you would have made a fine surgeon, Duncan,' Gran'ma said, eyeing the piece he had cut for her and hoping her flattering remark might earn a bigger share from her son.

'Not too much for me, Duncan,' old Auntie said. 'Especially that crackling. I dinna think my digestive system will cope with all that fat.'

'I'm sure I can cope with anything she doesna want,' Gran'ma said slyly.

When all were served, Duncan said grace and then with a nod gave the signal that everyone could begin.

Dinner proceeded in the usual way, all remarks and observations directed first to Big Dunk for evaluation. Billy saw how happy and content Laura was as she sat with her family at the table. She laughed and joked and joined in the conversation, and he noticed how her speech acquired a faint Scottish burr. She was so much at home literally and metaphorically, so relaxed and at ease, that seeing her thus he felt a pang of guilt to have taken her away from this comfort and security to a place like Gardenia Court. Somehow, he had to provide a house and a home for her. And soon.

After dinner, Duncan invited Billy and Hamish to his study for a post-prandial brandy and cigar. Uh-oh, Billy thought, here we go for the 'told you so' speech. He didn't have to wait long.

'So, Billy, how are you and Laura coping now you've been evicted?' Duncan said, swirling his brandy round the balloon glass.

'I think "evicted" is too strong a word, Mr Mackenzie. Mrs Dobson needed the flat for her son and his wife, that's all.'

'It amounted to the same thing, did it not? And now you're lodging with your own parents?'

'It's only a temporary situation. We're looking at houses for sale and I don't think it will be too long before we find something.'

'As I told you before you married, you need at least five hundred pounds in the bank before you should contemplate marriage.'

This was the cue for Hamish to join in, the prig.

'Jenny and I have taken your advice, Mr Mackenzie,' he sucked up. 'We have been saving for the last two years and should have well over five hundred by this time next year.'

Yuck! Billy thought. How I would love to give this prat a fourpenny one to add to his five hundred quid. Laura was lucky to escape from marrying this snooty-faced snob.

'As I said, Mr Mackenzie,' Billy continued, 'we've been looking at houses and think we may have found one on the edge of Regina Park.'

What was he saying? How could they afford it?

'That would please me a great deal,' Duncan said. 'To see you and Laura happily settled in your own home, especially now you're expecting a baby, would make me a happy man. And if you had a degree – that would be the icing on the cake as far as I'm concerned.'

'*I* should soon finish my degree in Business Management at Glasgow,' Hamish smirked. 'As you know, I am specialising in actuarial studies. My tutors expect me to get at least a two-one.'

'I'd like to give you one,' Billy muttered under his breath.

'I've no fears for you and Jenny,' Duncan replied. 'No, it's Billy here and Laura I'm a trifle worried about. I think they may have married too soon, before they have established a firm financial footing.'

'It's early days, Mr Mackenzie,' Billy said 'You don't know what the future may hold.'

What a pathetic answer, he thought to himself. I left myself open there all right.

'Exactly,' Duncan remarked, as Billy had known he would.

A little later that evening Hamish left with Jenny to join a family party at his own home. Billy was glad to see them go. With any luck, Hamish would fall down a manhole.

As the hall clock struck eight, Duncan announced that he had to go over to the 104 Club on Princess Road 'to take a look at the account books'.

Laura had explained to Billy that everyone in her family recognised that 'taking a look at the account books' was her father's euphemism for going to the club for a drink with his cronies.

Billy thought it odd to be going to the club on New Year's Day but the family did not seem surprised. Duncan's next suggestion bowled Billy over.

'I wondered, Billy, if you'd care to join me?'

This was more startling than his own dad's invitation to his local.

Laura smiled and looked pleased.

'Why, I'd love to, Mr Mackenzie,' Billy stammered.

'Then we'll get our coats and be off.'

It was a short drive to Princess Road. They entered the club up a flight of stairs and Billy walked into a new world, a man's domain and a haven of peace and quiet where men could put the rest of the world to rights, though at that particular moment a few members were concentrating their whole attention on snooker balls. Round the small bar sat four middle-aged gentlemen engaged in a discussion about the war in Korea and the possibility that Truman might drop the atomic bomb. One of the faces looked familiar and Billy was sure he'd seen it before somewhere but couldn't place it.

Remembering his dad's advice, he offered, 'Let me get the first round, Duncan. What'll it be?'

His father-in-law grinned as he replied, 'Sorry, Billy. Only members may order drinks. So you'll find it's a cheap night.'

Duncan ordered a bottle of Double Diamond for himself and a glass of Tetley's for Billy. Not a full pint, Billy noticed, but a half. What his dad called a 'gill'.

'Let me introduce you to my son-in-law, Billy Hopkins,' Duncan said to his friends.

'Billy, meet Pat Ryan. Pat is head of woodwind in the Hallé Orchestra.'

Wow! Billy was in distinguished company. He shook Pat's hand warmly.

'And you may have heard of my next friend, Billy. This is John Barbirolli – or I should say *Sir* John Barbirolli now.'

Sir John took Billy's hand in a firm grip. 'Happy to know you,' he said.

Billy swallowed hard and for a few moments remained dumb-struck. Was he dreaming? He had just shaken the hand of one of the foremost conductors in the world, the hand that had guided so many world-renowned orchestras, including Manchester's Hallé, the hand of the man who had succeeded Toscanini as conductor of the New York Philharmonic. Duncan really did move in the highest circles and here was Billy from Collyhurst Buildings being introduced into them.

The other two companions were Joe Clayton, owner of a string of chemist's shops, and finally Alfred Havekin, headmaster of a large Catholic secondary school.

Billy noticed the way the professional classes introduced people by first stating their name and then their occupation in order to establish social status. A person was thus defined by what he did. It usually went, 'Let me introduce Mr Jones the doctor . . .' Or dentist, solicitor, whatever.

So different from the working class. He couldn't imagine his dad saying, 'This is Joe Bloggs, the dustman.' But then, this exclusive club was nothing like his dad's local.

Duncan arranged to make up a foursome in a game of snooker with Joe Clayton, Pat Ryan and Sir John. How strange to see the great Barbirolli as one of the boys, coat off and chalking the end of a snooker cue. The last time Billy had seen him had been at the King's Hall, Belle Vue, when the stick in his hand had been considerably shorter.

Billy was left at the bar with Alf Havekin the headmaster.

'So, young sir, is it true what Duncan tells me, that you're teaching at St Anselm's Secondary?' Alf said.

Billy replied in the affirmative.

'How do you find working for Frank Wakefield, our famous rugby-playing scoutmaster?'

'I love working for him,' Billy said warmly. 'I have learned a lot from him, especially since he has his office at the back of my classroom and occasionally takes part in the lessons.'

'That's Frank Wakefield all over,' Alf chuckled. 'But which class do you teach?'

'The top class of fourteen to fifteen year olds.'

'Well done, young sir! It takes special talent to be able to handle the top class.'

Billy felt ten feet tall.

The rest of the evening flowed easily, as did the half-pints and the conversation. Billy said little but drank it all in. Towards ten-thirty, Duncan decided it was time to make tracks. As they were about to leave, he took Billy to one side.

'Do you have a bank account?'

'Yes, I do, Duncan.'

'Then put this in it,' he said, handing Billy an envelope.

A little puzzled, he opened the envelope. Inside was a cheque for one hundred and twenty-five pounds, equivalent to five months' salary.

Duncan smiled at him.

'Let's call it a delayed wedding present.'

Next day Laura and he had an urgent conversation in Billy's bachelor bedroom – the only place they could hold one in private.

'Do you think we can swing it, Billy?' she asked. 'Can we raise enough capital to go for that house in Regina Park?'

'Just about. We now have two hundred and twenty-five pounds, Mam reckons she can give us another hundred and also lend us whatever else we need of what she calls her "bob or two".'

'Oh, Billy, let's try for it. I'm sure that, given enough time, we can knock that house into shape.'

'But I thought you weren't struck on it?'

'That was when I thought we couldn't raise the money. I didn't want you to think I wanted it and you were letting me down by not being able to afford it.'

Women, he thought. I'll never understand 'em.

'Right,' he said. 'Our first move is to call in that financial wizard our Les has been going on about. What was his name again?'

'William Steele,' she said.

Chapter Five

The following week, Billy arranged to visit William Steele in his office on Mosley Street. Billy had emptied their savings account and had £225 in notes burning a hole in his inside pocket.

'Do you realise, Laura,' he said as he left the house, 'that I'll be worth coshing for the fortune I'm carrying this morning?'

He decided to walk to town as he was afraid some thief on the bus might spirit the money out of his jacket. He made it safely to his destination and took the lift to the second floor where he found the estate agent's office. Engraved on the glass door was a sign which read: 'Financial, Insurance and Brokerage Services: William Steele, Managing Director'. All most impressive.

William Steele was a rubicund young man with a smooth patter. He couldn't have been more than thirty yet was balding and had already developed a paunch, the sign of a rich diet or too many bread and butter puddings. He held out a hand in welcome and greeted Billy effusively.

'Good to see you, old boy. Your brother Les has told me all about you. I believe you have found a house and would like me to find you a mortgage?'

'Thank you, Mr Steele,' Billy replied. 'I'd appreciate your help and advice.'

'No need for all that formality,' he said. 'Call me Will. Everyone else does.'

'Right then, Will. We've found a house in Regina Park and made an offer of fifteen hundred pounds which has been accepted. We've raised enough money for a deposit.'

Steele then asked about Billy's salary and prospects and gave him details of the kinds of mortgages available.

'Les tells me you may be expecting a little stranger in the near future,' he said ingratiatingly. 'Leave it to me, old boy. I shall hold your hand throughout the nasty complex proceedings. I'm referring to the house purchase, of course, not the birth of your baby. Ha, ha.'

Billy joined in politely with the laughter, though he didn't think it was that funny.

'Now, as you're going to be a family man,' Steele continued, 'I'd recommend an endowment mortgage over a twenty-year period. If you take it with profits it will mean that at the end you will not only redeem your mortgage but have a tidy sum over to spend on a round-the-world trip with your missus.'

'How does it work?' Billy asked.

'You take out a mortgage loan with the Berkeley Building Society for the required amount. Alongside that you have a policy with my company, Steele Securities. We put your money into a wide range of investments in the Stock Market, mainly gilt-edged. At present we are earning high returns, but obviously these can go up or down. At the end of the period, your investments pay off the mortgage and any profits beyond that are yours to spend as you wish.'

'It sounds great,' Billy said. 'Where do I sign?'

Steele pushed across various documents he had already prepared. Billy handed over the money and obtained a receipt.

'You should now consult your solicitor about conveyancing,' Steele said. 'If you hurry him along there's no reason why we shouldn't exchange contracts in about four weeks' time.'

Half an hour later a euphoric Billy was on his way out of the building, his pocket very much lighter. It was a day of jubilation when he got back to Gardenia Court to give Laura the good news.

'I've done the business and found a mortgage with a building society,' he announced. 'They are willing to lend us eighty-five per cent of the cost of the house over a twenty-year term.'

'Oh, Billy, I'm so happy,' she said, hugging him tightly. 'Just think – a place of our own at last. And so soon!'

'That's me all over,' he said. 'A man of action, not words.'

'I must admit, though,' she said, looking at him intently, 'I couldn't help feeling we should have slept on it before you signed anything. Maybe had a chat with Daddy before we committed ourselves. Taken time to think it over . . .'

If there was one thing Billy did not want to do it was talk it over with Daddy. He was eager to show Laura he could look after her, could make decisions without the need for outside advice.

'What's there to think over?' he said. 'We take out a twenty-year mortgage and a "with-profits" endowment policy to cover it. And, hey presto! The place is ours. I don't know about you but I'm in a hurry to get into our own house and begin the business of making a home.'

'Of course I am, my love. I only hope you've made the right choice,' she answered. 'But what am I saying? Of course you have. I'm forgetting – you're my man of action. But twenty years . . . That'll take us to 1971. Why, we'll be forty-three years old!'

'That's right,' he laughed. 'Two old codgers! Grey-haired, ordering our wheel-chairs and polishing our walking sticks.'

'And I'm sure you noticed, Billy,' she grinned, 'that the company you've signed up with, "Financial, Insurance, Brokerage Services", makes up the acronym FIBS!'

Billy laughed, though it sounded hollow. 'Laura, don't be so suspicious. How does that song go – about accentuating the positive and eliminating the negative? Look on the bright side. The firm's a reputable one, recommended by my brother Les.'

'You're right, Billy. It must be my Scottish upbringing. We were taught to be canny. I'm sure everything's going to be all right.'

'Of course it is. Will Steele is completely trustworthy and honest.'

As Billy pronounced the name Laura looked at him steadily. It was a moment or two before the penny dropped.

'I didn't say a word,' she said.

'Ah, what's in a name?' he asked finally.

'Are we going to be able to pay for everything?' she wondered.

'Just about. My salary's twenty-five pounds and the mortgage is going to cost over nine pounds a month. That leaves three pounds for rates, coal, gas and electricity, and around thirteen pounds for all the rest – food, chemist, clothes, etcetera.'

'We'll never manage, Billy! Not on thirteen pounds. We'll never cover all the other bills. I shall have to go on working after I've had the baby.'

* * *

It was four weeks before they were given the keys to their new home: the terraced Victorian house in the quiet cul-de-sac named Pine Grove, though there wasn't any grove and only one pine tree. But it had the advantage of being only a mile from Laura's family home, and there was a small garden with a resident owl. The house was in severe need of repair and improvement but they didn't care. For them it was Buckingham Palace, a place they could finally call home.

They had little furniture and couldn't afford to buy more, not even the Utility kind. And on top of everything, they still had to find the solicitor's conveyancing fees.

'We'll never manage to pay for everything,' Laura sighed.

'No such word as "never". Leave it to me, Laura.'

'You're not thinking of robbing a bank, I hope?'

Billy borrowed £200 from his mother to add to the long-term loan he had already negotiated.

'I'll pay all of it back,' he told his mam, 'when my ship comes in.'

'That'll be the day,' she replied.

They now had enough capital not only to move in but to buy a few pieces of furniture from the Morgans, who were eager to retire to their Welsh cottage. A 'Jacobean' bedroom suite and an 'Elizabethan' dining-room suite was how the old folk had described their precious belongings. It would have been uncharitable to accuse the elderly pair of being crooks. Perhaps they thought their furniture *was* genuinely antique but the stuff turned out to have woodworm and had to be thrown out. The few bits and pieces were, however, enough to get Billy and Laura started. They also found a number of second-hand items in the Miscellaneous Sales columns of the *Manchester Evening News.* Once or twice, Billy was to be seen carrying things like a hallstand or a small kitchen table through the streets. He hoped he would not have the misfortune to bump into any of his pupils, but no such luck.

'Doing a moonlight flit, sir?' Paddy Daly, the class clown, called out one night as Billy humped a pair of kitchen chairs along Longford Place.

'Nah,' his companion John O'Neill, guffawed. 'Sir's got a second job as furniture remover after school, haven't you, sir?'

'Very funny, I'm sure,' Billy panted. 'Both of you see me after school tomorrow and we'll see about giving *you* some extra jobs since you find it so comical.'

'See ya, sir,' they called back. 'And if you need any help with furniture, all the lads in the class would be glad to help.'

'Thanks, lads,' he said. I'll remember that.'

Billy had been a teacher for three years at St Anselm's Secondary Modern where he was in charge of the top class of fourteen-year-old boys and girls. He loved the job and had a warm friendly relationship with all his pupils, thanks to the liberal policies of headmaster Frank Wakefield who encouraged Billy to take his class out on outdoor pursuits, like cycling and hiking. Map-reading and local studies were the avowed objectives, but Billy believed in the value of getting his charges out of the stuffy classroom and into the fresh air of the Peak District.

He and the headmaster had become good friends though the relationship was occasionally strained because Frank Wakefield had set up his office at the back of Billy's class, having lost his own room when the Luftwaffe dropped a bomb on it. At first Billy had found this arrangement daunting, especially since Frank was inclined to take part in the occasional lesson by offering comments and humorous observations. After a few months, however, the participation had developed into something of a double act and, while it could be entertaining at times, Billy yearned for a classroom of his own. Big changes were planned for the new school year starting in September when the seniors were due to move into their own premises at Stafford House in Regina Park. Billy could hardly wait.

Towards the end of January, in the depths of a severe winter, Billy and Laura collected their few possessions from the Mackenzies' and moved in. They also collected a beautiful blue Persian kitten from Billy's sister Polly, a true cat-lover.

'You can count this as a present to start your new home,' she said. 'I always think a cat helps to create a homely atmosphere. The great advantage of a cat is that it's so clean and you don't have to take it for a walk every day.'

'Thank you, Polly,' Billy said. 'Laura and I will treasure it forever, and it obviously has a high IQ and, judging from its snooty expression, an impeccable pedigree.'

'It certainly has,' she replied. 'If this cat could talk, it wouldn't speak to the likes of you and me.'

'It looks so calm and so wise. Let's call it Socrates and make it part of our family,' Laura suggested.

'We shall spend the next forty years here,' Billy happily predicted.

'You're right,' she said, 'but when I look round, I think we're going to need every minute of that time to lick the place into shape. There's so much needs doing.'

Laura had a point. The house *did* need a lot doing to it. For a start, there was a musty smell throughout as if the place had been unoccupied for some time – the old couple having virtually lived in the poky little kitchen (or 'snug' in estate agent's language) which was the only warm spot in the house, the rest being cold and draughty. The wind seemed to circle the building, trying every window and door, seeking a crevice or crack by which it might gain entrance. The rooms looked as if they hadn't been decorated since the turn of the century and the paper which still remained on the walls was of a depressingly brown floral pattern. Add to this the bare floorboards and Billy and Laura could see they were going to have their work cut out to make the house comfortable. Cooking facilities consisted of two gas rings, and the bathroom upstairs contained a Lilliputian bath and washbasin, the 'inside' toilet being located in the cellar. The final straw came when they tried to light a fire in the 'unique traditional fireplace' and the chimney belched great clouds of smoke.

Laura sat down in one of the fireside chairs and was about to break down in tears when Billy turned her sadness into gladness by saying: 'We'll plug in the electric fire. Cheer up, it could be worse.'

'How could it be worse?'

'Well, there might be no electricity,' he replied, plugging in the heater.

There was no electricity.

'Did you inform the Electricity Board and ask them to connect the supply?' Laura asked.

'Electricity Board? What's that?'

'There's only one thing to do,' she said, through her tears of laughter. 'Let's go up to our Jacobean bed and at least we can keep ourselves warm. We'll sort out the mess tomorrow.'

* * *

The next few months were spent in an attempt to create order out of chaos. The Sobel radiogram had to go, and with the proceeds they paid off the HP account with Campbell's store and bought instead a small Cossor wireless, had the chimney swept, and paid for a new gas cooker. Steve, his brother-in-law, came over and showed Billy how to put up wallpaper and together they decorated the dining room with a bright, contemporary design, stained the floorboards and put down a congoleum square – the cheapest floor covering they could find on Longsight Market.

At the end of February their funds ran out; they had what accountants call a 'cash flow problem'. It was colder than ever, their coal ration of two bags a month was used up and so was their money. Laura's pregnancy was more advanced. They sat in the little kitchen to keep warm.

'I've got an idea,' said Billy. 'In the cellar we have mountains of coal dust. Slack, I believe they call it. It won't burn easily, but why can't I make it into "coal eggs" by mixing in a tiny bit of cement and shaping it with my hands? Result – coal lumps. We can light a fire with those. They'll be like the real thing.'

For several hours, he sat freezing his backside on the concrete cellar floor putting his idea into practice, mixing and shaping the slack into lumps resembling 'cobs'. By the next night, the 'eggs' had hardened and were ready for burning.

'Do you think it'll work?' Laura asked doubtfully. 'I mean, I've never heard of coal dust being mixed with cement.'

'Of course, it'll work,' he said. 'Have some faith in my ingenuity. I can't understand why nobody's thought of it before. Perhaps I can patent the idea because every cellar in the land must contain heaps of useless slack.'

Laura remained unconvinced. 'I'm sure there must be some reason why it hasn't been tried before . . .'

They soon discovered the reason for themselves. When they lit the fire and placed the coal 'eggs' in position, there was a series of small explosions as if someone had thrown live bullets in the grate. After an hour of watching the fire spit and splutter bits of coal at them, Laura finally said, 'This is getting damned dangerous. It's like being in the trenches. I'm off.'

They abandoned the experiment and resorted to sitting in the kitchen with the gas burners turned on.

Billy was never allowed to forget this episode and it became incorporated into family lore. Formerly the expression 'water pipe' had been used to remind him of the nail-in-the-pipe episode. Now 'coal-eggs' came to replace it as a synonym for incompetence. Whenever he volunteered his services in the DIY department, Laura had only to give her Mona Lisa smile and whisper 'coal eggs' to cause an instant withdrawal of the offer. At first, Billy's pride had been wounded but then he saw an opportunity to turn it to his advantage. They had been entertaining Laura's parents to a slap-up dinner one night partly to tap Duncan for a loan and partly to show off their wedding present crockery and kitchenware. Billy was washing the dishes, the tureens and pans, the latter being particularly stained, when the idea struck him. He employed the brush and pan scrub on the stubborn stains but, try as he might, the marks refused to budge. So he sprinkled a liberal amount of Persil soap powder into the water and it seemed to do the trick. Soon, he had all the dishes and pans gleaming and arranged like soldiers on the draining board.

'Well, that's it, Laura,' he said triumphantly, as he put the last plate into position. 'Leave them to drip and then we'll put them back on the shelves.'

Later, when they had said their goodnights to Duncan and Louise, they turned their attention to the dishes.

'You see, Laura,' Billy observed, 'it takes a man to organise the kitchen chores and conserve energy. No need to dry the dishes with a towel; simply leave them to drip-dry themselves.'

It was when Laura began returning the dishes to the shelves that she noticed.

'Billy, every plate, dish and pan is smeared with soap powder. What on earth did you use?'

He pointed to the half-empty Persil packet.

'Not Persil!' Laura exclaimed. 'That's for washing clothes, not dishes.'

'I don't see why not,' he replied ruefully. 'It made the job easier.'

'Coal eggs!' she said.

From that day on, he was never allowed to touch another dish.

Chapter Six

It wasn't long before Laura had other things to occupy her. Since Christmas, her routine had consisted of teaching at school, cleaning and decorating the house, and in between visiting the Welfare clinic for check-ups and to collect her allocation of cod liver oil, orange juice and vitamin pills. Rennie's indigestion tablets were high on the menu, too.

'It's amazing, Laura,' Billy said one morning at breakfast, 'how in our society we surround the birth of a baby with so much fuss and formal ritual.'

'How do you mean?'

'In Western society, the mother goes to a pre-natal clinic, has to watch her diet with great care and avoid smoking and drinking. All her friends congratulate her and everyone's concerned she doesn't exert herself in the slightest way. And for the first baby at least, it's into hospital with an army of nurses surrounding her. When the baby's born it's taken from her and put in a cradle in an antiseptic nursery with a lot of other infants. After about ten days the mother gets up out of bed and from thereon she's treated like the Queen of Sheba with everyone dancing attention. The father's excluded and feels absolutely useless. What's worse, he's treated as a figure of fun and everyone jokes about his part in the process. "You've had your fun and now you can tie a knot in it." His only job is to hand out cigars when it's all over.'

'Well, what's wrong with that? It's tradition. How else would you have it?'

'I've been reading about the way it's handled in some of the South Sea Islands. The dad goes into a hut with a few of his mates and pretends he's having the baby. He writhes and yells at the pain he's going through while all his pals mop his fevered brow and console him with soothing words. It's called *couvade*.'

'Sounds like a madhouse to me. What happens to the mother while all this palaver's going on?'

'The mother-to-be goes off with a friend and has the baby without any more ado. Next day, she's back at work while the dad has to have a few days off to recover. I must say, it's got a certain appeal. Why, his missus even takes him his food and helps him through his convalescence.'

'I can see why men might like to adopt this practice. What good is all this supposed to do?'

'It's supposed to take away the pain from the mother and ensure an easy birth.'

'I've never heard such rubbish.'

'Oh, I dunno, Laura. I'm all for it. Why can't we do that here in Manchester?

'If that's what you want, Billy, you get yourself off to the South Seas and find yourself a Dorothy Lamour in a grass skirt. I'll stick to having it in a hospital on the National Health.'

'Maybe Titch and I will give it a whirl while you're in hospital,' he laughed. 'You can let me know afterwards if it works.'

* * *

On the Saturday morning of the Easter Bank Holiday, Billy was occupied splashing Walpamur on to the dining-room ceiling. His back and his neck were aching. Now I know how Michelangelo felt painting the Sistine Chapel, he was thinking to himself.

Laura was out with her young sister Katie on Stockport Road, rushing around the shops doing the kind of frantic shopping associated with a holiday weekend, as if the Martians had landed and were intent on destroying the nation's food supplies. As Billy slapped on the emulsion, a butcher's van came roaring into the Grove, its brakes screeching as it drew to a halt outside the house. Supported by the local butcher, Mr Burgess, and her young sister, Laura emerged from the van. She looked ashen and the front of her coat was covered in sawdust.

'What in heaven's name happened?' Billy exclaimed, rushing to her aid.

'She walked into my shop about ten minutes ago,' Mr Burgess answered. 'As she came through the door, she collapsed and fell forward on to her face.'

Billy was distraught to see his wife like this. He held her close, sat her down, and rushed off to make the English solution to all ills – tea.

'I think it was the sudden change in temperature,' the butcher said. 'She walked out of the cold right into the warmth of the shop, and that did it. Pouf! She simply keeled over and hit the deck.'

'I tried to stop her falling,' a worried Katie said, 'but I couldn't save her.'

'I shall be all right now,' Laura said tearfully. 'No harm done to the baby but my front tooth has broken. I shall look like a toothless old hag.'

Billy left off his decorating, and for the rest of the day Laura and Katie received the best TLC Billy could summon up. A few days later Laura visited her dentist and was much relieved when he fixed a crown to the broken incisor with such skill that it was undetectable. Laura's smile was as bright and as dazzling as usual. When Billy found that the NHS would be footing the dental bill, his smile was equally dazzling.

It was a Sunday evening in May when the call came. Laura bent down to pick up a spoon she had dropped and it happened – the waters broke. They went into the routine they had rehearsed so often that Billy could have recited it in his sleep. Nevertheless he had a list of 'Things To Do' pinned to the bedroom wall.

1. Get up and get dressed. Check I have two pennies for the phone.
2. Ring hospital and tell them what's happened.
3. Ring Laura's parents and pass on the news.

'Don't panic!' Billy shouted, his hands shaking. 'Stay cool and collected. Remember what the clinic said: take deep breaths. Keep your knees together until the ambulance gets here. Now, what was I supposed to do next?'

'Telephone for the ambulance,' Laura answered calmly. 'Do you have the two pennies?'

'That's right. The phone. The twopence. Where did we put them?'

'On the mantelpiece in the dining room,' she said patiently.

'And the number of the hospital? Where did we put it?'

'On the pad on the mantelpiece, with the coins.'

Billy fled out of the front door to the phone box on Longford Place and rang the emergency service.

'Hello! Please send an ambulance, I'm having a baby.'

'Right, sir,' said a matter-of-fact male voice at the other end. 'What address would that be then, sir?'

Billy gave the address. Next he phoned Laura's mother and passed on the news after which he ran back to Laura who was sitting in the dining room, her coat on, the pre-packed suitcase by her side.

She appeared unruffled but Billy knew how nervous she was feeling deep down. This was something she was going to have to do without him. Fifteen minutes later the ambulance arrived. As he helped her on board, she looked lost and forlorn, and his heart went out to her.

'Don't look so worried,' Laura said. 'Women have been having babies from the beginning of time. Remember your women in the South Sea Islands. Get hold of Titch and together you can act out the birth process.'

How he wished he could have taken a bigger part in the proceedings, perhaps gone with her to the hospital to hold her hand and comfort her.

'Sorry,' they'd told him, 'men not allowed. You'd only be in the way. This is women's work.' His only contact and his only news would be by telephone, and from a call box at that.

A disconsolate Billy returned to an empty house, his only company being Socrates the cat.

'Well, you wise old philosopher,' he said to his pet, 'there's nothing to do now but wait.'

The cat cocked its head and looked back at him solemnly.

At three in the morning, Billy rang St Mary's Maternity Hospital and asked for news. There was none except that Laura had been moved out to Coller House, Prestbury, in deepest Cheshire. That's miles away, he thought. Why had they done that? Was it significant? Perhaps only difficult cases went there. What was happening? How was Laura getting on? They could tell him nothing. At six o'clock, he rang again. Still nothing. Maybe it had all been a false alarm. There was no baby and it had been merely a case of chronic indigestion. That wouldn't have surprised him, considering the number of Rennie's Laura had been taking. As for there being a baby, he had never been able, *really* able, to take in the notion that such a complicated miraculous thing as a human being could be created by a simple act of love. Why, the greatest scientists in the world with their sophisticated laboratories and their complicated equipment couldn't make a baby while he and Laura had made one without the need of any such technological apparatus. A basic thing like a bed was all they had required.

At eight o'clock, Titch came over to stay with him as arranged weeks before. They intended decorating their 'unusual' L-shaped lounge while Laura was away. It was to be a surprise for her on her return.

Titch was reassuring.

'First babies are always longer in making their appearance. They're too comfortable inside there in the womb. Why, most of us men spend our lives trying to get back in. No wonder they're reluctant to come out. And, you never know, maybe they know something we don't.'

Fine, but what did Titch know about babies and birth except his own experience of getting born and what he had read in textbooks at teacher training college? What did men in general know about having babies anyway? And, come to think about it, why were most gynaecologists men? It was like having a car mechanic who had never owned a car himself.

At nine Billy rang for the fourth time. He had to wait while they connected him to Prestbury. Trembling, he inserted more coins in the box. Then at last: 'Mr Hopkins? Oh, yes. Your wife had a little boy this morning.'

Thank God it was a *little* boy, he thought. Even in circumstances like these he couldn't resist playing the Smart Alec. Nevertheless he reeled back with a jolt as if he had been hit with a charge of electricity. Of course he had been expecting the news but all the same it gave him a shock. So there had been a baby after all! He couldn't take it in. He phoned Laura's parents and stammered out the good news then rushed back home to share it with Titch. On Stockport Road, he bought a bunch of red roses and planned his route to Prestbury.

The hospital had reassured him on the telephone that there was nothing unusual about Laura being sent to the wilds of Cheshire; Prestbury was simply a rural retreat. All very well but getting to Coller House involved three buses and a long walk. It was past noon when he got there.

He was met by a tall, no-nonsense nurse who led him through a crèche lined with dozens of infants, cherub after cherub slumbering peacefully.

'Like little angels, aren't they?' he said, looking forward to seeing his first born. 'They all look the same.'

'You think so,' she said. 'How about this?'

She went along the row of cradles and pulled ever so gently on the legs of one or two neonates. No response. But at the third cot containing a red-faced, wrinkled Winston Churchill look-alike, there was an immediate reaction and the infant let out what sounded like a howl of indignation.

'There,' she said. 'What about that?'

'Sounds like a real stubborn type to me,' Billy said.

'I'm glad you think so 'cos he's yours.'

She consulted the card tied to the crib. 'Matthew Hopkins,' she read. 'A lovely name. Why Matthew?'

'Simple,' he replied. 'Today is the feast of St Matthew and we'd decided to name him after the saint whose feast day it was. Thank God he came today 'cos tomorrow is the feast of St Isidore and I don't think he'd have thanked us for that as a handle. Apart from that, Stanley Matthews is my favourite footballer.'

'Trust a man to think of football. Anyway he's eight pounds two ounces and he's beautiful.'

Billy took another peek. 'I'll have to take your word for it,' he said with a grin.

'You can hold him, if you like,' she said, thrusting the baby towards him.

Billy's arms came out automatically like the prongs on a fork-lift truck as he took his son from her. Despite his bravado and his feeble attempts at wit, tears sprang to his eyes. Here was his first-born son, fruit of his loins. It was an awesome thought, he reflected, that Laura and he had helped to create another individual soul, an autonomous being with his own personality and his own destiny.

'I'm a father,' he said.

'Obviously. You can hold him more tightly than that,' she said. 'He won't come apart, you know.'

'Why's his face so red?'

The nurse looked at Billy frostily. 'If you'd done the work he's done these last twelve hours, thrusting himself into the world, you'd have a red face as well.'

'Why twelve hours?'

'That's normal for the first one,' she said. 'It'll be easier and a little quicker next time.'

Billy took a closer look. Yes, it was a sheer miracle. Here was another human being complete in every respect right down to the soft down on his head and his tiny finger nails.

Laura was sitting up in the ward when he was allowed in to see her. She was wearing a new silk nightgown and looked radiantly happy. He gave her the flowers, then kissed her and held her close.

'Nice one, our kid,' he said. 'I always knew you had it in you.'

'Very funny. But thanks, Billy. I couldn't have done it without you. Well, what do you think of Matthew?'

'He's beautiful, and eight pounds two ounces is a superb achievement for your first effort.'

'I hope you don't think Matthew will be the first of twelve apostles?'

'Maybe not apostles. Perhaps of the evangelists.'

The nurse brought the baby to be fed. Lovingly, Laura took her son and began feeding him. Billy looked on fondly, deeply moved by the scene. And also envious.

'Laura, if you could only have seen the look on your face when you gave him the breast!'

'How do you mean?'

'It was the look you once reserved only for me.'

'Billy, you're jealous!'

'Don't be daft. But then, I suppose I am in a way. After all, he's in bed with my wife *and* getting her breast. Lucky little blighter!'

'You go and find your own mother,' she laughed.

'Somehow, I don't think she'd go for it,' he replied. 'We did our bonding twenty-three years ago. As for your bonding with Matthew, Laura, the nurse tells me you were in labour twelve hours! That's an awfully long time. What was it like? You can tell *me*. Was it as painful as you expected?'

'Let's put it like this, Billy. You remember all that business of *couvade* you were going on about, with the husband simulating childbirth to take away the pain from the mother?'

'I do.'

'If you and Titch tried it out it like you said you would, I can assure you, it doesn't work.'

After the customary ten days in hospital, Laura brought the baby home. From that day, their lives were never the same again. The baby and his needs dominated everything and their own concerns were pushed into the background as their lives acquired new priorities. It became a round of nappies drying on the kitchen rack; four-hourly feeds and sleepless nights; sterilising and mixing baby's bottles with the precision of a research chemist; gripe water, burping, bum rash and Vaseline.

For the first few weeks there was a stream of visitors who 'oohed' and 'ahhed' over the baby. Billy's sisters Flo and Polly provided a beautiful layette between them while Mam brought two sets of baby clothes that she had knitted, one pink, one blue.

'I was hedging my bets,' she said.

Flo reckoned that the baby had Laura's eyes and Billy's nose, Polly arguing the reverse. He has his own nose and his own eyes, Billy thought.

After six weeks' maternity leave, Laura returned to school and they were faced with the problem of finding a baby-sitter – not easy as they couldn't afford to pay an outsider. One within the family was difficult too. Billy's family lived too far away to make it practicable, and choices within Laura's family were limited. Her mother, Louise, was busy teaching her private music pupils at home, and at eighty-five Gran'ma was thought to be past it. That left old Auntie, aged seventy-four, who leapt, metaphorically speaking, at the chance to go round and look after things. It seemed like the ideal arrangement and things appeared to be falling nicely into place.

Chapter Seven

Throughout 1951 and the early part of 1952, Duncan never passed up an opportunity to persuade Billy to study for a degree.

'Work it out, son,' he said one day, 'it's logical. You need to raise your income, and the only way to do that is to get yourself promoted. And you won't get promoted unless you have better qualifications, preferably a degree with honours. Ergo, you must study and get one. QED.'

He sounds like our old maths teacher, Billy thought. Getting a degree was easier said than done. He had considered studying by correspondence through a college like Wolsey Hall or the Rapid Results College, but didn't go for the idea of working at home with a baby and a thousand and one domestic and DIY chores crying out for attention. It was Duncan himself who, having presented the problem, provided the solution.

'Many of our clerks at the Tax Office have signed up for an evening degree course in administration at the University of Manchester.'

'But I'm a teacher,' Billy protested. 'I don't want to be an administrator. I know nothing about law or accountancy. Besides, where would I find the fees?'

'Doesn't matter what the degree is in,' his father-in-law said. 'It's a degree and you can put letters after your name, that's all that counts. As for the fees, I'll help you out for the first year with a gift of half, but I shall expect you to find the other half yourself.'

'It's kind of you, Mr Mackenzie. Why are you doing all this for me?'

'I'm not doing it just for *you*, Billy, I'm doing it for my daughter and my grandson. And it's about time we cut out that Mr Mackenzie bit. Call me Duncan.'

Billy was touched by the little speech and the offer of help, but dropping the title 'Mr Mackenzie' and addressing his father-in-law as 'Duncan' was something his vocal chords instinctively resisted. It was like addressing the King as George.

'It sounds feasible, Mr Mackenz . . . Duncan. What does this degree involve?' Billy asked.

'Attendance for four nights a week and your own private study at weekends. As for accountancy, I can help you out there with a little private tuition. No charge. And that's saying something for a Mackenzie!'

'Thank you for your kind offer, Mr . . . Duncan,' Billy replied. 'I shall have to talk it over with Laura. If I take myself off to university every night, it's going to mean a lot of extra work being dumped in her lap.'

'She's a Scots girl, you'll find she's more than equal to it,' her father replied with a grin.

Duncan was right about his daughter. She was all for it.

'It'll throw a lot of work on your shoulders, Laura,' Billy said. 'It also means tightening our belts and we can forget about holidays for some time to come. Any spare cash will go on fees, books, fares, and I don't know what else.'

'Doesn't matter, Billy,' she said warmly. 'I'll back you to the hilt. If you can improve your qualifications, it could mean promotion and a better life for all of us. The alternative is that we go on as we are, just about keeping our heads above water. Always worrying if we can pay the next grocery bill or whether we're going to have the electricity or the gas cut off. We can't go on like that. This is a great opportunity and I think you should go for it.'

It's all very well this talk of taking a degree, Billy thought, but I'm not sure I have the brains for a university course. No one in our family ever aimed so high. When I went to grammar school and passed nine subjects in the School Certificate, that was the pinnacle of success as far as my family was concerned. There was nothing higher than that. When I went to a training college and qualified as a teacher, it meant I'd joined the middle class, much to the pride of my mam and the dismay of my dad. And now here's my father-in-law showing me another world and urging me on to higher things. Me, a university graduate? It's inconceivable.

Billy's mam was all for it. She still referred to the university by the name of its nineteenth-century founder, John Owen.

'I never thought I'd have a son who would be a scholar at Owen's College and going in for a cap and gown. Where will it end? I wonder. You'll be Prime Minister next.'

As expected, his dad didn't like the idea at all, despite the sentimental bosh he'd talked in the pub.

'Being a teacher is one thing, but going to that there Owen's College is going too far. Up to now you've only been *mixing* with the toffs. If you go to that bloody place, you'll *become* one of the buggers.'

'What have you got against it, Tommy?' Mam asked. 'What's wrong with our lad bettering himself?'

'All this education rubbish is no good – it'll break up the family. He'll become too good for us, and one day he'll get a big job in the south of England, maybe even London, God forbid, and that's the last we'll see of him for years, you mark my words.'

'You do talk rubbish sometimes, Tommy,' she said. 'If our Billy's got the brains he should make the most of himself.'

The consensus round him seemed to be that he should give it a go.

'Very well,' he told them all. 'I'll bow to the weight of opinion and register for the next course in 1952. I should have my head examined!'

Chapter Eight

Billy and Laura settled into domesticity. Matthew was nearly one and had lost his Churchillian look. Now he was more of a Botticelli angel who chortled and chuckled at Billy's games, such as being tossed into the air like a football, much to Laura's anxiety. 'Specially popular was Billy's act of balancing an object on his own head and letting it slither off into his hands, a trick which always sent the baby into fits of giggling.

'The most appreciative audience I ever had,' Billy observed.

Matthew had already taken his first faltering steps in learning to walk.

'He totters like my dad coming out of the pub on a Saturday night,' Billy remarked.

'More like a sailor on a rolling ship,' Laura said.

She was kept busy as a housewife with endless household chores: feeding her family, washing and ironing, looking after Matthew, fighting a never-ending battle against the Manchester grime, and forever trying to keep their tall rambling house warm – not an easy job given the permanent shortage of coal. One of Billy's jobs was to light the fire in the mornings, something in which he'd become expert as a boy when as a young entrepreneur he had earned his pocket money by providing a fire-lighting service for his Jewish neighbours in the Manchester Cheetham Hill district on Saturday mornings. Nowadays he got out of bed to do it with the enthusiasm of a condemned prisoner going to the gallows. On winter mornings, when they went to fetch Matthew from his cot, they invariably found his hands outside the blankets, fingers swollen like tiny cocktail sausages. Most evenings were spent in the tiny kitchen listening to the little Cossor wireless or reading books borrowed from Longsight Library. Making ends meet was a perennial problem especially when they found that, whilst the grocery and other bills came in weekly, Billy's salary was paid monthly, leaving a three-day shortfall at the end of the month.

'We always seem to run out of cash in the third week,' Laura said.

'That's one of the penalties we pay for being lower-middle-class,' he replied. 'Only the working class are paid weekly. Lucky beggars!'

When it came to clothes for Matthew, Billy's sisters had come to the rescue with hand-me-downs. All gratefully received. For other small purchases Laura had joined a small Co-operative Loan Club, a relatively painless way of buying clothes for themselves and the children. The scheme involved paying one shilling a week for twenty-one weeks for each pound borrowed. Five shillings a week, their limit, released a loan of five pounds to be spent at the Co-op Oufitters on Downing Street.

As for Billy, life was one long round of teaching during the day, lesson preparation and marking exercise books at weekends. Holidays were out of the question and there was little or nothing left for household repairs like pointing and painting that were urgently needed. Billy's one relaxation was his membership of the Holy Name choir. Every Sunday, he attended eleven o'clock Mass and helped to swell the bass section while his friend Titch sang on the other side of the choir with the tenors. Many of the choir members had already attended an earlier Mass and so at sermon time, after the 'Gloria', the male singers went for a stroll round the church to refresh their lungs with Manchester air and the smoke of W. H. Wills. They had once tried taking their sermon break in the church tower but the smell of tobacco smoke had lingered for weeks in the narrow winding stairway, arousing the suspicions of the rector, Father Doyle, SJ, and they had been compelled to change their venue. The sermon lasted exactly fifteen minutes and the smokers had timed their promenade to perfection. It was also an opportunity to exchange views on life in general.

'Laura and I are not exactly starving,' Billy told Titch one Sunday, 'but we're doing little more than existing from one month to the next. We live in what is referred to in literature as "genteel poverty". Now I understand what Henry Thoreau meant when he said that "the mass of men lead lives of quiet desperation". Sometimes I wonder what it's all about. Why are we all here?'

'I thought I was the pessimist round here,' Titch protested, 'and I object strongly to being usurped. But, Hoppy, I thought you knew the answer to your question?'

'OK, I'll buy it,' Billy said. 'Why are we all here?'

'We're here because we're here, because we're here, because we're here,' Titch sang to the tune of 'Auld Lang Syne'.

'Don't you ever take things seriously?' Billy asked.

'Never.'

* * *

At the end of each month Billy was invariably irritable. He had cut his smoking down to five fags a day though he couldn't really afford those, especially when the money ran out towards the end of the month. One Sunday evening, he wondered aloud whether all the efforts, the privations and the daily grind, were worth it.

'Of course they're worth it,' Laura said, kissing him on the forehead. 'One day our ship will come in, you'll see.'

'Are you sure the ship's not called the *Titanic*? It seems to me we spend half our lives waiting for good news, for something to happen, for the mail, for the cheque from Littlewood's. Always tomorrow, tomorrow. As Irving Berlin put it, "It's a lovely day tomorrow".'

'And what's wrong with that? We've got to live in hope,' she said.

'Thomas Carlyle had it right when he wrote:

What is Hope? A smiling rainbow Children follow
through the wet;
'Tis not here, still yonder, yonder:
Never urchin found it yet.'

'Oh, come on, Billy, you are an old grouch. Cheer up. At least we've got each other.'

'That's the one thing we don't have,' he said, shaking his head.

'I don't understand. Don't have what?'

'Each other. Not as long as we obey the Church's teaching on birth control. Sex is out except on rare occasions.'

'Cue for violins,' she said. 'Things do sound desperate.'

'At the moment that's the way I feel,' he said. 'I can't see the point in anything.'

'I think I know what's wrong with you,' she said mischievously. 'And what's more, I think I have the very thing here to solve all your problems.'

Billy's eyes lit up. 'You do?' he said gleefully. 'Shall I go ahead and warm the bed?'

'Not that,' she laughed, giving him a playful thump. 'But this!' She produced a packet of Three Castles cigarettes. 'Daddy buys his cigarettes in packs of two hundred and I'm sure he won't miss one packet. I took these some time ago and I've been saving them for an emergency like this.'

'Laura, you are the most wonderful person in the whole world and I shall love you forever,' Billy exclaimed as he joyfully lit up. 'Greater love hath no woman than this, that she will swipe cigarettes from her own father for her husband. Why, this fag has already changed my whole outlook and philosophy. Life *is* worth living after all.'

'I stole because I think your need is greater than his. In a way, though, you can thank your mother, Billy. She warned me before we married I should always have a packet of cigarettes in reserve for situations like this when you can be like a bear with a sore head.'

'One of these days, I shall give up the filthy habit,' he said, pulling happily on his fag.

'When?' she said.

'Tomorrow.'

'I'll believe it when I see it.'

'These fags solve my immediate need, but what about our long-term problem? It's so long since we made love, I think I've forgotten how to do it. Why can't we use some form of birth control?'

'You know it's forbidden, Billy, and we don't want to go

against the teaching of the Church. Not if we want to remain Catholics.'

'You don't have to remind me, Laura. Too many dos and don'ts, if you ask me. No artificial contraception. No recreation without procreation.'

'You make it sound like a prison sentence.'

'Sometimes,' he continued, 'I have the impression that our parish priest and the whole Catholic hierarchy are in bed between us, observing and issuing a stream of vetoes on every move we make. So we try a bit of this. "Not allowed!" O'Malley snaps. "We'll have none of that French hanky-panky, if you don't mind." So we try a bit of that. "Taboo!" the priest barks, watching with his beady eye.'

'You do exaggerate, Billy. It's not as bad as that, surely?'

'Do you realise, Laura, that you have twenty-two years of potential child-bearing left, and if we keep up our present rate of procreation, we could produce twenty-two kids by the time we're forty-four?'

'Don't frighten me so late at night,' she said, looking up from her cocoa. 'I'll have nightmares. What do you think I am – a baby factory? Twenty-two kids indeed! No one ever had that many kids.'

'You think not! According to the *Guinness Book of Records*, a lady in Russia had sixty-nine, though admittedly some of them were multiple births. And if I remember my history right, Queen Anne in the eighteenth century had eighteen pregnancies in sixteen years.'

'Impossible! I don't believe it.'

'All true, Laura. But we don't need to go abroad or into the past for big families. Mrs McCardle in Daneley Road has eighteen kids. People say she's thinking of having a turnstile fitted.'

'Very funny, I'm sure. But let me assure you, Billy, I shall not be challenging the Russian lady, Queen Anne or Mrs McCardle for the record.'

'Don't be so sure, Laura. Amongst the many legends about convent girls, there was one which said they have two choices. One, to remain in the convent and achieve permanent virginity . . .'

'And the other?'

'Leave, get married and achieve permanent pregnancy.'

'Or simply stop having sex.'

After the birth of Matthew, marital relations were restricted to one careful session per month. After a year of this, Billy was climbing up the wall with frustration and the print in the hall of Picasso's portrait of a young woman was looking more sexy every day. Not only that, both of them felt their temper fraying and they were snapping at each other. Something had to be done.

Billy decided to stop the guesswork and seek guidance on what the Church did and did not allow. He arranged to visit the great Father O'Malley himself, but he was a cantankerous old man whose only advice was to exercise moral restraint. If he could exercise it, he said, so could Billy. Besides, the purpose of sexual congress was the procreation of children and not one's carnal gratification. The very phrase 'sexual congress' sounded like a meeting of the Great Powers at the end of a war, Billy thought.

He fixed up an interview with Father McBride next, a young curate fresh out of the seminary. If the novice priest lacked experience, he might at least offer sympathetic advice. After the usual handshaking formalities, he and the curate lit up two of Billy's precious cigarettes while he explained how his wife was afraid of too many pregnancies and had severely restricted his conjugal benefits.

'But she can't do that,' the Father blustered. 'What about your marital rights! It's her bounden duty to grant you . . .' He was stuck for the word. Access? Billy thought.

'Mind you,' McBride continued, 'you can only insist on your rights provided you're reasonable. I mean, if you're demanding it three or four times a night, she would have a good case to refuse you.'

Three or four times a night! Obviously, Billy said to himself, he thinks he's dealing with Don Juan or Errol Flynn. Furthermore had he not heard about the one word that terrified men and had the bravest of them quaking in their boots? After making love, a woman had only to whisper that one word, 'Again!' to turn a man into a gibbering wreck.

The curate went on to point out that the only method permitted by the Church was the rhythm method. Billy had a fleeting, irreverent thought that this might have something to do with doing it in time to Gene Kelly's song 'I Got Rhythm' but dismissed this quickly from his mind. After all, he was in conversation with a holy priest under the sanctified roof of the presbytery. When Billy asked for a few details of the method, the curate seemed perplexed and gave the sort of hazy answer a politician would have been proud of. Obviously not a subject dealt with in the seminary study programme. Billy would have to seek help elsewhere.

He gave a full report to Laura who could shed no light on the mysterious 'rhythm method' as her convent education had not included it in the syllabus.

'In some ways, our two priests contradicted each other,' Billy said. 'The old priest insisted that sexual relations were strictly for procreation only while the young one seemed to be saying that at certain times relations were allowed, even if procreation was ruled out.'

All very confusing, they thought.

At Easter that year there was a reunion of Billy's old college chums in the Sawyer's Arms on Deansgate. He had been looking forward to the meeting all week as it was a chance to catch up on everyone's news and they'd all promised to be there. Apart from Titch, who always enjoyed a chin-wag with old friends, there would be Tony Wilde, nick-named 'Oscar' – not just because of his name, but because of the nature of his private life and the fact that he hero-worshipped the great aesthete. Also present would be Oliver Hardy, known simply as 'Olly', who fancied himself an authority on almost every subject under the sun, and would seize every opportunity to air his knowledge. Finally, there would be Nobby Nodder, the ladies' man, who never failed to entertain them with his lurid stories of sexual conquest.

Billy was delayed by one or two domestic chores and when he arrived, found his cronies already in full flow. Titch got him a pint in and then all attention was turned to Nobby, a lieutenant in the Royal Army Education Corps, who was holding forth about his latest exploits.

'I tell you, this little number from the WRAF was gasping for it,' Nobby was saying. 'She whipped off her clothes before I could get my hat off. "OK, Lieutenant, sir," she says, saluting me and lying back on the bed, "come and get it . . ." '

The group listened avidly to this tale of seduction, hanging on his every word. Good old Nobby, Billy thought, hadn't changed a bit from college days, forever going on about his conquests and how he had to fight the women off. No one believed him then or now but his anecdotes were always entertaining.

'We can all *talk* about sex and our sexual fantasies,' Titch said, 'but the only one who can claim any real experience is Hoppy here. The only married man among us and the only one who's getting it regular.'

'If only,' Billy sighed, taking a pull at his pint. 'The strict rules of the Catholic Church on contraception prevent any such thing.'

'Then change your church,' Oscar said. 'Join the Church of England, they're more relaxed about such things.'

'Lucky Proddidogs,' Billy said. 'Us Holy Rollers have to play it by the book.'

'I can't see the problem,' Nobby said. 'I simply *moucher la chandelle* or snuff the candle. I think a condom should be used on every conceivable occasion.'

'Condoms are out,' Billy said, 'they're "condomned" by the Church as not only sinful but unnatural.'

'No more unnatural than putting up an umbrella against the rain,' said Olly, seizing the chance to air his knowledge. 'Perhaps the solution for you lies in some of the old medieval methods.'

Olly seemed to have an inexhaustible list of suggestions and reeled off the methods: from juniper berries to the reciting of magic mantras, from coitus interruptus to coitus eucalyptus.

'No use, I'm afraid,' Billy said. 'A priest has advised me that artificial methods are out. The only one open to Catholics is one called the rhythm method, but I'm damned if I know what it is.'

'Ah, you mean the so-called safe period or calendar method,' said Olly, puffing on his Meerschaum pipe and looking very erudite. 'What is often referred to as the Vatican Lottery. It's too involved to go into now but I would recommend a book called *Birth Control Exposed* by an eminent Catholic doctor named Halliday Sutherland. That should put you right.'

Billy thought it time to change the topic of conversation from his marital frustration to more academic matters. He told them about his intention to register as an evening student at the University of Manchester for the degree of BA in Administration in the coming academic year. To his surprise, Oscar and Titch said they would be keen to join him and asked for more details, which Billy was happy to supply.

'It's the chance of a lifetime,' Oscar proclaimed. 'As you know, I work in a grammar school and I'm the only teacher in the place without a degree. And, besides, I fancy myself in mortar board and flowing gown. A regular Mr Chips.'

'And I'd like to do it, Hoppy,' Titch said, 'for a lark. I've nothing better to do with my time.'

'All very well for you two,' Billy sighed, 'signing up for the fun of it and to while away the time. For me, it's a matter of life or death.'

Talk switched to a consideration of the chances of Manchester United in the FA Cup but Billy's mind was preoccupied with getting hold of the birth control book at the first opportunity in order to investigate this mysterious rhythm method.

Later that week he ordered Sutherland's book from Longsight Library, causing the pretty young librarian to blush to the roots when he whispered the title, as if he had asked her for a copy of the *Kama Sutra*. In the past Billy had confined his borrowings to such innocuous titles as

The Key Behind The Door by Maurice Walsh or *The Robe* by Lloyd C. Douglas.

The book arrived a fortnight later in a plain brown-paper wrapper. It was handed over by no less a person than the head librarian herself, a frosty middle-aged woman, her face screwed up in disapproval and distaste as if she were holding a smelly nappy.

Billy and Laura took turns in studying the book and found the approved method involved identifying the so-called 'safe period'. There were only seven days around the middle of each cycle when conception could take place, and the trick was to avoid this so-called fertile window. Great news because that left about fifteen to twenty days available for 'whatchamacallit'. Billy's expectations rose. He read on enthusiastically but, as he did so, his hopes faded. The 'window' jumped about elusively and pinpointing it required the genius of a Euclid. The only way to be sure, the book told them, was to take the woman's temperature, keep a daily graph, and check for changes in cervical mucus. It was especially important to employ a thermometer before intercourse, a sudden rise in temperature being a sign that ovulation was in progress.

When Laura read this section, she put her foot down firmly and refused point blank to start each day by sticking a thermometer in her mouth, or any other orifice for that matter.

'It all sounds horrible,' she said, throwing the book down. 'Apart from the sheer inconvenience, it's so cold and clinical that it takes all the romance out of love-making. I'd rather take a chance on having another baby than go through that process with laboratory apparatus and what-not.'

Billy couldn't help but agree. 'It takes the X out of sex,' he said. 'I can just imagine a scene in a typical steamy novel:

'They could resist no longer. Urgently and passionately they made their way into the bedroom, tearing off each other's clothing as they went. Then they came at each other like two wild animals. "Yes, yes," he cried hoarsely. "Let's do it – now!" "Oh, yes, Conrad," she groaned. "I want you. I need you! I love you so much! But, darling, first could you bring me the thermometer and mucus measure from the bathroom cabinet? I have to check out my ovulatory cycle." '

In the end, they thought they'd had enough of long periods of abstinence and, after returning the book to the library, resolved to give the calendar method a go for a month or two but without the graphs, the thermometers and other paraphernalia.

'Let's hope this Halliday Sutherland bloke has got his sums right,' Billy remarked.

'It's in the lap of the gods,' Laura said.

Chapter Nine

Sex was not the only thing on Billy's mind that year. Ever since he had let himself be persuaded to read for a degree, he'd worried about it. Who did he think he was? he asked himself. What made him think he was capable of embarking on such an advanced academic course? Every day he asked himself the same questions: Do you have what it takes? Do you have the ability and the staying power to study at university level? Not only that, it will mean studying in your spare time after working a full day at school . . .

One day he spotted an advert in the personal column of the *Evening News*. 'Lacking in Confidence? Keep telling yourself you can't?' it asked. 'Then this book has been written 'specially for you. *How to Achieve Your Potential and Build a Positive Self-Concept* is available at all good bookshops.'

Exactly what I'm looking for, he thought, but pricey at £15 and so he ordered it from the public library. Three weeks later he collected it from the same suspicious head Librarian who now treated him like a sex pervert.

He took the volume up to his study in the attic and began the first exercise.

> You now have in your hands a guide which will teach you how to take control of your life and lead you to success and prosperity. Remember, you are what you think about. If you go about your life telling yourself 'I can't do this and I can't do that' how do you expect to succeed? You must learn to banish fear and replace it with a positive view of life. Stand before a looking-glass, narrow your eyes and giving yourself a bold stare. Say aloud, 'I am strong and confident.' Repeat this ten times.

Billy did as it suggested but found it impossible to look at himself without grinning like a jackass. This is barmy, he told himself, talking to my own reflection in the glass. People will think I've gone doolally if they see me. And if ever that face on the other side of the mirror starts to say things of its own accord, I'll *know* I've gone off my trolley.

Finally he obeyed the last instruction by taking out a piece of paper and writing out twenty times in capital letters: I CAN AND I WILL.

In the first week of June the trio of friends presented themselves at the Faculty of Economic and Social Studies in Dover Street and registered for the degree of Bachelor of Arts in Administration. It was to be a three- or four-year course depending on progress. In their first year they would be studying economics, government, accounting, and political thought. They were also required to study a modern language but when they saw the hordes opting for French, Spanish, and German, decided to go for unfamiliar Italian and found they were to be the only students on the course. After signing up, they needed a pint to recover from the excitement and so repaired to the College Arms where they practised writing BA (Admin.) after their names to get the feel of it.

Duncan had offered to pay half the university registration fee but Billy had still to find the balance and things were tight. How fortunate that Laura had her job, which acted as a cushion and helped them to make ends meet. But that cushion didn't last long. One day she came home to find Auntie dozing at the hearthside with the baby hanging precariously from her lap about to fall in the fire.

'That's it,' Laura said. 'No more.'

Next day she handed in her notice at school to take effect at the end of term.

'That's my degree course down the plughole,' Billy said. 'We'll be lucky if we can pay the grocery bills, never mind university fees.'

'I can't go to work worrying about the baby,' Laura replied. 'We don't have a choice – Matthew's health and safety must come first. And don't the psychology books tell us that a baby needs its mother for the first few years of life? Unless, that is, you want your son to grow up all bitter and twisted?'

There was no arguing with that.

'That's probably what happened to me,' Billy said. 'Either that or my mother dropped me on my head.'

He had more or less given up the notion of university study when Oscar of all people came up with an idea: a vacation job as waiters at the Middleton Towers holiday camp outside Morecambe. Oscar had done the work before and become a dab hand at serving. Or so he said. While the pay of £4 a week was poor, he reckoned all of that could be saved as the camp provided board and lodgings. Not only that, there was the possibility of extra work in the Wonder Bar. No pay but tips could be good.

It sounded like the answer to Billy's prayers though he did not like the idea of leaving Laura with the baby for four weeks.

'Our troubles are over,' he told her. 'In four weeks we could save maybe twelve pounds, enough for my half of the tuition fees.'

'You go ahead,' she said. 'If it means you can raise the money, it'll be worth it. My family's nearby, so I'll be all right.'

Billy and his two companions took the long-distance coach to Morecambe and the camp bus out to Middleton Towers where they were issued with uniforms and shown to a small caravan which was to be their accommodation for four weeks. The dining hall where they were to work was a vast cavernous place with seating for one thousand diners. They were each allocated a 'station' of thirty people and told it was their job to serve the diners' every need. There were three main meals a day: breakfast, lunch and evening dinner, each of which was served in two separate sittings. The food was prepared in a massive kitchen where they were to collect it and then deliver it to the dining tables. Cutlery and crockery were issued with instructions that it was their responsibility to wash and dry every item after every meal, losses to be replaced by them.

The kitchen was like nothing on earth, a stifling inferno which rang with curses and the clanging of pots and pans. In the middle were a number of glowing ovens where twenty cooks leapt about, their faces streaming with sweat despite their white caps and sweat-bands. Around the kitchen there was an arrangement of counters where a mob of gesticulating waiters clamoured with trays, every-one in a frenzy. Each sitting was the same delirium, the serving staff rushing about like madmen with only a few minutes to live. At breakfast the chaos lasted till ten-thirty. There was then a brief respite before the lunch pandemonium began at twelve-thirty after the staff had bolted down their own meal. But the biggest commotions of the day were the two sittings for evening dinner which began at five-thirty and ended at seven-thirty.

The kitchen was at one end of the hall and they soon found that the distance to a particular dining station varied in inverse proportion to their status on the staff. The higher the status, the nearer to the kitchen. The lower the status, the further away. Being newcomers, the trio had the lowest position in the pecking order and were given stations eighty yards away from the serving hatches, except for Billy who was a hundred yards. He reckoned he had to walk and run about twenty miles a day, carrying a heavy tray.

The kitchen was approached through an arrangement of 'in and out' swing doors up a ramp which became more and more greasy as food was spilled by hurrying waiters. Sliding through the door with a fully laden tray became a hazardous operation. To make the job more difficult, the enlightened camp authorities had allowed a wide choice of menu. Diners demanded individual meals of several courses which meant a huge team of chefs and waiters had to cook, serve and clean up afterwards.

'Why can't they make them all have the same bloody meal?' Titch complained. 'If we didn't have these *à la carte* menus we wouldn't have these complications.'

They skidded in and out of the kitchens, the diners' impatient demands ringing in their ears.

'Could you bring my porridge, please!' 'I'm still waiting for tea over here!' 'What happened to my bacon and eggs?' 'I distinctly ordered poached eggs – not fried.' 'Waiter, waiter –

what about some more coffee for my family, please?' 'More toast over here!'

As if the whingeing of the customers wasn't enough, their section supervisor, Joe Scrimshaw, was constantly at them to hurry up.

'You're too bloody slow, 'Opkins,' he snarled. 'Get a move on. Can't you see your diners are screaming for their grub?'

Billy slipped and slid, hither and thither, pouring sweat, harassed and toil-worn, in an effort to meet a hundred demands at once.

The more experienced Oscar seemed to take it all in his stride and even found time to offer helpful tips.

'Conserve your energy. Never go to the kitchen for a single job – try to do several things on each trip. If you're collecting a meal, wash some of your cutlery on the same trip.'

It sounded so easy!

Most of the jobs at Middleton Towers had been cornered by people from Ulster and the Manchester trio found it well-nigh impossible to gain access to a sink to wash up their crockery and cutlery. As Billy skated into the washing-up section, he was confronted by a dozen sinks and three dozen people jostling for a place.

'After you, Shaun!' 'When you've finished there, Maureen!' 'Make room for me there, Patrick!'

So much for Oscar's tips, of which he seemed to have an endless supply. He drew one more from his repertoire.

'When you give the punters coffee,' he advised, 'don't fill their cups to the top. They'll spill it and then you'll have thirty saucers to wash. Give them half a cup and tell them they can have more if they want it.'

All right in theory, but Billy had on his station a family of Sheffield steelworkers. He followed Oscar's advice and poured each a half-cup. A Gran'ma Buggins type, who appeared to be in charge of the burly workers, pushed the cups back indicating that she wanted them filled.

'You see, madam,' Billy explained patiently, 'these cups are larger than the usual coffee cups and so we pour only half. But of course should you require more, we shall replenish your cup.'

She listened expressionless, looked Billy straight in the eye and said: 'Fill the bloody things up, you daft bugger.' He did so and had thirty saucers to wash.

The same family gave trouble on another occasion. Billy had served out thirty meat pies – each in its own individual dish. One of the steelworker sons picked one up and tried to get the pie out with his knife.

'Hey, Gran,' he said, 'these bloody things are scalding hot.'

'Right,' retorted Gran, looking at Billy. 'Let this bugger burn his bloody hands – he's getting paid for it.'

Watched by a grinning Scrimshaw, Billy took the hot dishes and released the pies.

'Remember, 'Opkins,' he sneered, 'the customer's always right.'

Billy had noticed a private section right at the back of the hall – it seemed to accommodate around a hundred people. Most of the diners in this section were snazzily dressed and there was an air of affluence about them. Billy had an idea.

'Look,' he said, 'if the three of us could take over that private suite, we could work closely together, and with division of labour and economies of effort could make the work that much easier. The suite is a long way from the kitchens but take a look at the clientele – obviously well-off. The tips should be fabulous.'

Titch agreed readily. He was so done-in, he'd have agreed to anything. Oscar bowed to the majority decision.

The dining hall manager seemed more than happy to accept the arrangement, which puzzled them.

'Are you sure, Billy?' the manager asked. 'You realise there's a hundred people to cater for?'

'No problem, Mr Cartwright,' said Billy.

Very well,' he replied. 'I hope you know what you're doing.'

Next day they were given the private suite and, considering themselves to be three highly intelligent teachers, divided up the various jobs. The work was marginally harder but the operation ran like clockwork.

One of the diners, a smart, prosperous-looking gentleman with slicked back hair and a golden tan, remarked to Billy, 'This is the best service we've ever had. As far as I'm concerned, you can write your own reference and I'll sign it.'

A plump, middle-aged lady turned to Titch after he had gone to a great deal of trouble to obtain a special vegetarian diet for her. 'You are the most obliging, efficient waiter I have ever come across. First-rate. Absolutely first-rate,' she said.

At the end of that first day in the exclusive suite, the trio was highly elated.

'We're going to make a fortune in tips from this bunch of millionaires,' said Oscar. 'At least a pound from each of them at the end of their holiday.'

After two days of running themselves into the ground to please their benefactors-to-be, they discovered their true identity.

The rich-looking guy was the camp barber. The overweight female was an assistant in the camp post-office.

The rest of the hundred were all camp employees. Chances of tips? Zilch.

Billy remarked to Oscar one day that £4 per week seemed like poor pay considering the sweat involved.

'Your answer,' he said, 'is to do some extra work waiting on in the Wonder Bar. No pay – tips only. But when the holidaymakers are in festive mood, they can be generous.'

Billy agreed to give it a try and that same night turned up at the Wonder Bar. On the little stage there was a man playing an organ. As far as Billy could gather, he had only one tune: 'Stranger in Paradise' – a corruption of Borodin's famous melody from *Prince Igor.* Throughout the evening, Billy was run off his feet catering to the whims of the thirsty holidaymakers. The tips were not as generous as Oscar had predicted. Five elderly drinkers with Toby jug faces consistently ordered five Tadcaster Ales. 'Five Taddies,' they called. Eventually, they simply held up the fingers of a hand to indicate their order. Each time Billy complied ingratiatingly, sure that a tip would be on the cards eventually. But by the fifth order, when nothing was forthcoming, he'd had enough.

'Sorry, you'll have to get your own bloody Taddies this time,' he announced, wiping down their table to signal that it was last orders.

The evening came to an end at 11 p.m. and by that time Billy's legs had turned to jelly.

He counted up his tips. Five bob, he said to himself, for all that bloody work. Slave labour. But I suppose five bob is five bob.

At that point, an old man in a waiter's uniform approached him.

'I'm your bottle man,' he said.

'My bottle what? Bottle man?' Billy exploded. 'What the bloody hell is that? I didn't ask for a bottle man.'

'Your bottle man,' the old gent continued evenly. 'Who do you think has been keeping your tables clear all evening? Anyway, I get five bob for doing it.'

Billy thrust the money into his outstretched hand.

'Here, take it,' he said. 'Bloody Wonder Bar. Wait till I see Oscar! I'll give him Wonder Bar. "Stranger in Paradise"? More like "Stranger in Hades".'

Serving breakfast next day was the usual routine. On his way to the kitchen. Billy passed Titch who was looking distinctly hot and bothered, struggling with a heavy tray of breakfasts.

'I've had enough, I'm leaving,' Billy announced. He was also missing his wife and son after a four-day absence but he didn't tell Titch this.

Without a break in his tottering gait, Titch grimaced and nodded agreement.

They broke the news to Oscar who accepted their joint decision without discussion or argument.

'Right,' he said, 'we'll go at lunchtime. First we'll have our own lunch and then hand in our notice.'

'Don't you think we should serve lunch to the customers before resigning?' said Titch.

'No fear! We need to eat first to strengthen ourselves for the journey home. Then we go.'

At lunchtime Billy seized his last opportunity to take a snap of them in waiters' uniforms with his box Brownie. Then they went in to lunch – a slap-up affair as it turned out. At the main entrance to the dining hall they could see the hundreds of holidaymakers waiting for the doors to open, noses pressed against the window panes.

'Look at 'em all,' said Oscar, 'like animals at the zoo. Today they can bloody well feed themselves. Right, let's go.'

They marched over to the General Catering Manager's office – Billy and Titch nervous, Oscar cool as they come.

He knocked on the executive's office door.

'Come!' called Cartwright.

Oscar put his head round the door.

'We're off now, Mr Cartwright,' he said.

'Off? What do you mean "off?"?' said a puzzled Cartwright.

'Off – leaving,' replied Oscar. 'Resigning, departing, going home.'

'You can't go now,' said Cartwright fiercely. 'Not before lunch! We have a thousand people to feed in about five minutes.'

'Sorry,' said Oscar. 'But we have to go.'

'Well just serve lunch,' Cartwright pleaded.

'We've got to thumb lifts down to Bournemouth,' Oscar lied, 'so there's no time. Anyway, the work here is slave labour, the pay is a disgrace, and the living conditions are not fit for a pig.'

Seeing it was no use arguing, Cartwright blew his top. Purple with anger, he yelled, 'Get out! Get out! You've got five minutes to get off the place.'

They had already done their packing so there was no problem. As they made their way across the main square, loudspeakers across the camp boomed: 'Messrs Hopkins, Smalley and Wilde are hereby ordered off camp premises. If they are found here in the next five minutes, they will be arrested for trespass. They will not be allowed to use the camp bus and must find their own way back to Morecambe.'

They left in a hurry and made their way towards the main gate.

It was then that Billy discovered he had left his Brownie camera at his station in the dining hall!

'I'll have to go back for it,' he groaned. 'It's not mine. I borrowed it from Mr Mackenzie.'

Trembling, he went back to the dining hall. Chaos reigned.

The camp staff in the private enclave were sitting there fuming and ready to lynch him. The snazzy camp barber and the obese post office assistant seethed with fury as they doled out soup to their colleagues. Joe Scrimshaw had also been enlisted to serve. The sight of the hated supervisor pouring in sweat in an effort to keep up with the demands of the diners was meat and drink to Billy.

He collected the camera from the cupboard and tried to slink out but Scrimshaw grabbed him by the shoulder.

'You bastard,' he rasped. 'I've half a mind to throttle you.'

Billy struggled out of his grip and made for the door but before he made his exit, turned and addressed the camp barber. 'May I take it you won't be writing me that reference after all?'

When the bus from Morecambe finally pulled into Lower Mosley Street in Manchester, Billy felt a great sense of relief. Living in a caravan with Titch and Oscar had not been his idea of the high life and he had missed his family desperately even though he had been away only four days. It was so good to be home again with Laura and Matthew and to be back on familiar territory. Eight weeks later they received the pittance they had earned as waiters. Billy vowed never to take his family on holiday to Middleton

Towers and a few years later, when the camp was bought for use as a prison, Billy couldn't help thinking it was divine justice.

Meanwhile the money problem had not gone away. He still had to find his share of the university fee from somewhere, and the Middleton fiasco had set him back a few pounds in bus fares. There were still four weeks of the summer holiday left and it was vital he find another temporary job.

There was nothing for it but to try the Situations Vacant column in the *Manchester Evening News* to see if there was anything going. There was.

Chapter Ten

'Temporary cleaning staff required for British Rail,' said the clerk at the Hunt's Bank depot. 'Six-day week. Pay six pounds per week. Hours seven to five. Time and a half for overtime – double time for Sundays.'

'You said the job was for cleaning staff,' said Oscar. 'Which staff do we have to clean? And what kind of soap do we use?'

'Being funny,' replied the unsmiling clerk, 'won't get you anywhere. Report to the Head Railway Cleaning Executive at Victoria Station where you will be told what to do. Here are your green cards.'

At Victoria Station, they found the Cleaning Office (North West) executive suite and were ushered into a well-furnished room. A pipe-smoking executive checked them out to be sure they were qualified to do the job with the necessary physical attributes – namely eyes, ears, limbs – and weren't raving lunatics.

'These cleaning jobs,' he told them, 'are of the utmost importance to the forging of good relations with the general public. We at British Rail wish to create a positive image, and clean railway carriages are an important element in that process. If a passenger is faced with a dirty compartment it shatters the trust which the travelling public has placed in us. I know you won't let us down.'

'You can rely on us,' they said earnestly.

With an expression of deep concern, he looked into their faces. 'I take it you are not members of the NUR?'

'Oh, no,' they chorused, at the same wondering what NUR was. Some kind of secret society, perhaps.

'Very well,' the man said, relieved. 'Report to Mr Robertson, the foreman at Ordsall Lane Sidings, Salford, at seven o'clock tomorrow morning.'

Eager to make a good impression, the trio turned up at the sidings at 6.30 only to find the site deserted. They descended a flight of narrow wooden steps and stood outside the foreman's office. At 7.15 a gloomy little man in a trilby appeared and told them to wait until he had attended to some paperwork. At 7.30 the rest of the workforce drifted in, making first for the workers' canteen where they brewed up and took out their copies of the *Daily Mirror* to check on Jane's latest exploits

'We have sixteen lines here,' explained Mr Robertson the foreman when he had finished his clerical chore. Billy took a quick look out of the office window and saw a maze of railway tracks with dozens of carriages higgledy-piggledy on them. The foreman stroked his chin with a worried expression and Billy fully expected him to do a Robb Wilton and say, 'The day war broke out, my missus looked at me and she said . . .' Instead he continued, 'The trains come in from all over the country and it's our job to send them away again spick and span – inside and out. You will be inside cleaners and I'm attaching each of you to an experienced man who will show you the ropes. You'll spend your first day under instruction. Now, please sign here for your equipment.'

This consisted of a bucket, a large floor cloth, a polishing cloth, a chamois leather, a small hand-brush and pan, and one lavatory brush. These formalities completed, he took them over to the inside cleaners' canteen and introduced them to their 'instructors'.

Billy was handed over to one of their most experienced cleaners, Harry Tollitt, who had worked at the sidings man and boy for over thirty years. To Billy, aged twenty-three, he looked old, about fifty-five, with a rough-hewn face – a worker's face. He was dressed in blue overalls and wore a flat cap.

'Harry Tollitt,' announced Mr Robertson proudly, 'is one of our top workers and he knows the job inside out. You couldn't have a better teacher. Here's your first coach job, Harry – now show this new man how it's done.'

'Leave it to me, Mr Robertson. Right, follow me, lad,' Harry Tollitt said.

They collected several toilet rolls from a store tended by a spotty individual, then filled their buckets with a soapy liquid from a large vat of sickly-looking jelly which was being prepared by two specialists. Next, Harry led the way, climbing through several trains across numerous lines until they reached a third-class carriage on line six at the edge of the sidings.

'Now watch what I do,' he said. 'Most important, always leave clean toilets. Flush the pan and clean it with your lav brush, like this.' He added: 'The public is a dirty lot. Now put in a fresh toilet roll, clean round the wash bowl and the mirror, sweep the floor. Empty the litter bin. Be careful how you do it. See that notice which says 'Please place used towels in the bin provided' – well, some women think it means sanitary towels. So be careful how you empty the bin. See what I mean? The public's a dirty lot. Anyway, that's the toilet done.'

'What about the window, Mr Tollitt?'

'Never mind the bloody window. Let the outside cleaners wash it down. They think they're a cut above us inside cleaners – even got their own canteen. Besides, we can't do everything.'

They moved into the first compartment.

'Now, empty the ash trays on to the floor; look out for bloody chewing gum in them. Dirty lot! Sweep the floor and reach under the seat. Don't try to reach too far, we've only got small hand-brushes, remember.'

'And what about . . .' Billy was about to say. 'Oh, I remember: never mind the bloody windows.'

'That's right, you'll soon pick it up, son. Next, push your fingers down the back of the seats to see if anyone's left anything. I once found a fiver down there. But one of the other bastards working here had it in for me and put razor blades down the back when he heard. I cut my fingers to ribbons.'

Billy gathered that the compartment was now finished and they moved on to 'do' the others and the toilets at the other end of the carriage.

'Now for the most important thing of all,' said Harry. 'The corridor floor. Watch carefully.'

He dipped the floor cloth into the soapy liquid and, while it was still dripping, threw it down on the floor. The width of the cloth was a precise fit for the width of the corridor. Harry bent down and, with much panting and groaning, dragged the soaked cloth the length of the carriage.

'Always leave a wet corridor. When Robertson comes round to inspect, he likes to see a wet floor. It's proof that we've done it. Well, lad, that's it! Do you think you can do it?'

'I think so, Mr Tollitt,' Billy said. 'But what about the windows? And what do we do with these chamois leathers we've been given?'

'Will you stop going on about the bloody windows! You've got windows on the brain. As for the chamois, take it home and give it your missus for the windows at home.'

The whole operation had taken half an hour.

'What do we do now, Mr Tollitt?'

'Follow me,' he said.

They clambered through countless trains until they reached a carriage on a line at the edge of the sidings. Harry took out his well-thumbed copy of the *Mirror* and settled down to catch up on the rest of the day's news.

'One piece of advice,' he said. 'Never, never settle down in a first-class compartment. Robertson doesn't like it.'

At 10.45 precisely, he put down his paper and took out his fob watch.

'Tea break,' he announced.

They climbed back through the trains until they reached the canteen where the rest of the staff were busy scoffing their mid-morning snack. Each worker had a mug big enough to empty a normal teapot. Harry took out his brew – a mixture of tea, sugar and condensed milk – and filled his gargantuan mug.

'Didn't you bring a brew?' he asked. When Billy answered no, he said: 'Here, have some of mine,' and poured a liberal portion into a tin mug.

A little later, Billy's two companions arrived along with their mentors.

'I think I'm going to like this job,' said Titch.

'Easier than Middleton Towers,' added Oscar.

Following the half-hour break, they were given one more coach to clean, and followed the same routine. Harry finished reading his paper and then it was dinnertime with one hour off. The three apprentices ate their sandwiches and shared a bottle of Tizer. After the repast the entertainment began, courtesy of Harry Tollitt and his mates. There followed one dirty joke after another, each worse than the one preceding and each with a strong working-class flavour.

After a thoroughly entertaining dinnertime, it was time to go back to work for the afternoon. Mr Robertson came round with his slips and Harry and Billy were given one more coach which they finished by 2.15. Then it was the exhausting scramble once again across the lines to Harry's hideaway where, after a brief conversation, he put his head back and fell into a deep sleep, snoring loudly. At exactly three o'clock, he awoke with a snort and said: 'Tea-break.'

This is getting monotonous, Billy thought as they scrambled their laborious way to the canteen yet again. Afternoon tea completed, they were given their last job of the day. Harry made it last till six o'clock which gave them one hour's overtime at time and a half.

'This I could get used to,' Billy said to his companions. 'I might even take it up full-time because, with Sunday double-time, it pays more than teaching.'

The rest of the week passed uneventfully as the trio fell into the daily work pattern. In the afternoons, they each cleaned one coach then settled down to playing pontoon and poker. Everything went fine until the Friday when Robertson walked in on their card game.

This is it, Billy thought. Fair cop. We've been caught skiving. It means the sack after one week. Bang goes our cushy number, and bang goes my university fees. His fears proved to be groundless.

Mr Robertson looked wearily at them and the cards, clicked his tongue, and breathing heavily, delivered his remonstrance in his Robb Wilton voice.

'Look, lads,' he said, passing an anxious hand over his chin, 'if you must play cards, do it in third-class not in first.'

Sighs of relief all round.

On the Sunday they volunteered for work – they weren't going to miss the chance of double-time. No fear.

It was the same old thing – two coaches in the morning then reading all of the Sunday newspapers in the canteen. Around noon, Harry Tollitt appeared and announced to the assembled workers: 'Robertson's gone home and left me in charge. Right, lads, get your coats on and bugger off home. I'll clock everybody off.'

Which he did. Twelve inside-cleaners and twelve outside-cleaners were signed off and paid at double-time rates to go and sit at home and read the *News of the World*.

Billy and his friends stayed in the job for the rest of the summer holiday. After four weeks he returned the tools of his trade, his bucket and mop, the scrubbing brush, but not the chamois leather, to Robertson's office hut and collected his final pay. What sweet relief to have it all behind him! Clutching his pay packet, he rushed home to give Laura the good news.

'Laura, Laura!' he announced as he walked through the door. 'It's all over! No more slopping out corridors, washing windows, cleaning out toilets and wash basins. We're rich! I've counted up our savings and we've raised twenty pounds! Not only can I pay the balance of the university fees but there's a little over. Not much, admittedly, but it calls for a celebration. How about a night on the town?'

They booked a table at the Coq d'Or restaurant and ordered a bottle of wine and a four-course meal *à la carte*.

'Thank God those awful jobs are finished,' Billy said as he tucked into his melon starter. 'They've taught me one important lesson and that is that I never want to do such a mind-numbing job again. And to think, my poor old dad has been slaving at a similar job in Smithfield Market, working like a donkey, for the last fifty years. The way he's stuck it out fills me with admiration.'

'Unlike you, Billy, he had no choice. He didn't have your opportunities. You've been the lucky one in your family.'

'All the more reason, Laura, to do this degree and try and make something of my life. From now on, things are going to get easier, you'll see. It's all downhill.'

She wondered if she should tell him now but decided to wait till the end of the meal.

'I've got some news for you,' she said eventually after he had lit up a small cigar and picked up his liqueur glass.

'Sock it to me,' he said joyfully, sipping on his Benedictine. 'Nothing can surprise me now.'

'I'm pregnant again. The doctor confirmed it today.'

Billy didn't know whether to laugh or cry. 'But we were so careful! We used the safe period.'

'The so-called safe period,' she said, 'is anything but safe. We must have miscalculated.'

'No wonder they call it Roman Roulette,' he sighed. 'I told you we should have used a thermometer every day and kept a graph of your temperature.'

'Billy, I am not prepared to have my life dominated by an obsessive interest in temperature charts and ovulatory cycles.'

'I blame that bloke Halliday Sutherland. I'm sure he gave us a bum steer. We should have read Marie Stopes instead.'

'It's no use going over what we should or shouldn't have done, Billy,' said Laura, tears glistening in her eyes. 'The fact is we're having another and that's that.'

'OK, Laura. We'll have to accept it,' he said, taking both her hands. 'And rest assured, this baby will be welcomed and loved as much as Matthew. But money's going to be tight again from now on.'

'No matter,' she replied. 'We'll get by.'

Chapter Eleven

After the British Rail job, there was just enough money left to pay the balance of the fees and buy the set books. Early in October, Billy and his two companions attended the Dover Street Faculty of Economic and Social Studies for their first lectures.

The course titles alone were enough to make them nervous – Economic Theory, Political Thought, Public Administration, History of Local Government, Finance – but they found the appearance of their fellow students even more daunting. The great majority were male, and most were around Billy's age, but some of them were mature, middle-aged men with pipes, beards and thoughtful expressions while others with high foreheads and heavy pebbled spectacles looked like young Einsteins. In the row in front of Billy and his two friends sat a bald-headed man scribbling furiously in a reporter's notebook while next to him was a pale youth studying a book entitled *Economic Analysis* with frightening concentration.

'I can and I will. I can and I will,' Billy recited quietly to himself.

'Hoppy's finally flipped,' Oscar said to Titch. 'He's mumbling some kind of mantra.'

'What's got into you, Hoppy?' Titch whispered. 'Why are you muttering incantations?'

'I'm pumping up my courage, psyching myself up,' Billy replied. 'Feeding myself positive thoughts. These blokes around here make me jittery. They look like a bunch of Professor Joads from the BBC Brains Trust.'

'And those are just the caretakers,' Titch replied. 'Here's hoping we're not out of our depth. I don't even understand the titles of the courses.'

'You're not supposed to,' said Oscar. 'It's your first night and you've got the next three or four years to find out what they're about.'

Their first lecture was a general survey of the course by the Professor of Government, Bruce Macdonald. Yet another Scotsman in my life, Billy thought. The professor, a tall lanky figure who looked a lot less intellectual than his students, explained how, at university level, courses moved through their disciplines at high speed and it was up to each student to keep up as there would be no waiting for stragglers, no spoon-feeding. Private individual study was the key.

'I can and I will,' Billy recited quietly.

'Hoppy's rambling again,' Oscar said, looking up from his pad where he had been frantically scribbling notes.

'Something about making his will,' Titch said. 'He must be considering suicide.'

The professor went on to tell them that the subject of political science was a relatively new one, and that many of the students sitting before him today might well one day make a name for themselves in the academic world at home or abroad.

'I can and I will,' Billy repeated.

Macdonald turned to his subject and began tracing the development of local government in the Manchester area and the gradual improvement of health services there during the nineteenth century. It was a revelation and Billy's blood was stirred when it dawned on him that many of the professor's references had a direct bearing on the outbreak of cholera and the provision of clean water in Collyhurst and Cheetham where he had been brought up. He thought of St Michael's burial ground where as a kid, he had played football with his pals. Over forty thousand cholera victims lay there under the stone flags.

When the lecture was finished, Billy drew a deep breath. He had many questions to ask which would have shown his burning interest in the subject but the sight of the 'brains trust' panel around him inhibited him. His questions could wait for another day.

During that first week they were introduced to an unfamiliar academic world. By Thursday their heads were spinning with all kinds of strange concepts: trade cycles, indifference curves, and balance sheets. It was heavy going and the workload promised to be substantial. Their one consolation was that they had their Italian Studies to look forward to.

'Surely the study of a language cannot be as demanding as Social Studies,' Billy said to his friends on Friday evening as they walked across Oxford Road to the Arts Faculty. 'Italian should be a doddle.'

'Nothing can be as weighty as the stuff they've thrown at us so far,' Titch added.

'Nothing,' agreed Oscar.

They had another think coming.

'You begin this course,' said Course Director, Professor Adam Blackwell, 'knowing little or nothing of the language.

It is now October. By Christmas we expect you to have reached School Certificate level, and by summer you will be translating Charles Dickens into Italian. The course moves on at a good pace and there's no time to wait for lost sheep. You must keep up.'

'We can and we will,' the three friends chorused.

'As for literature, we shall study this year the greatest novel ever written, *I Promessi Sposi* by Alessandro Manzoni, the short stories of Giovanni Verga, and modern Italian poets. Next year, we'll meet Dante's *Inferno*.'

'We're already there,' Billy whispered.

'Wow!' said Titch. 'That's just for starters. Is it too late to switch to French?'

'Finally,' said Adam Blackwell, 'in the summer vacation we stipulate a month's course at the Università Per Stranieri at Perugia in Umbria as we expect a fair degree of fluency in the spoken language in your second year.'

'God knows where I shall get the money to go to Italy,' Billy remarked to his companions after the lecture. 'But I'll face that hurdle when I come to it.'

The only light relief in their study of Italian was furnished by the sessions on language taken by a handsome young Italian, Dr Giovanni Stefanuto. He proved to be touchy, and it took little to get his Irish, or in this case his Italian, up.

'Please repeat after me,' he began in his first lesson, '*Io sono un uomo.* I am a man.'

'And what a beautiful specimen you are,' Oscar whispered admiringly.

'*Io sono un uomo*,' the three students recited.

'And Laura will be so pleased when I give her this piece of information,' Billy added *sotto voce*, causing his fellow students to chuckle.

Stefanuto bristled. 'Please not to laugh. I not like it when you laugh.'

'Sorry,' they said.

'Now we learn about the weather,' their teacher said. '*Il tempo*. First, *fa caldo*. It's hot.'

'That's ridiculous,' Titch muttered. '*Caldo* should be cold not hot.'

'Quiet,' his two friends said. 'You'll get him mad.'

'*Piove*, it's raining,' Stefanuto announced.

That was it. The three students had only to look at each other to cause a fresh bout of giggling.

'Well, that should be easy enough to remember,' Billy said. 'It's peeing down.'

Stefanuto became incandescent. 'I no teach you!' he exclaimed. 'You make fun of me and laugh too much.' He stalked out of the room, slamming the door.

It took considerable time and effort to smooth his ruffled feathers. Professor Blackwell had to be brought in to explain Manchester humour to him and forever afterwards Stefanuto was ready to join in the fun. His lessons became the most enjoyable part of their course.

On Friday nights, after the last lecture, they took to retiring to the College Inn to assess and review the week's work. It began as a seminar in which they could exchange views and discuss difficulties they had experienced, but after two or three pints the session usually ended up with congratulatory pats of each other's backs and giving voice to their quiet satisfaction that after all their initial worries they were coping. The Friday night visit was about their only respite from self-imposed slavery. There was no let-up on Saturday and Sunday.

The first weekend, Billy moved the kitchen table, the one he had carried through the streets, along with a hard wooden chair up to the attic at the top of the house. The room was Spartan with its bare floorboards and lack of furniture and so Billy tried to add a cheerful note by painting the walls with bright emulsion paint. He avoided any kind of distracting ornament or picture but could see the back garden from the window and sometimes his eye wandered to the owl which sat on the upper branches of the sycamore tree, winking and watching and apparently supervising him. While Billy studied, Laura coped with the household and the baby below. Sometimes she found time to test Billy's Italian vocabulary and knowledge of irregular verbs. Every spare moment he went into the attic to study his books.

Sunday nights, however, were different.

His father-in-law had agreed to give him private lessons in accountancy and Billy was dreading it. Duncan had proved to be kind and generous in helping them out with the purchase of the house and furniture, but Billy still considered him a formidable character. He would no doubt be a hard taskmaster, intolerant of mistakes of which Billy was likely to make many, since he'd been studying the subject only three weeks and was still struggling with the rudiments of double entry.

'There's no need to be scared,' Laura said. 'He won't bite you. You must catch him in the right mood. Wait until he's back from Benediction and then walk over with your text books.'

'Doesn't he usually go to his club on Sunday nights? He won't like the idea of forgoing his drink with his cronies.'

'The way round that,' Laura smiled, 'is to visit the off licence and buy a couple of bottles of his favourite tipple, Double Diamond lager. That should soften him up.'

Billy collected his books and walked on to Stockport Road where he found a liquor store, bought two bottles of ale and made his way across to the Mackenzie household. As he stood on the threshold, Billy could hear young Katie practising her Czerny scales on the piano.

That's one thing Laura must miss since she married, he thought. Music and a piano. One of these days, we shall . . .

The doorbell was answered by Jenny who greeted him with a bright, cheery smile.

'Hello, Billy. Daddy said it would be you. He's expecting you.'

'Good to see you, Jenny,' Billy answered. 'How's it going?'

'Things are fine, Billy,' she said as she took his coat. 'Hamish and I are saving like mad to meet Daddy's target figure. We're hoping to raise six hundred by next summer.'

'Hope you make it, Jenny. Knowing Hamish's business acumen, I'm sure you will.' He was tempted to offer her sympathy over her choice of fiancé but thought better of it.

He decided to go into the kitchen first to greet the senior ladies before facing Duncan. As he knocked and opened the door, he was met by that familiar smell of freshly baked scones and bread.

Gran'ma as usual was rocking in her chair by the fire, no doubt waiting to sample the treats Louise was at that moment removing from the oven. Old Auntie gave Billy a welcoming smile, waiting for the chance to launch into one of her anecdotes.

'Good evening, Billy,' his mother-in-law said warmly. 'You've come to see His Nibs for a spot of tuition? He's looking forward to it. He loves showing off his knowledge.'

'I hope I'm not dragging him away from you?'

'Not at all, Billy. It will give us some peace for a couple of hours. We're about to watch *Dr Finlay's Casebook* and we'll enjoy it all the more without his running commentary.'

'Right, perhaps I shall see you all later.'

He knocked on the study door.

'Come in, Billy,' Duncan called.

He entered to find his father-in-law seated in his favourite armchair before a blazing fire, a picture of domestic bliss.

'Good evening, Mr Mackenzie,' Billy said. 'I hope you haven't forgotten our accountancy session.'

'Of course not, Billy. As a matter of fact, I've brought one or two Inland Revenue booklets which you might find useful. And I'm Duncan, remember? Did you bring your books with you?'

'I did, Duncan . . . and also these,' Billy said, producing the Double Diamonds.

Duncan gave him a broad smile. 'Now those should help us to think clearly and creatively. I'll get two glasses and we'll waste no time in getting down to work.'

'I should warn you that I'm a beginner at all this. I've done some preliminary work but the university moves so fast through the course, it's difficult to keep up.'

'We'll see what we can do to remedy that, Billy,' said his father-in-law enthusiastically. He offered his Three Castles cigarettes and they both lit up. 'Now let's take a look at these exercises.'

Soon the two men were hard at work on *Magee's Advanced Accounts*. Duncan introduced Billy to basic concepts, like profit and loss, the balance sheet, and how to make provision for various contingencies. Together they worked methodically for an hour through an involved and complicated set of partnership accounts, making provision for this, that and the other.

'There,' Duncan said, taking a sip at his beer and leaning back in his chair, 'that should do it. Now, add the totals on each side of the balance sheet and see what you get.'

Billy did a rapid calculation and was amazed to find they balanced at the first attempt.

'That's never happened to me before,' he said, shaking his head in disbelief. 'I usually find I've forgotten some tiny item.'

He was filled with a new admiration for Duncan's professional knowledge and skill and the clear way in which he explained things. Not only that, he showed a lively wit and it was obvious that he derived great enjoyment from teaching. At ten o'clock Katie took in two cups of cocoa which remained unnoticed amongst the books on the desk. At the end of the session, a new bond of friendship had grown up between the men.

'Give me a year,' Duncan said warmly, 'and I shall have you at an advanced standard. Give me two, and you could make Tax Officer grade! Three and you'll be after my job as Inspector.'

'Thanks for that, Duncan, but teaching's the job for me,' Billy laughed.

'I thought you might say something like that. Anyway, next time I'll let you in on some of the Inland Revenue wrinkles on how to estimate income without a set of accounts.'

'I'll look forward to it,' Billy said, and meant it.

Duncan shook his hand. 'Till next week.'

Billy called out goodnight to the rest of the Mackenzie family in the drawing room and Duncan walked him to the front door.

'Thanks for all your help,' Billy said. 'I was nervous when I arrived but I enjoyed it. See you next Sunday.'

'There's one thing you must not forget, Billy,' Duncan chuckled.

'What's that?'

'The Double Diamonds.'

Chapter Twelve

Billy was lying in bed studying Dante's *Inferno* for a university test and had reached the sentence '*Lasciate ogni speranza voi ch'entrate*' (Abandon all hope ye who enter) when Laura tapped him gently on the shoulder and said, 'Don't get excited, Billy, but I think it's time to get the midwife.'

The book fell from his grasp and his heart raced ten to the dozen. Even though they'd planned carefully for this moment, his mind was in a whirl. Now what was it he was supposed to do? First, stay calm and phone Laura's mother to alert her and Duncan. Second, get his old bike out and cycle round to Nurse McHugh. Where in heaven's name had he put the two pennies reserved for the phone? Of course, same as last time, on the mantelpiece, stupid! Stay calm!

'Right, Laura,' he said trying to sound in control. 'Leave it to me. One midwife coming up.' Matthew had been born in hospital but this one was to be born at home. Hence the panic stations.

Billy gave her a quick nervous peck and went into the other bedroom to check that Matthew was still asleep. He looked out of the window and saw that the few snowflakes he'd seen earlier had taken hold on the roadway. Just my luck, he thought. He dressed swiftly in his winter outfit: big overcoat, balaclava and leather gloves. He tucked his trousers into his socks and wrapped the woollen scarf that Laura had knitted round his neck. He looked as if he were about to join Scott on his Antarctic expedition, which was appropriate 'cos by the time he'd got his Raleigh out of the cellar, the snow was falling thickly. Billy hardly noticed. He rang Laura's mum from the local phone box, gave her the news and re-mounted his bike. Now for the midwife. No problem.

He found the address all right but not the midwife. On her front door she'd pinned a note: OUT ON A CASE. IF YOU NEED ME, I AM AT 27 COWESBY STREET, MOSS SIDE.

His stiff upper-lip composure crumbled like a collapsed cake. Where in hell's name was Cowesby Street? He had no *A to Z*. An absentee midwife was not part of the plan and he could see Louise and himself having to deliver this baby. Well, more Louise than me, he thought. The snow was coming down heavily, swirling round the lamp-posts and clinging to every object in sight, shrouding the houses, the walls, the rooftops, in ghostly white. There was no traffic, no pedestrians were about, and the deathly hush only added to the spectral scene. Desperately he lowered his head and pedalled furiously through the falling sleet to Moss Side Police Station.

'Yes, sir. How may we be of assistance to you?' said the desk sergeant, giving each syllable its full weight.

'Quick,' Billy blurted out, 'Cowesby Street. I need a midwife.'

'I see, sir,' the po-faced sergeant replied, giving him a funny look. Laboriously he brought out a road map and pointed Billy in the right direction. Cowesby was on the other side of the district and seemed as remote as Outer Mongolia.

After another half-hour cycling through the blizzard, Billy finally found it. The street was a small row of terraced houses between a brewery and a railway sidings. Even though it was midnight, the lights at number twenty-seven blazed out on to the snow-covered cobbles. Billy banged urgently on the door and after an interval of what seemed like an hour – it was ten minutes – the masked face of Nurse McHugh peered round the door.

'Yes, yes,' she snapped. 'What is it? We're busy here at the moment.'

Billy explained quickly who he was, the nature of his errand, and how he was worried out of his mind that time was running out.

Unperturbed, the nurse asked, 'How often are the contractions?'

Contractions? Which contractions? He wasn't having any contractions. Even when she told him she was referring to Laura, he still hadn't a clue. Nobody had said anything to him about contractions. He told her when and how the pains had begun, over an hour ago.

'Very well,' she said, still maddeningly calm. 'I'll be there as soon as I've finished here. Whatever you do, don't panic.'

Huh!

He rode back through the snow and found that Laura and her mum and dad were sitting quietly in the dining room having a cup of tea in front of a cheerful fire. Talk about British *sang-froid*! Shortly afterwards, Nurse McHugh arrived on her bicycle with her big black bag containing all sorts of mysterious bottles and instruments. Of course, a fresh pot of tea had to be brewed. Like a Sunday afternoon tea party. But not for Billy who opted for a large whisky and soda. Duncan joined him and had the same. After a while, the nurse suggested that Laura and she might go upstairs to attend to the business in hand.

'Is there anything I can do?' Billy asked of nobody in particular.

'You've already done it,' the nurse barked. 'The best way you can help is by staying out of the way. This is women's work.'

He was used to hearing this claim to monopoly but nevertheless it put him in his place once again and he felt useless. As far as the nurse was concerned the male was irrelevant once he had made his minor contribution to the creative process. At least Laura was not to be whipped off to the outskirts of Cheshire like last time.

She gave him a maternal kiss on the forehead. 'Don't worry, Billy my love,' she said. 'Everything's going to be all right.' Turning to the nurse, she said, 'Let's go and get this over with.'

Billy chain-smoked his Capstan full-strength while Laura's mum browsed through a copy of *Woman's Own* and Duncan smoked his Three Castles and read the *Financial Times*. From upstairs, Billy heard various sounds: voices calling, creaking floorboards, muffled moans and the occasional anguished cry. Then a long silence followed by the most wonderful sound in the whole universe, the cry of a newly born infant.

Ten minutes later, the nurse, still masked, leaned over the banister and called down: 'It's a girl! Ten pounds two ounces!'

Billy's heart leapt for joy. In that instant, all his tenderest feelings came rushing to the fore. A little girl! A daughter! Into his head came words from the musical *Carousel* about having fun with a son but having to be a father to a girl.

'You can come up and see her,' he heard the nurse calling.

See her! Perhaps hold her! Would she be anything like his new-born son?

It had been a couple of months before Matthew had come to resemble a member of the human race. What would this latest be like? Wait a minute! Ten pounds! Matthew had been an eight-pounder. Perhaps this time he'd spawned an Amazonian baby with a gargoyle face! A regular Pantagruel! Billy mounted the stairs with the grandparents in tow to take his first look at his daughter.

Laura looked flushed but glowingly happy as if she had completed a marathon, which in a way she had.

'Laura,' he said, kissing her on the lips, 'you're wonderful. I don't know how you do it.'

'Nothing to it.' She smiled. 'Not with a nurse like Nurse McHugh to ease the process.'

The mention of her name prompted the nurse to offer the baby to Billy. He took his daughter in his arms, oh, so gently and oh, so delicately as if handling a priceless Ming vase.

All his worries were for nothing because Lucy, the name already chosen for a girl, turned out to be the most beautiful infant in the whole wide world. No having to wait for a human appearance this time. With smooth, clear skin and an angelic expression on her face, Lucy was ready to join Bubbles in the Pears soap ads. The mysterious parental bonding process took place from the first moment Billy laid eyes on her.

'Laura,' he said quietly, 'you have surpassed yourself this time. She's beautiful. And look at those lovely blue eyes!'

'Don't see how you can see her eyes since they're closed,' Nurse McHugh said, bringing him down to earth. 'Besides, all babies have blue eyes at birth and they may change colour later.'

'Not this baby,' he replied. 'Blue eyes run in both our families.'

Duncan and Louise took their turn admiring their latest grandchild.

'If there were a competition for the most beautiful baby born in 1953, I'm sure she'd win first prize,' her grandmother said.

'Well, Billy,' Duncan said, taking Billy's hand in a firm handshake, 'now you have a son and a daughter, you have big responsibilities. It's more important than ever you get that degree.'

As if he didn't know.

The front doorbell rang and Nurse McHugh found she'd been called to yet another case, even though it was two o'clock in the morning.

'It never rains but it pours,' she remarked as she collected her bag of tricks and departed.

Shortly after that, Duncan and Louise left and Billy and Laura were alone with their new baby. It wasn't long before Laura was sound asleep but Billy remained awake, lying on his back, listening to the steady breathing and occasional snuffle of the new infant.

Fancy! he thought to himself. Me, Billy Hopkins, with a daughter! She's got to be handled differently from Matthew. No horse-play or rough-housing, none of this throwing her up in the air stuff and swinging her round. His mind leapt forward in time and he could see her as the May Queen at church. What a sight that would be! The eyes of everyone watching her as she climbed the ladder to lay the wreath on Our Lady's head as people sang, 'O, Mary, we crown thee with blossoms today'. But suppose she stumbled and fell! That would be a disaster. He watched in trepidation as she mounted the steps. Oh, my God, she's going to fall and hurt herself . . . 'Wait a minute,' he said aloud to himself. 'What am I thinking about? She's only an hour old and already I've made her Queen of the May and I'm worried sick in case she slips off the ladder. I must be going barmy.'

His mind turned to what Duncan had said about a degree being the key to success and getting on. That was Billy's dearest wish, to be successful and provide a better life for Laura and their *bambini.* He was determined to study hard, get high grades, win promotion and higher pay. With these thoughts going round and round in his head, Billy slept.

Next day he phoned his brother Les at work and asked him to pass the news around the family. It didn't take long for his mam and two sisters to put in their appearance and coo over the female addition to the Hopkins clan. Mam had knitted the usual baby clothes, this time in pink only.

'Somehow I knew it was going to be a girl, and I was right,' she said.

'You've forgotten to mention that you visited a fortune-teller,' Polly said.

'I did,' Mam replied, 'and she predicted a boy. I've never trusted these gypsies except to get it wrong. Believe the opposite of what they tell you and you'll be right nine times out of ten. No, I thought you'd be like the Queen and have one of each.'

'Anyway, she's a beautiful little girl,' Flo said, 'a true Hopkins!'

'If she's beautiful, she can't be a true Hopkins,' Billy said and received two digs in the ribs for his trouble. One from each sister.

Chapter Thirteen

Lucy was born in 1953 but the year was significant in other ways. In May there were two weddings. First, Billy's brother Les married Annette, a beautiful girl from North Manchester.

'How come an ugly puss like you won such a good-looking girl?' Billy asked.

'Personality,' Les replied nonchalantly. 'I'm unique. Some folk got it and some folk ain't.'

'Sure,' Billy said. 'You're unique like everybody else. And Strangeways is full of unique personalities.'

It was a quiet but happy ceremony at St Anne's Church on Ashton Old Road with a reception afterwards at the Grandsmoor Hotel. Billy was best man, which gave him a chance to get his own back for all the snide remarks Les had made at his wedding.

The second wedding was a grander affair.

Hamish and Jenny at last announced that they had succeeded in reaching not only the five-hundred-pound target Duncan had stipulated as a necessary pre-condition for a happy marriage but exceeded it by two hundred. Hamish had been appointed actuary to a Scottish insurance company at a princely salary and had bought a three-storey detached house on the outskirts of Edinburgh. He was Duncan's ideal son-in-law.

Naturally, before the wedding Hamish had arranged that he and Jenny should have thorough medical examinations to check there were no deadly diseases lurking in their genes. Hamish was convinced that he had every disease in the medical encyclopaedia, except maybe hypochondria, and on learning the disappointing news that he was free from defects, demanded a second opinion. Jenny too had picked up his neurosis and was convinced she was suffering from sleeping sickness though everyone had done their best to persuade her that England was relatively free from the *tsetse* fly.

'Maybe they should set up home in the Edinburgh Royal Infirmary,' Billy remarked.

The date of the wedding was set for 2 May but, at the insistence of Duncan, they had to postpone it by a week since it clashed with the Cup Final between Blackpool and Bolton Wanderers. The magic of Stanley Matthews winning his first cup medal took priority over a mere wedding, and on that Saturday the nation was glued to its wireless sets as Blackpool beat Bolton 4–3 with a last-minute goal.

The wedding was a lavish affair with a three-priest, sung High Mass at St Joseph's followed by a sumptuous reception at the Midland Hotel paid for by Duncan but no doubt requested by Hamish's family. Everyone, or nearly everyone, said what a really, really lovely couple they made.

'Soulmates,' the elderly lady sitting next to Billy said. 'I love the way he calls *her* his little bunny and she calls *him* her big teddy bear. They're as close as Siamese twins.'

Yuck, Billy thought.

He noticed the way Hamish always finished his little bunny's sentences for her, a habit, Billy thought with quiet satisfaction, that would drive her crazy one day.

Splendid though the wedding was, it was eclipsed by the Coronation of Queen Elizabeth the Second three weeks later. When the palace authorities reluctantly gave permission for the ceremony to be televised, there was a rush to buy sets. Titch and his family were amongst the first to acquire one and Billy and Laura were invited to join the elite viewing party. With Lucy in her pram and Matthew on the attached seat, they walked across to Fallowfield, a long walk but well worth the effort.

At Titch's home a dozen neighbours and relatives crowded the front parlour to view the pageant on a postage-stamp-sized set. 'Oohs' and 'ahhs' echoed round the room as the little crowd watched the royal coach being pulled at walking pace through the streets of London. The brilliance of the golden coach was lost, though, in the monochrome picture and the damp London weather, but the spirits of the audience were lifted by the sight of a beaming Queen of Tonga waving to the crowds as her open carriage filled with rainwater. When the Archbishop of Canterbury placed the crown on Elizabeth's head and she uttered the Coronation oath in a light but clear voice, a patriotic cheer went round the parlour and everyone felt proud to be British. There was similar patriotic fervour throughout the country and hope that, after the privations of post-war Britain, there would be a fresh beginning under this young Queen.

'You know,' Titch's mother said to Laura as they were preparing to leave for home, 'you put me in mind of the Queen.'

'What makes you say that?' Laura asked, looking pleased with herself.

'Well, *you* look like Queen Elizabeth while Matthew is the spitting image of Prince Charles. And as for Lucy there, she's the double of Princess Anne.'

'What about me?' Billy asked. 'Do me! Do me!'

Titch's mother regarded him for a moment, pursed her lips, and looked doubtful.

'No,' she said at last. 'You don't look a bit like Philip.'

'I had no idea,' Billy said as they wheeled the pram home, 'that I was married to royalty. One day I hope this commoner will be able to buy a TV fit for Queen Laura and her royal children. But with a bigger screen so that we don't need a magnifying glass to view the picture.'

'That'll be the day,' she said.

The prospect of acquiring a television, however, was remote because Billy had other problems on his plate in the summer of that year. The Italian class was due to visit the University of Perugia as part of the programme. While it was not a course requirement, Adam Blackwell had hinted that, to pass the oral exam, fluency was expected and this could only be acquired by 'total immersion' on a study-visit to Italy. For bachelors Titch and Oscar there was no difficulty. They were going.

Billy's problem was two-fold. First, the usual one. Money. The course would cost in the region of twenty pounds – an impossible sum since he wouldn't be able to take a holiday job.

Secondly, and more important, leaving Laura and his children for four weeks did not appeal to him. He could see no way out of the impasse.

'It's no use,' he said, 'I'm snookered. I shall have to forget the idea. Maybe I can speed up my spoken Italian by listening to Linguaphone records.'

'Don't give up. There must be some answer,' she said. 'Maybe we could ask the bank for an overdraft, or maybe Daddy will give us another loan.'

'We already have an overdraft at the bank and I don't like the look of that nasty little manager, Mr Wilson. As for your father, we already owe him a fortune. Best forget the Italian trip. I'll get by without it. I didn't want to go anyway, leaving you with the kids for a whole month.'

'But, Billy, getting this degree means so much to you. To us. Have faith, I'm sure something will turn up.'

'You sound like Wilkins Micawber. It would need a miracle, perhaps two, to solve things.'

A week later he got his miracles, and from two unexpected sources. On learning of his plight, Adam Blackwell called him into his office and told him he could help with half the cost from a special departmental award, set up with the express purpose of enabling needy students like Billy to study in Italy.

The other source was his brother Les. He and Annette intended buying their own home but while waiting for something suitable to turn up, they asked Billy and Laura if they could rent part of their house for a period of six months. A monthly rent of eight pounds was agreed. The arrangement was to everyone's advantage. The extra income would not only help Billy to pay for the trip but the tenants would also provide Laura with company while he was away. Annette was a friendly girl who loved children and she and Laura got on well together, an important consideration when they would be sharing a tiny kitchen.

It was a sorrowful parting from Laura and the children, though.

'I'll write to you every day, Laura, and I shall bring you back something Italian.'

'How about Beniamino Gigli?' she laughed through her tears.

* * *

Billy, Titch and Oscar caught the Manchester train to London and from there a connection to Dover. Everything ran smoothly. Even the crossing of the Channel, about which they had received so many warnings and so much urging to 'be sure to take your Kwells', was straightforward. A few hours later they arrived in Paris where Billy, despite his years of French, succeeded in getting them lost and on to the wrong train. After a sixteen-hour journey they arrived at Pisa where he sent a picture postcard winging its way back to Laura before changing trains for Florence.

Dearest Laura,
We have completed the first leg of what proved to be a nightmare journey. You can see from the picture overleaf where we've got to. Titch says the tower reminds him of a doodlebug on the launching pad, and moral decency prevents me from telling you what image it conjured up in Oscar's mind. Missing you and the kids terribly.
All my love, Billy

From Florence they took the local train to their final destination, Perugia. The trip from Paris had taken eighteen hours.

They found their *pensione* in a narrow medieval street, Corso Garibaldi, next to the university. Their accommodation, on the middle floor of a large building, was a spacious apartment with high ceilings and large shuttered windows which kept the place cool but failed to keep out the angry waspish buzz of the Vespas whizzing up and down the Corso at all times of the day and night. And judging from the number of obituary announcements on the notice boards at every street corner, a high death rate amongst the local motor-cycling youth seemed to be an accepted way of life.

The accommodation was owned and run by two elderly ladies, Maria and Francesca Cordi, who fussed and clucked like mother hens over their guests, treating them as members of the family. When Billy showed them snaps of his wife and two children he was treated like royalty, much to the annoyance of Titch and Oscar.

'*Che bella moglie et che bellissimi bambini!*' the old ladies cooed. (What a beautiful wife and children.)

'I object strongly to this currying of favour with the hotel management,' Oscar lamented. 'It's merely an attempt to get extra food.'

His complaint was not entirely justified as they found the food good but strange since everything was cooked in olive oil, and what looked like English new potatoes turned out to be heavy dumplings.

'I read somewhere,' Titch said, 'that olive oil helps Mediterranean people live a longer life.'

'With food tasting like this,' Oscar remarked as he cut into an oil-soaked piece of meat, 'who would want a long life?'

Evening dinner with the Cordi family was something of a formal affair. Billy and his companions learned a good deal of Italian as conversation flowed easily round the table, especially when the last course was rounded off by several glasses of the ladies' home-made but potent liqueurs, maraschino and peach.

Perugia itself was a medieval town which boasted two universities and several academies. A short walk from their lodgings was their Università per Stranieri. A programme of talk, tours and music recitals opened their eyes and ears to a new world of Italian culture, music, literature and art. On their trips to Florence and Assisi they were introduced to the works of the great Italian masters: the paintings of da Vinci, the sculptures of Michelangelo, the frescoes of Giotto, and the madrigals of Monteverdi. With his companions, Billy wandered spellbound through this wonderland wishing desperately that Laura could be there with him to enjoy it.

'How can we ever go back to Manchester with its greyness and drizzle?' Oscar murmured.

'Because where there's muck, there's brass,' said Titch. 'We're stuck there because of our jobs.'

'But are we?' Billy wondered. 'All I know is that this visit to Italy has made me realise that there is a great big world beyond our own city. There are things not dreamt of in our day-to-day life, things of breath-taking beauty to be seen and experienced. One day, I shall bring Laura and the *bambini* out here to enjoy them as we have.'

'You'll have to win the pools first,' Titch said.

Though mornings and evenings were spent at the university, in the afternoons the whole town went for a siesta. Not so the Englishmen. The three friends retired to a nearby park and, sitting on a bench, used little pebbles to bomb the thousands of ants which thrived in the Mediterranean sunshine. In the early evening around 6 p.m., they strolled down the main street, Corso Vannucci, to watch the Italian families taking the air, at the same time displaying their young sons and daughters to each other as potential marriage partners.

'My Jewish friends in Cheetham Hill, especially the mothers, would appreciate this custom,' Billy remarked. 'Look at all these lovely young ladies, Titch. Surely there's one amongst this lot for you?'

One evening, Titch thought he'd try his chances at a university dance arranged for the students.

'Please come and support me,' he begged. 'I'm not sure I'll ever attract a girl. I'm a teacher, I'm losing my hair, and I still live with my parents. Who would want me?'

'You never can tell,' Billy said. 'You might meet someone with strong maternal instincts.'

They agreed to accompany him though, for different reasons, neither Billy nor Oscar had any personal interest.

Titch spied an attractive *signorina* across the other side of the dance floor. The only problem was that the girl was surrounded by her extended family, acting no doubt as chaperones and protectors from characters like him.

'That's the girl for me,' he announced. 'I'll ask her to dance. Wish me luck. OK, I'm going in.'

Taking his courage in both hands, he strode decisively across the room and asked permission of the girl's uncle who gave him the once over.

'*Si*,' he said after a long pause. OK.

Next, he asked father and got his approval. Then the mother and grandparents. All of them looked him up and down and gave him a reluctant '*Si*'. Finally, Titch reached the girl herself.

'*Posso, signorina*?' May I, miss?

The *signorina* ran a practised eye over Titch, sizing him up as a possibility. She pursed her lips and came to a decision. '*No, grazie*,' she replied.

'Well, how did you get on?' Billy asked when Titch returned to his seat.

'I didn't understand all that she said but I caught the word "*piove*" somewhere in the dialogue.'

After their evening *passeggiata*, they rounded off the evening with a cappuccino at the local café, if they could afford it. The twenty pounds of foreign exchange they had been allowed was hardly sufficient to survive on, let alone pay for extra luxuries like cups of coffee. Billy had already spent a couple of his precious pounds on little gifts for his children, a hammering toy for Matthew and a fluffy dog for Lucy. By the last week they were each down to their last five pounds which they were keeping in reserve for a special purpose.

Titch and Oscar planned to make a day trip to Rome but Billy had other ideas. In a jeweller's on the Corso Vannucci he had seen a rolled gold necklace in the form of a daisy chain costing the equivalent of £4 in English money. Though it would leave him almost broke, he was determined to buy it for Laura.

'Hoppy,' Titch said, 'you must be off your head to swap a visit to the Eternal City for a rolled gold bauble.'

'I agree with Titch,' Oscar added. 'Here you are in Italy with Rome a few hours away. You'll be passing up a once-in-a-lifetime opportunity. Why not buy Laura a less expensive present such as one of those perfumed sachets I've seen the women selling in the marketplace?'

'Oscar,' Billy replied, 'you're the one that's mad. Imagine me getting home and saying to Laura, "I've brought you something special all the way from Italy. A pin cushion." She'd probably divorce me. No, it's got to be the necklace. As for Rome, I'll be back one day in my Roller.'

Billy bought the necklace and his friends made the trip to Rome and never ceased reminding him of the things he'd missed: St Peter's, the Coliseum, the Trevi Fountain, Piazza Venezia.

The return to Britain followed the same pattern as the journey out only worse as they suffered the additional inconvenience of a strike by French railway workers. It was a great relief to get back to their dear old Manchester. It was raining when they emerged from London Road

Station but after their horrific journey it was a sight for sore eyes.

'It's good to be here,' Titch sighed. 'It was raining when we left and it's raining now we're back.'

'Manchester,' said Oscar, 'is the only town where the buses have inflatable life jackets under the seats.'

For Billy's homecoming, the word 'joy' was inadequate. Bliss was nearer the mark. The children seemed to have grown during his absence. There was a good deal of hugging and tears running down cheeks, mainly Billy's. He handed over his gift to Laura.

'Billy, it's the best present I've ever had. But you shouldn't have. Was it expensive?'

'Not really, Laura. It didn't cost me all that much.'

Only a trip to Rome, he thought, that's all.

Some time later she asked, 'Well, Billy, was the trip worth the expense?'

'Every penny,' he answered. 'Not only did I learn a lot of Italian but I feel as if the scales have fallen from my eyes. I've come to realise that there's a great big beautiful world out there and one day we're going to see something of it.'

Chapter Fourteen

'The bank manager will see you shortly, Mr Hopkins,' the counter clerk said. 'If you'll kindly take a seat, we'll call you when he's free.'

They showed Billy into a little room to wait his turn. Ahead of him in the queue was a pale, thin man who looked as if he wanted to engage him in a discussion about their mutual financial plight. Billy avoided eye contact and adopted a deadpan expression. He was nervous enough without listening to someone else's sob story.

How he hated banks and bank managers; they always made him feel like a pauper holding out his begging bowl. But beggars, as they say, can't be choosers.

Billy was two months behind with the mortgage and they had a whacking great bill at the grocer's. But that wasn't why he was here. He needed to borrow £30 and he was desperate. To some people £30 might not have sounded like much, but for him it was a month's salary. He'd been studying every night and every weekend for the last three years because, as Duncan was forever telling him, a university degree was the only way to get ahead.

The nervous bloke was called first and shown into the *sanctum sanctorum*. In many ways an apt image, Billy thought to himself, for being in this waiting room was like going to Confession.

'Bless me, Mr Wilson, for I am broke. It's five years since I was last solvent.'

He strained his ears in an attempt to listen through the thick, heavy door but he couldn't make out a word they were saying inside. Judging by the tone of their voices, though, it didn't sound hopeful for the thin man. Or for himself for that matter. After ten minutes, the thin man came out looking shell-shocked, glanced over at Billy, shook his head and gave the thumbs-down sign.

It was Billy's turn.

Putting on a brave face, he entered the lion's den. Mr Wilson was a small, bald-headed man with a long nose on which was perched a pince-nez. He looked not unlike those drawings of Mr Chad that were seen chalked up on walls and Billy half expected him to begin the interview with, 'Wot no money?' Instead he gave Billy the non-person treatment by concentrating his attention on the file on his desk. At last, he looked up and gazed at him as if he was some kind of nasty insect.

'I see here from your file, Mr Hopkins, that you are constantly overdrawn at the end of each month. You have written so many cheques, you must have writer's cramp. It won't do. You will have to make an effort to live within your means. At the moment you are twenty pounds in the red. I take it that you've come to make good the deficit?'

'No, sir,' Billy stammered. 'I am an evening student at the University of Manchester. I am in the final year of a degree course and need the loan of thirty pounds to cover next year's tuition and examination fees.'

Mr Wilson was already shaking his head in disapproval as he asked, 'How have you paid the fees so far?'

'By working at summer vacation jobs and occasional bar work.'

'I'm afraid you must continue to find your fees in the same way. And there's the matter of this unauthorised overdraft which I expect you to clear immediately.'

'But my salary will barely cover it! I need more time . . .'

'You should have thought about that before you started spending the bank's money so freely. You state in your application that you're married. What age did you marry, may I ask?'

Billy didn't think it was any of the man's business and could see there was little chance of help from this quarter. But he answered the question.

'I married at the age of twenty-two.'

'Therein lies your problem,' Wilson said triumphantly, making a steeple with his fingers. 'You married too young. In this bank, we have a policy of discouraging our young men from marrying until they are at least twenty-five when their salaries are sufficient to support a family. So I'm sorry, Mr Hopkins, I must reject your request for a loan. You will have to rely on your own means to fund your university fees.'

He stood up to signal that the interview was at an end.

Wearily, Billy left the bank and made his way home through the Manchester drizzle. As he turned the corner into Pine Grove, he saw the faces of Matthew and Lucy at the front-room window. They gave him big smiles and cheery waves and he waved back. They both needed new shoes – new everything, when he came to think of it – and he'd promised to take them to Belle Vue Zoo if he was successful. Matthew was three, Lucy two, and they knew Dad always came home laughing, joking, and ready to tickle them. But not this time.

'Sorry, kids. Sorry, Laura,' he said as he walked through the door. 'Nothing doing. Maybe if I win Littlewood's, we can get the things we need.' A big maybe, he thought, I probably stand more chance on the pools than I did with that Scrooge of a bank manager.

Laura came forward and gave him a kiss.

'Never mind, Billy. Cheer up. It's not the end of the world. I'm sure something will turn up.'

There she was playing the Micawber role again. That 'something', he said to himself, would be borrowing from her father – again. They already owed Duncan £60. God only knew when he'd see his money. On the wireless, they were used to hearing comedians jesting about poverty with jokes which began with, 'We were so poor in our house that . . .' and finishing with punch lines like, 'My dad used to tell us ghost stories so we'd cling together to keep warm.' Funny? Maybe. But the real thing was not so droll.

Finally Billy had no alternative but to call on his father-in-law for fresh funds. The in-laws were invited round for tea and, at a pre-arranged signal from Laura, Billy invited Duncan to the Wagon and Horses for a quick half, to put the bite on him for a few quid. There was always a price to pay in the form of a penny lecture on marrying without sufficient capital and how they should have followed the example of Hamish and Jenny, now comfortably off in their own Edinburgh home. Billy knew it word for word – it was more or less the same sermon as the bank manager's.

He got the drinks in, a Double Diamond for his father-in-law and a glass of mild for himself. Duncan took a sip of his ale.

'A good lager,' he said.

Billy thought this might be the right moment to turn to the subject gnawing at him. He was about to speak when Duncan anticipated him.

'You'll be wanting to borrow some more money, I suppose.' He grinned and put his glass down.

'Why, yes,' Billy stuttered. 'How did you know?'

'Easy. Whenever you invite us to tea, it's usually for the same reason. How much?'

How much could I touch him for? Billy wondered.

'I need around fifty pounds to cover final fees plus a few odds and ends for the family,' he faltered. Billy thought he might ask for this bigger sum in case Duncan cut it back.

'You've been doing exceptionally well in our accounting sessions,' Duncan said, stroking his chin thoughtfully, 'and if you are doing half as well in your other studies, you should get a good degree. So I'll help you with these extra charges. I'll lend you half of what you ask. You must find the rest from your own resources.'

There he goes again, Billy thought. This was one of his father-in-law's more nauseating principles. 'It's the same when we give aid to the Third World,' he continued, launching into the usual homily. 'We must never offer the whole sum required otherwise they will look to us for easy hand-outs each time they run short. We must encourage them to be independent. Always best to leave a gap for them to fill from their own resources.'

Didn't he know, Billy thought, that people will learn to anticipate this ploy and ask for more than they need, knowing it will be cut? Then there's that favourite word of his, 'resources'. Fine, but in my case what resources? No use arguing, though. When Big Dunk gave his decision, it was as irrevocable as a football referee's.

Billy thanked him, realising there was only one thing left for him and that would be yet another holiday job during the summer vac, though he was supposed to spend any spare time he had studying economics and not practising it in some tedious job.

In July he and his two companions went in search of vacation jobs.

'One of these summers I may get a proper holiday in some exotic place like Blackpool or Morecambe,' Titch complained. 'Every year we end up in some monotonous job like British Rail.'

Oscar said, 'You'll have to wait until teachers are paid as much as plumbers, bricklayers and cleaners.'

They presented themselves at the Labour Exchange with little hope because in past years they had come away empty-handed. This time they were in luck. When the clerk told them that Kellogg's Corn Flakes in Trafford Park were looking for temporary workers to help with a sales campaign, they couldn't believe it. A job with this company was like striking gold because the firm had a good reputation for its generous wages and working conditions. It was night work, 10 p.m. to 6 a.m., but the pay was £15 a week. They didn't need to be told twice about getting over there right away. The trio caught the first bus to secure a place at the front of the queue.

A smartly dressed American executive explained the nature of their duties.

'On the back of each packet is a 'specially designed cartoon face,' he said. 'We want all the kiddies out there to cut out the face and attach it to a coloured balloon. We're gonna call these fun images "Doodleoons". Your job will be to put a balloon in each packet.'

'How many packets?' Billy asked eagerly.

'We keep all twenty conveyor belt lines running twenty-four hours a day in three shifts of eight hours. Our throughput on each shift is around one million packets, give or take a few thousand.'

'Are the night workers a mixed staff?' asked Titch with an innocent expression on his face but ideas of romance in his heart.

'No, the staff on night-work are all men. During the war, females were permitted to do nights but not now.'

'Pity,' Titch muttered.

The following night they reported to Barney Brennan, the foreman, who allocated each of them an assembly line and a tray of balloons. The lines were arranged in pairs but it was impossible to talk to your neighbour because of the roar of the machinery. The open cereal boxes rolled down the conveyor belt rapidly and at first it was difficult to keep up with them. Within an hour or two, the young men had become robotic parts of the process and had little trouble keeping up with the relentless speed of the conveyor belt. Their skill was such that, with hardly a glance, they could flick a balloon into a box several yards away. The biggest problem was boredom. Billy determined to learn all Shakespeare's sonnets by heart and propped up the slim volume on his heap of balloons.

' "Shall I compare thee to a summer's day?" ' he recited over the thunderous factory roar.

Barney spotted him and snatched the book away.

'No reading on the job!' he bellowed.

At one o'clock in the morning, after three hours of mind-boggling work, it was time for the first fifteen-minute rest period. How quickly the break shot by and how slowly time crawled when they were engaged again on their soul-destroying job.

Night after night, hour after hour, they sat in a stupor on their high stools flinging their rubber missiles into the boxes.

'In some future overpopulated world,' Billy called, 'I can see the government providing condoms by this method.'

'And of different colours,' Titch shouted.

'Not forgetting a variety of flavours,' Oscar yelled.

The weeks went by and the long summer vac came to an end. Time to finish and return to the classroom.

But not for Billy.

Kellogg's had a rule about pay for those leaving its employ. If an individual left of his own accord, he was paid up to his last working day. If, however, the company dismissed the worker as redundant, he was entitled to an extra fortnight's pay in lieu of notice. At the end of the promotion, the casuals left to go back to their normal full-time pursuits as students and teachers. Billy, being stubborn and desperate for that extra pay, decided to stay on though it meant working at two jobs, night and day: nine o'clock till four at school and ten at night to six in the morning at the factory. He reckoned that, with careful planning and precise timing, he could fit in three to four hours' sleep a night between half-past four and half-past eight. But it was vital that he did not sleep in the morning as he was likely to fall into a deep slumber from which it would be difficult to wake in time for school.

After the other temps had left, Billy was summoned to the executive office.

Uh-oh, he said to himself. They have a complaint about my work.

He knocked on the office door and waited.

'Come in, Billy boy,' said the American. 'Take a seat. We've been watching you at work.'

Ah, here we go, Billy thought. They've rumbled me. This is where I get the push.

'And we've been most impressed by your efficiency,' the executive continued. 'Most impressed. So we've decided to move you up to higher grade work. Starting next Monday, you will be promoted to the sugar-frosted section.'

The new job involved depositing a small toy submarine in each of a million packets. Before Billy could start work there was a high-powered meeting of engineers and executives at the conveyor belt to debate the logistics of getting the toys into the cartons.

'If we put them in before the grease-proof packet operation, the item will catch the sensitive arm and the whole line will shut down,' said the chief technician.

'The only answer,' Barney said, pursing his lips and sucking his teeth, 'is to pull the grease-proof aside and drop the submarine down the side of the box.'

There was a general murmur of agreement amongst the administrative staff and the dilemma was resolved. It was left to Billy to implement the decision.

This task proved to be more mind-numbing than the balloons because these toys could not be thrown but had to be placed carefully and individually in each packet. In order to keep up, Billy became an automaton, a cog in the machine. At home in bed there was no respite because the noise of the engines vibrated in his head and in his dreams he continued to thrust celestial submarines into an endless line of boxes.

He stuck it out for four weeks. In the early stages, he felt tired but managed to carry on. After a week, he became light-headed and tottered about punch-drunk. At four o'clock each day, he came out of school, reached home at 4.15 and, as he went through the back garden gate like a sleepwalker, Laura was already pouring his cocoa, which he picked up without pause on the way to the bedroom. No time to stop. He drank it down as he changed into pyjamas. When his head hit the pillow, he went out like a light. No sooner had he closed his eyes, or so it seemed, than Laura was shaking him and telling him it was time to go on the night shift.

Trance-like he continued the routine. Sometimes his head nodded forward and he almost swooned into unconsciousness but with a jerk forced himself to stay awake.

Finally, came that wonderful night. Barney approached him one Thursday and, placing a hand on his shoulder, bawled the good news in Billy's ear.

''Opkins! The summer promotion is over this week. You're finished! Collect your cards in the morning!'

Billy looked at him dreamily, hardly able to take it in. Then the message registered.

'Finished? Really finished? I don't believe it.'

Euphoria! Billy wanted to waltz around the factory floor with the foreman.

'I've cracked it! I've cracked it!' he shouted over and over again.

Next day, he collected his cards, his normal week's wage and a fortnight's extra pay. It was £45 in total! A fortune! At last their heads had bobbed above the water. They could pay the university fees, outstanding grocery bills, buy the kids some shoes, and cover the bank overdraft with a little over. And who knows? Maybe a short holiday to Blackpool or Llandudno in the long summer break after the final examinations. His cup was not merely full, it was brimming over.

Chapter Fifteen

Billy was sitting – as usual – in the attic at the top of the house poring over his books. Laura had suggested earlier that afternoon that they take the kids for a walk through Birch Park and over to Platt Fields to feed the ducks. He'd had to say no because soon the finals would be upon him. Feeding ducks was a subject that couldn't have been further from his mind at that moment for he was up to his eyes revising. It was four weeks to doomsday and his whole future rested on the outcome.

In the garden below, Matthew was playing with the second-hand, three-wheeler bike Billy had bought for his son's third birthday. The rag and bone man had described the bike as 'practically new and a snip at ten shillings'. He had made no mention of its tendency to lose its front wheel and chain and Matthew had spent more time fixing it than riding it. Lucy as usual was busy making mud pies in a mound of dirt which served as a flower-bed. How Billy envied them their freedom and their childhood! He felt sorry for himself. Since the age of sixteen, he thought, I seem to have spent half my time in lectures or with my head in a book. When do I get to enjoy life? There wasn't even the consolation of a spot of love-making since Laura had put the shutters up after the birth of Lucy and it was back to separate beds and the monastic life.

Billy had complained, 'Sometimes I feel like a monk who has taken vows of poverty, chastity and obedience.'

'Poor old Billy!' she'd laughed. 'Wait now till I blow the dust off the violins. At least you have peace to get on with your work.'

True, he said to himself. Nevertheless it didn't solve his problem and he'd tried to use up his excess energies in his job, in playing Saturday-afternoon football for the Damian Old Boys' team, and in losing himself in study. Two years had gone by since Lucy's birth and Billy was sure he'd developed a nervous tic.

At suppertime one night, after they had put the kids to bed, Billy plucked up the courage to broach the subject that had long been gnawing at him, namely the question of sex or the lack of it. The safe period had proved to be far from safe and the rhythm method unrhythmical. Furthermore Mother Nature had cleverly arranged her rhythms so that the safe period was the very time they felt least in the mood for love. And vice-versa. If they felt amorous, it was sure to be the riskiest time. Their mood swings were a better indicator than a calendar or a thermometer. They just couldn't win.

'I was reading something by Somerset Maugham the other day,' he began. 'He claims that a man marries to have a home, but also because he doesn't want to be bothered by sex and all that sort of thing.'

'He's being cynical,' Laura said. 'Marriage doesn't mean no sex at all.'

'Maybe not. Perhaps once-in-a-blue-moon sex.'

'You do exaggerate, Billy.'

'I don't think women appreciate what a big problem sex

is for a man. Sometimes I think they don't have any interest.'

'If that were true, it would be goodbye to the human race. A woman's needs are different, that's all.'

'Nevertheless, less urgent and less demanding. Aristotle once said that for a man the sexual urge was like being chained for life to a maniac. And an unpredictable one at that.'

'Well, Billy, the maniac will have to stay chained up for the time being unless you want to challenge Mrs McCardle for the record.'

That was that, and for a while longer they resigned themselves to a life of almost total abstinence. For them the rhythm method, except within wide limits, had proved hopelessly unreliable.

Then one day, unexpectedly, there was a breakthrough. In the most unlikely of places, a Catholic newspaper, Billy spotted an advertisement for a device which promised to solve their problem.

TAKE THE GUESSING OUT OF THE SAFE PERIOD WITH OUR SCIENTIFICALLY PROVED CALCULATOR, THE ORACLE. BASED ON FINDINGS AT THE BLETCHLEY PARK RESEARCH STATION WHICH CRACKED THE ENIGMA CODE. APPROVED BY THE VATICAN!

They sent off their cheque by express post. Delivery was promised within twenty-eight days and, observing strict abstinence during this period, they waited impatiently for the goods to arrive. When the package landed on the doormat, they tore it open with bare hands, eager to have sight of this piece of technological wizardry which was about to transform their lives. The gadget consisted of four small rotating drums which required four simple facts to be fed into them: the longest and shortest menstrual cycles, the date of the commencement of the last period, today's date. And, hey presto! The fertile and infertile periods were revealed in a little window. At last! Their newly liberated sex lives had begun!

'How can we be sure it'll work?' Laura asked.

'It's bound to work, Laura,' Billy declared. 'It's based on science!'

Towards the end of May it was time for final degree examinations and Billy and his two companions were dreading it. Billy was particularly anxious as he had invested so much in terms of money, time and effort. Everything was riding on the outcome: his reputation, his chances of promotion and his hopes for Laura and the kids. Failure was unthinkable. So many people would be watching out for the results: his own parents, brothers and sisters; the Mackenzie family, especially Duncan and not forgetting his arch-rival Hamish. No two ways about it, Billy had to pass if he was to hold his head up in public.

They had already taken the Italian oral and that had seemed to go well. They had been lucky in their external examiner, a Professor Giuseppe Orlandi from the University of Florence. He asked lots of questions about Perugia, Assisi, and Etruscan art and culture, and so they were able to converse on subjects they knew something about. The professor had rounded off the oral by shaking Billy's hand and saying, '*Grazie tante e buona fortuna.*' (Thank you so much and good luck.) To which he had replied, '*Grazie a lei, professore, e altrettanto.*' (Thank you, professor, and the same to you.) Had that been the right thing to say? It was a bit like saying, 'And you, mate!' And what did that bit about good luck mean? Did it mean he'd be lucky to pass?

The results were not disclosed immediately as they were part of the overall mark. Not only that, examiners enjoyed keeping their victims in suspense.

Meanwhile, the trio had submitted their final dissertations and now they ticked off the days and got their heads down to hard revision for the written exams. In an effort to spot likely questions, they fine tooth-combed past papers. But would the same questions be repeated or would they be changed? Would the right questions come up? It was a guessing game.

'In economic theory, they won't ask about monopolies,' Titch said. 'They asked that last year.'

'I don't think we can bank on any of this speculation,' Billy said. 'It's too much like a lottery. Maybe the lecturers might throw us one or two clues.'

In the weeks immediately preceding the exams, students hung on to every word their tutors uttered. They were listened to as if the gods themselves had spoken from Mount Olympus.

'It might be worth your while to read Stiegler on imperfect competition.'

That was enough to send a rumour whizzing round the students who took it as gospel.

The real problem was in applied economics where the tutor had been taken into hospital at the beginning of the year and the students had been left to flounder with written notes only.

The examinations were held in the Whitworth Hall, a large barn of a building with stained-glass windows like a church. Outside the main entrance on Oxford Road there was a sandwich board man bearing the legend: PREPARE TO MEET THY GOD FOR THE END OF THE WORLD IS NIGH.

'No doubt the university authorities have sent this Cassandra to cheer us up,' Oscar observed.

'He's probably one of the examiners,' Titch added.

Inside the building, a mass of examinees from every country on earth had congregated to begin the process of regurgitating the vast amounts of knowledge they had assimilated during their years of study. The passageway was thronged with them and the air was filled with the babble of strange accents, dialects and languages. As well as British students from every corner of the kingdom, there seemed to be representatives from every nation on earth that accepted British qualifications. Beefy men from the Dominions standing around nonchalantly as if waiting for the pubs to open; Africans from every corner of that continent waiting nervously, some still swotting from text-books in the precious few seconds before the doors opened; bespectacled Indian gentlemen impeccably dressed conversing calmly amongst themselves or with their female counterparts clad in flowing silk saris.

'I had no idea,' Billy said, 'that there were so many students taking the Admin degree. There must be around a hundred here.'

'Don't forget we're in with the full-timers,' Titch replied. 'There's no distinction made between part-time and full-time students in the exams.'

'And those lucky blighters have all day to do their swotting,' complained Oscar. 'But do you notice that our original seventy part-timers are now down to thirty? The rest couldn't stand the pace.'

Billy and his companions went with the other students into the hall which was set out with rows of desks positioned at strategic distances to prevent cheating. The senior invigilator gave out last minute instructions, and then, glancing up at the clock, said, 'Turn over your papers and begin.'

The first examination was in economic theory. Billy looked down at the paper. The first question was on monopoly. Good old Titch, he thought, trust him to get it wrong. It's a good job I took no notice of him. The other questions were all on familiar ground.

About halfway through, candidates manifested individual differences. One or two earnest types scribbled furiously and made frequent journeys for extra answer books; a few others stood up, handed in their scripts, and after bowing to the platform left the room. Either they're brilliant or they're stumped, Billy thought.

After a while, the invigilator announced, 'You have twenty minutes left.'

Of course Billy had given too much attention to the first question and left insufficient time for the last, but that was par for the course.

He left the hall feeling light-headed and a little punch drunk. Shortly afterwards Titch and Oscar joined him and all three lit up Senior Service.

'Well, Hoppy, what did you think?' asked Titch.

'Not bad,' Billy replied. 'I answered five, that's the main thing. Good job we ignored your advice about monopoly.'

'I shouldn't worry too much about it,' Oscar said. 'I've heard that the way they decide the results is by lottery. Nobody reads the scripts, they simply put all the examination numbers in a hat. The first ten out get firsts, the next ten are failed, and the rest are given seconds, either first or second grade.'

Over the next week they took the rest of the examinations. In the accountancy paper, Billy's heart leapt for joy when he saw the first question was one which Duncan, with unbelievable prescience, had anticipated.

'An old lady of your acquaintance wants to invest her life savings in the company whose balance sheet is shown below. What advice would you give her and why?'

Billy knew the answer by heart for it was standard material from Inland Revenue manuals. The rest of the questions had also been dealt with thoroughly in Duncan's Sunday night classes, and for the rest of the time allotted Billy became totally absorbed in grappling with accountancy problems until nothing existed for him but that examination paper.

On the way home, he called on Duncan to discuss the paper and as they carried out a post-mortem, his father-in-law became more and more excited which was unusual for a Scotsman.

'That's right! And that's right too!' he called. 'And your final accounts balanced, you say?'

He shook Billy's hand firmly and said, 'I'd be surprised if you haven't got a first in the subject.'

The next day, the trouble began. In applied economics. The trio were dreading the paper as they'd had no lectures in the subject and no guidance whatsoever. In the Whitworth Hall they sat waiting as the invigilator, a corpulent man in a faded gown, handed out the paper. Billy closed his eyes in a prayer to St Jude, patron saint of lost causes, and picked it up. In mounting panic, he read the first side, turned it over and scanned the last few questions. Their worst nightmares had come true. There wasn't a single question they could answer. He looked over to Titch who raised both arms above his head in a gesture of despair. Oscar had turned red and was staring ahead of him with an expression of incredulity. What a rotten trick fate had played, Billy thought. Have all my efforts, all my sacrifices, all the privations been in vain? Pipped at the post? He looked around the hall. Most of the other students seemed to be in the same state of shock and some had put their heads down and covered them with their arms. Then a thought struck Billy. We're all in the same boat and they can't fail everybody; it would reflect badly on the academic standing of the tutors.

He looked down again at the paper. Answer five questions, it said. Very well, if that's what they want, that's what they're going to get. He began writing and where he didn't have a clue, he turned the question round to fit the stuff he had prepared. Halfway through the exam, Titch attracted Billy's attention with a 'pssst', and signalled that he'd had enough. He bowed to the platform and handed in his paper. Oscar followed shortly after. This seemed to trigger a wave of departures and soon only a handful remained. Billy wrote on blindly, knowing that most of the time he was answering on topics he'd only hoped would appear. At the end of three hours, he had written five answers to five questions which had not been set. With a shrug of his shoulders, he surrendered his answer book and left the room.

His two companions were waiting for him.

'I have spent three hours writing undiluted rot,' Billy said. 'That's the end of my big dream. What about you two?'

'No use,' Titch said. 'I know I've muffed it 'cos I managed only three and my answers were complete rubbish.'

'Same for me,' Oscar said. 'Let's go drown our sorrows in the College Inn. We can always re-sit next year.'

'That thought fills me with horror,' Billy said. 'I don't think I could face another year going over the same subject, borrowing money from my father-in-law, looking for a vacation job.'

Six weeks later, the three friends were once again sitting in the College Inn. It was Judgment Day. The exam results were due to be published at noon.

'Have you ever noticed,' said Oscar as he sat down in the bar lounge, a pint in his hand, 'the number of ways you can say "I failed"? You can say flunked, fluffed, ploughed, flopped . . .'

'How about: buggered up, laid an egg, made a cock of it?' suggested Titch.

'Or blew it, missed the bus, came a cropper?' Billy offered.

'It's all so bloody public,' Titch whined. 'The way they put the results on the notice board for all to see. It's like a list of people due for execution.'

'In Japan, you'd be expected to fall on your sword,' Oscar said.

'Not such a bad idea at that.' Billy laughed nervously. 'Come on, drink up and let's go and see what cards fortune has dealt us.'

The corridor of the Faculty of Economic and Social Studies in Dover Street was packed with a crowd of anxious students waiting to learn their fate. There was a subdued air about them like a political party that had lost an election. At noon precisely an assistant registrar emerged from her office and pinned up a large printed sheet on the notice board. There was a mad rush to get near it. Titch forced his way to the front but there was so much pushing and jostling, it wasn't easy to take in the details. At last he emerged from under someone's legs.

'You're not going to believe it,' he said breathlessly.

'Come on, Titch, sock it to us. We can take it,' said Billy.

'Congratulations, Hoppy! You are now a graduate of the University of Manchester. Not only that, you've been awarded the degree with distinction and are the only one with that honour. It says you've been awarded the NALGO Prize for the best degree of 1955.'

'If you're kidding me,' Billy said, 'that's the end of a beautiful friendship. Come on, tell me what really happened?'

'You'll see for yourself as soon as this crowd thins out,' Titch replied.

Some time later they were able to check the results for themselves. They were pleased to see that they had all been awarded firsts in Italian, but after that their grades varied. Billy had achieved a first in Accountancy and an average of upper seconds in all other subjects. The biggest surprise of all was that, along with six other candidates, he had passed applied economics with a lower second. Oscar and Titch had been referred in that one subject, which meant a re-sit the following year.

'It could be worse,' Titch said. 'Next year should be a doddle with only one subject to take, and maybe this time the lecturer will turn up for a few sessions.'

Billy rushed home to give the good news to Laura.

'So it's all been worth it,' she exclaimed, holding him close. 'The penny-pinching, the studying, the going without . . . it's all behind us. But what on earth is the NALGO Prize and how much is it worth?'

'NALGO stands for National Association of Local Government Officers and the prize is worth twenty pounds.'

'We're rich!' she exclaimed.

When Duncan heard the results, his face broke into a wide grin and he took Billy's hand in both his and shook it firmly. For one anxious moment Billy thought he was going to be embraced.

'Well done, Billy,' Duncan enthused. ' I knew you could do it.'

'I should soon be able to start paying you back all that money I've borrowed from you over the last few years,' he said.

With a nonchalant wave of his hand, Duncan said, 'Billy, you can forget all that. This result is sufficient compensation for me.'

Billy only hoped his father-in-law hadn't been carried away in the heat of the moment. As for his own parents, they were proud but a little hazy about what it all meant.

'In Italian and accountancy,' he told them, 'I got a one.'

'Eeh, that doesn't sound like a very high mark,' Mam said doubtfully.

'No, Mam,' he explained. 'I got a first and won the NALGO Prize for 1955.'

'Does that mean you came first in class, then?'

'I suppose that's about the size of it,' he said.

But it was Dad who proved to be most confused as he told everyone in his local that his son had won the Nobel Prize for his degree.

Billy's birthday that year was a double Red Letter Day, for it was also graduation day. Laura, along with her parents plus Billy's mam and dad, made up the celebratory party that attended the Whitworth Hall for the ceremony. The University was to be honoured by the presence of their Chancellor, Lord Woolton, who would preside over the degree-awarding ritual.

'I never liked that man,' Mam said. 'He was Minister of Food during the war and kept us half-starved. I'll never forgive him for that disgusting Woolton Pie.'

'Not only that,' said Dad, 'he's a big wig in the Tory Party and I never thought I'd see the day when a son of mine would be shaking his hand.'

Billy's mam and dad were dressed in their best outfits as befitted a formal, solemn occasion. Dad sported his funeral/wedding gear consisting of a dark suit, waistcoat watch and chain, and his pot hat. Mam wore her finest coat and hat, along with a velvet blouse and her 'Mother' brooch proudly displayed lest the world be unaware of her social status. The guests assembled in the hall while the graduands arrayed in their new gowns and mortar boards, hired from Wippell & Company, Clerical Tailors of King Street, were shepherded into orderly lines by a team of registrar's assistants who fussed around them like sheepdogs.

To the sound of Handel's 'Hail the Conquering Hero', the candidates processed into the hall. There was a thunderous noise of scraping chairs and feet as the assembled guests struggled to rise and the graduands were directed to their seats in strict sequence.

The ceremony began when Professor Macdonald, the Dean, mounted the stage. Lifting his mortar board, he proclaimed: 'My lord, on behalf of the Faculty of Economic and Social Studies, may I present to you for the degree of Bachelor of Arts in Public Administration the following candidates. First, with Distinction, William Hopkins . . .'

Billy self-consciously rose and made his way on stage to the sound of tumultuous applause. The registrar who was there to receive him checked his name and whispered, 'Congratulations.' 'Thank you,' Billy whispered back and went forward to shake Woolton's hand. As he did so, a voice from the body of the hall cried out, 'Nice one, our kid.'

Woolton laughed along with the rest of the other guests.

Oh, no, Billy thought. Not Mam again! Calling out like she did at our wedding!

He was mistaken. The voice came not from Mam but from Titch, high up in the gallery at the back of the hall, and Billy soon found that there was no need for embarrassment as barracking was part of the accepted procedure. The candidate immediately behind him was announced as 'Andrew Bull' which brought forth noises of a lowing herd from the students up in the gods, while 'Dorothy Pickles' inspired someone to yell, 'Give 'er the money, Barney!' and a candidate with the unfortunate name of Margaret Tarras-Wahlberg elicited the response, 'What was that? Come again?'

After the ceremony, there was a sherry reception in the main quadrangle. Mam didn't look comfortable as she took her glass from the porter. Her little finger was raised just a little too high and Dad rejected the proffered schooner proclaiming that he would prefer a pint of Tetley's.

They were joined by Duncan and Louise who shook Billy's hand warmly.

'Congratulations again,' they said.

Then turning to Mam and Dad, Duncan said, 'Well, Mr and Mrs Hopkins, you must be proud today of your son's achievements.'

'Oh, we are, thank you,' Mam replied. 'Never in my life did I think I'd have a son who would go to Owen's College and win a cap and gown.'

'It's all very well,' Dad started. 'As long as his head doesn't get too big for that cap . . .'

There he goes again, Billy thought. He thinks education always results in bigger proportions of the body, like 'a swelled head' or 'too big for his boots and breeches'.

They were joined by Professor Macdonald who came to add his congratulations. Even Duncan and Louise deferred to such an august presence while Mam curtsied and Dad removed his pot hat, holding it clasped to his middle. This meeting with a higher-up would provide him with rich material for his pub cronies and would be worth at least two free pints. Billy could almost hear him.

'Yes, I spoke to this professor fellah and gave him what-for about having that bastard Woolton as his master of ceremonies . . .'

Professor Macdonald, however, turned to a more serious matter.

'Billy, I read your dissertation on "Apathy in Local Government" and think there is possibly a Master's thesis there. Come and see me after the vacation and we shall look into it.'

'There you are,' said Duncan after the professor had gone. 'A chance to get an even higher degree.'

'Oh, I dunno, Duncan,' Billy replied. 'I think I've had enough for the time being.'

'I agree wholeheartedly,' Laura added. 'We all need a rest from the hard grind of academic study. It's time we started to enjoy life.'

'I'll drink to that,' Billy said, helping himself to another sherry.

* * *

Later that evening, he found it difficult to settle down to a quiet night at home.

'It's been such an exciting day, Laura,' he said. 'What do you say we celebrate by going out to dinner? I'm sure your sister would baby-sit for us.'

'That's the kind of offer I can't refuse,' she said. 'Besides, I wanted to have a natter.'

'Sounds serious.'

It was a wonderful meal in the Manzil. After coffee, in an expansive mood, Billy ordered two Benedictines. It was then that Laura dropped the bombshell.

'Billy, I think I'm pregnant again.'

His heart skipped a beat. 'But you can't be . . . The Oracle's infallible, according to the blurb that came with it.'

'I don't understand it either,' she replied. 'We, or the Oracle, must have got it wrong somehow.'

Billy could see their new-found solvency disappearing down the plughole.

'You know, Laura,' he said, 'I've become nervous about taking you out to dinner because it's always then you give me the news you're pregnant.'

Chapter Sixteen

In early-September, Billy made an appointment to see Professor Macdonald.

'I have been most impressed by your academic achievement,' the professor said. 'Have you considered working for a higher degree? You could do the MA by thesis only, and I'm sure we can fund your research from special grants 'specially set up for the purpose.'

Billy's inner reaction was not one of unbridled enthusiasm. He had spent almost half his life studying for some examination or other and had been hoping to put academic work behind him. Nevertheless, the idea held its attractions for him. An MA would almost certainly lead to promotion somewhere within the education world, perhaps to a Further Education college or something similar. And, there was little expense involved and no lectures, unless one counted the occasional tutorial with the professor.

'I haven't given it any thought as yet, Professor,' he answered. 'Do you think I'm capable?'

'You're certainly capable if we could find a suitable topic for you. With hard work, you could have your Master's within the year. Your dissertation on local government might offer possibilities. For example, there is a grave problem in the recruitment of staff into local government services here in the North West. You might tackle something like that.'

The professor made out a strong case for the research, how important it was for local government and how, furthermore, a Master's degree would enhance Billy's career prospects. Billy was sold.

He reported back to Laura later that night.

'They've chosen me to do research into apathy in local government.'

'Great news,' she said. 'But why have they picked you?'

'Nobody else was interested,' he laughed. 'I've got to find out why no one wants to work in local government.'

'I would have thought that was obvious,' she said. 'The pay's no good and the jobs are boring.'

Why did Laura have to make everything sound so simple?

Though the work for the higher degree proved to be demanding and money was still tight, the research grant and relief from having to find tuition fees meant things had become a little easier. They decided to allow themselves one luxury. A television! Billy finally gave into pressure from his family and bought a set. He'd sworn he'd never have one in the house as he believed it not only discouraged reading and the use of the imagination but also destroyed family conversation and culture. He'd heard that many families no longer had a meal together but sat gawping with a TV dinner on their laps. There were even homes with more than one set!

But the constant harping at school and at home had gradually worn him down. Everywhere he went people talked about the things they'd seen on the box the night before. Conversations invariably opened with gambits like, 'Did you see that thing on TV last night . . .?' Billy had no choice but to give in. All for the sake of his family, of course, because they were feeling deprived and socially inferior. Matthew had fallen into the habit of watching at his pal's at night and could never reciprocate the hospitality. Then again, as Billy told Laura, in his job he needed to keep in touch with current affairs. The arguments for buying one became irresistible and he bought a set on the never-never from Forsyth Brothers on Deansgate. It had retractable doors and Billy could never work out what they were for. Were they there to protect the screen or to disguise the fact that it was a television and something to be ashamed of?

As he feared, Matthew and Lucy soon became telly addicts. Billy and Laura viewed with them, of course, to check that they were not watching unsuitable stuff. The kids became obsessed by the adverts and it wasn't long before catchy tunes and jingles echoed through the house. Though not yet three, Lucy knew them all by heart from 'Murray mints, Murray mints, the too-good-to hurry mints'; 'The hands that do dishes/Can feel soft as your face/With mild green Fairy liquid'; and 'A Double Diamond works wonders'.

Except for the occasional children's programme, however, Billy found little time to watch because the research he'd taken on was a huge task. Sometimes, he felt like a tiny mouse nibbling at a giant piece of cheese. For months on end he spent his spare time checking references in Manchester's Central Library, visiting local authorities across the North West, and writing up his findings in that old familiar place, the attic.

From his window, he could see the kids in the garden below. How he wished he could be one again without the responsibilities of a mortgage and an endless stream of bills. How he longed to be down there with them playing with their toys. Not that they had much in the way of those. Matthew still had the second hand bike but had long since given it up as a bad job. At Christmas, Billy had been a little better off and had managed to buy a wheelbarrow for him and a doll for Lucy, but she was more interested in the wheelbarrow than the doll.

'Typical,' Billy said to Laura, 'she refuses to accept her allotted sex role.'

'Maybe she's going to be the first female navvy.'

The wheelbarrow had been bought from Ned Bolton, the local joiner, who produced an array of wooden toys for sale around Christmas time. The toys were well made and, most important, inexpensive. Billy had taken Matthew over to Ned's workshop to view the selection and he had made his choice. But Billy had had to take Ned to one side to enlist his co-operation in the matter of perpetuating the Santa Claus myth.

'Look, Ned. My little boy still believes in the old gentleman and I'd appreciate it if you would tell him that you're making these toys for Father Christmas. That you'll be sending them across to Greenland so he can give them out on Christmas Eve.'

'No problem,' Ned said, giving Billy a big wink. 'Many parents round here make the same request.'

Indeed Ned himself was not unlike Santa Claus with his portly frame, silver hair and rubicund cheeks. With a solemn expression, Matthew listened to Ned and seemed well satisfied with the explanation.

Some time before Christmas, he got into trouble at his nursery school when Rebecca Tintwistle, his erstwhile girlfriend, pushed him over and he retaliated by pulling her pigtail.

'That was naughty, Matthew Hopkins,' his teacher snapped. 'If you don't behave, Santa won't bring you anything this Christmas.'

'Oh, yes, he will,' Matthew retorted. 'You see, we know his brother.'

Ned Bolton would have been pleased.

Lost in these thoughts, Billy turned back to his books but a squeal of pain from Lucy made him look up again. Matthew had accidentally stumbled and tipped her on to the garden path. Billy left his books and ran down to pick her up but Laura beat him to it.

'I've got a sore arm,' Lucy wept.

'Never mind, Lucy. Mummy will make it better,' Laura said, picking her up. 'Let's go inside and we'll find you something nice.'

'It was an accident,' Matthew said. 'I tripped over a stone. I couldn't help it, honest.'

'Not to worry,' Laura said. 'Nothing to be alarmed about. No bones broken.'

Billy returned to his study and put the matter behind him. Kids, he thought. No peace. There's always something.

Later that night, Laura and Billy were going through the nightly routine of seeing the kids to bed, which involved a wash-down in the kitchen.

'Come along, Lucy,' Laura said. 'Time for bed and for your nightly wash. Look at the state of you! You could grow potatoes in your hair.'

'Don't want a wash,' Lucy sulked. 'Don't want to go to bed.'

'Come along, my girl,' Laura said. 'No arguments. Time for 'bye-byes.'

'I want Daddy to give me a television wash,' Lucy pouted.

'Oh, very well,' Laura said. 'You spoil that girl,' she said to Billy.

'So what!' he replied. 'If a father can't indulge his little daughter, what's the world coming to?'

Laura was probably right. Maybe he did spoil the girl. But that didn't mean he didn't love Matthew. Of course he did. He took both kids to the park, played football and rough and tumble games with Matthew, went on trips to Belle Vue Zoo. He was proud of his little family and never more than when they went dressed in their best to Mass on Sunday, greeting the neighbours who nodded to them along the way. He had a right to be proud – Matthew, though only five, was taking piano lessons from Dora Wilson of the Royal Manchester College and had shown distinct musical talent. That said, there was still something about a little girl that made her different. Perhaps it was her fragile and vulnerable nature or her daintiness that brought out the protective instincts in him as her father. He wasn't supposed to have a favourite in the family but at school, the staff had picked up on his love for his little girl and begun calling him 'doting dad', while Greg Callaghan, the school's armchair psychologist, had talked knowingly about Freudian complexes of the Electra kind. Billy didn't care. Lucy was turning out to be a bonny little creature with big blue eyes and curly brown hair.

That curly brown hair was at the moment encrusted with half the mud from the garden. Both she and Matthew looked as if they'd stepped out of a Norman Rockwell painting. When Lucy was born, Billy had had visions of her dressed in silks and satins and all that stuff. Some hope. She always wanted to join in the rough romps of her brother and his pals and Billy hoped she wasn't going to develop into a tomboy. How different she was from Valerie, the little girl born to Laura's sister Jenny earlier that year. According to Jenny, her daughter was a genius. Laura said her sister had played Mozart and Haydn records to her bump during pregnancy because she'd read somewhere that it made the foetus musical. She and Hamish had even put the baby's name down for a violin course. Nothing like starting them early, she'd said. Thank God, Billy thought, they lived up there in Edinburgh so he wouldn't have to listen to such claptrap.

On this particular night Laura took Matthew to the other side of the kitchen to wash him and get him ready for bed. Matthew was five and about as resistant to the application of soap and water as Socrates, their Persian cat.

When it came to Lucy, however, Billy had no such problem for he'd made her nightly ablutions the subject of a soap ad. The routine always worked.

'Here we have a little girl who has come in from the garden. And now we are going to use our lovely soap on her beautiful skin. IT'S SOFT, SMOOOOOTH, LUXURIOUS, AND CREAMY. See how easily it goes on to her – cool, refreshing, radiant.'

Lucy usually glowed with pleasure under the spotlight and the commercial clichés that Billy showered on her. Not this time. As he applied the soapy lather to her hands, she yelped in pain. Gently he tried again.

'Ouch, ouch!' she cried. 'Please don't touch me there, Daddy. It hurts a lot. A very, very lot!'

Hello, he thought. She's taking this TV ad business a bit too far.

'She's trying it on as usual,' Laura said. 'She's after sympathy.'

Softly Billy put his finger on the same spot and got the same reaction. Lucy howled.

'There's something definitely wrong,' he said. 'It's the fall she had from the wheelbarrow. She may have sprained her wrist. I'll take her to Casualty tomorrow.'

On Saturday morning the Casualty department of the Royal Infirmary was filled to capacity with the usual motley crowd, the aftermath of a Friday night in Manchester: drunks with blood-shot eyes muttering curses at unseen enemies and threatening to kill the effing doctors, black-eyed prostitutes screeching oaths at the medical orderlies, lunatics cackling to themselves, and a miscellaneous collection of bandaged and plastered casualties sitting or lying around in bizarre postures.

It was two hours before Lucy's name was called to meet a young, tired-looking houseman who listened to the story, checked her arm and passed them on to the radiology department where, after another two-hour wait, X-rays were taken. Finally they were ushered into a room with several illuminated display screens round which a group of medical students was gathered. They were scrutinising the X-ray plate with puzzled expressions.

'Here comes the little girl, now,' said the tutor. 'Well, have you spotted anything yet? You'll have to look carefully.'

With creased brows, the students peered closely at the plate. They were clearly flummoxed.

'Why do they always send me a bunch of blind students every year?' the tutor whined. 'Use your eyes, for God's sake! It's a hairline fracture.'

Then one of the students spotted the Manchester University tie Billy was wearing.

'It's a hoax,' he declared, grinning in Billy's direction. 'You're having us on. There *is* no fracture!'

'Is that so?' said their boss. 'Then what about this?'

He took hold of Lucy's arm and deliberately squeezed the affected spot. She squealed and her face crumpled into tears.

'She didn't like that very much, did she?' the tutor said, smirking at his students.

Billy's hackles rose. Perhaps it was the long wait. Perhaps it was his anxiety. Whatever it was, he took the doctor's arm in a vice-like grip and growled in his ear, 'You bastard! Do you normally use small children as guinea pigs to emphasise a point? I've half a mind to report you to the Medical Council.'

Peering nervously over his wire glasses, the tutor recoiled as if expecting a punch on the nose.

'Sorry about that,' he stammered. 'It was an entirely reflex action to demonstrate to these slow-witted students the importance of accurate observation.'

Meanwhile, one of the brighter youngsters was pointing excitedly to the X-ray plate.

'I see it! I see it! A hairline fracture of the radius.'

'Good! Good!' the specialist said. 'At last someone has used his eyes.'

That doctor little realised how close he'd come to being thumped. And perhaps Billy little realised how close he'd come to being arrested and thrown off the premises. The students seemed amused by the incident, seeing their mentor taken down a peg.

Lucy was hurried through the plaster of Paris section. Feeling sorry for herself, she sniffed back the tears as her arm was encased in the white gooey cement though she was secretly proud of her robot arm, knowing full well that her playmates would be green with envy when they saw it. At home she became the centre of attention as her many visitors signed their names on the plaster. There was another bonus when she found she could use it to bash Matthew when he frustrated her, which was often.

In mid-February there occurred an event in the family which dwarfed degrees and research into local government. Laura was due to have their third baby at the end of January and booked into St Joseph's Maternity Home in Whalley Range in the hope of a little peace and quiet away from the other two children. This time the baby was undecided about making its entry into the world but finally made up its mind to be born ten days late. Another boy, and another giant weighing ten pounds. He had dark hair, a red face, and feet that already looked too big. His nose had become misshapen somehow in delivery and one eye was bloodshot. He struck out with a clenched fist, opened his mouth and yowled. This time they had an infant resembling not Winston Churchill or the Pears soap ad but Rocky Marciano after ten rounds with Joe Louis. Billy, now an old hand, knew however that in a month or two this latest arrival would be ready for baby beauty competitions. They called him Mark as the third member of their Evangelists and it looked as if they were on course to rival, if not the Russian lady, then at least Mrs McCardle of Daneley Road.

During the day Billy took Matthew and Lucy across to Laura's mother while he himself went to work. He collected them in the early evening and took them across to see their mother and the new baby. The two children examined their brother with curiosity and took turns in holding him, Lucy wondering if she could add him to her doll collection. They were more interested, however, in finding out when their mum would be coming home.

'It won't be long now,' she told them. 'Only a few days more. Is Daddy looking after you well?'

'I suppose so,' Matthew said. 'He reads us a story every night before we go to sleep.'

'And is he making you nice dinners?' Laura asked.

'He reads us a story every night,' Matthew repeated.

'Today is Shrove Tuesday, Billy. Why not make them pancakes?'

'Good idea, Laura. There's one small problem, I don't know how.'

'There's a recipe book in the kitchen drawer.'

Billy and the kids left the hospital feeling miserable and lonely. Everyone wanted Mum to come home. But determined to demonstrate his culinary skill when they got back, Billy parked both children on kitchen stools so they could watch.

'Now you're going to see a master chef at work,' he announced. 'So, *bambini*, what's it going to be? Name it and I'll cook it.'

'Pancakes, Dad?' they chorused. 'Our favourite.'

'Pancakes coming up,' he said, taking out Laura's recipe book from a kitchen drawer. 'Now, let's see what we need . . .'

'You need four eggs, flour, a pint of milk and a pinch of salt,' Matthew informed him. 'You also need to put cooking oil in the frying pan. That's the way Mum always makes them anyway.'

'Yes, yes, I know,' Billy said. 'It's here in the book. Let's do it.'

He lit the stove and turned the jet to high, poured oil into the pan and assembled the ingredients. First, he cracked open the eggs with a knife, put them with the other things into a bowl and stirred them vigorously with a tablespoon.

'Mum doesn't use a spoon,' Matthew said. 'She uses the whisk to mix them properly.'

'Well, I'm not Mum,' Billy said irritably. 'This is the way dads mix things.'

'I like the way daddies do it,' Lucy simpered. 'Daddies do it best.'

'Thank you, Lucy. It's nice to know I've got at least one supporter in the ranks.'

Billy's attention was suddenly distracted from the mixing process when the fat in the pan began to sizzle and splutter. Panic-stricken, he poured the squelchy mixture into the pan.

'That's too much, Dad,' Matthew shouted. 'That's not a pancake, it's more like a sponge cake.'

'Look, Matthew, I know what I'm doing. Let me do it my own way.'

'But, Dad . . .'

'I know, I know – it's not the way Mum does it.'

'No, Dad. It's smoking like mad . . . it's on fire! It'll be burnt black.'

'That's the way I like it,' Lucy said. 'Now you have to toss it and turn it over, Daddy. I'll bet you can do it. Show Matthew how daddies do it.'

Billy took the handle of the pan and burned his hands.

'Bloody pancakes,' he yelled.

'Mum always uses oven gloves,' Matthew said calmly.

Billy grabbed the gloves and threw the contents of the pan high in the air. The mush landed on the kitchen floor.

'Bugger it,' he said. 'Look, kids, how about egg in a cup with toast soldiers?'

'We had that last night and the night before,' Matthew sighed.

'Egg in a cup is a special recipe,' Billy said. 'Only three people in England know how to make it. The Duke of Edinburgh, Winston Churchill and me.'

'I like egg in a cup,' Lucy said. 'It's my favourite.'

'When's Mum coming home?' Matthew asked.

Later that night, in a quieter moment after he had put the two children to bed, Billy retired to his attic-study to smoke a ruminative cigarette.

Well, I certainly made a mess of that meal, he said to himself. Like Matthew, I can hardly wait for Laura to get back and take over. But sometimes I can hardly believe it's all happening. Ten years ago I was a bachelor with hardly a care in the world except maybe where my next packet of fags was to come from. Now I've a wife and three kids to care for, along with a mortgage and whacking great bills at the end of every month. I've got to get a better-paid job if I'm to provide a decent standard of living for them. We can't go on living this hand-to-mouth existence. Maybe this Master's degree is the answer. Perhaps that will lead to higher things and after that I can start to relax and take things easy.

To everybody's relief, Laura came back a few days later to take over the household. Two children in the home had been something of a challenge but a third seemed to transform it into a zoo. Once again, the world revolved around baby routines and their life became one of four-hourly feeds, sleepless nights, soiled nappies, endless washing, milk dribbles, baby sick and sticky fingers.

In June, Billy completed his Master's thesis. His mam and dad were truly puzzled by this latest development.

'I don't understand any of it,' Mam said. 'First they make you a Bachelor when you're a married man with two children, and now they want to call you Master Billy Hopkins which to me at any rate means a kid not old enough to be called Mr.'

'It's a great honour,' he explained. 'It means I can put MA after my name.'

'That's even worse,' Mam said. 'Ma is a name common American people use instead of a respectable word like Mother or Mam.'

'And if he gets two of these degrees,' his brother Les added, 'we can call him Mama.'

'I'll tell you what all this means,' Dad declared, responding as it were to some inner tribal reflex, 'master means boss. Our Billy is joining the toffs as one of the boss class. That's what it means. I warned you this would happen one day.'

No use contradicting him, Billy thought. This was an argument he knew he couldn't win.

Chapter Seventeen

When Billy heard that Gavin Power, the Inspector of Schools, was coming to see him, he felt a momentary pang of alarm. Then he thought, What the hell? Nothing can faze me now. I've finished two degrees and all that hard academic graft is behind me at last. I can put my feet up and start to live a little. He was looking forward to the holiday at Squire's Gate holiday camp in Blackpool which they had planned with the kids. That was before the Inspector made his visit.

After the usual routine of checking schemes of work and hearing Billy teach, the Inspector said, 'Have you ever thought about doing an advanced course in education? The Leeds Institute is organising a new one in secondary education and I would recommend it strongly. The competition to get on it is fierce as only six students are accepted, but if you were successful Manchester could offer you a maintenance grant and secondment on full salary. Talk it over at home and let us know what you think.'

Not again, was Billy's first reaction. Is there no end to it? He had spent his whole adult life with his head in a book, long enough to have qualified as a doctor or a dentist, though, he thought ruefully, his pay was a mere fraction of theirs. Surely he'd done enough! As for Leeds, it would mean being away from home again, leaving Laura with the children. No, the whole idea was preposterous and out of the question.

Laura was less sure. Despite all Billy's hard work and study, a better job had not materialised. While she didn't like the idea of his being away, if this final effort led at last to promotion and a higher-paid post, perhaps it was worth it. After all, she was near her parents and could enlist their help if need be while he was away.

Big Dunk, who had become Billy's mentor, had no such hesitation.

'It's the chance of a lifetime,' he said. 'They're offering you a big prize on a silver platter. A grant *and* secondment on full pay! You'd be a fool to turn it down. Take it! Who knows where such an advanced qualification might lead?'

Still unsure, Billy travelled over to Leeds for an interview which was conducted by a small committee of high-powered academics. It had been many years since he'd had to face such a panel and he was highly anxious about the prospect. To calm his jangled nerves, he bought a packet of Relaxotabs from a chemist's on the station concourse. Half a tablet was enough to calm him without affecting his alertness. It was as well he took only half since the interview proved to be a severe grilling about his interests, his private reading, his academic and teaching career. The following week Billy learned that he had been accepted as one of the six students, and Manchester LEA followed up with a generous grant. Billy wasn't entirely ecstatic as he had a vague feeling he was being swept along by the tide of events and was still unhappy at the prospect of seeing Laura and the kids only at weekends. But, he supposed, if it were in their best long-term interests, he'd have to accept the situation.

By this time, Titch had finished his degree and was keen to try for a place on the Leeds course, too, though he knew competition was cut-throat. He applied and was invited over for interview the following week, but when he heard about the third-degree methods the panel employed, he pleaded with Billy to accompany him for moral support. They took the train together during the half-term break and as they walked up to the university from the station, Titch became more and more tense.

'Look,' Billy said, 'you need something to relax you. Take half a Relaxotab, it worked for me.'

Titch took the packet eagerly.

'I'm feeling so tense,' he said, 'I'm sure half a pill won't be enough.'

He took three.

They continued their way up Copperas Hill, past the Brotherton Library, until they reached the Institute half an hour before the interview was due to begin. They were shown into a small office where they found two other nervous-looking candidates, both middle-aged, a man and a woman. Billy noticed that Titch yawned once or twice and hoped the tablets were not putting him to sleep. But as the minutes ticked by Titch was looked distinctly drowsy and his yawns were coming faster.

'Would Mr Smalley please come this way,' the clerk announced at last.

Titch's eyes were closed and Billy had to nudge him. He awoke with a jolt.

'Time for your interview,' Billy said.

Like a sleepwalker, Titch followed the clerk into the main office.

When he emerged half an hour later, he was still yawning and could hardly keep his eyes open.

'What sort of things did they ask?' Billy inquired on the train back to Manchester.

'Something about Greek philosophy,' he said dreamily. 'I forget the details. But I remember they wanted to know if I subscribed to the philosophy of Morpheus, the god of dreams.'

At that, his head dropped forward and he enjoyed 'the honey-heavy dew of slumber' all the way back to Manchester.

Titch did not get into Leeds.

In October Billy started the Leeds course. Laura and he had decided that it would be best if he took digs during the week and returned home on Friday nights for the weekend.

Billy checked the postcard ads on the university notice board and found lodgings a mile away with a widow, Mrs Gina Gattesco. To Billy, she was middle-aged, in her mid-forties, her Italian origins manifested in her dark hair and eyes. She had been born in Turin and had married an English businessman of Italian extraction when he had been visiting that city. Her husband had been her senior by twenty odd years and had died of pneumonia some three years earlier.

The rent was a reasonable two pounds a week, and for that Billy was given the front room as his sitting-room and study. The arrangement was that Mrs Gattesco would supply his breakfast and evening meal. It seemed ideal and Billy paid her a month's rent in advance.

'I don't need to take a lodger,' she told him, placing a hand on his arm, 'as my Enrico left me well off, but I like to have male company in the house. It makes me feel secure.'

Billy could have sworn she fluttered her eyelashes at him.

His first evening meal was excellent consisting of minestrone followed by a well-cooked steak with vegetables, and finishing with a sorbet dessert and a cappuccino, although he could have done without her detailed explanations of the origin of each item on his plate.

'I grew that spinach in my garden. The potatoes were the best King Edward's on Leeds market. The broccoli came from an Italian greengrocer . . .'

Otherwise a perfect meal, and he told her so.

'Don't you worry, Billy,' she said. 'I'm going to take good care of you during your stay in Leeds. But the name "Billy" seems strange on my lips. May I call you Guglielmo? That's Italian for William.'

'If you go on producing meals like that, Mrs Gattesco,' Billy joked, 'you can call me anything you like, even Dracula.'

She laughed at his joke. Placing her hand on his, she said, 'Please call me Gina. I think we're going to get on well, you and me. Remember, I am here to serve you.'

Early next morning, Billy was awakened by Gina shaking him gently. She was dressed in a silk dressing gown and as she leaned over him, he could smell her perfume.

'I thought you might like to start the day with a nice cup of tea,' she whispered.

'Gina, you are most kind.'

He dressed quickly and was soon ready to start his first day at the Institute. Gina had his breakfast prepared. Once again, she stood over him watching him eat.

'I love seeing a man with a good appetite.'

'I shall have to watch my waistline.'

She placed a hand on his shoulder. 'I think a little weight here and there might be good.'

Billy stood up. 'Well, time to go to work.'

She examined him closely. 'You are a handsome man, though I think maybe you should try parting your hair on the other side.'

She brushed his hair with her hand to try the effect.

'Yes, Guglielmo, that is much better. And I love that salt and pepper suit you're wearing. It makes you look so businesslike, but that tie is *terribile*. It doesn't go with the suit at all. Wait now. My husband left many ties and I'm sure I can find one more suitable.'

'That's all right, Gina. I'm not one to worry about clothes . . .'

Too late. She was back with one of her husband's ties. She put her arms round Billy's neck and began removing his tie. He got a whiff once again of that heady perfume as she brought her face close to his. This is getting out of hand, he thought.

The first day of the course was spent finding his way about and being introduced to tutorial staff and the fellow students who were to be Billy's companions for the coming year. One in particular, Tony Barrett, who hailed from Sunderland was around his own age and Billy found he had much in common with him. Both had a working-class background and both had worked for their degrees part-time while holding down a full-time job.

'Like Mr Bounderby in *Hard Times*, we were both raised in a ditch,' Tony Barrett laughed.

'And both pulled ourselves out by our own bootlaces,' Billy added.

'Bootlaces! You were lucky if you had boots. We used to pray every night for a pair of boots,' chuckled Tony.

Billy knew he was going to get on with him and when they discovered that Tony had digs close by, they arranged to walk to the Institute together each morning.

When Billy got back to his lodgings on the first evening, Gina was already waiting for him with a cup of tea.

'While you were out, Guglielmo, I pressed your other suit and polished your brown shoes.'

'That's kind of you, Gina,' a bemused Billy replied. Nice to have these cuppas, he thought, but where was it all leading?

There followed another excellent meal. Once again, she stood over him supervising him like a head waiter.

'Do you like Italian opera, Guglielmo?' she asked suddenly.

'I can't say I know too much about it.'

'Then I must educate you,' she said huskily. She put a record of Caruso singing a love serenade on the turntable. 'There. Music to aid the digestion,' she said, touching his hand lightly.

Gina was definitely a touchy-feely type, a hand-and-arm squeezer. When she found that Billy had studied Italian as part of his degree, she became excited.

'But your accent is perfect,' she rhapsodised when she heard him say a few words. 'I must take you in hand until you speak the language fluently.

'Si, Gina, ma le parole non mi vengono alle labbra facilmente.' (Yes, Gina, but the words don't come easily to the lips.)

'Then we must see what we can do about it,' she purred.

Billy enjoyed practising Italian but deep down was ill at ease and could hear alarm bells ringing. Gina was taking him over. He felt as if he were sliding down a slippery slope into a sea of trouble.

This is getting bloody dangerous, he thought. It's like one of Nobby's tall stories, an attractive widow crying out for comfort and solace.

His first week at the Institute was gruelling and the demands on him relentless. Great lists of books to study and papers to write came at them in a steady stream. By Thursday night, Billy's head was spinning and he was in a state of collapse. He had the usual evening meal of minestrone and risotto, accompanied by the running commentary.

I have to get out of this, he told himself, before I'm in over my head.

On Friday morning he nearly was, for when she appeared with his tea she was minus the dressing gown and wearing only a black night-dress. As she leaned over him, she stroked his hair and murmured, 'Guglielmo, you look so lost in that big bed. Wouldn't you like some company?'

Wow, he thought, what do I do now? Let's see you get out of this one, an inner voice whispered.

'It's a tempting offer, Gina,' he said. 'But I have a nine o'clock lecture and I shall be late.'

Wait till I tell the boys back home, he thought. They'll never believe me.

After lectures that day, Billy went home for his first weekend break. On the train ride back, he thought about the position he'd landed up in. When it came to temptation, Oscar Wilde had said he could resist anything but that; on the other hand, the Lord's Prayer asked not to be led into it, and hadn't St Paul said somewhere that when faced with it, the best thing to do was to run like the wind, or words to that effect. It was the last option that Billy chose. Damn it, he was only human, and if Gina went on giving him the glad eye, he might succumb, especially since Laura had put the shutters up for fear of having another baby. On reaching home, he had a frank talk with his wife and put her in the picture.

'Right,' she said, 'on Monday morning you go and see this Italian *signora* and collect your things and get out of there in double-quick time.'

'But I've paid her a month in advance,' Billy protested.

'Never mind about that. Better to write it off than put our marriage in danger. From now on, you travel daily to Leeds and you stay here where I can keep my eye on you.'

This was a Laura he didn't know. When her home and family were in danger, she was a she-cat defending her territory.

On the Monday, he found time to visit Mrs Gattesco and give notice. He made some excuse about being needed at home, told her to forget the rent he'd paid in advance. The news did not go down well.

'But I thought you'd be happy here,' she protested. 'I could make your time in Leeds so comfortable. And I loved having you.'

Nearly true, Billy thought. We certainly came close.

'What about that handsome young man who called for you each morning?' she asked. 'Perhaps he might be interested in a few home comforts?'

'I think he's already fixed up.'

'Well, remember, Guglielmo, if you change your mind, I am always available.'

There was only one thing left for Billy to do and that was to get out of there, as they say in Italy, *rapidamente come il vento,* like the wind.

Though the Gattesco episode was put behind them, the problem of sex was still in the forefront, at least for Billy. He had read in one of Laura's magazines that the birth of a child was often a cause of tension and that sex, or the lack of it, could drive new parents apart. Several husbands had reported that they hadn't done it for months; in one case for two years. While in Billy's case the tap hadn't been turned off completely, it had been more or less back to separate beds after the birth of Mark.

'You're not attracted to me any more, Laura,' he complained one morning.

'No, it's nothing personal like that,' she said. 'Of course I still love you, but I don't fancy the idea of producing any more children. I find the three we have are very demanding and enough to keep me more than occupied. The so-called safe period doesn't work, and as for that Oracle thing we bought, you may as well chuck it in the bin.'

It was one bright day before Easter that Billy found the answer, or at least thought he had. He was in the Manchester Central Library doing research into Comparative Demography when he stumbled on the philosopher's stone. He was consulting a book entitled *A History of Ancient Contraceptive Practices* when his eye was drawn to an account of Ming Dynasty customs. As he read on, he became more and more engrossed and could hardly believe what the book was telling him. Now he understood what the man who'd found the Koh-I-Noor diamond had felt like. There it was in black and white – the panacea! The solution they had been seeking all those years! Why had no one told them about this before? Perhaps it was a Vatican secret the hierarchy had kept for itself.

He could hardly wait to tell Laura of his discovery.

'Laura, Laura!' he called as he strode through the front door. 'Eureka! At last I've found the answer to our problem.'

She emerged from the kitchen wiping floury hands on her pinafore.

'What is it, Billy? What's all the shouting about?'

'You will shout too when I explain what I have found. Tucked away in an old tome, I've discovered an ancient Chinese contraceptive method first learned in 400 BC by the Yellow Emperor.'

'Not another calculator?' she said dubiously.

'No, Laura, nothing like that this time. It's birth control without tears. What's more, it's approved by the Pope. It's a method that depends on contemplation and thought control. To be successful, you need inner calm and tranquillity. The Chinese called it *coitus reservatus* and it's possible to achieve orgasm without ejaculation.'

'Impossible.'

'Not at all. Instead of being overwhelmed by a waterfall, we ride over the top of the waves. Like surfing. The Chinese have been using it effectively for thousands of years.'

'If it's so effective,' she said, 'how come the Chinese have a population of one billion?'

But Billy wasn't to be put off by cold logic.

'I suppose the method was too sophisticated for your average peasant.'

'And we've got to remember all this stuff about calmness, contemplation and meditation while having sex?' she said. 'It doesn't sound easy to me.'

'I'm sure it would help if we were to concentrate on

something that was a complete turn-off. I could think of ugly old hags and you could think of England.'

'It's a funny thing,' she said, 'but whenever I think of England, I always see the English football team.'

After heated discussion she reluctantly agreed in the interests of research to give the ancient contemplative method a try.

After leaving Mrs Gattesco's board and lodging, Billy's routine became tough because the only train that would reach Leeds in time for the first nine o'clock tutorial was the slow one leaving Manchester at 6.30 a.m., which in turn meant setting out from home at 5.30. If the train was on time, it pulled into Leeds Central at 8.50 from where he had to sprint the length of Copperas Hill to make it for his lecture. There was no way of hiding in a crowd of fellow students since there were only six on the course and his absence would have been noted immediately. Billy came to know every little station along the route: Stalybridge, Greenfield, Slaithwaite, Huddersfield, Dewsbury. Some nights, if there were evening sessions or visits to other colleges, he arrived home at midnight and had to be up at the crack of dawn to catch the early morning train next morning.

The course itself was ultra-modern and the two tutors running it were imaginative in their approach. It soon became obvious that the small elite group of which Billy was now a part was being groomed for plum positions on the educational tree. Visits to famous schools like A.S. Neill's Summerhill or Bedales; giving impromptu talks or votes of thanks to visiting celebrities, or nerve-wracking public performances of one kind or another were the daily fare. The underlying philosophy was very much of the liberal school of thought. The students were fed a straight diet of Jean Jacques Rousseau and John Dewey, and the zeal with which it was presented made it more of a brainwashing exercise than an education course.

Towards the end of their time at Leeds, students were treated to a series of recruitment talks on openings available in a wide variety of educational fields. Speakers waxed lyrical on opportunities in administration, teacher training, further education, and finally in developing countries. Although the talk by the Colonial Office representative was more like a rousing political speech than a recruitment drive, Billy found it particularly moving.

'Say the word "Kenya" to the average Briton,' the officer began, 'and what do they think of? Wild life, the Mau Mau rebellion, primitive farming. But Kenya is also a place with its eyes on the future and that means education. However, there is a desperate shortage of qualified people to staff its schools and colleges and that's where you could help. No other country on this vast continent has such an urgent need at the present time. We appeal to you to give the idea of becoming an education officer some thought. The Colonial Office can offer attractive permanent pensionable posts or, if preferred, four-year contracts at the end of which you may return to resume your career here. Most of you present today will teach for forty years or so and here is a chance to devote your career, or at least part of it, to a worthwhile cause which you will find fulfilling and which will give your life meaning and purpose.

'The Mau Mau rebellion is over, Jomo Kenyatta is locked away, and the country has embarked on an optimistic journey that will be in vain without the help of professionals like yourselves. This is a critical turning point for the country, and indeed this vast continent. Kenya is a place of astonishing beauty and abject poverty, a place where hope and despair live side by side. It is the place where we became human, the root of our civilisation.'

The speaker told the audience that it was not necessary to make a commitment there and then but that anyone completing an inquiry form would be provided with further information. There were no takers and it looked as if the talk had fallen on stony ground. Disappointed, the visitor gathered up his papers, but one listener had been enthralled by the speaker's eloquence. Feeling sorry about the poor response, Billy thought he'd make up for his fellow students' apathy by putting his own name forward, though the idea of taking his family to Kenya was about as alien as taking them to the planet Jupiter.

'So you see yourself as a white hunter?' Tony Barrett chuckled.

'Oh, sure,' Billy replied. '*Sanders of the River*. I can see it now – me in my pith helmet directing Paul Robeson and his gang of natives rowing up the Zambezi.'

'The Zambezi is in Southern Rhodesia.' Tony grinned. 'In Kenya you'd be dealing with the aftermath of the Mau Mau, and who can tell? They might set Jomo Kenyatta free.'

'Then I should want danger money,' Billy laughed. 'Only a crazy man would take a job out there.'

Six weeks later he learned that, along with his fellow students, he had passed his examination and had been awarded the Diploma in Secondary Education. Tony Barrett got a lecturer's job in a prestigious training college and Billy was appointed Head of English in a less prestigious Manchester school located in the district of Beswick.

'What next?' Mam said, when he told her of this latest development. 'Surely not another lot of letters after your name?'

'Now I can add DSE,' Billy said.

'It sounds like one of them medals they give to Battle of Britain pilots.'

'If he gets any more bloody letters after his name,' Dad said, 'they'll never fit 'em all on his gravestone.'

Trust him to think of something cheerful.

Chapter Eighteen

The new job was daunting. Billy was twenty-nine years old and as well as teaching classes and running the school library, he was to be in charge of the English teachers in a secondary school in one of the toughest districts in Manchester. The school was a hundred per cent male in both staff and pupils, and the headmaster was an ex-regimental sergeant-major who ran the school with an iron hand.

The building itself was an unusual piece of architecture. Its square tower made it look more like a town hall than a school. Billy's Uncle Eddie had told him that the place had been used as a casualty station for the wounded sent home from the trenches in the Great War. His uncle had been most impressed to learn that Billy had been appointed to a position in this hospital school, and Billy liked the sound of the title Head of English in Holbrook Hospital School as it was reminiscent of famous schools like Christ's Hospital of Charles Lamb fame, though the two institutions could not have been more different.

The headmaster, Eric Sharpe, met Billy a week before term was due to begin and gave him the briefest of interviews. Billy was made to stand before his desk like a private on parade and he had the strange sensation that his turnout was being closely inspected. Did he have razor-type creases in his flannels? No! Gleaming shoes? Definitely not. He half expected to be put on a charge for not being up to standard.

'I hope you'll be happy here,' the Head began. 'You have been selected from a shortlist of five candidates and come highly recommended by Gavin Power, the School Inspector. You are to be Head of English, a high-profile position as English is the school's largest department and the subject is at the core of the curriculum.'

'I know how lucky I was to be appointed,' Billy said, 'and I shall do my best to live up to the responsibilities of the job.'

Sharpe stared straight at him as if exasperated at the interruption.

'We have well over eight hundred boys here,' he continued, 'all from poor, deprived backgrounds, some of them criminal. So I run a tight ship as it's vital that we maintain strict discipline at all times. Without that, no teaching can take place. I hope you agree with that?'

'Of course, Mr Sharpe,' Billy said eagerly. Do I have a choice? he wondered.

'Our pupils come from chaotic homes and need order in their lives,' Sharpe went on, 'and it's our job to give them a well-regulated environment where they know what to expect if they break the rules. In the past there has been too much corporal punishment in this school and I have devised my own system to cut it down to a minimum. Teachers were hitting out with the strap indiscriminately and it had to stop.'

'I'm sure Jean-Jacques Rousseau would have approved

heartily,' Billy said warmly. What a stupid thing to say, he told himself.

Sharpe glared at Billy as if he'd exposed himself. 'Yes, yes,' he snapped, 'I'm sure he would. Anyway, the problem in a big secondary school like this is that we have lots of subject specialists and it's difficult to keep an eye on each individual pupil as they come under so many different teachers in the course of a day. You'll learn how my system works as you go along.'

'I look forward to seeing it in operation,' Billy said earnestly. 'Anything that cuts down on corporal punishment is OK in my book.'

Once again, Sharpe gave him that funny look. 'I'll take you to the staff-room and introduce the rest of the masters,' he said.

As they pushed open the staff-room door, all eyes turned to examine the new man. Billy gave them all a friendly good morning though inwardly he was consumed with terror, and expected to be shown up as a fraud at any moment. What was he, a slum kid from Collyhurst, doing in a place like this, masquerading as some kind of expert in the teaching of English? Someone was bound to see through him sooner or later.

Sharpe presented him to the Deputy Head, Charlie Henshaw, an older teacher with a ready smile and a bluff personality.

'Welcome to the madhouse.' He grinned. 'If you're not crazy already, you soon will be, working here.'

Billy then met the rest of the staff including those with some responsibility for teaching English. They were mainly middle-aged, friendly enough but seemed wary and suspicious.

Two teachers were designated as Billy's deputies as they

were English specialists. The younger of the two who introduced himself as Dave Charlton was a tall, lanky individual brimming with enthusiasm.

'I'm looking forward to working with you,' he said, shaking Billy's hand firmly. 'You must have learned lots of new ideas on that Leeds course. I'd have given anything to get on it myself.'

The other teacher was around forty, a ruddy, weathered-looking man who gave his name as Albert Afford. He wore baggy corduroys, a thick tweed jacket, an open-necked check shirt, and two days' stubble on his chin. Judging by the look of distaste on the Head's face, Afford was not flavour of the month but Billy learned later that the boys adored him since he was easy-going and took them hiking, camping, and climbing in the Peak District. It was a relief to find his two colleagues were both likeable people. Billy soon made friends with them and it wasn't long before they were on first-name terms.

'You won't be popular in the staff-room, Billy,' Afford told him when they were out of the Head's earshot.

'Why not?'

'Mr Chilton, one of the regular staff, applied for your job and when they gave it to you, he took the huff and left in high dudgeon, as they say.'

'Not my fault,' Billy said.

'Doesn't matter. They're a clique in the staff-room, all ex-servicemen as was this bloke Chilton, and they resent you getting the top job instead of their mate. They also consider you an upstart and too young for the post.'

'Thanks, Albert, for that,' Billy said, 'but it's too bad. They're stuck with me.'

Why, oh, why, did I ever leave my old job at St Anselm's? he thought. I was safe, secure and happy there.

* * *

Billy went home with his head and his briefcase full of schemes, syllabuses and lesson plans. For the whole of that week he was immersed in organising programmes of work for the English staff.

A week later he had his first day of teaching classes of boys from eleven years of age to sixteen. A nineteenth-century psychiatrist once claimed that a criminal type could be recognised by his facial characteristics, those of the Neanderthal. The idea had long since been discredited as rubbish but, Billy thought, if there was even a vestige of truth in the theory, then a fair proportion of the pupils who passed before his eyes that first day were destined to do time as guests of Her Majesty at some future date. Many of the boys in the upper forms were so brawny they couldn't fit behind the desks and it was obvious that the school furniture makers had not taken the trouble to measure their prospective customers.

In the first few lessons, Billy tried to gain some idea of standards by requiring them to write a composition.

'Take out your exercise books,' he said.

'You're not going to ask us to write on "My Birthday" or "My Favourite Hobby" or boring stuff like that?' one thickset lad asked.

'What's wrong with that?' Billy said.

'Boring, boring, boring,' the rest chanted.

'OK, OK,' he said. 'Write on any subject that interests you. Films, TV, football, whatever.'

With a sigh, the class got down to work and soon there was no sound but the scratching of pens. Billy determined to talk the matter over with Dave Charlton and Albert Afford. At his first conference with them that day, he raised the subject of motivating the boys in their charge.

'I came across an idea in a progressive school in Leeds,' he told them. 'It's revolutionary but I know it'll work 'cos I've seen it in operation with my own eyes, but it will need the co-operation of other members of staff.' He explained his plan.

Dave Charlton was all for it immediately.

'Let's give it a go,' he said.

Albert Afford was doubtful.

'You'll find the other blokes on the staff against any new idea,' he said. 'They prefer to stick to their trusted old ways, but if you can get Eric Sharpe behind it you'll have no problem as they're all nervous of him. Let them try arguing with an ex-RSM.'

Afford was right about the staff being afraid of Sharpe. The next day at break-time they'd congregated in the staff-room for their cuppa when the Head suddenly burst through the door. The whole room froze.

'Who the hell is on playground duty?' he bawled.

'I am,' a red-faced Dave Charlton mumbled. 'I came to get my cup of tea.'

'Then bloody well get down there. Now! There's a big fight going on in the playground,' Eric yelled.

Dave Charlton, minus his tea, left in double-quick time.

'The teacher on duty must get down to the playground immediately the bell rings,' Sharpe ordered, addressing the rest of the staff.

Later that day, when Sharpe had cooled down, Billy outlined his English-teaching idea to him and was surprised at the enthusiastic response.

'Exactly what's needed,' he said, offering Billy a cigarette. 'This school needs the occasional kick up the arse. That's why you were appointed, to inject fresh ideas into our moribund staff. Don't worry about their opposition. What I say in this school goes. Let me have the detailed plan as soon as you can and we'll implement it first chance we get.'

Billy was looking forward to his second week at the school, mainly to get down to the job of running a department but also to learn more about Eric Sharpe's 'system' for reducing corporal punishment.

Monday began as usual with school assembly in the main hall. Hundreds of boys standing in line made an awesome sight. The staff stood at the sides; the music teacher Vic Curzon sat at the piano, and Eric Sharpe waited arms akimbo on the stage. This was a different scene from the small informal assemblies of St Anselm's, and for some reason Billy sensed an air of expectation, of foreboding even. The Head called out the names of a dozen pupils who slowly mounted the stage. Perhaps, Billy thought, they were to receive some kind of award for achievement. If this were so, why did the boys, who ranged from junior form members to seniors, look so scared?

'They're the kids put on report last week,' whispered Albert Afford. 'They're for it.'

The Head announced the title of the hymn for that day, 'The Church's One Foundation', and the whole school lifted its voice in unison. Billy joined in though deep down he still felt guilty about singing Protestant hymns, especially ones about the Church which he knew referred to the Anglican church and not his own. My God, he thought, it's a throwback to the Rechabite Hall all those years ago in Collyhurst when I took part in 'heathen' rituals for the sake of a few potted meat sandwiches and a game of Snakes and Ladders.

As the last notes faded away, a hush fell over the hall.

The boys on the rostrum had lowered their heads and turned pale. What is going on? Billy wondered. He hadn't long to wait.

Eric Sharpe glowered at the most junior victim, a one-eyed boy called Joey Duckett.

'Why are you on report?' he asked ominously, inspecting the lad from head to foot.

'Talking in class, sir,' the young boy stammered.

What happened next shocked Billy to the core. Sharpe went berserk. Red as a turkey cock, he exploded in a fit of anger.

'Talking in class? You nasty little creature! You obnoxious little boy,' he roared in the lad's face. 'Stand up straight. Look at the state of you! Muddy shoes, dirty clothes, snotty nose . . . you're a mess! What are you?'

'A mess, sir,' the young wretch stuttered.

It was pure theatre and the whole hall looked on in silent horror as if watching a Shakespearean tragedy. Billy too was mesmerised.

The boys waiting their turn were now quaking in terror as Eric Sharpe went along the line castigating them. If anything, anticipation was worse than the reality. The last boy in line, a gargantuan fellow with coarse features, cringed in terror when Eric Sharpe reached him. It was an eyeball-to-eyeball confrontation.

'And you? Why are you on report, Dawson?' he asked threateningly.

'Answering back, sir,' came the answer.

Sharpe blew a fuse and became apoplectic with rage.

'Answering back!' he seethed. 'You horrible individual! How dare you answer back to one of *my* teachers, in *my* school? Take a look at yourself. You're not a human being, you're a troglodyte! What are you?'

'A troglodyte, sir.'

It sounded like the name of an alien race from outer space. Billy was sure that Des Dawson did not know what a troglodyte was. Neither did most of the school, including the teachers.

Dawson remained standing ashen-faced. He had been annihilated.

The drama over, the victims returned to their places looking shaken and Sharpe led the school in a recital of the Lord's Prayer.

'So this is the much-vaunted "system"?' Billy whispered to Albert Afford as they returned to their classes. 'Now I see how Sharpe has eliminated corporal punishment. He's simply replaced it with something infinitely worse: personality destruction.'

'You can look forward to this performance every Monday morning, Billy,' Albert murmured. 'But that's not the end of it. Now the twelve wretches must report to the Head every dinnertime and if they have one black mark that day, he gives them two of the strap on the hands.'

'The Nazis could have learned a thing from this system,' Billy remarked. 'Surely not all the staff are in favour of this Gestapo method?'

'Nearly all the old-timers are,' Albert answered. 'Except Charlie Henshaw. He's the only teacher who understands these kids as he was raised in this district.'

As Billy went to teach, he wondered what kind of place he had come to. And, crucially, could he stick it out? The treatment he had witnessed that morning went against the grain of everything he believed in.

* * *

Billy's first class was in the school library where he tried to inculcate a love of books and literature in the boys. For most of the pupils there were no books at home, apart from the occasional football or comic-book annual, and reading was confined to the popular press.

'My mam was going to buy my dad a book last Christmas,' Joey Duckett told him, 'but my auntie said that was no good 'cos he already had one.'

'Very funny, Joey, I'm sure,' Billy said. 'But what's happened to the book you borrowed last week?'

'My little brother spilled condensed milk on it, sir, and so my dad chucked it in the dustbin, sir.'

'Then you'll have to replace it, Joey. That was an expensive book.'

The book had been an illustrated volume on Africa and Billy suspected that Joey had borrowed it because it featured several naked peasant women.

'I haven't got no money, sir.'

'Then you'll have to get your dad to buy another for us,' Billy said, though he had little hope of seeing a replacement.

'He can't, sir. He's on the dole.' Then, in an aside to his desk companion, Joey whispered, 'Besides, he's pissed every night.'

'I heard that, Joey. It's disgraceful. Now go and tell Mr Henshaw what you said. He'll know how to deal with you.'

Poor old Joey. He always seemed to be in trouble. He was away for some time and Billy wondered what had happened to him.

At break-time, he found out. As he collected his tea and biscuit, Charlie Henshaw came over to him, chuckling. 'What was all that about with young Duckett? He came over to my office and said, "Mr Hopkins told me to tell you that my dad gets pissed every night." He clearly thought I needed to have this vital piece of information.'

As Charlie and Billy stood laughing together, a school prefect interrupted to tell Billy that Joey Duckett was waiting at the staff-room door to see him. Billy excused himself and went out to see the lad.

'Well, Joey, what can I do for you?'

'Please, sir, I've been home and my dad got this book for you to replace the one he threw in the bin. Will it do, sir?'

It was an illustrated volume of Impressionist painters. Billy was deeply moved.

'Of course it will, Joey. Please thank your dad and tell him I'm glad he cleared the matter up.'

Billy returned to the staff-room and told Charlie Henshaw what had happened.

'It goes to show,' Billy said, 'these boys do have a conscience. Look at the book Duckett's dad has sent us.'

'Here, let me have a look at that,' Charlie said, taking the book from Billy. 'Just as I thought,' he exclaimed, turning it over. 'Manchester Public Libraries.'

The following weekend proved to be a busy one at home. The promotion had eased their money position and they went into town to check out pianos at Forsyth's and Swan's. The lack of a piano was something that had niggled Billy since the early days of their marriage for Laura was an accomplished performer. She had never complained but he felt that she missed playing and he was determined to rectify the omission as soon as he could.

'The way things are going,' he remarked one day, 'we'll soon catch up with Hamish and Jenny. Next thing you know, we'll be having a new kitchen with one of those big fridges with a deep-freeze compartment.'

'Those cost the earth,' Laura answered. 'We've a long way to go before we can think about such things.'

It was a strange coincidence that they had mentioned the names of Hamish and Jenny for the next weekend Jenny came back to Manchester with her two daughters. Billy and Laura took the family over to the Mackenzie home to meet them.

'It's over,' Jenny announced to the household which had gathered in the big kitchen. 'Hamish is unbearable. Silas Marner was a spendthrift by comparison.'

'Hamish is a careful man,' Duncan said in his defence. 'That's why he's worth a bob or two,' he added, throwing Billy a meaningful look.

'Careful isn't the word for him,' Jenny said vehemently. 'He's a skinflint of the first order.'

' "Take care of the pennies and the pounds will take care of themselves" is not a bad motto,' her father protested.

'Hamish takes care not only of the pennies but also the farthings. He gives me a weekly household allowance and I am supposed to account for every last ha'penny. Friday night there's always a big inquisition. Talk about cheese-paring! It's "Why did you spend half a crown on biscuits? Why a shilling on soap powder? Is that the cheapest you could buy it?" and so on. I'm sick to death of it.'

'There's nothing wrong with having a tight budget,' Duncan countered.

'But we thought you were doing so well up there in Edinburgh,' Laura said. 'We heard nothing but good reports. Private education and special violin lessons for the bairns. What happened?'

'Hamish was good in the early days,' her sister said, 'but the last couple of years, his true nature has come to the fore.'

'How do you mean?' Billy asked. 'I always thought he was not only affluent but generous to boot.'

'There are hundreds of examples I could give you,' Jenny replied, 'but you'll get some idea when I tell you he switched off the freezer the other night, ruining a whole lot of food. Said it was a waste of electricity.'

'Good God!' Laura exclaimed. 'And there's Billy and I praying every night for such a luxury item as a fridge.'

'It gets worse than that,' Jenny went on. 'Now he's taken to saving hot water. When I make tea, he pours the surplus hot water into a Thermos flask to be used when we make the next pot.'

'It minds me of a man I knew in Bishopbriggs . . .' old Auntie began.

'Haud your whisht!' Gran'ma said. 'Let Jenny tell her story.'

'Thank the Lord you've never gone that far, Duncan,' Louise said, 'though at times you too can be tight-fisted.'

'I think the word "canny" might be more appropriate,' he said.

'Anyway,' Jenny said, 'I'm not going back till he mends his ways. The final straw came when I saw him going through the dustbins to see if I'd thrown any food away.'

'A few days on his own,' her mother said, 'should make him see the light.'

Louise was right. A week later Hamish was on the phone pleading with Jenny to come back. A fortnight later he came down to Manchester in person and implored her on bended knee. Jenny relented but wrung out of him, before her family as witnesses, the promise to change his habits and turn his one-way pocket into a two-directional freeway.

Billy could hardly contain his feeling of *Schadenfreude* as he and Laura made their way home.

'To think,' he said, 'you nearly married this character. I must say, though, I like the idea with the Thermos flask. Maybe we should be economising too.'

'Don't even think about it,' Laura said, digging him playfully in the ribs. 'Now what about that piano we were talking about last week . . .'

The following weekend they bought a piano from Swan's in Longsight, second-hand but in superb condition. The instrument had a beautiful, pleasing tone, but what made it unusual was that it was also an Aeolian piano-player and came with two hundred piano rolls, some of them recording famous performances by Rubinstein and Paderewski.

Young Matthew found that he could play it from a standing position by clinging to the grips and pumping furiously at the foot bellows. When he had finished, the mechanism folded away and became an ordinary piano which Laura took full advantage of. Billy spent the rest of Saturday up in the attic preparing his grand plan for school to the accompaniment of Liszt played by Laura and Chopin pumped out by six-year-old Matthew.

On Sunday morning, Billy attended the eleven o'clock Mass at the Holy Name Church and the choir took its usual 'sermon stroll' for a smoke and a chat to catch up on each others' news. As Billy walked along Oxford Road with Oscar and Titch he told them about Eric Sharpe's ranting and raving at the Monday assemblies.

'He sounds like a regular Caligula,' Titch observed.

'You must find it particularly hard, Hoppy,' Oscar said, 'after that idealistic course at Leeds.'

'You'll have to confront him and tell him where he gets off,' Titch said, 'but rather you than me. I wouldn't fancy having a set-to with any of the RSMs I met in the army.'

'I have an advantage over you then,' Billy said, ''cos I was never in the army and he doesn't scare me. Besides, I've met tougher guys in Collyhurst, my own dad for one.'

Billy then told them of the latest development in the Hopkins household, the piano, and invited them round for tea that afternoon to hear a demonstration. He said nothing about the player-piano facility.

'Things are looking up then,' Titch said. 'Next thing we know, you'll be buying a car.'

'That's a long way off,' Billy said. 'Say another five years if I can put up with working for a martinet headmaster.'

They had reached the main doors of the church and as they were about to enter, Titch turned and said nonchalantly, 'Oh, it slipped my mind, Hoppy. I've had a request for a reference from the Colonial Office. Something about a job in Kenya. You're not thinking of emigrating to the dark continent, surely?'

'Oh, no!' Billy exclaimed. 'I'd forgotten all about that. I applied for details on the spur of the moment when I was studying at Leeds. I was the only one to fill in a form as I felt sorry for the visiting speaker. I didn't think for a minute that anything would come of it. Anyway I might get a free trip to London if they call me for interview.'

They went into the church together. Time for the 'Credo' and 'Palestrina'.

In the afternoon, Titch and Oscar appeared for tea and to hear the new piano. Before they went into the front room to view the instrument, Billy took them to one side.

'I want to let you in on a family secret but I must insist on absolute discretion before I tell you.'

'Sounds intriguing,' Titch said.

'I simply love family secrets.' Oscar said. 'I do hope it's a scandal of some kind.'

'Afraid not,' Billy said. 'It's young Matthew. We think he's been possessed.'

'Good God!' they exclaimed together. 'How do you mean, possessed?'

'As you know, he's only six but the other day, we found him playing Chopin's "Minute Waltz" and he's never had a lesson in his life. We think he's been taken over by the spirit of some great musician . . . Rubinstein, Paderewski, maybe even Chopin himself. You may have read about a similar case in California. She was called Audrey Rose, I believe.'

'You're having us on,' Titch said. 'I don't believe a word of it.'

'I'll prove it to you,' said Billy. 'Wait in the hall and I'll get Matthew to play something, but you must stay out of the room until he has finished or you may disturb the spirit.'

Matthew who had been primed for the ruse, was more than ready to join in the fun. Alone in the room, he pumped out a creditable performance of Chopin's 'Revolutionary' and then quickly folded the mechanism away.

'You can come in now, Dad,' he called. 'I've finished playing.'

The piano had been restored to 'normal' and Billy's two companions fell for it. Over tea they could talk of nothing else. It was a miracle. Was Billy going to put Matthew on the stage? Was he going to inform the press? What about taking him to a medium to ascertain the identity of the spirit? Or even a priest to be exorcised? After tea, Billy disabused them and put them out of their misery, and after a good laugh all round Laura gave them a demonstration of 'real' piano-playing.

At the beginning of that week, Eric Sharpe gave his usual Monday morning display of fury. As he marched along the line of recalcitrant pupils, seething and hurling vicious abuse at his wretched victims, he soon had them shaking in their shoes. Billy too was fuming. He couldn't stand idly by while this reign of terror continued. Either he took some kind of action or he would have to leave the school. And he'd only just got there!

After assembly he went to see Sharpe in his office. Billy had prepared his speech well but nevertheless he had butterflies in his stomach as he knocked gently on the door.

'Come in,' Sharpe called. 'Yes, Mr Hopkins? What can I do for you?'

'Mr Sharpe,' Billy began angrily, 'I am very unhappy about these Monday morning assemblies. I find them hard to take, especially after the course I recently attended. They go against every liberal principle we were encouraged to adopt. I don't know what you hope to achieve by the dressing down you give the boys but I personally find it most distressing.'

Eric Sharpe lit a cigarette. His hands were visibly shaking. No one had ever talked to him like this before.

'Hopkins, you don't understand,' he growled. 'You with your ideals and your ideologies! You live in cloud cuckoo-land and the leafy lanes of Regina Park. You haven't a clue about boys like these. They need order in their chaotic lives. You think we should use soft words and rational arguments but fear is the only thing most of them understand. I can assure you, the boys who appear on stage never need a repeat session. It keeps them in their place.'

'I know I'm less experienced than you, Mr Sharpe, but as for understanding "boys like these" as you put it, I was raised in a Manchester district which has the edge on Beswick when it comes to toughness and I'm sure fear is not the answer. By all means give them a rocket, if they deserve it, but does it have to be so vitriolic? After all, they're not in the army.'

Eric Sharpe was much concerned about his reputation as a headmaster and any suggestion that he was less than perfect worried him, especially in the eyes of a young idealist like Billy who also had the ear of Gavin Powers, the Inspector of Schools. It would be an exaggeration to say that Sharpe changed overnight but Billy noted a slight moderation in his tone the following Monday. He was certainly not gentle, but not quite as aggressive as he had been.

In his third week at the school, Billy introduced his 'big idea'.

'From now on,' he told his senior English class, 'there will be no more writing of compositions with titles like "What I did on my holidays" or "My favourite hobby".'

The announcement was greeted with a cheer.

'But what are we going to do instead?' one boy asked suspiciously.

'We're going to write novels, that's what we are going to do.'

There was a long silence while they took this in. Then came a howl of protest.

'Us, write books?' 'This new teacher's gone bonkers.' 'He's round the bend.' 'I can't write a novel! What does he think we are?'

'How do you mean, sir?' Dawson asked at last. 'Books . . . that sort of thing?'

'That's right, and I am going to show you how to do it.'

'Can't be done, sir,' he declared. 'Most of us here are thick. We can't put two words together, never mind write a book.'

There was scepticism not only among the pupils but also among the staff.

'This is what comes of appointing a whippersnapper with new-fangled ideas.' 'Most of the kids in this school can hardly write their name, never mind a book.' 'With their background, the only kind of books these kids will ever write will be pornographic.'

Billy took it all in his stride because he was confident that the idea would work once he got it up and running. With Sharpe behind him, there was little effective opposition.

Throughout that first term, all classes spent their 'composition' lessons writing up their 'books'. The early lessons were concerned with choosing subjects to write on, planning the outlines, saying who the book was aimed at, and organising the work into chapters. By half-term, there were over five hundred books in production. There was a wide variety of subjects, from fairy tales through science fiction to ghost stories; many efforts were re-hashes of television programmes seen or stories they had heard elsewhere, and countless tales concluded with the *Alice-in-Wonderland* ending 'it was all a dream'. But among the heaps, there sparkled the occasional diamond. One boy wrote a superb saga of the Peninsular War that was worthy of publication.

On the last day of term, Eric Sharpe called Des Dawson on to the stage. Uh-oh, Billy thought, poor old Des is for it again. The boy himself must have had similar thoughts because he was trembling as he mounted the steps. But Sharpe had summoned him, not to lambast him but to hand him an award.

'It gives me great pleasure,' the headmaster announced, 'to present this book, *Years of Victory* by Arthur Bryant, to the writer of the best school novel. Well done, Des. Let's give him a round of applause.'

Red with embarrassment but smiling with pleasure, Dawson returned to his place in the body of the hall.

Not bad for a troglodyte, Billy thought.

The book-writing episode involved other disciplines in the school. The Art Department had the boys producing illustrations and covers; Handicraft worked on book-binding. The final versions were written up by the pupils in their best handwriting. At the end of the first term there were several hundred finished novels for the Head to show off to the Inspectors who rhapsodised about the idea and tried to promote it in other Manchester schools. The image of the school and Sharpe's reputation as a leader were at an all-time high and if he could have awarded Billy a medal, it would have been a Victoria Cross. In the staff-room, the English Department were hailed as heroes who had brought honour to the school which redounded on them all. Billy was in.

Gavin Powers, the Inspector, was the most pleased of all, as his sponsorship of Billy appeared to have paid off, thus enhancing his own status among his fellows.

'You have a good name at the Education Offices,' he told Billy, 'and if you keep up this good work, I can see you as headmaster of a school like this one day.'

'That would be wonderful, Mr Powers.'

As Billy said it a shudder passed through him as if someone had walked across his grave. He had a momentary vision of his career mapped out for the next thirty years and the Inspector's encouraging words filled his heart not with joy, but dismay. He could even see himself becoming like Eric Sharpe and running 'a tight ship'. Is that my lot? he asked himself. Is that all there is? Surely there must be more to life than that?

Chapter Nineteen

'Kenya! You must be going off your head!' Laura exclaimed when Billy told her he'd been invited for interview at the Colonial Office. He had requested information about working there on a whim but the Civil Service wheels had begun to turn. Only when he received a letter along with a railway warrant inviting him to attend in London did he fully appreciate that the matter was becoming serious. Then he thought, a visit to London with expenses paid? Why not? It would be a short welcome break from his ever-demanding job.

'There's no harm in attending for an interview,' he replied. 'In no way am I committed to taking a job with them. I'm simply curious, that's all.'

'All very well,' she continued, 'but Friday the thirteenth is hardly the most auspicious day to travel to London by train.' She was right for there had been the most horrific train accident the previous week in the fog with ninety-two killed and over a hundred seriously injured. However, Billy wasn't the superstitious type and had written back accepting. At school, not wanting to let the cat out of the bag, he reported himself sick on the Thursday afternoon and took the overnight sleeper to Euston.

Now here he was, standing outside the Colonial Office in Great Smith Street.

There was something about the atmosphere in that part of London that fascinated him. Being interviewed in an office close to Whitehall and the Houses of Parliament, he sensed that he was close to the centre of power, where it was all happening, where the big decisions were made. A small voice inside him whispered about the big wonderful world out there.

Feeling jittery, he entered the Colonial Office building through a magnificent entrance hall and reported his presence to a uniformed male receptionist who checked his credentials and asked him to wait in a small ante-room. Whether this ploy was part of some deliberate plan Billy never did discover, but it was there that he became hooked. As he sat waiting to be called, he could hear various phone conversations in the adjoining office.

'I'd like to book two first-class airline tickets to Dar-es-Salaam for the third of February,' a voice said.

'We have a family going out to Kampala on the twelfth, can you arrange accommodation for them?' said another.

'We'd like to make first-class reservations for Dr Mowbray and his wife going to Fiji, departing the fourteenth. They will require sea passages plus their heavy baggage . . .'

Faraway places with strange-sounding names. These snippets were enough to set Billy's imagination soaring. He was about to be interviewed for the job of education officer in Kenya, a challenging position on the African continent and at a much higher salary. A feeling of excitement coursed through his veins. What a wonderful opportunity for him, and what a wonderful experience for Laura and the kids. Life in another world, another culture.

Why not? Suddenly the idea of returning to his job in a Secondary Modern school in Beswick left him with a sinking feeling. Was that to be his whole future? Or was the door of opportunity opening for him this very day?

The interview itself went well. The senior civil servants on the selection board congratulated him on his qualifications and the industry he had displayed in achieving them. There were no awkward questions and the offer of a job seemed to be a foregone conclusion.

'The appointment would be as an education officer in the Colonial Service,' the chairman of the panel told him.

'Education officer? You mean, school teacher?'

The chairman laughed.

'The concept is a little wider than that. As an officer, you can be called on to work in any branch of education as schoolmaster, administrator, inspector, teacher-trainer and so on. Even be seconded to other government work, if necessary.'

The more details they filled in, the more attractive the job became.

As they described the living conditions – a fully furnished house at a nominal rent, a large garden, one or two servants to help with the chores, the high standard of living, the pay and generous non-contributory pension plus superb educational facilities for his children, the magnificent climate, the sports facilities, the glorious holidays in the game parks and at the Mombasa coast – his sense of adventure was aroused. Billy was sold.

'Finally,' the chairman of the board said, 'to help you make up your mind, we can arrange for you and your wife to attend a four-day orientation course at Farnham Castle in Surrey. Any queries you may have will be answered there by a panel of experts.'

All the way back to Manchester he was in a frenzy of excitement. The day had fired him with a longing for this wonderful land that offered so much in the way of sunshine, sport, and the promise of prosperity and self-fulfilment. If Laura agreed, their lives would be turned upside down. Everything depended on her reaction. Without her, it was out.

Laura wasn't enthusiastic – at first. She was less impulsive and needed time to mull things over. She raised many objections: the children's education, tropical diseases, insects, wild animals. Besides, what about the job at Holbrook? He had only just been promoted, their money worries were easing, he had begun to be accepted by the staff at Holbrook – and now he was considering throwing it all in to go off on some wild goose chase in wildest Africa. And what would they do with the house? What about the furniture? The whole idea was too risky. In his eagerness, Billy brushed these objections aside. He had answers for them all.

'Laura,' he said, 'I feel as if the tide of events is sweeping us along. Opportunity knocks but once and then she's gone and the chance is lost. For the rest of our lives regret will linger, taunting us with what might have been. Here in England I sometimes feel like a hamster on a treadmill stuck in the same dull routine for years and years, just an endless line of classes and me growing old like Mr Chips. At least you have a more interesting day at home, you're your own boss looking after the house and the kids.'

'Oh, yes, Billy. I lead such a sophisticated lifestyle! Today I dressed the kids and saw Matthew and Lucy off to school. Came back and hoovered through the house, changed Mark's nappy, then went shopping to stock up with toilet paper and Shredded Wheat, bought fish fingers for tea, collected the kids from school at half past three, did some weeding in the garden and then rinsed out your shirts and underpants. This took me until five o'clock, the hour of your return, and then I made tea. All very exciting.'

'Exactly my point, Laura.' Billy chuckled. 'We could both be doing the same old things for the next thirty-odd years. Let's do something different with our lives while we're still young. Here's a chance to see something of the world, to raise our kids in a new exciting environment. Let's take the risk and go for it.'

'You do make it sound attractive, Billy,' she wavered, 'but I need time to take it in. It's happening too quickly.'

A few days after the interview they arranged to leave the children with Laura's mother for a few days and travelled to Farnham Castle for the promised orientation weekend. Along with other prospective expatriates who were planning to work in every corner of the globe, they were treated to a series of talks from a team of experts who had worked in the country of their choice. Every conceivable field was covered and they were given advice on matters like health and medical facilities, education of children, immigration requirements, insurance, and travel allowances. To Billy and Laura, some of the advice seemed a trifle bizarre, like that from the doctor who recommended that the best way to fight malaria was to take no precautions at all but to let the mosquitoes bite and so build up a natural immunity. Perhaps the strangest and potentially most profitable advice of all came from a man who had recently returned from Kenya after a four-year tour of duty. In his striped suit and pencil moustache, he resembled a music-hall spiv.

'There is a desperate shortage of quality prestige cars,'

he told them. 'If you could take a Daimler or a Jaguar out there, you'd make your fortune.'

'We could never afford such a car,' Billy laughed. 'We'd be lucky if we could manage a tandem, never mind a luxury car.'

'You could buy a second-hand one with a government loan and export it as your heavy-baggage allowance,' he said, giving Billy a conspiratorial nudge.

Billy grinned.

'We'll remember your words if we decide to go.'

'And that's by no means sure,' Laura added, shaking her head. 'We've got lots of thinking to do before we make up our minds.

Towards Christmas, Laura stopped dithering. It wasn't due to anything Billy had said but to something more powerful than any argument he could have advanced.

The Christmas shopping season was in full swing when it descended on the town. Smog! A mixture of smoke and fog from a thousand factories and a million domestic fires, it wrapped itself round the city in a great, choking, eye-watering cloud. It seeped into the houses, leaving a dirty grey film on everything and everyone. Every family, including Billy's, was affected by it. They coughed and spluttered as if they had inhaled poisonous gas.

On Christmas Eve, while out shopping on Stockport Road, they could just about make out through the gloom the hoarding offering a £10 migrant fare to Australia. One half of the poster depicted a dreary grey street of back-to-back houses with miserable slum-dwellers, and the other contrasted this with a suntanned Australian family enjoying the sunshine on Bondi Beach. That poster said it all.

'Billy,' Laura declared, 'I can't take any more of this foul climate. I've made up my mind. Let's go.'

'You mean, to Australia?'

'No. Stop fooling about. I mean to Kenya.'

Laura was on board.

Their friends were in no doubt that they had gone stark staring.

'You're the one possessed, not young Matthew,' Titch said. 'What were you thinking of when you applied? And what does Laura think about it all?'

'She's quite keen, ya know.' Billy had been waiting patiently all day to say that to someone.

Titch groaned. 'Didn't anyone ever tell you that the pun is the lowest form of wit?'

Laura's family were not thrilled when they announced their plans.

'You won't find it easy to keep up with your music out there,' Louise observed. 'I shouldn't think there are too many pianos in the African bush.'

'Then I shall take up another instrument, like the recorder or the flute,' Laura answered. She'd caught the bug and was sounding as enthusiastic as Billy.

Big Dunk was dead set against it and voiced his objections in no uncertain terms.

'What about all the work you've done getting higher degrees? All my work with you in accountancy? Just as it's paying off with promotion, you want to take yourself off and waste all that effort!'

'It won't be wasted, Duncan. I shall make full use of everything out there in East Africa.'

'In the Inland Revenue we reckon that the only men who enter the Colonial Service are those who can't make the grade at home. Men who have scraped a third at university and are mad about organised sport. You're by no means one of those.'

'That's an old myth, Duncan. The job offers a challenging career and a chance for real responsibilities.'

'It's a big risk you're taking, Billy,' he protested. 'I don't like the idea of you taking my daughter and grandchildren to darkest Africa. And what about Jomo Kenyatta and the Mau Mau? How can you be sure all that trouble is finished?'

'Duncan, the Mau Mau rebellion is over. As for Kenyatta, he's locked away in the Northern Frontier District of Kenya, miles away from anywhere. They're not going to let him out in a hurry.'

'Don't be too sure, Billy. There'll come a time when these African countries will demand independence like Ghana did under Nkrumah. Leaders like Kenyatta will be released to head the new state. What then?'

'We shall be home long before that happens, Duncan. In any case we should be given generous compensation, I should imagine.'

'I don't know what's got into your head, Billy. It's a form of temporary insanity. Wild horses wouldn't drag me out there at a time like this. They'd have to treble my salary.'

'Duncan,' Billy protested, 'here in Manchester I'm on seven hundred and fifty a year and that includes my Head of Department allowance. This Kenya job is offering fourteen hundred and I can get a loan for a car up to half my annual salary. The job is permanent and pensionable and I'll be a member of Her Majesty's Overseas Civil Service. What's more, tax is low out there. The first tour of duty is for four years and at the end of that I get six months' leave on full pay. It's the opportunity we've been waiting for and I don't think I should pass it up.'

Billy's own family reacted more emotionally. Mam in particular was upset.

'Billy, oh, Billy,' she said. 'What in God's name has got into you? You can't just take off into the jungle with your wife and kids.'

Dad was more matter-of-fact.

'It's one of our Billy's daft ideas. He has a different one every week. Next week it'll be the French Foreign Legion. Besides, if they had any more kids out there in Africa, they'd turn out to be black, wouldn't they? Stands to reason.'

As far as Billy could see, his dad acknowledged only two places in the world. There was 'Here' and there was 'Not Here'. 'Here' was safe and secure, but the 'Not Here' place was dangerous and to be avoided at all costs.

Later that day when they had got back home, Laura turned to Billy and said, 'When your dad made those remarks about having kids out there, I think he must have second sight or have looked into a crystal ball.'

'You mean those daft remarks about having black kids? I never know whether Dad's plain barmy or acting the goat.'

'No, I mean about having kids out there. You see, Billy, I think I'm pregnant again. Baby number four will probably be born in Kenya.'

His heart skipped a beat. 'But you can't be! The Chinese reservatus method we've been using for the last year was foolproof, according to the book.'

'Perhaps we missed out some tiny detail,' she replied. 'Or perhaps the method was more suited to oriental emperors than full-blooded, fecund Western males.'

For a moment, Billy thought he was going deaf. The word he thought he'd heard wasn't in her vocabulary. Or was it?

Eric Sharpe hit the roof and went into RSM mode when Billy handed in his resignation.

'Damn and blast it!' he exploded, turning purple with rage. 'You've only just taken the job and you're off already. If we'd known you were going to stay such a short time, we should never have appointed you. We turned a good man down to give you the job.'

'I am truly sorry, Mr Sharpe,' Billy said with both hands upturned. 'I didn't know the East Africa job was going to come off when I joined Holbrook. In some ways, I feel as if I'm being blown along by the wind of destiny. The moving finger writes and all that.'

'Ah, Kismet!' Eric Sharpe barked.

At least, that's what it sounded like.

Once Billy and Laura told the Colonial Office they were going, the Civil Service machine went into action and things fell into place automatically. In no time the whole family had been immunised against a range of tropical diseases – smallpox, yellow fever, and typhoid. Billy himself was required to attend at the Liverpool School of Tropical Medicine where he was given a thorough medical examination and declared fit for tropical service.

Two weeks after all these formalities had been completed, they received a bulky registered letter in an official-looking envelope. They knew what it was but all the same it was with great excitement that they opened the package. It contained a banker's draft for two hundred pounds to buy tropical kit for Billy ('What about the rest of us? Don't we need tropical kits?' Laura asked), a railway warrant, and air tickets for the whole family to fly out from London to Nairobi on 24 April, 1958.

Laura and Billy read up on health in the tropics and the various precautions they should take. The dangers seemed endless. They learned about malaria and the anopheles mosquito, about *tsetse* flies and sleeping sickness, about rabid dogs, and bilharzia, a disease caught from water snails. Enough to put off the faint-hearted. Only great enthusiasm could overcome such a frightening list of perils and Billy sometimes had the feeling that Laura was going along with it all against her better judgement.

One day Titch mischievously gave Billy and Laura a book to read, Robert Ruark's *Something of Value*, and overnight they changed their minds about going. In gory detail, the book told the story of the Mau Mau rebellion and its blood-curdling savagery. How could they take their family to such a dangerous place? What guarantee was there that the insurrection had been finally put to rest? Next, they went to see the film of the book and that was the clincher. Kenya was definitely not for them. The movie depicted in grisly detail some of the Mau Mau atrocities, like the brutal murder of an entire settler family, one not unlike their own.

Billy and Laura decided to settle for their quiet, uneventful routine. At least the kids weren't going to be cut up by Mau Mau machetes in Manchester.

'We'll have to return the air tickets and the railway warrant but I've already spent the kit allowance,' he remarked.

One day, Titch visited them to check on the latest. Billy was slapping Walpamur on the ceiling in the kids' bedroom.

'Well, have you finally made up your minds?' he asked, dodging the splodges of distemper Billy was spraying about the place.

'Definitely not going,' he answered. 'Thanks to the book you so kindly lent us.'

'Oh, that is good news, Hoppy,' Titch said warmly. 'But what about all those injections you've had? All for nothing!'

'Not at all,' Billy said, sploshing on the paint. 'If ever there's an outbreak of yellow fever in Manchester, we shall be the only family to survive. Furthermore, if ever the climate of Manchester hots up, I'll be the only one equipped with a pith helmet.'

But destiny had a way of imposing its will, no matter what Billy and Laura thought they had decided. As Shakespeare put it:

> *There is a divinity that shapes our ends/*
> *Rough-hew them how we will.*

Further reading revealed that the Mau Mau in Kenya was clearly a thing of the past. The country had settled down and law and order had been restored. Furthermore, in the district where they were to be posted, there had never been any trouble. Marangu, the capital of the region, had not suffered a single attack even at the height of the rebellion. Billy and Laura thought afresh, they talked, and then they thought and talked some more.

Eventually, they came to a decision.

It was on again. More or less. Until the next twist of fate.

* * *

In February, they began dithering once more, and for good reason. On the sixth of that month, the city of Manchester was plunged into mourning on hearing the news of the Munich air crash disaster with the loss of the 'Busby Babes'. Manchester lost seven of its United team, three staff members, eight journalists, and Matt Busby was left fighting for his life in a German hospital. Billy and his family were due to fly out within a few weeks and the news stopped them in their tracks. Was it an omen? they wondered. Fortune seemed to be sending them contrary messages and they were constantly blowing hot and cold. Given the precarious nature of flying, they might be lucky if they made it to Nairobi at all. Again, everyone around them seemed to be against their going: both sides of the family, their friends, the staff at Holbrook. Perhaps the wisest thing was to forget it, put it behind them and settle down once and for all. It wasn't too late; Billy was sure he could get his job back and, after all, things were getting easier and the days of penny-pinching seemed to be over.

Then destiny made its final move.

One evening in early-March, on his way home from school, Billy called at his local newsagent to pick up his *Evening News* and there it was on the front page.

> WILLIAM STEELE ADMITS DIVERSION OF £10M FUNDS
> Government statement is expected today
> Mr William Steele today admitted that he secretly channelled more than £10 million of investors' money from Steele Securities, his crashed investment company, into his own personal bank accounts. Clients are shattered by the affair. Many have lost their life savings. See inside pages where we report

on the bizarre personal life and jet-set lifestyle of William Steele whose company was wound up this morning.

In a deep state of shock, Billy boarded his bus and read the details. Steele, the paper said, had spent enormous sums of money on his fast and furious life-style: a private jet, fleet of prestige cars, luxury yacht, château in Bordeaux, and a half-million-pound estate in Derbyshire. Billy couldn't bring himself to read on for he knew that it spelled personal ruin for him and his family. Laura had been right in her early suspicions. The man's name alone should have been sufficient warning: Will Steele.

'What does it all mean for us, Billy?' Laura asked nervously when she heard the news. 'How bad is it?'

'It's more than bad, I'm afraid, Laura. It's a disaster. Our mortgage was covered by Steele Securities and now that's worthless, the Berkeley Building Society is sure to foreclose and we shall be left with nothing.'

'How did he manage to hide things for so long?'

'Apparently he always paid the interest on the mortgage but not the capital itself. Now we shall be forced to sell the house in order to pay back the outstanding balance.'

'How much do you think that will be?' she asked, anxiously biting her lower lip.

'Around twelve hundred pounds.'

'But that's a fortune! We can't hope to find such a huge sum.'

Billy's predictions turned out to be accurate, and the following week a letter from the building society confirmed the news.

'There's one good thing to come out of this,' he said

ruefully. 'No more wavering. Now we shall have to go to Kenya.'

Before the Easter holidays began, the staff at Holbrook held an end-of-term party. Eric Sharpe gave a speech and said one or two kind things about Billy, how sorry he was to see him go and what he'd achieved in such a short time. Then on behalf of the staff he presented Billy with a Swiss Army knife remarking how invaluable it was in removing stones from horses' hoofs and how useful it might be in cutting a way through the African bush and defending himself against Mau Mau terrorists.

Once their hand had been forced, Billy and Laura began selling off their furniture, what little they had. Denis Glynn, the Holy Name choirmaster, took the pianola after removing the mechanism and dumping the rolls; Eric Sharpe bought the television set with the sliding doors. He came round to pay and to collect it.

'I see you have sold most of your furniture,' he remarked, looking round the 'best' room.

'Sold!' Billy exclaimed. 'We haven't sold anything yet. This is all we've ever had!'

Albert Afford at school agreed to buy the house at a price of £1500.

'It may take me a week or two to raise the twenty per cent deposit,' he'd said.

'That's fine by me,' Billy answered. 'You'll have no problem getting a mortgage but make sure you check out the mortgage provider.'

'I hope Albert's other name isn't "Can't",' Laura remarked.

A fortnight before the final farewell, Billy recalled the wide-boy advice offered to him by the gentleman on the Farnham orientation course. Never one to pass up a chance to make extra money, the week before they were to set off he scoured the Cars For Sale columns in the *Manchester Evening News*. And there it was, the car he was looking for.

> FOR SALE 1954 DAIMLER CONQUEST. 6-CYLINDER. 2.5 LITRES. MECHANICALLY SUPERB. RADIO AND HEATER. SPOT LAMPS. COLOUR BLUE. BODYWORK NEEDS A LITTLE ATTENTION. PHONE WHITTLE LE WOODS 254367. £500 O.N.O.

Billy cursed when he saw the address for it meant three bus rides to get there. Why do people selling things always have to live miles away? he wondered. The vendor, Mr Harry Ramsbottom, had done his best to cover up the bodywork's blemishes with touch-up paints but there was no hiding the rust on the sills and doors. Billy offered him £400.

'Nay, nay, lad. It's worth more than that. It cost a penny or two when it were new. Do you know why it's called Conquest?'

Billy had to admit that he didn't.

'Its new price in 1954 before tax were one thousand and sixty-six. D'ye get it? 1066.'

'Good story,' Billy said, 'but that price was when it was new. It's far from that now. Look at the corrosion – you can poke your finger through it. Four hundred's my final offer.'

Mr Ramsbottom tried for £450 but Billy was already walking away.

'Awreet,' he said, calling after him. 'Four hundred it is. You're a hard man.'

Billy paid cash for it from the government loan and arranged for the car to be delivered to an export company at Salford Docks for onward shipment to Nairobi via Mombasa. The cost was well within his baggage allowance. He could expect to collect and clear the car through customs in about three months' time, they told him.

'I suppose you'll be driving this flash car round East Africa,' Titch remarked. 'One of the bloated plutocrats.'

'Not on your life,' he replied. 'This car is an investment and will be sold to some rich coffee farmer who has more money than sense. If I buy a car at all, it will be a less pretentious affair. A Ford or a Vauxhall.'

Once the decision to go was made, Billy's mam and dad threw a farewell party. It was like Christmas all over again with the little flat bursting at the seams. Mam had cooked a massive Lancashire hot-pot supper, Dad had ordered his usual firkin, and the drink and the talk flowed.

Billy's sisters and their husbands were all for the move to Kenya.

'You've only got one life,' Flo said. 'I believe in living it to the full.'

'You'd never forgive yourself if you didn't take this opportunity,' Polly added.

Her husband Steve was more philosophical.

'Sometimes you have to get off the treadmill and look around you to see what life is all about. We envy you and Laura. We only wish we'd done something adventurous when we were younger.'

Mam was less enthusiastic. She had the idea that they'd be living in a tree house like Tarzan and Jane and Billy would get to work by swinging on a rope through the forest.

'Eeeh, Billy, I don't think you should take Laura and the kids out there, living in a mud hut among all them lions and tigers, to say nowt about the snakes and the crocodiles.'

'It's nothing like that, Mam,' he said. 'We'll be living in a modern house with all mod cons, electricity, hot water, a fridge and all that.'

She wasn't to be put off by facts.

'Then there's this flying business,' she continued. 'It's not safe. I tell you, I don't trust them there aeroplanes. If God had wanted us to fly, he'd have given us wings. No, mark my words, it's safest to stop at home.'

'Nowhere is safe, Mam. You can get knocked down crossing the road. This job in Africa is my big chance to do something with my life.'

'You're restless, Billy,' she said, 'always wanting to be in some other place; the place where you're not. The other side of the hill is always greener. You're just like your brother Jim.'

'And look what happened to him,' his dad chipped in. 'He wanted to see the world, and what did he see? He saw the sea. And not even that, he saw the bottom of it instead.'

At the mention of Jim, Mam's eyes misted over. 'I seem to have spent my life saying goodbye to you, Billy,' she wept. 'First when you were evacuated to Blackpool during the war, then to that college in London, then when you went off to be married. Now to Africa, for God's sake.'

Laura put an arm round her to comfort her.

'It's not forever, Mrs Hopkins,' she said. 'We'll be back in four years' time. It'll soon pass.'

Her words of solace didn't help, however. Four years seemed like a long time to Mam

'Dad and I are seventy-two this year and we won't live forever. It's to be hoped we're still here when you get back.'

'Make sure you are,' Billy said. 'And who knows? Maybe you can come to Africa for a holiday.'

'That'll be the day,' said Mam. 'Why, I've never even been to London. The furthest I've been is Walsingham when I went with the Union of Catholic Mothers.'

Billy's brother Les had a different angle, a socialist one. 'You've been reading too many adventure stories,' he said. 'You see yourself as the big *bwana*, the lord and master, with the Africans bowing and scraping to you. As for that huge salary you'll be getting, you'll be taking the bread out of the poor peasants' mouths.'

'Hardly,' Billy replied. 'More like the bread out of your mouth since it'll be the British taxpayer footing the bill.'

The rest of the evening was given over to the usual communal sing-song and they picked the old war songs with goodbye themes: 'Wish Me Luck As You Wave Me Goodbye', 'I'll Pray For You', and Les's rendering of 'Goodbye' with the accompanying waving of hankies which had become a family ritual. Finally, when the company sang 'Now Is the Hour, (When We Must Say Goodbye)', everyone blubbed, and Billy and Laura were choked up themselves.

It was an emotional farewell when it was time to go. Dad looked grave as he shook Billy's hand and the tears sparkled in Mam's eyes when she said, 'If you've decided to go, there's nothing we can do or say to stop you. You've buttered your bread and now you'll just have to lie in it. It's like the war when I used to say if your name's on the bomb, it'll hit you no matter what you do. What has to be, will be. Make sure you write regularly and let us know how you get on.'

'Goodbye, Mam. Goodbye, Dad.'

And this time it wasn't only Mam whose eyes were wet.

* * *

D-day – the day of departure – came round. The last view they had of Manchester was of Big Duncan who had come round to see them off. It was drizzling lightly and he had brought his big black umbrella. As the taxi carried Billy, Laura and his three young grandchildren away, Duncan waved a hand in farewell, looking sad and perplexed, and when they turned the corner, he was still standing there, shaking his head in disbelief.

Chapter Twenty

When the train pulled out of London Road station on that Thursday in April 1958, their hearts were filled with sadness as they realised it would be four years before they saw their beloved Manchester again. They had spent the previous week in 'This is the last time we shall . . .' frame of mind as they attended to last minute preparations for their journey. There was no room for second thoughts now. They were committed. Matthew and Lucy were beside themselves with excitement at the idea of the adventurous life that lay ahead.

In London they booked into a small B & B near Victoria Station and strolled round the district in the afternoon. Next morning they took a taxi across to Victoria Terminal and engaged a porter to carry their luggage, consisting of a large trunk and two suitcases. Billy passed a machine which offered life insurance and decided to take out a policy for £20,000 naming his mam and dad as beneficiaries, and posted it back with a cheque to his brother Les. If they were going to die in an air crash, at least the old folk at home would benefit. The picture of Mam and Dad cashing in on their deaths caused a lump in his throat and he had to swallow hard. At least the old folks would see to it that they all had beautiful gravestones.

At the BOAC check-in counter he deposited the heavy trunk on the weighing machine and the receptionist tagged it and sent it on its way down the conveyor belt.

'Why is he allowed that big trunk while I can only have this itsy-bitsy suitcase?' a grumpy man in the queue complained.

'Well, first, you must get yourself a wife and three children,' she replied.

They took the bus out to Heathrow and the nearer they got to the airport, the more excited the kids were and the more nervous Laura and Billy became. In fact, nervous was an understatement. Petrified was nearer the mark because the memory of the Munich air crash was still fresh in their minds.

They passed through customs where a smartly dressed officer checked their hand luggage for contraband goods, though, given the current austerity in England, they couldn't imagine what these could possibly be. In the departure lounge, they bought Cokes for the kids and tea for themselves and settled in front of the huge indicator boards to watch for their flight, Argonaut No. 2416. The boards clicked and clacked as they flipped over to provide fresh information. Against their flight there appeared the words DELAYED BECAUSE OF TECHNICAL FAULT. Billy felt the adrenaline course through his body and noticed Laura's hands shaking as she raised the cup to her lips.

Technical fault! What did that mean? A wheel or a wing had fallen off! How could they be sure the mechanics had stuck it back on properly?

A couple of hours and several cups of tea later the Tannoy told them to report to Gate 6 for boarding. Billy hoped the engineers had had enough time to identify and fix the fault, whatever it was.

* * *

Aboard the aircraft, they were welcomed by a glamorous air stewardess in BOAC uniform who showed them to their seats.

'Welcome aboard Argonaut 2416 to Nairobi,' she announced through the PA system. 'We shall be flying at twenty thousand feet and our first stop will be Rome.'

She demonstrated the use of the oxygen masks which would drop from the lockers above their heads if they lost air pressure. They looked up anxiously to check that the masks were indeed in place. Most frightening of all, she told them about the inflatable life jackets under their seats and showed them how to put them on 'in the unlikely event that we have to ditch in the sea'. Each jacket was equipped with a whistle to attract attention and a torch for signalling 'in case we come down in the dark'. 'Whatever you do,' she explained, 'do not inflate them while you are in the plane otherwise you will not fit through the emergency exit. You must wait until you hit the water.' All very reassuring.

'That'll be the English Channel, or after Rome the Mediterranean,' Billy informed Laura.

'Thanks,' she whispered back. 'That piece of information will be invaluable when we're floating around in the dark in our rubber dinghy.'

'Right,' he said, 'if we end up in the sea, you look after Mark and I'll take care of the other two.'

'But we can't swim,' Laura protested.

'No need,' he said. 'We have Mae West life-jackets.'

'Next,' the stewardess continued, 'we may experience a certain amount of turbulence and the occasional lightning strike. These are quite normal occurrences and nothing to be concerned about. We hope you have a comfortable flight and if there is anything we can do for you, don't hesitate to call us. Remember: BOAC Takes Good Care of You. Now please fasten your seat belts and make sure your seats are in the upright position.'

There was a roar from the Rolls-Royce engines, a shuddering of the aircraft, and they moved slowly along the runway. They hadn't travelled far when the aircraft made a sharp right turn, there was an almighty surge of power as if an invisible hand had grabbed hold of them and they were propelled faster and faster down the tarmac. Billy had read somewhere that the most dangerous times in flying were the take-off and the landing. OK, God, here we are if you want us, he prayed quietly to himself. But if you do decide to take us, please make it quick. It was a prayer he was to repeat ten times on the journey. Suddenly the vibrations ceased. Billy gave a sigh of relief as the wheels came up with a bump and the plane started to climb. The flight became smooth and they looked back at the airport receding rapidly behind them.

As they gained height, their ears popped and the ever-helpful stewardess came round distributing boiled sweets and newspapers. They had to make sure she didn't give a sweet to Lucy or Mark or they'd have had choking children on their hands.

'The best way to clear the air passages is to pinch your nose and blow,' the stewardess advised.

Before long they hit air pockets and the plane dropped twenty or thirty feet into the void. They bucked and rolled so violently that even the cabin crew had to take to their seats. Billy looked through the windows and saw fiery lightning flashes in the distance. When he heard a passenger behind reciting 'Litany for a Good Death', a chill ran down his spine and he thought their last hour had come. He held Laura's hand tightly, both of them 'white-knuckle' passengers. The kids, however, were loving it and, each time they fell into what seemed like an abyss, they hooted in delight.

'Whoopee! This is like the Bobs at Belle Vue,' Matthew yelled.

Not that he had ever ridden the vertiginous roller-coaster, he was much too young for that, but he had seen it when they went to look at the wild animals and never ceased pestering for a go.

Three hours later they were looking down on St Peter's in Rome and Billy could not believe his eyes. Three hours! The journey to Italy had taken eighteen nightmare hours when he'd visited Perugia with Titch and Oscar two years back. At Fiumicino airport they were allowed to disembark and stretch their legs while the aircraft refuelled. As they sipped their drinks in the bar, they gazed in awe at the frenzied activity around them: transit buses zooming in all directions, baggage handlers whizzing across the tarmac, planes from every nation on earth landing and taking off. Billy thought back to the quiet uneventful existence they had been living back in Manchester. This indeed was the high life.

A few hours later they were flying over the Mediterranean, which happily they crossed without getting wet. As they came in over the ocean, he could see the lights of Benghazi's Benina airport. The runway didn't look too wide and he marvelled at the skill of the pilots who would be landing this giant bird on such a narrow strip in the dark. They were given half an hour to visit the small seedy airport café where they drank glutinous black coffee and sickeningly sweet soft drinks, but it was the Arabic music playing on the radio that held their attention and brought home to him the fact that they had truly left their native shores behind and were in a foreign land.

They flew on through the night and in the early hours of the morning landed at Khartoum but were banned from disembarking in case any of them took pictures of the air installations or aircraft, information which might prove useful in the next Anglo-Sudanese war. Although it was three o'clock in the morning, it was like an oven and the humidity was overpowering. Their discomfort was added to when a small bearded man in a huge turban boarded the aircraft and sprayed everybody with DDT.

After Khartoum people took the opportunity to take a cat-nap, but with the excitement of all that had been happening Billy wasn't in the least drowsy. He looked around at his sleeping family and felt a pang of remorse. What had he done, uprooting his wife and children from their secure familiar surroundings to take them on this expedition into the unknown? Too late to entertain such thoughts now, though.

He gazed out of the cabin window at the world below. There was no moon that night and from the cloudless sky a billion stars looked down on the dark earth, pinpricked with the tiny lights of countless village fires glowing in the black landscape. But far off on the distant horizon he detected the merest hint of light and, as he watched, the pale band gradually became tinted first with pink, then violet, yellow and red, faint at first but suddenly and breathtakingly radiant, filling the whole sky with a glorious spectrum of colours. Darkness turned to brilliant gold, illuminating the interior of the plane. It was like watching God paint a masterpiece in the sky. An African dawn. His first.

* * *

The stewardess brought round coffee and rolls, and woke the dozing passengers. Shortly after that, they flew across a magnificent stretch of blue water, more like an inland sea than a lake, and the stewardess told them to fasten their seat belts as they would shortly be landing at Entebbe in Uganda. There they had a longer stay and were given enough time to visit a restaurant where they ordered tea and sandwiches. An African waiter dressed in an immaculate *kanzu* with a red sash at the waist and a fez on his head approached.

'Why is that man wearing a nightshirt and a red plant-pot on his head?' Matthew asked.

'Shush!' Laura said. 'He might hear you.'

The soft-footed waiter greeted them with a polite bow of the head. '*Jambo, bwana. Jambo, memsahib.* What can I get for you, please?'

He brought a large silver tray with a matching tea-pot, china cups and saucers, and little white plates of cucumber sandwiches with the crusts cut off. Billy noticed his spotless hands and manicured nails.

'And the *bwana ndogo na memsahib ndogo*?' the waiter inquired. 'What would the little lords and the little lady like to drink?'

'The children would love Cokes, please,' Laura said.

Billy thought back to the time they had visited Blackpool where the snootier restaurants displayed signs like: NO YOUNG CHILDREN or NO CHILDREN UNDER TEN. They had been forced to go downmarket to Fred's Caff where the waitress greeted them with, 'What'll it be, luv?' as she wiped down the Formica-topped table, then said, 'Sorry, we don't serve half-portions for kids. Only full meals. Please yourself, luv.'

And now here they were on the balcony restaurant of Entebbe airport overlooking Lake Victoria and they knew their lives had changed.

The final leg of the journey to Nairobi was relatively short being no more than an hour and a half. They had barely settled down before there was an announcement.

'This is Captain Evans speaking. We shall shortly be commencing our descent into Embakasi International Airport and expect to land in about fifteen minutes. Passengers on the left of the plane should be able to see the peak of Mount Kenya through a break in the clouds.'

Eagerly, they looked through the window and caught a glimpse of the magnificent mountain shrouded in mist.

'Look, Mum,' Matthew called excitedly. 'It's covered in snow!'

'Local time is 10 a.m.,' the captain continued. 'The weather is fine and the temperature is 30 degrees Celsius. Please return to your seats, fasten your seat belts and extinguish cigarettes. We trust you've enjoyed your flight with BOAC and hope to welcome you aboard once again in the near future. Thank you.'

The rhythm of the great engines changed abruptly and the plane descended steeply. Soon the world turned topsy-turvy as they rushed at a crazy angle over daub-and-wattle villages, roads, railways, rivers and bridges.

Getting through the airport system was no problem. The customs officer seemed interested only in the importing of erotic material and when he saw them with three small children, gave them hardly a second glance as he chalked their luggage and waved them through. Obviously they didn't look like shifty-eyed smugglers or dissolute porno-merchants.

A junior African Immigration Officer scrutinised their passports, Billy's work permit giving him the right to live and work in the colony, and finally their vaccination certificates. When he was sure everything was in order he firmly stamped their passports making every object on his desk bounce.

Bleary-eyed, they emerged from the formalities to be met at the arrival gate by a smart, military-looking man of about fifty. He had a toothbruth moustache and was wearing a panama hat. He held aloft a small black slate with the name HOPKINS chalked on it. Billy waved to him.

'You must be the Hopkins family,' he said, shaking Billy's hand then Laura's. 'I'm Henry Blewitt, headmaster of Marangu High School. Welcome to Kenya.'

'Thank you,' Billy replied warmly. 'You were quick spotting us.'

'Easy,' he grinned. 'I recognised you by the size of your family and your pallid complexions.'

The Head took charge of proceedings, barking a series of commands in Swahili to the African labourers he had brought with him and who were standing by awaiting orders.

'*Lete sanduku ya bwana na tia ndani gharri. Upesi sana.*' 'Bring the bwana's luggage and put it in the lorry. At the double!'

The men gathered up their belongings and threw them into the waiting truck.

'*Polepole!*' Blewitt yelled. 'Carefully!

'These bladdy people,' he confided. 'I'll never understand 'em. They don't know the meaning of "carefully". They'll break anything and everything.'

He led them out to his car, a battered old Wolseley which he had parked in the shade of a jacaranda tree. Even so, the interior of the car was swelteringly hot and there were yelps from the kids when they felt the scorching leather upholstery on their backsides. With all the windows wound down, they soon cooled down as they set off for Marangu, fifty miles distant.

Chapter Twenty-One

They drove out of the airport along the main tarmac road which connected Nairobi to Mombasa three hundred miles away.

'You speak Swahili fluently,' Billy remarked, in an effort to make conversation and in order to get into the new boss's good books.

'Well, I've been out here over ten years,' said Blewitt. 'I was a major in the Indian Army during the war. Came from India when the balloon went up there, after they gained Independence in 1947. Bit of a come-down after life under the Raj. Now *that* was something.'

Not another bloody military headmaster, Billy thought. Last time it was a Regimental *Sergeant* Major, now it's a *full* Major. So I suppose, in a way, I'm making progress.

They drove along quietly for some time as they drank in the new exciting scenes around them. The silence was broken by Matthew.

'Dad, why has that tree grown upside down?'

Blewitt laughed. 'That's a baobab tree,' he said. 'Clever of you, young man. It's known locally as the upside-down tree and that one's probably more than a thousand years old.'

Matthew glowed under the praise.

'I saw it before you did,' Lucy pouted. 'I bet I'll see a wild animal before you do, too.'

The first new sensation Billy was conscious of was the smell – sweet, smoky, acrid – rich and deep, the smell of Africa. Earlier that day it had rained and there was an odour of damp earth mixed with rotting matter and decomposing organic life.

As they turned into the open country, they gazed entranced at the passing landscape and thrilled at their first glimpses of wild life.

'A giraffe! A giraffe!' Lucy squealed. 'I told you I'd see an animal first.'

'You always want to be first,' Matthew protested.

'Quiet, you two,' Laura said. 'No fighting.'

On the left side of the road, the giraffe bent their dappled necks down to the acacias, and bushbuck grazed nervously on the rich grassland.

'Look, big doggies and horsies!' cried Mark, pointing to the animals on the other side of the road.

The 'doggies' were a herd of tail-wagging Thomson's gazelle, or 'Tommies', bounding across the plain; the 'horsies' fat-bellied zebra, looking like polished toys, feeding lazily in the bush.

'I suppose,' Billy said, 'that when those zebra move to the other side, you have to stop for the zebra crossing.'

'Very droll,' Henry Blewitt said, 'but I don't think you're the first to make the remark, and I don't suppose you'll be the last either.'

So much for my feeble attempt at wit, Billy thought.

They were passing a cluster of round mud huts and roadside trading stalls that indicated a small village.

'Are there any elephants or lions around here?' Matthew asked.

'Elephants are found about a hundred miles down this road at a place called Voi in Tsavo National Park, but there are plenty of lions around here at the Athi River township.'

'Oh, good!' Matthew exclaimed. 'Then we'll be seeing them soon.'

''Fraid not,' Blewitt said. 'During the day, lions stay hidden, sleeping in the bush and the reeds, but they come out at dusk around six-thirty. They're attracted by the smell of the meat from the Kenya Meat Commission plant which we are passing at this moment.'

They turned their heads to gaze at the factory which was emitting a powerful aroma of cooked meat.

After twenty miles or so, they turned off the tarmac and joined a corrugated murram road which led directly to Marangu. That was the end of the smooth ride. From thereon they bounced around as if inside a cocktail shaker.

'This won't do your car springs much good,' Billy remarked.

'True,' Blewitt replied. 'You need a four-wheeled Land-Rover for this kind of road. Fortunately it's only another twenty miles and this old car has done the journey many times.'

They passed several African pedestrians, the men unencumbered and walking ahead with the women shuffling behind like pack-horses, their backs bent low under enormous burdens suspended by leather straps that bit into their foreheads. Further on, they passed a young woman with a baby slung on her back, as well as a large container of water balanced delicately on her head. She walked with the poise of a fashion model on the catwalk. Later, they came across a young boy tending a herd of hump-backed cattle. They slowed down as they overtook a man wobbling about on a bike carrying his wife and child on the handlebars and a load of baskets on his back.

They shuddered round a rutted hair-pin bend, up a steep hill, and there nestling below in a valley was their first view of Marangu. A few minutes later they came to a sign which read MARANGU HIGH SCHOOL. They turned left into a gravelled driveway which wound through a whitewashed, stone-ringed drive, past the main entrance where a Union Jack fluttered on a tall mast. They stopped outside a red-tiled bungalow with a long verandah and an enormous garden rich in every kind of tropical plant. On the lawn, stretched out on a sun-lounger, was a lady in a light blue summery dress, the colour setting off her golden tan. Next to her in a high chair sat a baby being fed by an African nanny while nearby a young boy of about Matthew's age was sailing a toy boat in a little rubber paddling pool. Alongside sat a fierce-looking bulldog riddled with bloated ticks.

'Here we are,' Blewitt said. 'Come and meet my family.'

They piled out and the Major introduced his wife and children.

'Daphne, this is Billy and Laura and their children, Matthew, Lucy and Mark. The boy over there in the pool is my son, Arnold.'

'So pleased to make your acquaintance,' Daphne said, coming forward with outstretched hands. 'I do hope you had a pleasant journey? I'm sure you must be feeling worn out. Let me order you a sandwich and some drinks. Coffee or cold drinks?'

'Cold drinks and a sandwich would be welcome,' Laura replied.

'Sixpence, bring five cold Fantas!' she said, barking the order in Swahili to the waiting servant. 'And make a few sandwiches, half sardines and half honey. If your children are anything like my Arnold, they'll prefer something sweet.'

'*Ndiyo, memsahib*,' Sixpence replied with a bow.

What an unusual name for a servant, Billy thought, and noted how Swahili seemed to be used exclusively to shout orders at servants. In the list of useful phrases he had learned before setting off, he had noticed how the expressions were couched in the imperative. Clear the table! Prepare food! Make tea! Sweep the floor! He liked particularly the command for making toast, '*Choma mkate*!' which meant literally, 'Burn bread!'

As if she had read his thoughts, Daphne said, 'You have to give your orders clearly or these people are bound to get it wrong. Our last servant was ghastly. He once prepared a pudding decorated with toothpaste and whenever he broke something, he would remark "Its time had come" or "*Shauri la Mungu*". It was an act of God. We've employed this boy on a month's trial to see how he gets on.'

'And what about you, Daphne darling?' Henry Blewitt said. 'Can I get you something?'

'A sherry, Henry darling, if you please.'

Henry went off to get her drink. Evidently the servant couldn't be trusted to get the sherry or perhaps he didn't have access to the drinks cupboard.

'I do hope you will be happy here,' Daphne said. 'Kenya is vastly different from England. I come from Surrey and it took me some time to adjust to conditions here. It's no place for the scream-at-a-mouse type of housewife, I can tell you.'

'I'm sure I'm not that type,' Laura said. 'Insects and mice don't worry me in the least. We've been so looking forward to coming that now we are here, we can hardly believe it. It seems like a dream.'

'I know the feeling only too well,' Daphne said. 'It can seem quite surreal but you can put much of that down to the long flight and the change of time zones.'

'I'm sure we'll get used to things here eventually,' Billy added. 'We're ready to fit in wherever we can. As you say, it's different from home.'

'And which part of England is home?' Daphne asked haughtily.

'We come from Manchester.'

'Really! How terribly interesting!' she exclaimed, stifling a yawn and making it sound as if it was the most boring thing she'd heard that day. 'I suppose you were teaching at Manchester Grammar School, were you?'

'No, I was a teacher at the Holbrook Hospital Secondary School.'

Henry was back with the drinks, a sherry for her and a scotch and soda for himself. Obviously drinking time began early in these parts.

'Sherry dry enough, darling?' Blewitt asked.

'Perfect, Henry darling,' she answered, sipping her drink.

'I heard you say just now that you were a *teacher*,' Blewitt said to Billy. 'You mean, you were a *schoolmaster*, not a teacher. There's a world of difference. We reserve the term "teacher" for elementary-school types.'

'Is this Holbrook Hospital place a public school?' Daphne asked. 'It sounds like it. Like Christ's Hospital, the Bluecoats school.'

The only thing public about it, Billy thought, was the fact that it was open to the general public while the public school she was thinking about was not. He kept these thoughts to himself.

'Sorry to disappoint you again,' he replied. 'It was a secondary modern school.'

'Good God!' Blewitt said. 'You mean, an elementary school?'

'Not quite,' Billy answered. 'Elementary schools were abolished in 1944 by Act of Parliament. Now all secondary schools are equal.'

' "A rose by any other name . . ." ' Blewitt replied. 'I suppose you yourself went to a public school, though. What?'

'Negative again,' said Billy. 'I went to an ordinary grammar school.'

He seethed inside. The snobbish bastards, he thought. What kind of place had he come to? This man was his dad's nightmare in the flesh. A snooty, public-school man who sneered at the working class. He wondered what Blewitt would have said if he'd known that Billy did his first degree by part-time evening study, but he held this piece of information back.

'Pity about that,' Blewitt said. 'You see, here at Marangu, we are a boarding school with all that implies and I try to run things on the lines of an English public school.'

'The Major is an old Etonian and he taught at Wilmingon,' Daphne added proudly. 'He's also an Oxford blue in rowing.'

The Major preened himself.

'We are educating the future leaders of this country,' he said, 'and I've made it my life's work to create another Eton here in the heart of Africa. Our motto is *Floreat Marangu*. May Marangu flourish. It's imperative that we create and maintain the highest standards.'

'I agree wholeheartedly,' Billy said. Better get on the good side of this stuffed-shirt.

'I insist that our boys wear straw boaters whenever they go into the town, as they did at my old school,' Blewitt went on. 'Gives the place a spot of class, I think.'

You and your wife have enough class for the whole bloody school, Billy thought.

'Next, and most important, I have introduced classics in the curriculum this year. No man is educated who has not studied the Ancient Greeks and Romans.'

Oh, sure, Billy said to himself. Caesar's Gallic Wars. Just the thing to study in an impoverished third-world country like this where contaminated water, disease and starvation are the order of the day.

'As Thomas Arnold put it,' the Major wittered on, 'our aim is to produce Christian gentlemen who are fit to take up the highest positions of responsibility. Public-school values are what we must aim for.'

'A tall order, headmaster,' Billy remarked. 'What exactly are these public-school values?'

'Well,' Blewitt continued loftily, 'take the question of sneaking, for example. Suppose a chap has committed a misdemeanour, say. Ask a public-school boy, "Who did it?" and he'd rather have his eyes gouged out than split on a fellow. But ask an elementary-school type and he'd answer rightaway, "Jones did it".'

That's me in my place, Billy thought.

'I believe strongly in the old Latin tag *Mens sana in corpore sano*. A healthy mind in a healthy body. We must produce men who can take pain and hardship without blubbering.'

'What do you have in mind?' Billy asked warily. Surely this prig didn't want to introduce a Tom Brown system of fagging and beating?

'A cadet force would be best but Government Inspectors are against it. So we have to rely on athletics and organised sport.'

'I'm all for that,' Billy said, though the words stuck in his throat.

'What about you, Mr Hopkins? What games do *you* play?' the Major asked suddenly.

'At home I played a little tennis, also football for the Old Boys' school team,' Billy said, pleased that he could answer positively at last and boast at least a couple of sporting skills.

'Football, eh? Oh, good,' Blewitt said warmly. 'Rugby, I trust!'

'Soccer,' he answered ruefully. 'I played centre-forward.'

Blewitt looked aghast. 'Good God! You mean that lower-class game where the players indulge in back-slapping and bear-hugging if one of their number happens to score a goal? Here we leave that sort of thing to the Africans.'

It was no use. Whichever way Billy turned, he was a disappointment. What in heaven's name was he doing in this snooty place?

By this time Sixpence had returned with the refreshments. The Fantas were good, really cold, and they all slaked their thirst, the children noisily. Then they turned their attention to the sandwiches. But there was something wrong. Even though they were ready and willing to adapt to the strange customs of this Lord and Lady Muck, these sandwiches were taking it too far.

'Mum, my butty tastes funny,' young Mark said, spitting the mixture out on to the grass.

'And so does mine,' Lucy said, doing the same.

'And mine!' echoed Matthew.

Daphne examined one of the sandwiches. 'I don't believe it!' she squealed. 'That stupid Sixpence has made each and every sandwich half-honey and half-sardine.'

'Sorry, *memsahib*,' a mortified Sixpence said. 'I thought you ordered half-half.'

'I'll never understand these bladdy people,' the Major exclaimed.

Poor old Sixpence, Billy thought. As far as the servant was concerned, he'd followed the instructions to the letter. Besides, for him their food was foreign muck and, when all was said and done, he was *making* the sandwiches, not *eating* 'em.

Chapter Twenty-Two

After fresh sandwiches had been made and eaten, the Major drove them across to their own house where they found their luggage had already been deposited. Laura could hardly wait to get her first look at the place where they were to spend the next four years.

They were not disappointed. Like the Blewitts' place, it was a bungalow with a good-sized garden containing a wide variety of tropical plants from frangipani to poinsettia, and several beautiful jacaranda trees. This place more than made up for the Blewitts' snobbery and Laura's face beamed when she saw it. The Major introduced them to a young sandy-haired colleague, Mike Sherwood, and his pretty wife Jill. Mike was dressed in khaki shorts, knee-length socks and a battered trilby, and was busy giving orders to a labourer in the garden.

'*Mzuri, Makau. Tosha sasa.*' (OK, Makau, that'll do.)

'Mike and Jill will show you the ropes,' the Major said, 'and so I'll leave you in their capable hands.'

'Welcome to Marangu,' Jill said, offering her hand and giving them a warm and encouraging smile.

'Yes, welcome to Marangu.' Mike laughed when Blewitt had gone. 'The place where time stood still and we're still in the thirties. We've been given the job of showing you around but it's a case of the blind leading the blind as we've been here only three months ourselves. First, we'll leave you to it so you can look around for yourselves, then we'll pass on any little tips we've picked up. What do we call you, by the way? Mr and Mrs Hopkins sounds too formal.'

'This is Laura,' Billy said, 'and I'm Billy but my friends call me Hoppy.'

'Then Hoppy it is,' said Mike.

'I expect you'll want to unpack,' Jill said, 'so we'll let you get on with it. See you shortly. We'll bring our two little girls over to meet your kids.'

'Billy, am I glad to be here!' Laura exclaimed when they were alone.

'To be in your own home at last?'

'Not so much that,' she said. 'It's Mark. He's needed his nappy changing since we got off the plane. I'm sure the Blewitts could smell it. I hope they didn't think it was us giving off the pong.'

'They'd have simply put it down to the smell of elementary-school types from the slums of Manchester.'

Laura went into the bedroom to do the necessary and finding that Jill had thoughtfully left some basic provisions, including soap powder, washed the nappies which had accumulated on the journey out. Meanwhile the kids had rushed into the garden to try out the swing which some previous resident had bequeathed while Laura and Billy examined every corner of the house: the high-ceilinged living-room and bedrooms; the large bathroom; the spacious kitchen with its wood-burning stove; and the sturdy government furniture.

Laura went into the garden to hang up the nappies and

could not believe her eyes. It was a different world, a place of birdsong and fragrant perfumes.

'The garden's massive. Where does it end?' she exclaimed.

'As far as you want to cultivate it,' Mike said as he returned with Jill. 'Up to the river if you like, but that's about a mile away and would need an army of gardeners. You could practically run a small farm here.'

'This is my idea of the Garden of Eden,' Laura enthused. 'And what plants! I can't wait to explore and take a closer look.'

'Take care.' Jill smiled. 'The garden just about sums up Africa – beautiful but with all kinds of hidden dangers. Like a rose with thorns.'

'Surely not?' Laura said, shaking her head. 'Those flowers and plants don't have any thorns.'

'You think not?' Jill replied. 'Take the frangipani. Gives off a delicious scent and has the most radiant colours, but try breaking off one of the flowers and you'll find it exudes a milky white liquid that burns like mad if it gets on your skin. A sort of defence mechanism for the plant, I suppose. It's also poisonous and is used by hunters on the tips of their arrows. So keep the kids away,' she added, looking at young Mark.

Just then there was a squeal from Lucy who had wandered off to inspect the bathroom as she always did in a strange house.

'Mum, Mum, come quick! There are two little crocodiles on the ceiling.'

They all rushed to her aid but Mike simply chuckled.

'Those will be your two resident lizards, geckos by name. They are your friends 'cos they eat up the mosquitoes. The same goes for the spiders in your wardrobes. We got a shock when we first set eyes on *them*; they're the size of saucers, but they too will eat up any harmful insects flying around.'

'Talking of mosquitoes,' Billy said, 'we were told that there's no malaria here in Marangu.'

'Don't believe everything you hear,' Jill said. 'Marangu may be five thousand feet above sea level but nevertheless we sleep under nets and I'd advise you to do the same. The things to watch out for are jiggers, ticks and ants.'

'We have ants in England,' Billy said.

'Not like the *siafu* African ants, Hoppy, I can assure you,' Mike said. 'The rain brings them out and if you are plagued by them, they form endless black rivers over the garden, across the veranda, and through the kitchen. Nothing can stop them. Of all the insects in Kenya, *siafu* are the ones I fear most. There are many horror stories about them, like the cow in labour or the pullet and her chicks that were devoured and stripped to the bone by a seething mass of them. And everyone in the school knows the story of our drunken cook who fell asleep in the hen coop and was eaten alive. If by accident, you walk into them when they're massing, don't hesitate. Run into someone's – anyone's – house and yell "Ants!" and they'll point you to the bathroom. They're ferocious and before you know it, they swarm into your nose, hair and eyes. Be sure, too, you stand the legs of your meat safe in tins of water or ants'll eat you out of house and home.'

'My God,' Billy exclaimed. 'At this rate we can't let the kids out of our sight for an instant.'

The Hopkins kids at that moment were playing in the garden with Mike's two little girls, Phoebe and Chloe. By the look of things, they were getting along like a house on fire.

'Given a few weeks,' Jill said, looking out fondly at the children, 'your kids will be alive to the dangers around them. All the same, it pays to be vigilant at all times. Always examine the insides of your shoes in the morning. You never know, a scorpion or a tarantula spider may have taken up residence during the night. And watch out for ticks. If you find any crawling up your legs, pluck them off and squash them in your fingers. If they dig into your skin, they'll itch like mad and leave a little lump which will develop into a sore if you scratch it.

'We may as well get all the bad news over at once,' she laughed. 'I hope you're not the kind who comes over all a-tremble at the thought of creepy-crawlies?'

Then she regaled them with stories of rhinoceros beetles the size of mice, lethal snakes and bugs that went for the eyes, and giant centipedes with a poisonous sting.

'Life in the tropics is pleasant,' she continued, 'as long as you are constantly on your guard. For example, you have hung up those nappies to dry but make sure they are pressed thoroughly afterwards with a hot iron.'

'Why, what's the problem?' Laura asked.

'There is a bug called the *tumbu* fly which lays its eggs in damp clothes. The eggs later hatch into maggots and like to burrow beneath the skin, growing fat and causing boils. The way to destroy them is to close off their entrance opening with Vaseline, which cuts off their air supply. This forces them to the surface, and then they can be squeezed out like cherry stones. Fat, hideous, wriggling white maggots.'

'Sounds delightful,' Laura said. 'What about those other things we've read about, the jiggers? What are they?'

Mike chuckled at the question. He was obviously enjoying himself. 'They're a kind of blood-sucking flea that burrows under the skin and lays its eggs there. Don't let the kids walk around bare-foot because that's where they like to strike. If you get bitten, the best thing to do is let one of your servants extract the thing along with its nest with a hot needle. I was bitten and old Makau there had it out in no time.'

'I noticed that reference to " your servants",' Billy said. 'Somehow I can't see us with a retinue of servants.'

'That's what they all say, Hoppy,' Mike laughed, 'But in time they succumb. We employ three: a gardener, a houseboy and an ayah.'

'I'm used to managing things myself,' Laura said. 'I'm sure I don't need a whole lot of helpers getting under my feet.'

'We shall see,' Mike said non-committally.

Billy grinned. 'Any other good news to reassure us?'

'Not really.' He smiled back. 'Except maybe about the successors to the Mau Mau terrorists. A new organisation calling itself the Land Freedom Army has sprung up but I don't think they will amount to anything as the security forces have got things under control.'

'Is that why we have steel grilles up at all the windows and doors?' Laura asked.

'Partly. It also deters burglars,' Mike replied. 'Though not altogether because now they use a device like a long fishing rod to hook out your clothes. We never leave our windows open when we go out unless Makau is around.'

'Maybe we should be equipped with weapons to defend ourselves in case of attack?' Billy laughed nervously.

'We're not allowed to carry guns or anything of that sort but I've brought you something just in case,' Mike said solemnly.

He handed Billy a heavy golf club.

'Here you are, Hoppy. A good whack with a number one wood should frighten off any potential intruders.'

'It's not all bad news,' Jill said reassuringly. 'Think back to England and the fog, the rain, the grey damp climate. People at home spend most of their time in traffic jams or standing up in trains trying to get to work. At least you've left all that behind. Kenya has a superb climate, good schools, and your kids will thrive here.'

'We do hope so,' Laura said. 'I'm wondering if we've come to a land inhabited solely by reptiles and insects.'

Jill laughed. 'Oh, it's not so bad, once you get used to it.

'Finally, you will have noticed that I've got some basic rations in for you until you can get to the *duka* yourselves. Tomorrow, Mike will take you on a conducted tour of the *boma*, the shops, and the European Country Club.'

'European? Aren't Africans allowed to join?' Billy asked incredulously.

'Afraid not,' Mike answered. 'The only Africans allowed in the club are the servants and the menial workers.'

'That's crazy. After all, it's their country.'

'Doesn't matter. The old colonial farmers reckon they need a place where they can relax away from the natives.'

Mike and Jill departed with their children, leaving the others with food not only for their stomachs but for thought as well.

Later in the evening, after the sun had gone down and they had put the kids to bed, Laura and Billy sat on the verandah and looked out at the township of Marangu which was aglow with little lights. The balmy air carried the aroma of night-scented jasmine mixed with the smell of wood-smoke, cooking, and the tang of the dank earth. And the night sky glittered with stars.

* * *

They'd had an exhausting day and Laura went to bed early. Along with the children, she was asleep in seconds.

Not so Billy.

He sat in an armchair facing the two glass-panelled front doors, hyper-sensitive to every creak in the house, expecting the Land Freedom Army to break in and attack at any moment. Gradually things grew quiet. He held his breath and listened. There was no noise save for the monotonous chirping of the crickets with their shrill 'brr brr', and the occasional shriek of some far-off bird. Somewhere in the distance he could hear hyenas howling and fancied he could distinguish the roar of a lion, sounds that added mystery to the night. After a while, his head fell forward and he dozed off.

Suddenly he was awakened by the most fearful squealing and scurrying on the verandah behind him. Taking a firm grip on his golf club he leapt to his feet, ready to do battle for his family against any enemy, animal or human. He drew the curtain aside and there, transfixed in the light, was what he thought was a leopard with a chicken in its mouth. He learned later that the animal in question was a genet or spotted civet cat and that the chicken had belonged to Joshua Kadoma, a colleague who lived next door. He rapped on the window and raised the club. It seemed to do the trick because the animal shot off into the bush still carrying its prey.

At that moment, Pine Grove with its resident owl seemed a long way off on a distant planet.

A few hours later he awoke with a start from a fitful sleep when dawn began to break with a faint lemon glow on the horizon and every rooster in Kenya lifted its head and gave the new day a strident welcome. Billy looked out at the garden in the early light and was faced with his second challenge. Striding purposefully towards the house was an African dressed in a tattered army overcoat and a Balaclava. His dress seemed more appropriate for Siberia than equatorial Africa. He was coming from the direction of the servants' quarters carrying a flaming torch aloft, and judging by the determined expression on his face, it looked as if his intention was to set fire to the house. The hair prickled on the back of Billy's neck. My God, he thought, what a welcome to our new home! First a fierce wild animal in a fight to the death with a defenceless chicken and now a murderous arsonist. For the second time, he prepared to do battle for his family. When the intruder disappeared round the side of the house, that was it. Time to act. Brandishing the club above his head, Billy leapt out and confronted the fiend.

'What the hell do you think you're doing?' he yelled, ready to strike.

Then he recognised the man. It was Makau, Mike's servant.

'*Bwana* Sherwood asked me to light your boiler so that you would have hot water,' he answered, nervously eyeing the raised weapon. '*Mzuri, bwana*?' (Is that OK?)

'*Mzuri*,' Billy replied softly.

Collyhurst was never like this, he thought.

Chapter Twenty-Three

A little later, the rest of the family appeared and Laura prepared a breakfast of tropical fruits which Mike and Jill had kindly sent over. Paw-paw, mangoes and avocados became a regular feature of their breakfast fare, very different from the porridge and the Kellogg's Corn Flakes they were used to.

Mike came over when they had finished to help with the selection of domestic staff from the queue which had formed outside the kitchen door. Laura once again said that she had no intention of employing an ayah, preferring to look after the children herself. They decided to conduct interviews on the verandah.

'How much do we pay them?' Billy asked.

'The going rate is forty shillings a month for a cook/houseboy and thirty for the gardener.'

'That doesn't sound like much. How can they live on that?'

'Most African families live only on what they can produce from their *shamba* and the pittance they raise from the sale of their vegetables or from basket-making. You'll be paying your cook/houseboy nearly five hundred shillings a year which to him is a fortune. Don't forget that in addition you have to supply them with uniform, accommodation and rations.'

'Sounds like the war. What are these rations?'

'Each servant receives a daily ration of *posho,* a sort of maize-meal, plus a once-weekly ration of meat, salt, sugar and tea. So they don't do too badly. They usually save all their wages unless they spend them on *pombe*, the native beer.'

They set up tables and chairs at the back door and prepared to interview the candidates. Billy felt like David Livingstone choosing native bearers for a dangerous safari into the interior of darkest Africa. Heaven knows what his mam and dad would have said if they'd seen him hiring servants, especially Mam since she had been one herself. As for his socialist brother Les . . . it didn't bear thinking about. He'd have muttered something doom-laden about slavery and exploiting the workers.

The first applicant was an old silver-haired man called Golden Boy Githuku. Eagerly he offered his identity card and a reference written on a grubby piece of paper which read:

> To Whom It May Concern
> Golden Boy was formerly a book-keeper for a Nairobi tailor but has been unable to find suitable work in Marangu, his home town. He has tried his hand in the kitchen and can cook simple meals. He is also a useful odd-job man. I have had to let him go as we are returning to England. You will find him honest and a good worker but because of his age, getting rather slow.

Golden Boy watched their reactions anxiously. '*Mimi mpishi mzuri na mfundi,*' he said. (I am a good cook and handyman.)

'Perhaps a better name for him might be Silver Boy,' Billy observed. 'He looks like an old-timer. How old would you say he is, Mike?'

'Between forty-five and fifty. That's old for Kenya, Hoppy, the average life expectancy is only around forty-five. Not only do you want someone younger but you need a cook/houseboy – one who can cook, clean the house, and do your washing.'

'Thank you, Golden Boy. We'll let you know,' Mike told the old boy in the manner of an agent rejecting an actor. 'Don't call us, we'll call you. Next,' he called.

'I feel sorry for him,' Laura said.

'We can't employ everybody,' Billy told her.

The second candidate named Teetotal Mwale was rejected out of hand before he had got a word out. He was drunk and smelt strongly of alcohol.

'He's been drinking jungle juice,' Mike said. 'Made from bananas. It's lethal. Obviously he hasn't followed the advice of his own name. Next!'

Their third man had an unusual name even for Kenya: Dublin City Sitaka.

'I can cook Irish stew,' he grinned, revealing a row of gleaming white teeth. 'I cook for Irishman for many years.'

'I suppose that's where you got your name,' Billy said. 'Why did you leave your last job?'

'My *bwana* has gone back to his country and now I have no work, but I need to save many shillings to buy goats to pay for a bride in my village.'

'His former employee is the retired District Foreman, Paddy Flynn,' Mike explained. 'He's worked for Paddy as cook and general dogsbody for fifteen years. He comes highly recommended and I'd advise you to take him before someone else snaps him up.'

'Very well, but what a peculiar name!' Billy remarked.

'I've heard worse,' Mike said. 'The older Africans often adopt English words as titles believing they will give them the white man's power. I've met servants with names like Whisky, Lucky Strike and Rolls-Royce. On the other hand, many who have been educated by the missionaries have landed up with Old Testament names like Moses, Eliud, Daniel. Girls are often named for the way the mother was feeling at the birth. So they give their daughters names like Gift-from-God, Reward-from-Heaven, God-Bless-Us, Happiness or Cheerful.'

'And what's this about buying a bride?' Billy asked.

'It's the customary price a man must pay to the father of his intended. If his bride doesn't produce any kids in the first couple of years, he can ask for his goats back.'

'Sounds as if he's insisting on a guarantee when he makes his purchase.'

'That about sums it up,' Mike chuckled. 'It's insurance against an unproductive wife.'

Billy determined to abbreviate their man's name to Dublin if they decided to employ him, which they did. All this time, Laura had been listening quietly to the proceedings but now she voiced her opinion.

'I agree that Dublin is probably the best choice but I still feel sorry for Golden Boy,' she said. 'Can't we find him some work around the house? As an odd-job man, say, until he finds something else. He's getting on and I'm sure he could do with the money, even though it's not much.'

'You have to be hard sometimes,' Mike said. 'You can't employ all the Golden-Boys in Kenya.'

They could see, however, that Laura was upset at the idea of sending the old man away.

'Oh, very well,' Mike said. 'If you like, we could share him between our two families until he finds something permanent.'

'OK,' Billy said. 'Then he's hired as a shared temporary odd-job man. I must need my head examining because I'm sure we can't afford it.'

The job of gardener was considered last. The candidate was a tall, lanky Kikuyu called Twiga, an appropriate name since it meant 'giraffe' in Swahili. With a bright smile, he thrust the usual documents at them. The identity card was in order but his reference was in French. It read: '*Pas employer cet homme. Il est voleur*.' (Do not employ this man, he is a thief.)

Billy was angry when he read this. Not with the man but with the unfeeling brute who'd sent this man out with this condemnatory reference.

'Do you know what this letter says?' he asked Twiga.

'No, *bwana*. But I think it says I am a good gardener, isn't it?'

Mike told him the true import of the poisoned letter he was carrying around and asked him why his previous employer had written it. Twiga explained how the cook of the house had given him some of the food left over from a party his boss had held the night before. His employer had become angry and sacked him on the spot.

'I know this farmer,' Mike said. 'A cantankerous bastard if ever there was one.'

There was no need to interview any of the other applicants. They had found their gardener. A member of one of the bloodiest tribes of Africa, maybe, but probably all the candidates in the queue had revolutionary connections.

Dublin went home to his village to collect his belongings but Golden Boy and Twiga remained as they didn't seem to have any. The old man went to the servants' quarters while Twiga accompanied them on a tour of the garden.

'We'd like to grow our own vegetables,' Laura told him. 'Is that possible?'

'Yes, madam. You do not even need seeds. If you want tomatoes, you squash a big tomato into the soil of the *shamba* and tomatoes will come in a few weeks.'

As they were speaking, a flamboyant red and green lowrie glided across the garden and perched on a nearby tree from where it croaked a song of welcome.

'What was it Churchill wrote about Africa?' Laura exclaimed. 'Something about, "Birds as bright as butterflies; butterflies as big as birds".'

'That bird that flopped clumsily across the trees may have beautiful plumage,' Billy said, 'but the noise it makes is hideous. Surely there are better songbirds than that?'

He had always fancied himself as a whistler from his earliest days in Collyhurst when he'd warbled his way to school. He puckered up his lips now and blew a tune across the garden. To his amazement, there was an answering call.

'My God!' he exclaimed. 'Have you ever heard anything as beautiful as that? This is an ornithologist's paradise.'

He tried again, this time a more elaborate melody and was rewarded with a precise imitation from some invisible bird in the thick undergrowth.

'I've read somewhere about birds like this,' he said. 'It's a species of African parrot that mimics the songs of other birds in the forest. It's said that it can imitate to perfection a whole range of sounds from a saw to a siren. I'll see how clever it really is.'

He trilled a few bars from 'The Blue Danube' and was not disappointed. Back came the familiar melody with a few variations added. Billy was deeply impressed. He determined to ask Mike about it after lunch and was soon put right. It had been Mike himself answering Billy's calls, believing that *he* had been communicating with a bird of paradise.

'If the pair of you *were* birds,' Laura remarked, 'you'd be a couple of cuckoos.'

Chapter Twenty-Four

In the afternoon, Mike escorted them on a tour of the *boma* while Jill opted to stay behind with her two daughters.

'I've already done the guided tour,' she said. 'Several times.'

It was a two-mile walk along a dusty path that twisted like a snake, making the distance seem twice as long. Along the way crickets kept up their high-pitched chorus in the long grass and they stepped along carefully in case of snakes or safari ants. They passed several brown ant-hills tapered like church spires.

'Termites,' Mike said. 'Their citadels have taken ages to build. If you dug into one, you would find a bloated white queen at the centre producing thousands of eggs year upon year.'

When they reached the *boma* their first impression was that they had walked on to the Hollywood set of Dodge City and they half expected Gary Cooper to come riding on horseback down the main street. The town boasted three general stores, a bank, a post office, a garage, and two churches, one Protestant, the other Catholic. That was it. Town of Marangu, chief city of the region.

Their first port of call was the market-place which that afternoon thronged with a wide diversity of customers from across the district. They had come down from the surrounding hills in their hundreds to form a boisterous crowd that jostled and haggled for the goods on display. There was an abundance of fruit and vegetables on offer at 'give-away' prices and stall-holders tried to force them to buy by thrusting their produce into their hands. There was much shouting, laughing, name-calling and noisy bickering as they bartered for merchandise. Ragged children followed them about, offering their services as porters and hoping to snatch up any stray fruit that might fall from their baskets.

This was a throw-nothing-away society. In one corner handymen were busy recycling and repairing detritus that would have found its way on to the rubbish dumps long ago in England. Nothing was rejected: odds and ends, bits and pieces, rags and bones. If a thing had the remotest use, somebody picked it up and restored it. Here was a man selling bottles and jars of every shape and size; over there was another making sandals from discarded car tyres, next to him an entrepreneur offering old tin containers. The most desperate of them all had set out his stall of bent nails and rusty screws on little white doilies. It was a colourful vibrant spectacle and over the busy scene hung the rancid smell of cassava and dried fish, plus a million swollen-bellied bluebottles.

'This beats Sainsbury's supermarket any day,' Laura laughed as they strolled through the market taking in the sights, the sounds and the smells. 'I think I have enough fruit, vegetables and fish to last a month.'

As they came through the gate of the market, they met a blind leper woman sitting on the stone step, breast-feeding her baby. She held up a claw-like hand begging for alms. Laura thrust two shillings into her palsied fingers.

'You made her day,' Mike said. 'Most people give her a couple of cents.'

'Asante, asante, bwana Sherwood,' she croaked.

'Laura gives the money, you get the credit,' Billy said. 'How come she knows you?'

'I usually drop her a few coins when we do our shopping. She relies on what she can beg but her fellow Africans are terrified to go near her even though she's a burnt-out case. The dread of leprosy goes way back despite drugs having brought the disease under control. Old habits die hard and your average Kenyan will run a mile if he thinks there's the slightest chance he'll contract it.'

Though it was only a short walk from the market to the township, the heat was overpowering. It seemed to tremble visibly on the air, as if they could reach out and touch it. There was plenty to interest them on the short journey. Along the verandahs, a succession of workers plied their trades against the rhythmic racket of hip-swaying African music blaring from little black radios: here, a watch-repairer concentrated with screwed-up face, his total attention on the workings of a customer's clock; there, an old tailor pedalled furiously on his treadle, with swathes of fabric flowing through his nimble fingers as he created a dress for a waiting client.

They called next at the Marimba Stores which sold everything imaginable. And if an item wasn't in stock, they'd get it for you 'tomorrow when the truck goes to Nairobi'. The store was run by the Singh family whose sole purpose in life was to provide an all-encompassing service for the people of the town. A request for an unusual article, like a gold-plated tap, a lady's crinoline dress or a set of false teeth, would be met with an obsequious, 'Yes, please. Anything else, please?'

'Watch out for yourself here, Hoppy,' Mike warned. 'They'll sell you the shop on credit if they get the chance. Anything you buy at home they can get for you here, at a price. Sometimes I think the whole country runs on tick. Only the Africans seem to carry cash. You may have seen those holed coins which they string together. But for us *Wazungu* everything is on the slate and some government officers owe the whole of their gratuities at the end of a tour.'

Young Dalip Singh, a tall, turbaned youth, stood smiling at the counter. On the wall behind him was a huge picture of a young Queen Elizabeth complete with Coronation crown and golden cloak, holding the sceptre and orb in her hands. As soon as they entered the shop, Dalip greeted them.

'Good afternoon, sirs and *memsahib*. You are most welcome in our emporium. You like cold drink, please.'

Sipping their ice-cold Fantas they sat on the high stools and ordered their provisions. As it was their first shopping expedition, they stocked up with everything they could think of: gardening tools and seeds, groceries, soap power, medicines, pharmaceutical needs like toothpaste, not forgetting the aspirin which instinct told them they were going to need. And, most important, a charcoal iron to kill those *tumbu* flies. The order filled several boxes and the bill was big enough to bring old Malkit Singh himself from the back of the shop to welcome them personally as new European customers.

'As you are a member of Her Royal Majesty's Britannic Government, *bwana*, we shall be happy to open an account in your name. Anything you ask for shall be yours at the drop of your hat, *memsahib*, and we shall be most revered to deliver it to your home,' he said, bowing from the waist. 'Now, before you go, anything else, please?'

From the Marimba Stores they walked down the High Street as far as the tailor, Fundi Mrefu, where Billy was measured for khaki shorts and socks, Mike dismissing his UK clothes as too good for everyday use.

'No one wears a pith helmet today,' he said. 'It's *nineteen* fifty-eight, not *eighteen* fifty-eight.'

'I hope this isn't too expensive,' Billy said. He could see his cash rapidly disappearing.

'A few shillings only,' Mike answered. Turning to the tailor, he said, 'You'll give the *bwana* here a big discount, you old pirate, won't you?'

'For a new *bwana*, best material, lowest price,' Fundi agreed. 'Ready tomorrow.'

'They give good service,' Mike explained, ''cos the school buys its uniforms here.'

Adjoining the tailor's was 'Jimmy's Garage' and Mike presented the proprietor, Khalid Khan.

'Jimmy's is the only garage in town,' he said. 'And Jimmy is regarded as God by local car-owners.'

'Everybody calls me *Doctor* Jimmy,' Khalid announced. 'I am PDH, AMC, SKJ . . . I don't know how you say it. But I am doctor for motor cars. When you buy, bring to me. I know everything about engines. I can tell when anything's wrong just by listening. No need to open bonnet.'

'A modest chap,' Billy said as they walked away.

They passed the Kailas Kinema where a queue of Kikuyu natives and goatskin-caped Masai complete with spears and clay-ochred hair were lining up for the first house performance of *Carry On, Sergeant*, starring Dora Bryan and Kenneth Williams.

The European Country Club was set in spacious grounds which included a couple of red clay tennis courts, a dilapidated squash court, a cricket pavilion, a rugby ground, and a pock-marked nine-hole golf course. The club itself consisted of a dingy-looking, single-storey building with a long wooden verandah and a roof of rusty corrugated tin. The place hadn't seen a lick of paint in years. As they walked through the car park, Mike looked round the various cars and said, 'Usual crowd here. Finnigan, Tonkses, Nelsons, and all the rest.'

'How do you know?' Billy asked.

'In a small town like this, you can identify everybody by their car. Everyone knows who drives which car. And whose wife's entertaining whose husband.'

'No secrets then?'

'Not a chance,' Mike chuckled.

Inside there was a bar, and a hall-cum-lounge filled with seedy-looking armchairs which on festive occasions could be pushed back to provide space for dances, film shows, tombola, or whatever took members' fancy as entertainment. Laura opted to stay in the lounge with the children while Mike and Billy went into the bar to order drinks.

Over near the window, a fat man in baggy shorts puffed away at a cigar, his attention riveted on the fruit machine into which he was feeding the small fortune of silver coins which he jiggled in his hand. Sitting on high stools around the bar-counter was a crowd of bar-flies who, judging by their serious expressions and lack of conversation, were intent on drinking the place dry. Sitting at a table near the window two weather-beaten women dressed in blue jeans, flannel shirts and ankle boots, and looking more like two tough old men than ladies, were putting pink gins away with total concentration. Billy consulted his watch. It was 5.15. Obviously in this place serious drinking didn't wait until the sun was over the yard-arm.

'The two leathery-looking ladies over there,' Mike whispered, 'are the Nelson sisters, famous around these parts for fighting off a Mau Mau gang single-handed. But let me introduce Mr and Mrs Reginald Tonks from the District Commissioner's office,' he said, approaching a couple who were knocking it back as if it was the last day on earth.

'Lovely to see a new family,' Tonks said, rolling the whisky round his mouth. 'Meet Mrs Tonks – the only wife in Marangu who drinks more than her husband.'

'What's good for the goose . . .' Mrs Tonks said. 'I drink to stop Reggie from drinking so much. Every drink that goes down *my* throat is one less down *his*.'

'Tell that one to the Marines,' Reggie mumbled. 'Anyway, what'll you have? Vat 69 or Haig?'

'A bit early for spirits for me,' Billy told him, 'but thank you all the same. Perhaps another time.'

'Never too early for a scotch and soda,' he boomed. 'My boy, there is one piece of advice I always give newcomers: never have more than two drinks in the evening.'

Billy thought this a sound piece of advice until he saw what Tonks put into his own glass.

'Chui,' Tonks called to the old, pock-marked bartender in his gold-buttoned uniform, 'straight Vat 69 for me, Haig for the *memsahib. Upesi sana.*'

It was a tumblerful of whisky with a mere hint of water and a similar quantity for his wife.

'I love the sound of whisky being poured into a glass,' said Tonks. 'Something special about the way it plops. I love the way it gurgles in the bottle and the way the light catches the amber colour.'

'Chui is a strange name,' Billy remarked, changing the

subject. 'Is he addicted to Spearmint gum or chewing tobacco?'

'Not really,' Tonks replied. '*Chui* means leopard and the *mzee* there would knock spots off any leopard, eh?'

'Looks as if he already has,' Billy chuckled.

Next to the Tonks sat a handsome middle-aged man who was smiling broadly in Billy's direction. He didn't wait to be presented but introduced himself.

'Hello,' he said warmly, holding out his hand. 'Welcome to our little town. My name's Joe Finnigan and I'm the district education officer round here.'

'Glad to know you,' Billy said taking the outstretched hand. 'What does the District Education Office do?'

'Good question.' He grinned, and took a sip of his beer. 'Lots of people reckon we sit on our arses all day drinking tea. But we administer education services, mainly primary schools, right across the area. The job also involves inspecting and organising courses for teachers.'

'Administration! That's a field I'd give my right arm to get into,' Billy said.

'Don't do that, you might need it to push a pen one day. If ever a vacancy occurs in my office, though, I'll remember what you said. Perhaps I should warn you that our administrative district is about the size of Wales and takes in both the Masai and the Kamba tribes,' Finnigan told him.

'Thanks. I have a degree in administration and I'd love to get into it if ever there's an opening.'

There were various other people sitting around the bar but Billy's eye was drawn to a glamorous-looking lady who was enjoying a joke with her three male companions.

They gave their drinks order and returned to the hall to wait for them to be brought by one of the waiters.

'Who's the girl sitting at the far end of the bar?' Laura

asked when they got back. 'She could be Marilyn Monroe's double.'

Laura had a point because the girl in question had it all: blonde hair, voluptuous figure and bedroom eyes at half-mast. It wasn't easy to tell whether she was trying to look sexy or was simply short-sighted. The three fawning young men around her hung on her every word and followed her every movement as she crossed and re-crossed her legs, exposing generous portions of thigh.

'The young lady you are referring to,' Mike whispered, 'is Georgina Roberts, biology teacher at the Women's Training College. She comes from Altrincham, I believe. Isn't that your part of the world?'

'It certainly is,' Billy said warmly. 'Perhaps I should introduce myself.'

'Eyes off!' Laura said, nudging him. 'Remember, you're a married man and a father.'

'As if I could forget.' Billy laughed. 'Anyway, a cat may look at a queen.'

'And that's about as far you'll get,' Mike laughed, 'because there's keen competition to win her attention. The three gentlemen hankering after her are Vic Green, a doctor from the African hospital, the man in the police uniform is Inspector Andy Towers of the Kenya Constabulary, and the fair-haired one with his tongue hanging out is Roger Bedwell, a teacher on our staff. You'll meet him later in the week. There's a competition to see who can bed her first. My money's on the policeman.'

'It's nice to see romance flourishing among the young bachelors and spinsters,' Laura remarked. 'That's what makes the world go round.'

Mike roared with laughter. 'You've *got* to be joking. The three men are bachelors but Georgina's married.'

'But where's her husband?'

'Richard is a District Officer and is away on safari a lot, sorting out *shauris* or problems in the little villages in the bush.'

'That doesn't justify his wife getting up to such shenanigans,' Laura said primly.

'Maybe not,' Mike said, 'but the problem is that her husband takes their Land Rover and so she has no transport. Not that it matters because she doesn't drive anyway.'

'That's still no excuse,' Laura said, looking distinctly concerned.

'There's a well-known saying in East Africa,' Mike laughed. 'Are you married or do you come from Kenya?'

'I don't believe it,' Billy protested. 'You're trying to shock us?'

Mike laughed again. 'There's a joke that goes round in these parts. A farmer is supposed to have said to his son, "My boy, it's time you took a wife." "Yes, Dad," the son says. "Whose wife shall I take?" You must have heard of the Happy Valley Syndrome. It was invented here in Kenya.'

'I'll bet the Marimba Stores does a roaring trade in chastity belts,' Billy chuckled.

'That's right,' Mike said, 'also sets of spare keys. It's a problem in all the colonies, not just Kenya,' he continued. 'Too many bachelors kicking their heels and buzzing around married women like bees round a honey pot. And many married women with little to do but assemble at the club for elevenses easily become involved in affairs.'

'I shall have to keep an eye on you,' Billy joked with Laura.

'With three children and another on the way, I have enough to keep me busy, thank you very much,' she replied, digging him playfully in the ribs.

The draught from the whirling roof fans had attracted people into the hall and there were a few sitting about reading the tissue air-mail editions of the *Daily Telegraph* and *The Times*. Around the sides stood one or two barefoot servants in white uniform and fez, waiting to bring orders from the bar. A waiter brought soft drinks for the kids, a sherry for Laura and two frosted bottles of Tusker beer for Mike and Billy.

They had hardly taken their first sip when they were approached by Henry Blewitt and a distinguished-looking gentleman of around sixty years of age accompanied by an equally superior-looking lady. Mike leapt to his feet and Billy thought he'd better do the same in case they were in the presence of royalty.

'Glad to see the Hopkins family's making itself at home,' Blewitt said. 'I trust Mike's looking after you. Now, it's a great honour,' he said deferentially, 'for me to present the President of the Club, Sir Charles Gilson, and his wife, Lady Gilson.'

'How do you do?' the elegant pair said. Laura and Billy wondered if they should curtsy or kiss their rings. 'Hope you'll be happy here, Hopkins,' the great man intoned.

'Thank you, sir,' Billy said. 'I'm sure we shall.'

'We've been here only a couple of days and we love it so far,' Laura added. Except, that is, for the snobbery, the heat and insect life, Billy thought to himself.

They exchanged a few trite remarks in this vein and then Blewitt took his VIP companions into the bar for drinks and more serious discussion.

'Sir Charles is chairman of our board of governors,' Mike told them. 'Blewitt thinks the sun shines out of his arse and spends all his time sucking up to him. He expects us to do the same. Sir Charles is a powerful guy, and he can make or break you in these parts.'

Though they had been in the town only a couple of days, Billy could discern the pecking order. Being a snob himself, Blewitt worshipped power and position in others. Sir Charles and his lady probably kow-towed to the Governor of the Colony who in his turn looked up to royalty back home, and so on right up to the Queen herself. As for his own position in the structure, Billy realised he was at the bottom of the heap having, in Blewitt's opinion, taught in the wrong school, attended the wrong university and played the wrong kind of football. He could see that the only way to be accepted in Marangu was to win favour with Sir Charles himself. How was he, a lowly peasant, to do that? Maybe I should grow a forelock, he thought.

'I suppose it's best to keep on the right side of the bigwig?' he queried.

'Short of kissing his feet,' Laura remarked.

'Or any other part of his anatomy,' Billy added.

'Too true,' Mike replied. 'Whatever you do, don't get into his bad books 'cos he's the leading landowner in the region and all the other farmers hold him in high regard, especially since he's also president of the club.'

'Some club!' Billy exclaimed. 'It's a ramshackle place. I've seen better Sally Army doss-houses in Salford. It needs a few bob spending on it to make it look half decent.'

'That's the burning issue Sir Charles has on his mind,' Mike said, supping his beer. 'The place nearly closed down a few months back because of lack of funds. As far as the settlers are concerned, us civil servants are fly-by-nights. We come and go and if the place had to shut up shop tomorrow, we wouldn't give a hoot. But for them the club is everything; it's their regular meeting place, and at weekends their social lives revolve around it.'

'Judging by the amount of drinking that goes on, Mike, it should be making big profits.'

'That's one of the mysteries. It seems to make a loss every month and no one has been able to understand why. They suspect someone has his hand in the till. But who?'

When they left the club at around six o'clock, the sun was a great red ball on the horizon and they were suffering from heat exhaustion. They covered the two-mile walk back in an hour. What joy it was to find that Dublin, their new cook-houseboy, had prepared poached egg on toast, with the crusts removed, of course. A simple first meal and counted a success.

After the meal they watched, fascinated, as Dublin spat on the new charcoal iron before thumping it down on the nappies as he incinerated any *tumbu* fly eggs lurking in the folds.

Not only were they ravenously hungry but, after a day walking in the hot sun, they were shattered. Billy realised that for a young family such as theirs, a car was a must, even though he'd never thought he'd own one. Perhaps more important, he hadn't a clue how to drive one. The matter was urgent and he'd have to act quickly before he became too busy teaching at school. The Daimler coming from England wouldn't be arriving for months and, besides, that was an investment and not for everyday use. He'd settle for a less pretentious model. When he asked Mike why he hadn't bought a car to date, his fellow teacher brushed it off with a mumbled 'somehow, haven't got round to it'. But, having experienced the heat, Billy was determined not to put the matter off.

Chapter Twenty-Five

Next day, he hitched a lift with the Marimba Stores truck and went into Nairobi.

When they reached the outskirts, the squalor gave him a shock. They drove first past gaudy Indian residences until they reached the native quarters along Racecourse Road with its teeming bazaars of *dukas* and roadside stalls selling fiery snuff, cheap cigarettes, bolts of bright Manchester cotton, fifth-hand clothes, rubber-tyre sandals, sickly-sweet tea, fly-blown sticky buns, and native *pombe* that was more like porridge than beer. Crowded up against each other competing for space were a number of doss houses and ramshackle bars with names like 'Hotel Metropole', 'The Waldorf' or 'Las Vegas Casino'. Billy wondered if Sinatra's Rat Pack was booked to play there.

As they moved through the district the din became louder: goats bleating, children howling, wirelesses blasting out raucous African music, and somewhere high above the racket a muezzin calling the faithful to prayer. An endless stream of peasants thronged the roads on foot, on bicycles, or packed like sardines into buses and overloaded trucks. Everywhere people carried the most unlikely possessions on their heads: a sewing machine, an easy chair, a kitchen table. And always there were women bowed double under their burdens of firewood, food, or crates of live chickens. Overhanging the scene were the smells which merged into one overall pungent essence of decayed meat, rotten fruit, animal dung and human sweat.

Suddenly the squalor was behind them and they entered a city centre of contemporary white-rendered buildings, a bustling cosmopolitan place of fashionable shops, hotels and cinemas, dominated by the ultra-modern Legislative Council. The traffic was busy in the centre and the air was filled with the noise of blaring motor horns and clamorous bicycle bells. They drove along Delamere Avenue, past the statue of Lord Delamere and the helmeted African *askari* who used his baton to direct the traffic with the artistry of a juggler of Indian clubs.

Billy called first at Gill House, the head Education Office for the colony, and filled out the forms for the balance of his car loan entitlement of £300 or six thousand shillings. Next, he drew out some cash from Barclays DCO and made for Hughes the Ford dealer where he found a wide variety of second-hand Fords, mainly Zephyrs and Consuls, all recently serviced, plus one or two continental makes. He opted for a green Zephyr and completed the formalities. Ten minutes later he was a car owner, the first member of the Hopkins family ever to be so. Billy's dad would have reckoned he had betrayed his class and joined the toffs. I'd better not take up horse-riding or polo, he thought, or Dad'll disown me.

'There's only one snag,' Billy said to the car salesman as he signed the forms, 'I can't drive.'

'No problem,' the salesman said with alacrity, anxious not to lose the sale. 'I'll lend you an African driver to take you back to Marangu. Give him board and lodgings for the night and his bus fare back and everyone's happy.'

His next visit was to a second-hand furniture shop where he bought a settee and an Axminster carpet. If we're to spend the next four years in Kenya, he thought, may as well make ourselves comfortable.

Last visit was to the Nairobi dog pound where he selected a golden Labrador puppy. In Manchester, the kids had been forever pestering him for a dog but he'd never been keen on having one in a big city. A dog, like kids, needed freedom and space to run about, and Kenya was the ideal place for that. In some ways, too, a pup was an outward sign of commitment to their new home and life style.

For lunch, he grabbed a quick sandwich at the Norfolk Hotel. At three o'clock he met the Marimba Stores truck and arranged for them to collect the items of furniture, and then with his Ford driver, a little man named *Simba* (lion), and the Labrador, began the fifty-mile journey home.

They drove through the outer districts of the city, through Karen, past Embakasi Airport, and were soon out in the country. Billy sat in the back with the pup which was whimpering nervously. He stroked it, talking baby language to allay its fears. He was looking forward to arriving home like Father Christmas with his gifts. How excited the kids would be when he drove up. Their first dog! What would they call it? As for Laura, she would be in seventh heaven when she saw the furniture and the carpet which would help to give their government furnishings a homely touch.

They had covered about twelve miles when they spotted a large blue Bentley parked at the side of the road. Beside it was Sir Charles Gilson. Billy told the driver to pull up behind him. Maybe this was his chance to earn a few merit marks with the big *bwana*, the uncrowned king of the *boma*.

'Car trouble, Sir Charles?' he said, winding down the window.

'Nothing serious,' the farmer replied. 'A puncture in the nearside front wheel, that's all. A bloody nuisance, though, as I have to get back to Marangu for a committee meeting at the club and I'm already running late.'

Billy got out of his car. This was too good an opportunity to miss.

'Can I be of any help, sir?'

'Yes, you could, my good man, by getting the spare wheel out of the boot,' said Sir Charles, handing him the keys.

Billy got the jack out first, and handed it across. Next he undid the nut securing the spare, lifted it out and rolled it across.

'Thank you so much,' Sir Charles said as he began jacking up the car. 'You've been a great help. Sorry, I can't remember your name. I've such a terrible memory but I shan't forget your help.'

'Hopkins, sir,' Billy said, anxious to impress the name on his mind. 'Hopkins. I'm the new teacher, correction, schoolmaster at the High School.'

At that moment the heavens opened. There was a sudden gust of wind and a downpour of tropical rain, forcing them to race back to their respective cars. The shower stopped as abruptly as it had started.

Sir Charles wound down his window and called over, 'Everything's under control now, Hopkins. Grateful for your assistance. Perhaps I'll see you in the club one of these nights. Must buy you a drink.'

Billy's driver started the car and they continued on their way. Billy was in clover. What a lucky break! He seemed to have started off on the wrong foot with Blewitt. Wrong accent, wrong university, wrong background and all that. Well, here was one in the eye for him. Sir Charles was now Billy's mate and soon-to-be drinking companion.

All the way back he basked in the knowledge that he'd had such a fruitful day, having pulled off a string of masterly coups: a car, a dog, furniture, and finished up by winning favour with the most important man in the *boma*. Wait till he gave Laura the news. How happy and proud she'd be. An hour later, the car pulled up outside their front door. When Matthew and Lucy saw them coming, they rushed out with whoops of delight that could be heard all round the compound.

'Is it ours, Dad? Is it *really* ours?'

'Yes, it really is!' Billy said, equally delighted with the car.

But when they saw the pup, their joy reached fever pitch.

'Let's call him Sandy,' Matthew shouted. 'He's the colour of the beach at Blackpool.'

'No, Ginger's a better name!' Lucy said.

Billy resolved the dispute by christening the pup Brandy which was what he poured himself to celebrate his highly successful safari. Throughout this display of rejoicing, Laura watched with a quiet smile. She too was pleased. And when, a little time later, the Marimba Stores truck trundled down the drive with the settee and carpet, her smile became broader still.

Billy thanked the African driver and, having paid him, organised lodgings for him with Dublin, their servant.

Mike and Jill Sherwood came over to inspect the new purchases. Jill admired the furniture and the dog but Mike turned green with envy when he saw the car.

'My God, Hoppy,' Jill exclaimed, 'you've been here only a matter of hours and you've set us an example of how to get things done. You certainly don't let the grass grow. Mike could take a lesson from your book.'

'OK, OK, Jill,' he said. 'I get the message. But tell me, Hoppy, do Hughes have any more cars like this for sale?'

When Billy told him there were several, including a blue Fiat 1800 which had taken his eye, and at the same price, Mike's eyes lit up.

'I'll go into Nairobi tomorrow,' he said, 'before it gets snapped up. You've shown us the way all right.'

The four adults settled on the veranda to enjoy a drink and Billy told them of the encounter with Sir Charles and how he had helped him.

'That was a stroke of luck and no mistake,' Mike said. 'It looks as if you've fallen on your feet since you got here. With Sir Charles on your side, you can't go wrong.'

'I'm so glad,' Laura said, 'that something's gone right. I was beginning to think that our faces didn't fit around here.'

'We'll succeed,' Billy said earnestly. 'Give it time. We've only just got here.'

Their euphoria lasted two hours. It came to an abrupt end when Henry Blewitt's car came tearing along the drive and screeched to a halt alongside the verandah where Billy sat reading, wondering if he dare have another brandy and ginger. Blewitt emerged from the car, slamming the door behind him. He was bristling.

'You really have blotted your copy book,' he stormed. 'You bladdy idiot! You've not only ruined your own reputation but also that of the school!'

Billy was baffled. What on earth had he done? Had he

inadvertently knocked down a child on the road? What had caused Blewitt to blow his top?

'What am I supposed to have done?'

'You stopped to help Sir Charles along the road?'

'Why, yes. He'd had a puncture and I got the stuff out of the boot for him.'

'That's not the only thing you did,' the Major exploded. 'You also drove off with his bladdy keys, leaving him stranded forty miles back in the middle of nowhere.'

Billy's face turned bright red. He slapped his hand to his trouser pocket. And there they were. The keys!

'Sir Charles had to find a Sikh mechanic to start the car by shorting it out. He missed the committee meeting at the club. He's furious.'

'It was a complete accident,' Billy protested. 'I was distracted by a sudden downpour of rain. The question now is: how do I make amends?'

'The first thing to do is return his bladdy keys and apologise. I should get down to the club right away.'

Chapter Twenty-Six

Billy called Simba the driver out and had him take him to the club. In some trepidation he entered and found the usual crowd hanging round the bar, Georgina with her entourage, the fat man in the baggy shorts feeding the one-armed bandit. Sir Charles was sitting at the bar drinking with the Tonkses.

'Sir Charles,' Billy said, holding out his keys, 'how can I ever apologise for driving off with your keys like that?'

Sir Charles got down from the bar stool and took him over to a table near the window.

Uh-oh, Billy thought. He's going to thump me. Blewitt's words had led him to expect an explosion of fury but, to his surprise, Sir Charles was calm. Billy was puzzled.

'It was damned inconvenient,' Sir Charles said with a grin, 'but in the circumstances, understandable. It was that sudden shower of rain that did it. Anyway, your intentions were good. I promised you a drink, so what'll you have?'

Here is a true gentleman, Billy thought. Unlike that bastard Blewitt who inflated the incident into a catastrophe. Billy was still a bit suspicious, though. He had learned that when a person was outwardly as calm and reasonable as this after a mishap, he was probably seething underneath or had some ulterior motive. Perhaps Sir Charles was after something.

'A Tusker would go down well,' Billy replied, thinking that he was exceeding his normal drinking quota, certainly having far more than he ever drank in Manchester.

'Chui, you old rogue,' Sir Charles called to the elderly bar boy, 'a large whisky and soda for me and a Tusker for the *bwana* here.'

'*Ndiyo, bwana mkubwa*,' Chui answered.

'I must say, Sir Charles, you are taking it well,' Billy said when he'd got his beer in his hand. 'I thought you'd go berserk at my stupidity.'

'We're all human,' the other man said equably. 'Could have happened to anyone. Anyway, it's behind us now and it wasn't exactly the end of the world. Besides, I wanted to have a little chat with you and welcome you to Marangu and the club.'

Ah, here it comes, Billy thought. Now I'll find out why he's being nice. Too nice.

'I hope you'll be happy up there at the school despite some of Blewitt's funny ideas.'

'Funny, Sir Charles?'

'All those strange notions of creating Eton in the African bush. In many ways, you're doing the country a great disservice by educating them.'

'Disservice, Sir Charles? How do you mean?'

'Kenya is a rural economy and needs farmers with agricultural skills. What you people are producing is an army of clerks, a bunch of pen-pushers with a distaste for any work that puts soil under their finger nails. If Blewitt has his way, the educated African will handle nothing dirtier than a fountain pen, lift nothing heavier than a pencil.'

'Surely after secondary school they can go to agricultural college?'

'How many do? No, they see education as a passport to a pensionable clerical job in one of the ministries.'

'There's no harm in that,' Billy argued. 'They simply want to better themselves and look after their families.'

'Sure, but Blewitt forgets that only a couple of generations ago, the tribes round these parts were killing and occasionally eating each other.'

'Surely not?'

'The Mau Mau revolt taught us that for many tribesmen, civilisation is no more than a superficial skin. Beneath it still lurks the primitive man. We've only to consider some of the vile oaths that were administered, like the eating of the brains of another human being, preferably a European child.'

'But that's all in the past, behind us now,' Billy said hurriedly.

'Don't you believe it! Many of the Mau Mau are still hanging about waiting their chance to re-establish the cult. The life of the ordinary peasant is still ruled by superstitious fear and practices.'

'For example?'

'For a Kikuyu there are at least fifty ordinary domestic incidents that demand the slaughter of a goat to appease evil spirits – such minor accidents as water spilling while *posho* is being cooked, or a child falling from its mother's back, or a man gashing himself while cutting meat; occurrences like these all require the sacrifice of a goat. Or if a crow settles on the roof of a hut, it means that hut has been cursed with a death *thahu* and must be burned at once, and more goats have their throats cut. If a man falls ill, it is because he has been cursed by an enemy and only a witch doctor, a *mundumugu*, can lift the curse by consulting the bones and entrails of a sacrificed chicken.'

'We have similar practices in Britain with our rabbit's feet, horseshoes, crystal balls, and horoscopes.'

'Except that some of the things that happen here are violent and involve murder. For example, first-born twins are killed at birth. The explanation normally advanced for this atrocious practice is that feeding two infants at the same time puts too much strain on the mother. But there can be no logical reason why breech-birth babies too are suffocated at birth.

'Aren't the wrongdoers prosecuted for murder?'

'If it's discovered, yes. But most of the time the peasants hush it up. Most Africans don't regard a child as a person until it's one year old. And these are the people to whom you want to teach Shakespeare and the poetry of Tennyson!'

Billy was stuck for an answer. He didn't accept all that Sir Charles was claiming and thought much of it could be taken with a pinch of salt. It seemed to him he ought to stick up for his principles so as not to appear a timid yes man.

'We can but try, Sir Charles. I came out to Africa with the idea of passing on some of our western values, introducing students here to the best that's been thought and said in the hope that some of it might rub off.'

Sir Charles smiled.

'You'll learn in time.'

Then Billy remembered his dad's advice about always getting your round in. Mercifully he had managed to stay out of Sir Charles's bad books but forgetting to put his hand in his pocket might undo that at a stroke.

'What can I get you to drink?' he asked.

'No,' Sir Charles replied decisively, 'tonight, the drinks are on me. Same again?'

Now Billy *knew* he was after something.

The club president returned with the drinks and turned to the subject that was obviously on his mind.

'Henry Blewitt tells me that you've had training in accountancy . . .'

Billy thought, So that's it! Accountancy.

'This club,' Sir Charles continued, 'is the social and you might say spiritual hub of the community, the only general meeting place we've got. It's vital we keep it going but there's something wrong somewhere and I can't put my finger on it. We do a roaring trade yet seem to make a loss every month. If this goes on we can't survive, and closing down would be a tragedy.'

'Where do I come in?'

'We need someone like you to take a look at the accounts, carry out a thorough audit and find out what's going wrong. I'd do it myself but running a big farm doesn't leave me the time. We'd be able to pay an honorarium, of course.'

'I'm not sure I'd be much help, Sir Charles. I have no practical experience of running a business, and apart from that I've only just got here and believe my new job is going to keep me more than busy. Especially as I might be dealing with cannibals.'

'Very well, Mr Hopkins. I understand your concerns but when you've settled in, maybe you'll think it over then. As chairman of your board of governors, I can put in a good word for you up at the school and make sure they don't overburden you. You'd be doing a great service for the community here. And, incidentally, you can drop the Sir Charles stuff. Call me Charlie.'

'And I'm Hoppy,' he answered through an alcoholic haze

Billy felt it was time to go home. Earlier, he'd drunk a couple of brandies and here in the club three Tuskers. He was feeling decidedly woozy.

'I'd better make a move, Charlie,' he said. 'My wife will be wondering what's happened to me. Which way is the gents' toilet?'

'I'll join you, Hoppy,' said Sir Charles, giving him a friendly slap on the back. 'Follow me.'

Instead of going to the toilets at the back of the bar, he led Billy outside into the gardens.

'This is the toilet we bar-flies use,' he said. 'MMBA.'

'MMBA?'

'Miles and miles of bloody Africa! We don't waste water down the drain. We use it to irrigate the bushes here.'

Something strange happens when men accompany each other to the toilet. For some reason that Billy had never been able to understand, they became more friendly and confidential. Perhaps it was connected with the idea of sharing release.

'Let you into a secret, Hoppy,' said Sir Charles. 'Can't stand that bloody headmaster up at the school. Bloody snob! Have you ever heard such rubbish as wanting to create a public school in the middle of the *bundu*? Why, many of your schoolboys have to be taught how to use a WC when they first arrive. Instead of sitting down on the lavatory seat, they stand on it and squat.'

'I suppose that's because they're used to using a different kind of toilet,' Billy said tactfully. 'Perhaps they consider it more hygienic, avoiding contact with a seat that someone else has sat on.'

'Too bladdy right! Now *you're* the kind of man I can relate to. No airs and graces about you. Must have you and your family over for a spot of tea one of these days.'

Men who pee together, Billy thought irreverently, take tea together.

He said his farewell to Sir Charles and made his way through the bar towards the exit to the car park where his driver would be waiting. He called out goodnight to the Tonkses who were imbibing their nightly ration of Scotch with dedication and, as he reached the door, was surprised to be addressed by Georgina Taylor.

'Hello,' she called, turning away from her three admirers who seemed to cling to her like tickbirds on a lioness. She got down from the bar-stool and came over to shake Billy's hand.

'Mike Sherwood tells me that you and I hail from the same part of the country,' she said. 'I'm from Bowdon near Altrincham, and you're from Manchester.'

'That's right. We probably speak the same alien language. What else did Mike tell you?'

'He told me you're married with three children and that you're nick-named Hoppy.'

Billy laughed. 'He seems to have told you everything.'

'Not quite everything.'

They sat down together at one of the small bar tables and exchanged a few personal details, finding out they had one or two mutual acquaintances and shared common experiences. Billy had once taken a class of pupils rambling in Dunham Park not far from Georgina's home, and her husband had attended St Bede's Grammar School in Manchester. Frank Wakefield, Billy's former headmaster, had come from Altrincham and Georgina knew of the family.

He got home around 9.30. Laura had already put the children to bed. He told her he'd made friends with Sir Charles; how Charlie in fact wanted him to manage the club and had promised to invite them up to the big house for tea some day. It cut no ice with his wife. He then told her about Georgina and his conversation with her. That certainly didn't help matters.

Laura simply said, 'I hope you're not going to make this drinking a habit.'

Chapter Twenty-Seven

Next day, Mike went into Nairobi to buy the Fiat. He came back that night bubbling with enthusiasm like a kid with a new toy.

'My God,' he babbled, 'what a car! I did seventy all the way back. Those Italians know how to produce a work of art. I wish you could have seen the lights sparkling on the dashboard as I came over the hill out of Nairobi. Blue lights, yellow lights, green lights – it was like Piccadilly Circus. Incidentally, one particularly flashing red light kept spelling out the word "*freno, freno*" over and over again. You studied Italian, Hoppy? What's it mean?'

'If I remember rightly, Mike, *freno* is a horse's rein or a restraint of some kind. Wait a minute . . . it was telling you about your brakes.'

Mike's face had turned the colour of the *freno* warning. 'My God! I must have had the handbrake on the whole of the way back.'

Jimmy confirmed the diagnosis when he got the car.

'Brake linings burnt to a cinder. You need to replace the master cylinder. As I always tell my customers when they buy a new car or a new anything, RTBH. Read the bloody handbook!'

* * *

Towards the end of the week, Blewitt arranged a staff meeting to prepare for the new term. Mike called for Billy and they walked over to the staff-room together.

'When we first met,' Billy began, 'you said, "Welcome to Marangu where the date is 1930". What did you mean by that?'

'I meant that in some ways, people in this part of the world are stuck in a time warp. The ethos of this school belongs to a public school of the thirties: the motto, the song, the uniform, the curriculum. Most of the stuff we teach is irrelevant.'

'In what way?'

'I teach maths and one of our text books is Longman's *Modern Arithmetic*. An excellent book in many ways but it still includes the fatuous old sums about tanks and cubic feet and gallons of water – whoever uses them now? Some of the problems are about taps filling and emptying baths, when our students have never even seen a bath.'

They had reached the staff-room by now and Billy took note of the fierce-looking bees, some of them as big as golf balls, buzzing under the eaves. He hoped none of them would decide to join them in the meeting. The room contained a number of Public Works Department items of furniture, a table with several straight wooden chairs arranged around it, and one or two rickety arm-chairs.

A few members of staff were already in attendance and Mike introduced them in turn.

'This is Horace Nuttall, he teaches Latin and Greek.'

Nuttall was an elderly man with mutton-chop whiskers and a pince-nez. He was dressed as if he had stepped out of the nineteenth century in his formal black suit, waistcoat with watch chain, and winged collar. His handshake was limp and effeminate and his voice high-pitched.

'Nice to make your acquaintance,' he said. 'You and I are both language teachers and hopefully shall complement each other. Good English depends on a knowledge of the classical languages. Have you any Latin or Greek?'

'A little Latin, mainly Church. *Dominus Vobiscum* and that kind of thing.'

'Ah,' he said, disappointed. 'Pity, but I suppose a little is better than nothing.'

Maybe one of these days I'll get something right, Billy thought.

Sitting at the table were two Africans, one smiling broadly in welcome, the other a sour-looking individual.

'This is Joshua Kadoma,' Mike said, indicating the surly one, 'our chemistry master, also secretary of the local branch of the Kenya African National Union, KANU for short. So you'd better watch what you're saying.'

Kadoma forced himself to grin though it looked as if it had cost him.

'Our other Kenyan teacher is Job Karioki,' Mike said. 'He teaches biology and religious studies, though I've never worked out if there's a connection between them.'

'You should study *Genesis*,' Job laughed, 'it's more revealing than Darwin. Welcome to Kenya,' he said warmly, giving Billy a firm hand-shake.

'And this is our American colleague,' Mike said.

'Hi,' said the young man with the crew cut. 'Great to see a new face around here. I'm Buck Kramer from Madrid. No, not Spain but New York State.'

'Buck here is recently married and spends most of his time in bed with his wife, Charity,' Mike grinned. 'He claims to be teaching physics when he can drag himself away from the marriage couch but I don't think the students understand his accent. We certainly don't. He's been sent to replace Geoff Moulton here who's just been promoted to the headship of a school north of Mombasa. The lucky bastard. Geoff, I mean.'

'That remains to be seen,' Moulton guffawed, giving Billy a matey shoulder-thump at the same time as holding out his hand in welcome. 'I hope you like it here but if ever you fancy a posting to the coast, drop me a line and I'll see what I can do.'

'You've already seen this last character,' Mike said, indicating the fair-haired young man in the arm-chair. 'Roger Bedwell. He was the one at the club, trying to look down Georgina's cleavage.'

'Some hopes,' Bedwell sighed. 'I couldn't get near her for the medic and the copper.' He addressed Billy. 'I caught a glimpse of your wife the other night. She's a stunner, reminds me of Elizabeth Taylor.' With a glint in his eye, he added, 'I look forward to getting to know her.' He made the word 'know' sound lascivious.

Billy said with commendable calmness, 'Laura's certainly beautiful, that's why I married her. Now she's pregnant, she's at her most radiant. If anyone here in Kenya takes a fancy to her, though, he will have to accept the whole package. Three children, with a fourth on the way.'

It wiped the leer off Bedwell's face.

The door of the staff-room opened and in strode Henry Blewitt, his gown flowing behind him, a mortar board perched on his head, and his tick-ridden bulldog waddling in attendance. The staff rose to its feet.

'Good morning, gentlemen,' he said. 'Please be seated.' He fitted a cigarette into his holder and accepted the light which Roger Bedwell was quick to offer.

'Thank you, Roger. Now, I have a number of items to get through so let's get down to business.

'First we welcome a new member of staff, Mr Hopkins, who will be taking the place of Mr Stewart who returned to the UK last term. Mr Hopkins last worked at Holbrook Hospital School in Manchester. Not a public school, I hasten to add.

'I'd like to begin today by reminding my British colleagues that out here in this colony, we are all representatives of the British Empire [pronounced *empah*] and I must stress the need to keep up standards at all times.'

Billy took a surreptitious look at Blewitt's mangy dog. You should take that mutt to the vet's for a start, he thought.

'I have many plans for the school,' the Major continued. 'For example, I should like to have an Army Cadet Unit as they do in public schools at home and am doing my utmost to persuade the Education Authorities, though they seem to be afraid we shall create a dangerous private army.'

'I'm all for it, Henry,' Bedwell enthused. 'As you and I had at our *alma mater*. A cadet force would instil a spot of discipline.'

'I would support such a force,' Joshua Kadoma said, 'and am sure KANU would also. Such a force could form the basis of a future officer class.'

'Splendid,' Blewitt said. 'It's good to know we have the support of our African colleagues in something. We must maintain our ideals in every possible way. For example, I expect members of staff to wear a gown when teaching, and if you have a mortar board, so much the better, wear that too. Lends dignity to the profession of schoolmaster.'

'Poppycock!' Geoff Moulton hooted. 'This is Africa not

England. What do you hope to achieve with all this public-school nonsense?'

Blewitt looked put out. 'What do you mean, nonsense! We're trying to produce Christian gentlemen here.'

'I say again,' Moulton bellowed, 'poppycock! You're trying to preserve this school in aspic along the lines of some outdated nineteenth-century philosophy, when what our schoolboys really want are decent grades in the Cambridge School Certificate so they can get clerical jobs in the Civil Service.'

Blewitt frowned. 'Each man is entitled to his own opinion but here in Marangu I am endeavouring to promote public-school values. We have begun teaching the classical languages this year and I can see a day when our fourth-form students will converse in Latin and Greek.'

'I am sure that day will come about, Headmaster,' Horace Nuttall purred.

'Meanwhile, we must encourage the speaking of English by forbidding the students to speak their own tribal languages. English at all times must be our watchword.'

'Poppycock,' Geoff Moulton muttered again under his breath.

'Now, I turn to boarding matters,' Blewitt continued, ignoring him. 'I have allocated duties for the term and asked Buck Kramer here to type them up for us. Did you manage to do it, old chap?'

'I sure did,' Buck replied. 'And if you got some thumb tacks, I'll pin the schedule up on the bulletin board.' He pronounced schedule with a hard 'k'.

'You mean,' said Blewitt testily, 'that if I have some drawing pins, you'll pin the duty roster on the notice board.'

'Yep, I guess that's what I mean in Limey language.'

'I'm sure,' the headmaster went on, 'I don't need to remind you of your responsibilities when you're on duty. The most important thing is to ensure that the Union Jack is hoisted in the morning and taken down at sunset.'

'One day,' growled Joshua Kadoma in an aside to Billy, 'that flag will be torn down and replaced by that of an independent Kenya.'

Blewitt either did not hear or chose to disregard him.

'I'd like to bring your attention to some of the problems we experienced last term,' he continued. 'It is essential that when you're on duty there's no sneaking off to the club for a quick one. You're on call for the whole twenty-four hours, remember.

'We must also supervise the kitchens at every meal and make sure the cooks are not drunk and meals are served on time. We were getting lax last term and once or twice the *posho* was burnt. That kind of thing can cause discontent among the student body. Next thing you know, we'll have a riot on our hands.'

'Talking of standards, Headmaster,' Mike said, 'can we put an end to the practice of serving meals from galvanised buckets? It makes the food resemble pig swill. Can we not buy some decent tureens and make the meal a civilised affair?'

'Point taken,' Blewitt said, 'but it's a matter of affording them on a tight budget. I am allocated the sum of one shilling a day to feed each student and that doesn't allow for fancy-serving utensils, I'm afraid. But I'll look into the matter.'

'Thank you, Major,' Mike said, giving Billy a wink.

'Talking of budgets,' Blewitt droned on, 'we must tighten up on the collection of fees. Boys failing to bring them must be sent home at once. The bursar has expressed deep concern over this matter.'

Mike whispered to me, 'Blewitt *is* the bursar! He wears different hats and talks about the other role as if it's carried out by another person. Schizoid, if you ask me. At the moment, he's playing the headmaster.'

'We've got to be patient when it comes to the collection of fees,' Job Karioki put in. 'We must remember that often a whole family, perhaps a whole village, has scrimped to put one son through secondary school. They always pay but may need time to raise the money.'

'All very well,' Blewitt sneered, 'but meanwhile I have to meet the bills of the maize suppliers, the tailor, and countless other tradesmen.

'Now I come to the allocation of administrative duties. We shall continue as last term with Mr Sherwood in charge of stationery, and Mr Kramer the library. Mr Hopkins will take over the hardware store.'

'Be glad to, Headmaster,' Billy said, eager to show his willingness to be part of the team. 'What does that involve?'

'Keeping inventories of stock, issuing implements for ground maintenance, and seeing that the tools are well maintained.'

'What kind of tools, Major?'

'*Jembes*, they are African versions of the spade, sickles, and *pangas*.'

'Pangas! Weren't they the machetes used by the Mau Mau to hack up their victims?'

Joshua Kadoma laughed. 'They were, but they also have peaceful uses like weeding and pruning.' Narrowing his eyes, he said menacingly, 'But they must be kept bayonet-sharp at all times if they are to be of any value.'

Billy swallowed a couple of times. I, he said to himself,

the one who was terrified by the stories of the Mau Mau atrocities, will now be in charge of issuing *pangas* to African schoolboys, some of whom are Kikuyu! When I took this job, I never for a moment thought I'd be employed keeping Mau Mau machetes in razor-sharp condition.

'And now for allocation of subjects,' Blewitt said. 'Everyone will teach their usual subjects and I am giving Mr Hopkins English though he can also help Mr Sherwood out with junior mathematics teaching as he has qualifications in accountancy.'

'Wait a minute,' Billy interjected vehemently, 'I object to teaching maths. I've never taught the subject in my life and I should hate to make a mess of it. The only maths needed in accountancy is the ability to add up a row of figures. My special subject is English.'

'Look here,' Blewitt reproved, 'that's not the spirit. Not the spirit at all. Everyone has to buckle down to it here in the colonies. Flexibility is the keynote, what?'

At the mention of accountancy, Moulton's ears had pricked up.

'You do accounts?' he exclaimed. 'I could use your talents in my new school. How would you like free holidays at the coast for your family and yourself?'

'What's the problem?' Billy asked, thinking to himself that Duncan's training in accountancy was proving to be a valuable asset.

'The last head was sacked for fiddling the books,' Geoff Moulton explained. 'Something about virements, whatever they are. It seems he got into a fair old mess.'

'I'll help if I can,' Billy said, 'but that doesn't help me here in Marangu, having to teach maths.'

Buck Kramer came to his rescue. 'Look, Headmaster, you've been telling me for some time now that we

Americans don't speak English so I don't mind forgoing some of my classes and substituting a little junior math in their place.'

'Very well,' the headmaster conceded, 'as long as you remember the word is "maths" in the plural.'

'Thanks, Buck,' Billy murmured. 'I owe you one.'

Phew! A lucky escape, he thought, but not a good start to his first staff meeting as he had caused things to be moved around.

'We come now to the matter of school reports,' Blewitt announced, 'to which parents attach great significance. We've got the results of last term's exams and must now fill in comments on each student. Please let me have these individual observations as soon as possible for the school records. Mr Hopkins will take over Mr Stewart's form, 3A, and if he would kindly fill in the report forms, I'd be most grateful.'

Uh-oh. More trouble. Billy had to object again. 'But I don't know any of the students, Headmaster, so how can I fill in these reports?'

'Look, don't argue with me, my good man. Just fill the bladdy things in.'

'But . . .' He realised it was no use arguing with this man.

'I'll give you some help,' Job Karioki said softly. 'I know most of those students well.'

'Thanks, Job. I owe *you* one.'

At this rate, I'm going to be in everyone's debt, he thought. I seem to be, as my mam used to put it, a Spaniard in the works.

'That's settled then,' Blewitt said, eyeing Billy with a baleful stare. 'Finally, I want to turn our attention to the organisation for the sports meeting to be held at the end of term. As usual, I'll be responsible for the smooth running of the operation but individual events will be taken by the following. Running Events: Mr Sherwood, Mr Karioki, Mr Kadoma. High and long Jumps: Mr Bedwell. Throwing Events: Mr Hopkins.'

'I hate to object again, Headmaster, but I know absolutely nothing about these events. Haven't the first clue. And aren't some of our students Masai?' Billy asked.

'They are indeed.'

'That means that I, an absolute beginner, will be teaching African tribal warriors how to throw javelins or in other words spears?'

'Correct.'

'But I've never thrown a javelin, a discus, or indeed a hammer in my life.'

'Then you'd better bladdy well learn, my good man. Didn't they have any of these sports events at your last establishment?'

He made the word 'establishment' sound like Borstal.

'I'm afraid not.'

'Then, my dear fella, you'd best get a bladdy book out of the library and start boning up on the subject.'

'A good meeting,' Joshua Kadoma said sarcastically as they broke up. 'Some fine decisions made. Now, if you'll excuse me, gentlemen, I must bugger off as I have another meeting to attend, this time the local branch of KANU – which will make more sense than that fiasco.'

As Mike and Billy walked back along the path, Billy remarked, 'My first staff meeting. Not what I would describe as a roaring success.'

'Oh, I dunno,' Mike said. 'You made your position clear and let His Lordship know you can't be pushed around.'

At home Laura anxiously enquired, 'Well, how did it go?'

'Don't ask,' Billy replied. 'You're now looking at one of the school's chief administrators. I'm responsible for issuing *pangas* and sickles to our Kikuyu schoolboys and I'm to make sure they're sword-sharp at all times. I'm to teach English throughout the school, and finally I've been given the task of instructing the Masai in the art of throwing spears. So, all in all, a success.'

Chapter Twenty-Eight

Now Billy had acquired a car only one problem remained: neither Laura nor he knew how to drive. He thought of asking Mike to teach them but Jill warned him off.

'You and he get on well together,' she said. 'Don't jeopardise that friendship by asking Mike to give you driving instruction. Back in Britain, he tried to teach me and we nearly came to blows. I was ready to divorce him. He has no patience.'

'That's because you can't tell your left from your right,' her husband retorted.

'Only because you gave me contradictory instructions like, "OK, reverse! Go ahead!" Or when I asked you if you wanted me to turn left, you said, "That's right!" We were like Abbot and Costello.'

Billy could see they were about to get into an argument recalling the episode. Then Jill suggested Job Karioki as his teacher.

'He's taught one or two ladies at the club and they said he never once raised his voice in anger. He really does have the patience of Job,' she said, giving her husband a dirty look.

'With some of those scatterbrained *memsahibs* at the club, he'd need it,' Mike remarked.

'If you like,' Jill continued, ignoring him, 'we could get him to teach you and I'll teach Laura myself in the Fiat.'

'God help her,' Mike said. 'The blind leading the blind.'

So that was how Job became Billy's driving instructor. He came round one Saturday morning, and for the first session Matthew and Lucy were allowed to sit in the back provided they kept quiet.

'The test will be conducted by Andy Towers,' Job informed his pupil, 'and he has a fearful reputation. Fails nearly everyone first time.'

'Except, according to Mike, the pretty ladies from the club.' Billy grinned.

'I don't know about that,' Job said diplomatically. 'What I do know is that he's a hard taskmaster and doesn't allow for errors.'

'Why so strict?'

'He has to be. Marangu is a small town with few of the features you would expect to meet in a city like Nairobi. We don't have traffic lights or pedestrian crossings; there are no busy streets and only one roundabout. So he has to be severe in the test and try to put you through the conditions you'd find in a city. You'll need to know the Highway Code backwards, of course.'

After these introductory remarks, they turned to the practical business of driving. Job was a good teacher and soon had Billy drilled in the ordered sequence of movements to set off, though at first his clumsiness resulted in jumpy starts.

'Kangaroo petrol?' Job laughed. 'Don't worry about it. That's normal for beginners and you'll soon be starting easily and smoothly. Just remember the routine.'

Not that there was much chance of his forgetting since he had two critics in the back watching his every move.

'Don't forget to signal before you start, Dad,' from Matthew.

'Don't forget your mirror, Dad,' from Lucy.

'OK! OK!' Billy said. 'No need to tell me!'

It wasn't long before he got the hang of it and after five or six lessons was driving along smoothly and confidently. Job was thorough and took him through the whole gamut of procedures from hand signals to three-point turns, reversing into narrow spaces, emergency stops, and the like. When it came to starting on a steep hill, he placed a matchbox under a rear wheel.

'This is an old Andy Towers trick,' he said. 'If you roll back and touch the matchbox, he'll fail you. And remember, always be courteous to other motorists on the road and, most important, be especially kind to pedestrians attempting to cross the road since we don't have zebra crossings.'

One day the two of them were driving along the main road when they passed a signpost which read: TIKALE 5 MILES.

'Tikale is my home village,' Job remarked. 'A few of our own students went to the primary school there as I did.'

'Let's go and take a look at it,' Billy said. 'I'd love to visit one of our feeder primary schools to see what goes on at the stage before our students come to us.'

'All right, let's do it. Take the next road on the left.'

They turned off the main road and drove for several miles along a narrow cart track until they came to a little village of mud and wattle huts. In a clearing set apart from the village there stood half a dozen rectangular mud huts with thatched roofs. Outside each building was a rock garden with brightly coloured flowers and plants.

'Well, this is it,' Job said, 'my old primary school where I first learned to read.'

'It looks compact and neatly laid out.'

'Yes, the villagers are proud of their school, and so they ought to be since they had to build it themselves.'

They found the school office where the headmistress, a Mrs Kanyuka, greeted them warmly and took them on a tour of the school. It was an eye-opener for Billy.

First they visited the admission class which was housed in one of the larger huts. The room was packed to the rafters with infants who sat cross-legged on the clay floor. It was so congested that there was no space for a teacher's desk let alone a blackboard or cupboard. There was little light save from narrow windows set high up towards the top of the walls. To Billy there seemed to be a multitude of little black faces staring up at him as if he were the first white man they'd ever seen. Their eyes and teeth seemed to glow in the dim light.

'Say "Good morning" to our distinguished visitors,' said Mrs Wambui, the class teacher.

'Good morning, sir,' the infants chanted in their sing-song way.

'Good morning, children,' Billy replied.

'I hope you are well?' Job said.

'We are well, thank you,' the children chorused.

'It's a large class,' Billy remarked to the teacher. 'How many are there?'

'About a hundred and fifty,' she said, 'give or take twenty or so. I can't keep an exact register as the number varies from one day to the next. They come and go.'

'I suppose it's all the children from the village,' Billy put in.

'Not all. Only about half the local children come to

school. It's a question of finding the fees of ten shillings a term. Some families have several children and cannot afford to send them all and, if they have a son at secondary school as well, it makes it 'specially difficult.'

'Sometimes,' Job added, 'the whole village contributes towards sending one of their deserving sons to secondary school.'

'Deserving sons?' Billy asked. 'How do they decide who's deserving and who's not?'

'At the end of primary school, the children take selection exams for the intermediate school, and at the end of that for secondary school. Only five per cent of boys get into secondary so those who reach us are the cream of the crop. Even fewer girls go to secondary school, of course.'

Billy was intrigued. This explained why education in Kenya was regarded as a great privilege and helped him understand why many of their students were impatient when they were given a public holiday, like Empire Day, and had to take part in a tree-planting ceremony.

'A complete waste of time,' he'd heard them complain, 'when we should be in the classroom learning.'

Billy turned to Mrs Wambui and asked, 'How do you manage to teach such a large class of children without books or basic equipment like pens or pencils? Not even chalk and slates.'

'Mainly by chanting things together, and we take many of our lessons outdoors where the children can write with a stick or their fingers in the sand.'

Billy thought of teachers back in England complaining that thirty or forty in a class was on the high side. They thanked the teacher and the children for their time and moved on.

The headmistress then conducted them to one of the higher classes, Standard Five.

'This class isn't so bad,' she announced proudly. 'It has only seventy-five pupils.'

The boys and girls sat five to a desk but, after the admission class, it did seem less overcrowded. They went through the same routine of wishing each other good morning but Billy was glad to see that this class seemed better equipped since they had a few tatty text books to share, two between five. They also had pencils but no exercise books and were having to make do with scraps of paper off-cuts which the teacher had begged from the government printers in Nairobi. There was an arithmetic lesson in progress and the pupils listened with rapt and reverential attention as if at a church service.

'Most of my pupils,' the teacher explained later, 'are hoping to go to secondary school if their families can find the fees. Unfortunately that usually means only the boys as it's generally regarded as a waste to send a girl.'

'How would you like to meet my family?' Job asked as they came away from the school. 'They live in the village only a short distance away.'

They passed across a field and, as they did so, Job turned to Billy and said, 'Meet my two brothers, Daniel and Samuel.'

He looked around but could see no one. Job went across to a hole in the middle of the field and called down.

'Daniel! Samuel! Come up here! I want you to meet a friend of mine.'

After a few minutes, two muddy figures appeared from the earth having climbed the rope ladder which led to its innermost depths. Wiping the clay from their hands on a piece of rough material, they came forward, big smiles on their faces.

'Glad to meet you,' they said together, shaking Billy's hand.

'They are digging a well,' Job explained. 'How far have you got, boys?'

'We're down about twenty feet,' answered Daniel.

'Another thirty and we should find water,' added Samuel.

'Don't you already have water in the village?' Billy asked, puzzled.

'They have,' Job replied, 'but it's five miles away and it's a long way for our women to walk carrying heavy buckets on their head. And when they get the water, it has to be boiled and filtered and boiled again. The boys are trying to find a fresh source.'

'Don't they worry about the sides of the hole collapsing on them?'

'They do but when they come to water, they'll shore up the sides with wood until a more permanent structure can be put in place.'

He turned to his brothers and said to them, 'We'll let you get on with it. Best of luck with your search.'

Billy came away from the scene feeling deeply moved and couldn't help reflecting how easy they had it back at home in Manchester where they simply turned on a tap and there it was, clean water. Taken for granted. He vowed never to complain about a water bill again.

They made their way through the village of mud and wattle huts until they reached Job's family home. At the door, he introduced his grey-haired father who clasped Billy's hand in both his and shook it warmly.

'Welcome to our home, sir,' he said. 'Please come in and sit with us.'

The hut consisted of a single room which served as living room, kitchen and bedroom for the whole family.

Job's mother came forward next to greet Billy. Gripping the wrist of her right hand with her left, she shook his hand firmly, curtsied and said, 'We are honoured, sir, that you have come to visit us.'

Now Billy had an idea of what it was like to be a member of the royal family. But when Job's younger sister, Martha, approached them on her knees bearing a tray with three cups of tea for the men, he felt like a visiting emperor. No one protested at Martha's behaviour as it seemed to be the accepted norm. They made polite conversation for a while and it was obvious that Job's family was exceedingly proud of their son and his achievement in becoming a teacher. And now here he was showing a *mzungu* how to drive. They finished the tea and Billy thanked the family for their hospitality and apologised that they had to leave to continue with the driving lesson.

'I am sure my son will teach you well,' Job's father said as they departed. 'One day we hope he will own a car of his own.'

As they came through the village, passing hut after hut on the way back to the car, they were surrounded by dozens of wide-eyed young infants who stared at Billy as if he were a creature from another planet. The children's general appearance, though, worried him no end. Not only were their eyes encrusted with flies but most of them had the pot belly he'd seen on so many African children along the road, as if their tummies had been inflated with a bicycle pump. He asked Job about this.

'It's due to malnutrition,' he said, becoming suddenly serious. 'The kids don't get enough to eat and what they do eat is the wrong kind of food, mainly *posho* or maize meal, pure starch and carbohydrate.'

'Don't they get *any* meat?'

'Very little. That's the trouble. They are suffering from *kwashiorkor* which in dialect means "red boy"; you can see the tell-tale signs in their reddish-orange hair. Protein-deficiency is the problem. But what can we do? I give my parents a third of my salary to help them out.'

When he uttered the word 'protein' a notion formed in Billy's mind. Only the glimmering of an idea but he wondered if in some small way it might offer a solution. He remembered how his dad had always been going on about how rabbits were the best source of protein and often brought one home along with a bag of vegetables from his work in Smithfield Market.

'They produce lovely white meat,' he used to say. 'Better than poultry, and there's hardly any bone.'

Some week-ends Mam had made delicious rabbit pie that melted in the mouth. Maybe they could introduce rabbits into the African diet? He filed the idea away at the back of his mind for possible future action. Meanwhile he had to get through the driving test and so it was back on the road with Job.

A fortnight later, Laura and Billy booked their driving tests with Inspector Towers for a Saturday morning. Billy was to be first off at ten o'clock, and Laura next at eleven. They were both nervous as they had heard such stories about Towers and his severity but their respective teachers had assured them that they were ready.

At the appointed time, Job and Billy drove down to the police station and made their presence known. As the clock was striking ten, Towers appeared and invited Billy into his office for the first part of the test, an oral examination on the Highway Code. Billy had done his homework thoroughly and this was the one part in which he felt most confident.

He began with the usual road-sign recognition test and had no problems with questions about the various signs for cattle grids, mandatory signs, prohibitory signs and the like. Nor did questions about the order of traffic light sequences or listing the situations when it was dangerous to overtake give him any difficulty. So far so good, he thought. Then Towers, poker-faced, said, 'Let's go on the road.'

They started off and Billy went through his routines automatically: smooth gear changes, emergency stops, reversing into side-roads, parking in narrow spaces, three-point turns, starting on a hill. He executed them all without a hitch and throughout took great pains to be courteous to other road-users. As they drove through the crowded market, he slowed down and waved hesitant pedestrians across the road; on the open road he signalled to motorists on his tail that he was ready to be overtaken by turning his left indicator and waving them on as was the custom in Kenya. He saw with satisfaction how Towers made notes on his clip-board as he did this. Points in my favour, he thought. As they drove back to the police station, he felt sure that not only had he passed, he had done so with flying colours.

They stopped outside Towers' office and he made great show of consulting his notes before pursing his lips and turning to Billy.

'Sorry, but I can't pass you on that performance.'

Billy was thunderstruck. The bastard! he thought. He's taking it out on me because I'm not one of the pretty faces from the club.

'No,' continued the policeman, 'I can't pass you.'

'May I ask why not?' Billy said testily.

'For several reasons. First, I don't like your signal for slowing down. I hate that floppy arm stuff; I like to see a smart stiff arm as you move it up and down. As for that "I have stopped" signal, there's no such thing. It's used by policemen to stop the traffic and by Nairobi bus-drivers.'

Billy could feel his hackles rising as he asked, 'You said "several reasons". What are the others?'

'You gave instructions to other road-users – a thing you must never do. You told pedestrians in the market that it was OK to cross and you told other drivers that it was safe to overtake. What if your instructions had resulted in an accident! You wouldn't have a leg to stand on in any insurance claim. *You* would get the blame.'

He handed Billy a slip of paper giving the reasons for his failure.

'Apart from those things, you drove well,' he said. 'Good morning.'

Billy told the result to Job who had been waiting, and gloomily they drove back home so that he could give the bad news to Laura.

'I'm so sorry to hear that,' she said, 'but if *you* didn't pass, what chance do *I* stand? You're a much better driver than me.'

An hour later she was back, with her driving licence in her hand. Billy was happy for her, of course, but he couldn't stop the bile from rising in his throat.

'Well done!' he croaked. 'At least we have one driver in the family.' Nevertheless it hurt getting the words out.

That evening, Mike and he went down to the club so that Billy could drown his sorrows in a few bottles of Tusker. He was so miserable, he felt like crying into his beer.

'What happened to you, old boy?' Reggie Tonks mumbled, knocking back his scotch and giving an involuntary shudder as it hit bottom. 'You look like an alcoholic who's knocked his drink over.'

'Failed my driving test today, that's all. That bastard Towers had it in for me.'

'Don't talk to me about Towers,' Tonks groaned, ordering another shot. 'He had me up before the bench a few weeks ago. Accused me of drunk driving. Said I was zigzagging along the main street. The stupid bugger! At the station, he told me to walk along a chalk line but I showed him. I walked the line on my hands and said, "Let's see *you* do that." That stopped him in his tracks all right. Anyway I told Tim O'Shea, the magistrate, that I was weaving from side to side along the main street because I was avoiding the people. For some strange reason, O'Shea couldn't stop laughing.'

'So what happened in the end?' Mike chuckled.

'I was fined and banned from driving for six months. Now I have to employ a chauffeur to bring me and the *memsahib* to the club. Damned inconvenient.'

Georgina came into the club next. She looked in Billy's direction and said, 'So what happened to you, Hoppy? You look as if you've just come from a funeral.'

'He has,' Mike said. 'His own. Your good friend Andy Towers failed him on his driving test this morning.'

Georgina smiled.

'There's only one thing to do. Dust yourself down and start all over again.'

'It'll probably be the same result,' Billy whinged, not to be consoled. 'Besides, I don't think I *can* drive better than I did today.'

Georgina looked at him steadily. 'Next time you will pass, Hoppy,' she said. 'I guarantee it.'

'How can you be so sure?' he asked, unconvinced.

Slowly and deliberately, she put a cigarette in her holder and lit it. Taking a puff, she narrowed her eyes and adopted her best Mata Hari expression.

'I have ways of persuading him,' she murmured.

Two weeks later, Billy re-took the test. This time he was so nervous, he was shaking and made mistake after mistake. He reversed and hit the kerb; starting on a hill, he rolled back and crushed the matchbox; his three-point turn became his twelve-point turn.

'Is there any point in carrying on?' he asked halfway through.

'Go on,' Towers ordered.

They came to the end of the ordeal and Billy waited to be given the black spot again.

Instead the Inspector smiled broadly. 'Well done!' he said. 'I am pleased to inform you that you have passed with a first-class performance. Much improved and a much better effort.'

Elated, Billy drove home with his Kenya Driving Licence in his pocket. That night as he celebrated with Mike in the club, he sent a double Martell over to his good friend Georgina.

'Cheers, Hoppy,' she said, raising her glass and giving him a big wink.

Chapter Twenty-Nine

A week after the staff meeting came the first day at school for Billy and also the two children. Matthew and Lucy were due to begin at nine o'clock at the European primary school and were to catch the bus with the Blewitts' boy, Arnold, outside the main gate. Billy's starting time was an hour earlier. The kids were feeling nervous and so was he. Despite his eleven years' teaching, starting a new routine, meeting new people, getting used to unfamiliar ways, were enough to cause colly-wobbles.

The ever-helpful Mike called for him at 7.30 and together they walked along the murram path which led to the school hall for morning assembly.

'Watch out for the safari ants,' Mike warned, pointing out several black ribbons of *siafu* which marched across their path. 'Notice the soldier ants which form a gauntlet for the workers to pass along, like SS guards. Occasionally we see a procession of nothing but soldier ants parading in lines which can stretch for miles. Whatever you do, don't walk into them or you'll know about it. When you've been here for a while, you'll hardly notice them and stepping over them will be automatic.'

The school hall which served also as the dining hall still retained a whiff of the boys' *posho*-and-beans breakfast when they joined the other members of staff seated on the stage. They were all there, Roger Bedwell complete with his Alsatian guard dog. Horace Nuttall sat at the piano in the main body of the hall, music obviously being one of his other accomplishments. Five minutes later, the Major, accompanied by his ubiquitous bulldog, strode on to the stage and the whole school, including the staff, rose to its feet. Billy stood up and looked around the staff with their canine companions, and then down at the students gazing up at them. He had the oddest feeling that he was playing the part of a guard in a film about a stalag POW camp.

The morning assembly began with the Lord's Prayer, followed by a brief homily on the theme of gratitude illustrated by the story of 'Androcles and the Lion'. The sermon finished, Blewitt gave the signal for everyone to sit down.

'As members of our little community,' he began, 'we should always be proud of each other, but when I saw some of you in the township last Saturday, I was ashamed to be your headmaster. I have never seen such an untidy bunch: scuffed shoes, unwashed faces, and untidy uniforms were the order of the day. You looked like Fred Karno's Army! Some of you were not wearing your hats, and many of those I did see were looking distinctly frayed. Your straw hats are expensive and not to be used for games of Frisbee-throwing or flying saucers which I believe has become the practice amongst some of you.'

One or two students grinned at each other but Blewitt soon put a stop to such levity.

'I must warn you,' he barked, 'that if there is a repeat of this sloppiness in dress, the offenders will be gated and put on *shamba* work for a month.

'And on the subject of discipline, I must insist that while you are here in this school, you speak only English. Swahili and tribal languages are forbidden. It is for your own good because, if you wish to succeed at your examinations, you must learn not only to *speak* in English but to *think* in English. I have asked the staff to keep their ears open and to bring any breaches of this rule to my attention. You may rest assured that the culprits will be severely punished.

'I come now to the subject of school fees. Without them I cannot run the school. I cannot feed you, supply uniforms, buy books and stationery. You may think the sum of three hundred shillings a year expensive but let me tell you that the fees at Eton and Harrow in England are over a hundred times yours. Count your blessings.'

At a nod from Blewitt, Nuttall played a few arpeggio chords on the untuned piano and Billy expected a hymn like 'In Our Work and In Our Play', or some such. Instead he was astounded to hear the boys break out into their own school song, sung to the tune of the 'Eton Boating Song'.

Lovely tropical weather,
Sun in a cloudless blue sky,
Wind as light as a feather,
Rustling in the trees,
Here we all pull together,
And we're happy to pay our fees.

With the song still echoing round the hall, the staff, along with their dogs, marched to the school office to collect their registers.

'I'm sure you'll find things run smoothly on your first day,' Blewitt said to Billy. 'Get to know your students first, their names and their backgrounds. At eight-thirty, it's fee-collection time and the bursar will expect to see your boys with the term's fees, namely one hundred shillings.'

'What do we do if boys don't have the fees, or only part?' Billy asked.

'That's up to the bursar,' he replied. 'Send the boys anyway and he will decide.'

Billy remembered that Mike had told him Blewitt *was* the bursar. Perhaps the headmaster didn't know what his *alter ego* would say. Weird, he thought.

Softly whistling the 'Eton Boating Song', Mike and he made their way to their classes.

A concrete path ran around the classrooms which were open on both sides to allow fresh air and cool breezes to blow through although, Billy thought, the arrangement was also an open invitation to a host of inquisitive insects. They reached Mike's room first where they parted after he'd pointed Billy in the direction of his own room, a hundred yards on around the next corner. With register and books in hand, Billy strode along the path trying to look confident though inside he was as terrified as he'd been in those distant days of 1947 when he'd entered his first classroom at St Anselm's.

As he turned the corner, his ears were assailed by the noise of shouting and excited voices. Uh-oh, he thought. Trouble. He had been led to believe that African students were disciplined and obedient. This didn't sound like it.

The nearer he got to his classroom, the louder the noise became. He entered the room and found the place in an uproar. There were boys, young men would be a better term, standing on desks, waving their arms and yelling at the top of their voices.

'What on earth is going on?' Billy demanded. 'What's all the commotion?'

'A snake in the classroom,' a tall boy answered.

'Snake!' Billy said, reeling from the shock. 'Where?'

'Over there against the wall,' the youth said, indicating a large brown snake. 'It's a boomslang.'

'Poisonous?'

'Very, sir. Its neck is inflated which means it's angry and ready to strike.'

'Get it out of here at once,' Billy gasped. 'And stop fooling about, playing these silly games.'

'Sorry, sir,' said another boy. Taking the wide classroom sweeping brush from the corner, he swept the reptile out of the room where it wriggled off into the long grass. Order was restored and the boys now stood to attention like ramrods.

'Good morning, 3A,' Billy said, mustering a nervous smile. He hoped they hadn't noticed his trembling hands.

'Good morning, sir. We are well, thank you,' they chorused, though Billy hadn't asked after their health. He learned later that it was a stock answer to the morning greeting.

He turned his attention to the register. There were no strange first names like Golden Boy or Sixpence but one or two had been given optimistic names by ambitious parents, like Learnmore Luanda, Workhard Wambui, and Cleverboy Mboya. Most of the other names were Biblical; there was Abraham, Jonah, Shadrach, Samuel, two Elijahs, three Moses, and one with the sobriquet Lucifer. Billy felt as if he were dealing with characters out of the Old Testament. At least he was able to pronounce these forenames if not their family appellations. He could not get his tongue round names like Agachikundemi or Mwangimuriungu.

'I'll call you Abraham,' he told the latter.

His pronunciation of other names like Ngombe or Ncube which required strong nasal resonance for which he lacked the physical equipment, produced howls of laughter. It was, however, his attempt to pronounce the name Samson Banana that brought the house down.

'The stress, sir,' a red-faced Samson pointed out, 'is on the last syllable and so I am called BA-NA-*NÀ*.'

It reminded Billy of the Lancastrian with the name Sidebottom who insisted on being called 'SIDI-BOTT-AM'.

'Sorry,' he said. 'I'll try to remember.'

He was learning fast. The whole of the time he'd been calling the register, he'd been acutely aware of the hornets which had entered from the open side and were zooming menacingly around the room like Stuka dive bombers with their wheels down ready for landing. He prayed it wouldn't be on him.

When he'd finished the administrative formalities, it was time to get down to some introductions. He told them his name and that he was from Manchester in England.

'Ah, Manchester United,' said the tall boy, who turned out to be a Masai by the name of Ngombe. 'Bad accident at Munich. But Bobby Charlton was saved.'

'Yes,' Billy agreed, 'though we lost many of our greatest players, eight in total as well as twenty other people. How do you know about the tragedy?'

'We read old copies of *The Times* in the school library.'

Billy found that the rest of the form was made up of members of the Kikuyu, Kamba and Luo tribes, with two or three Masai also. All of them had their sights set on becoming clerks in government service in Nairobi. Not one had ambitions to work on the land. Sir Charles had been right on that score and Billy wondered if he was also right about this kind of education not being in the best interests of the country. That was a big question which properly speaking was down to the statesmen in Nairobi and Westminster to settle. How the students made use of the education they received was a matter of personal choice. Billy's job was to further literacy. What they did with it was their own business.

But before he could get down to teaching, he needed to have some idea of the standard of their written English.

'I'd like you to write something for me.'

'What subject?' a Kikuyu called Abel Makombe asked.

'The subject doesn't matter,' Billy said. 'Write about your birthday.'

One or two in the class pursed their lips and shook their heads. The others didn't look too happy either. Perhaps they're nervous of me, Billy thought.

'We can't do that, sir,' Makombe began.

'Look, no need to worry about it,' Billy said, interrupting him. 'It's not a final test or anything like that.'

'But . . . but . . .' Makombe protested.

Billy became a little hot under the collar.

'Don't argue,' he said, addressing the class in general. 'Just do it.'

The students shrugged their shoulders and began writing. They had to break off for a while when the head's prefect called to tell them they were to report to the bursar's office for payment of fees. Billy escorted the class to the other side of the school to complete this chore. At the door of the office marked 'Bursar' he lined up the boys to await their turn.

He sent in Ngombe first who quickly emerged with his receipt for one hundred shillings, the fees for the term. Next Makombe went in and Billy heard him ask Blewitt for permission to go home that weekend to collect the fees from his father.

'I'm only the bursar,' Billy heard Blewitt say, 'and don't have the authority to give such permission. You must ask the headmaster tomorrow morning.'

No doubt when Makombe went to see the bursar again, he would be asked what the headmaster had decided.

Back in class the students went on with their task of writing about their birthday and for a while there was no sound but the scratching of pens on paper.

It was during this period of quiet industry that Billy heard blood-curdling screams that made his hair stand on end. It was Lucy! He would know that scream anywhere. What in God's name had happened? Was she being assaulted by terrorists of the Land Freedom Army? Had she been attacked by a wild animal?

No time for speculation. He leapt out of class and dashed in the direction of the sound. He found Lucy dancing a frantic war dance like one possessed, with Matthew standing by distraught, not knowing what to do.

'She's walked into a line of soldier ants, Dad,' he exclaimed. 'She's covered in them.'

'Daddy, Daddy,' Lucy wailed, 'please help me. There are thousands of ants biting me all over.'

'You go on to school and let them know what's happened,' Billy ordered his son.

Then he grabbed Lucy in a fireman's lift and rushed her to the nearest house, Joshua Kadoma's. He ran on to the veranda and opening the French window, yelled, '*Hodi!*' (May I come in?)

'*Karibu!*' Kadoma's servant answered.

'*Siafu!* Ants!' Billy shouted.

Without a word, the servant pointed to the bathroom. There Billy took off all Lucy's clothes and began plucking off the countless ants that were clinging to her, each one biting voraciously. Their grip was so tenacious that when he pulled them off, the body came away from the head leaving their pincers buried in her flesh. He put her in a warm bath, dried her off and carried her back home where she whimpered out her tale of woe to Laura. That was how Lucy started school. By having the day off. But she never walked into ants again.

Billy returned to class to check the essays his English class had been writing.

'Pens down,' he ordered. 'Abel Makombe, let's hear your effort.'

'Yes, sir. This is what I have written. "May all the blessings of God and all his angels and saints be showered down on my father for the glorious gift of a bicycle on the auspicious occasion of my birthday." '

'That's a good opening,' Billy said. 'A little flowery and ornate perhaps, but a good effort. Let's hear from you, Moses Kanyuki.'

The tall Kikuyu got to his feet.

' "My birthday was a splendiferous celebration," ' he began, ' "and there was a convocation of the entire village to circumambulate the magnificent ritualised commemoration of my birthday. The elders of the village retired to the assembly hut to confabulate together about this unparalleled event." '

Moses looked up proudly from his work and gave a big smile. Wow, Billy thought, this boy has not only swallowed the *Oxford English Dictionary* as the main course but taken in *Roget's Thesaurus* for dessert. As for that bit about the elders going to the big hut to confabulate together, it sounded vaguely immoral. Obviously the lad was enthusiastic and Billy didn't want to kill that, whatever happened. This had to be handled with kid gloves.

'Quite good,' he said diplomatically. 'You have a way with words and evidently like big words that you can wrap your tongue around. The trouble is: not everyone will understand them. Why not try simpler words? Instead of "confabulate", say "talk" or chat".'

'But what is wrong with "confabulate", sir? It's a beautiful word and I like big words that taste good and you can roll around the mouth.'

'Many years ago,' Billy answered, 'my English teacher taught me the value of the short, easy-to-understand word. He used to say: "In promulgating your esoteric, psychological, superficial sentimentalities, beware of platitudinous ponderosity. Eschew all conglomerations of flatulent garrulity and asinine affectations, and let your unpremeditated descantings possess a clarified conciseness, a coalescent consistency, and a concatenated cogency." '

The class listened spellbound. There was a long silence followed by spontaneous applause.

'That is the most beautiful English I have ever heard in my life,' Moses exclaimed. 'What does it mean, sir?'

'It means, "Don't use big words".'

'Please, sir, I beg you,' said Moses. 'Write it on the blackboard so that we may learn it.'

Billy could see this was an argument he could not win. 'I shall type it out for you, but remember that good English prefers the short word when possible. Your verbosity apart,

Moses, your birthday sounded like a big occasion. Exactly when were you born?'

'I don't know, sir.'

'What do you mean "you don't know"? You must know how old you are.'

'No, sir. I think I'm about fourteen but I am not sure about the date.'

There was a murmur of agreement from the form.

'You see, sir, in our African tribes, the date of birth is not important.'

'Can you pin your birthday down to a particular year?'

'Roughly, sir. We measure time by the seasons or by some natural event. If, for example, there was some disaster, like a plague of locusts or a drought, our families might remember a year as the Year of the Locusts or the Year of the Drought. But apart from that, the year is not recorded.'

God help this country if they get the Welfare State, Billy thought, when they would need dates of every event, both major and minor, from births, marriages, deaths and divorces, to the date the dog died.

'What are more important in our society,' Abel Gichuru explained, 'are the circumcision ceremonies. After a harvest, the boys and girls who are initiated are given a general name according to some big event that has taken place at the time and that gives us a rough idea of the date of the ceremony.'

'What kind of names?' Billy asked.

'Names like "Forest Fire" or "Golden Harvest" or "Much Rain".'

'Next time,' Billy said, 'I shall ask you to write about that. I suppose you do remember the date of that?'

'Naturally,' Abel replied. 'It is a year we can never forget for it is the date when we become men and the girls become women.'

Billy was aghast. 'Did I hear you right? Circumcision of girls?'

'But of course,' Abel said. 'How else could they find husbands?'

Billy's first dramatic morning at school ended on that note and he felt that somehow he had learned more than he had taught, received more than he had given.

Chapter Thirty

In the afternoon, he was due to take the top form, 4A, for the set texts in English Literature. He wondered how they would cope with Shakespearean language since many were struggling with modern English, which was their third language after their tribal one and Kiswahili. In addition to *Hamlet*, they were studying George Eliot's *Mill on the Floss*, and English essayists like Hazlitt, Belloc and Chesterton. Most preposterous of all was Herman Melville's *Moby Dick*, especially since none of them had seen the sea, and the language and obscure Biblical references in the book were totally incomprehensible to them. When he arrived, he found several studying *A Crash Course in English Literature for the Cambridge Certificate* which offered the set books in condensed form, promising 'certain success in three weeks' if they would only memorise the critical terms contained therein.

'How does it work?' Billy asked Godfrey Odinga, a tall Luo boy.

'We learn off certain key phrases which can be used in any situation. For example, "George Eliot is the high priestess of 'mature' fiction. Her novels are full of complex interactions between complex characters." This tells the examiner that I know the writer is a woman, but with a few minor changes I can use the same wording for any other author.'

'Clever,' Billy conceded, 'but it doesn't guarantee that you understand the book you're writing about.'

'That doesn't matter,' Odinga replied. 'We're not here to understand; we're here to pass the exam.'

Billy found that there was a long list of such 'useful' phrases and that most of the form had committed them to memory since much of the set literature was beyond them. Many boys spent their time pacing up and down the dormitories chanting formulae like weird religious mantras. 'The author found his tragic material in the commonplace lives of English working people' or 'The book is a heterogeneous set of whimsical humorous memoirs', this last referring to Laurence Sterne's *Tristram Shandy*.

As they read through the literature in class, Billy had to explain every word and phrase they met. It was uphill work.

'When Hazlitt says,' Billy banged on, 'that "Rules and models destroy genius and art" he is saying that creative genius needs to be free from restrictions and restraints.'

Solemnly the class hung on every word he uttered, looked at him uncomprehendingly, then with heads bent, meticulously wrote down everything he'd said, no doubt thinking they would try to unravel its meaning when they got back to their dormitories where they would commit it to memory.

As they laboured through the text, outside there was a cloudless blue sky. Billy could see the bright green fields running down to the river, and watched the peasants working in them, tilling the soil with their *jembes;* the mothers, with babies wrapped astride their backs, bending over the earth, singing as they planted new seed. Viewing them like this from the classroom, he felt a physical ache at being so ludicrously employed; a glorious day and they were wasting it on tedious and meaningless exercises. Kenya was an undeveloped country blighted with poverty, ignorance and disease. His students came from homes of mud huts and shanties, with no running water, no electricity, and hardly a table or a chair, and yet here he and his colleagues were inculcating English culture and classical languages.

'When Belloc says,' Billy droned on, 'he hopes that it may be said of him that while "his sins were scarlet, his books were read", he is making a play on the word "read" which could be taken to mean the colour red. It is called a homonym, that is, a word that sounds the same as another.'

'Why are sins scarlet?' Odinga asked. 'Why not some other colour? Why not black?'

'The expression was first used in the Bible, "Though your sins are scarlet , they can be made as white as snow". Scarlet is a bright crimson colour, like a stain that everyone can see,' Billy said desperately. He could see Belloc's wit going down the drain as he tried to analyse it. Humour, he thought, is like gossamer. If you try to dissect it, it crumbles in your hand.

He paused to let them finish scribbling, then continued his tedious dissection of English literature.

When it came to Shakespeare, he had hopes that the bard would be of greater appeal despite the Elizabethan English since the subject matter was concerned with basic raw human emotions, like hatred, revenge and love, while the plots involved murder and intrigue. He found instead that the boys' interpretation of the plays was bizarre.

He suspected there might be a problem with the study of *Hamlet* when a tall Masai named Nathaniel Ngombe said, 'Last year we read *Macbeth*. We were told that he was an evil man and his wife a fiend, but we thought he was a great statesman in an age of violence and he fought well against his enemies. We had great admiration for Lady Macbeth because she was a dutiful wife and stood by him and encouraged him to be ambitious and make something of himself.'

A novel interpretation of the Scottish Play, Billy thought. What would they make of *Hamlet*, the set book? he wondered. Their understanding of this tragedy was even odder.

'In the opening scene,' Billy began, 'the ghost of the king, Hamlet's father, appears.'

'We don't think that's possible,' Ngombe declared. 'We don't believe it was a message from the dead chief at all; it was an omen sent by a witch-doctor.'

Billy forged on with the tale. 'The dead king's younger brother, Claudius, has married the queen barely a month after the funeral.'

'He did well!' a Kikuyu called Karanga commented, beaming and announcing to the rest of the class, 'I always said the *Wazungu* are like us. In Kenya also the younger brother marries the elder brother's widow, and becomes the father of his children.'

How could Billy explain Hamlet's disgust and rage at this marriage? For the time being, he skipped over the famous soliloquy and continued the tale with the ghost reappearing to talk to Hamlet. 'When the latter learns that his father was poisoned by his uncle, he swears to revenge his father by killing the uncle.'

This idea troubled the class.

'For a man to raise his hand against his father's brother, especially the one who has become his father, is a terrible thing,' Odinga observed. 'If he wants revenge, he should appeal to his father's circumcision brothers who will decide the best course of action.'

The subplot of Polonius, Ophelia and her brother Laertes became totally confused. The class claimed that Ophelia had been bewitched by Laertes who wanted to sell her body to witch-doctors to pay his debts.

'*Hamlet* is our favourite story from Shakespeare,' Ngombe said when Billy had finished his summary. 'But it's necessary, sir, to look behind the words to see its true meaning and in order to understand it. We look forward to further study of the play with you, sir, so that we can pass the School Certificate paper in English Literature.'

Billy knew from that first day he was going to have his work cut out getting them through the exam. Once again, he saw the futility of trying to superimpose an alien culture on another society through the study of an alien literature in an alien tongue. Who were those people in Cambridge who decided on the English Literature syllabus, and had they ever visited the victims of their decisions?

Chapter Thirty-One

Billy and his family had been in Kenya a month when Matthew's seventh birthday came round. They were anxious to arrange a party for him so that he could make friends with other children from the *boma* and so that they themselves could establish social contact with other parents.

With these aims in mind, they decided to splash out. Laura made full use of her baking skills and produced a range of things she knew kids loved. Courtesy of the Marimba Stores she was able to provide small sausages on sticks, sandwiches with sweet fillings, cakes, biscuits, and three kinds of jelly.

Billy arranged a whole lot of games he thought would appeal to children of Matthew's age group: there were prizes of sweets and board games for everyone in a treasure hunt, a guessing game, a simple quiz, ball games, and Mike had volunteered to entertain them with magic and conjuring tricks. There was even a colourful party hat for every child.

This was more than a kids' party. It was to be the Hopkinses' introduction to Marangu society, and if they could impress and amuse the children, the parents too might be won over. It was especially important for Billy after his gaffe over Sir Charles's car keys as the story had gone round the *boma* like wildfire.

They invited all the children on the school compound: Blewitt's son Arnold; Mike's two daughters Phoebe and Chloe; Joshua Kadoma's two sons Samson and Enos; also Sir Charles's daughters Priscilla and Gwendoline; the hospital doctor's daughter Kathleen, along with the children of the town magistrate and the district commissioner.

They began arriving in the early afternoon in a wide assortment of cars, from Peugeots to the Gilsons' Bentley. For Laura and Billy much was riding on this affair. But kids are kids the world over and when they had them all sitting down, there was laughter and giggling as everyone tucked in. Laura's cakes and scones were a success and they could see glowing reports would be relayed back to the parents. Next it was fun in the garden as Billy brought out every game he could remember from his Collyhurst days: blind man's buff, hide and seek, kick can, giant strides, Queenie-o-co-co. Everything was going swimmingly and they were looking forward to Mike's conjuring act which he'd been rehearsing all week. Then it all went wrong.

Lucy was the first to get it. She began scratching furiously at her neck and then her legs. The other kids followed suit and soon the whole lot of them were at it, tearing madly at their faces, arms, legs and hair. One or two whirled around feverishly like spinning tops; others writhed about on the floor in an attempt to escape whatever was irritating them.

'Oh, my God!' Billy exclaimed. 'What's happening?'

Laura was bewildered as were Mike and Jill. This was something outside Jill's lexicon of creepy-crawlies.

Whatever it was, it was invisible. There was only one answer: the hospital physician, Doctor Anderson! Billy ran to the school office to phone the hospital but was told that all doctors were out on calls. He explained the symptoms to the African orderly.

'Sounds like the caterpillar itch,' he said. 'Do you have calamine lotion?'

He didn't. Neither did the Sherwoods.

'Right, Hoppy,' Mike said. 'Let's get down to the Marimba Stores. *Pesi-pesi.*'

Dalip Singh was as unruffled as usual as he supplied them with king-size bottles of the solution.

'You like cold drink, please?' he asked as they fled out of the door. 'Anything else, please?' he called after them.

At home the two ladies were trying to cope with their little whirling dervishes. The calamine gave a little relief but not much. They had to wait till Kathleen's father, the doctor, put in an appearance before they could offer a more effective cure, an astringent.

He explained that the itch had been caused by invisible caterpillar hairs floating in the air.

'Typical of this continent,' he added. 'Nothing done by halves. There must be trillions of moulting caterpillars in the district.'

The doctor solved the problem for the children but not for Mike who had been affected so badly that his features had swollen to leonine proportions. He was ordered to hospital immediately and remained there for a week.

'Another effort gone wrong,' Billy remarked. 'One of these days, things will go right for us.'

'I hope so,' Laura said. 'We can't keep up this run of bad luck forever.'

'Don't be so sure,' Billy said, darkly.

Chapter Thirty-Two

Before he'd left Manchester, Billy's cronies from the Damian College Smokers' Club had held a farewell party for him at the Sawyer's Arms on Deansgate. They'd reached that time in the evening when the drink takes hold and friends become sentimental and confiding. Billy's good friend Oscar had taken him to one side to offer some advice.

Placing a hand on Billy's shoulder, he said tipsily, 'Hoppy, you're going to find the change traumatic.'

'Which change? You mean, going to Africa?'

'That, yes, but also something else. You'll find the change from day school to boarding just as much of a shock. I'm working in one and I know what I'm talking about. The work in the classroom will probably be more or less the same but you'll find looking after your charges twenty-four hours a day is a different kettle of fish. The routine is usually based on the premise that "the devil finds work for idle hands" and every moment of the little darlings' time is taken up by some activity. I find it's more like an army camp than a school.'

Oscar proved to be right. Billy's first days on duty at Marangu High School were reasonable as he worked with Mike who showed him the ropes and the routine, but it wasn't long before he was expected to 'fly solo' and on a Saturday at that.

At 6 a.m. he began by wakening the boys from their slumber. Best to start on a positive note, he thought.

'Rise and shine,' he shouted cheerfully, though he himself was feeling exactly the opposite. Wearily, the boys dragged themselves from their warm beds and to encourage them Billy quoted Scott's immortal lines:

Breathes there a man with soul so dead
Who never to himself hath said,
'I'll have five minutes more in bed.'

No one appreciated the humour.

There followed the public-school panacea for all ills and temptations of the flesh: a cold shower. While the boys of Livingstone Dormitory were suffering under the freezing jets of water, Billy found that Godfrey Odinga had remained behind and was painstakingly applying Pond's vanishing cream to his face.

'What's all this about, Odinga?' he asked. 'Are you trying to make yourself invisible?'

'No, sir. One day I want to be an office clerk and according to this picture, I must have a light skin if I'm to be successful.' From his locker he took out a tattered copy of the African magazine *Drum* and pointed to an advertisement portraying a pale-skinned African executive, obviously high-powered as he was dressed in a Savile Row suit and was seated at a desk containing lots of telephones. More importantly he was surrounded by a bevy of admiring caramel-coloured beauties. The ad read:

WILL YOU BE READY WHEN THAT BIG JOB COMES ALONG? MAKE YOURSELF MORE PRESENTABLE BY GIVING YOURSELF A SMOOTH, LIGHT COMPLEXION WITH POND'S VANISHING CREAM. IT REALLY WORKS. NINE OUT OF TEN EXECUTIVES USE IT.

What a crazy topsy-turvy world we live in, Billy thought. We're never happy simply to accept ourselves as we are but must forever be trying to be what we are not. Whites spend hours on the beach or under sun-lamps baking themselves to acquire a dark sun tan. Now we have the ludicrous situation of an African boy trying to make himself less dark in the hope of securing an office job.

Once Billy was sure that his charges were up and running, he dashed across to the kitchens to make sure the cooks were awake, recovered from their hangovers from the night before, and were preparing the *nsima* or light porridge for breakfast at 7 a.m. Before breakfast could begin, he found the Head Boy and went with him to the front of the school to raise the Union Jack on its flag pole. As far as the Major was concerned, the school could be set on fire as long as the flag was flying at the top of the mast. Next Billy went into breakfast to say grace and, once the students began eating, it was a mad scramble home to bolt down his own breakfast.

After the boys had finished their meal, it was laid down that there would be *shamba* work for one hour. Billy dished out the tools from his hardware store: *pangas*, *jembes*, and sickles. The students were soon about the school, clearing and tidying up the compound: whitewashing rocks, weeding, and cutting back the long grass which grew so rapidly in the rainy season that one could almost see it getting longer by the minute.

This aspect of school life was one the students hated with a particular loathing and treated with contempt.

'This is women's work,' they complained. 'In our villages, no self-respecting male would do such menial tasks.'

'Stop whining,' Billy ordered, 'and get on with it.'

Their final task of the morning was to clean the dormitories ready for the headmaster's tour of inspection at 10 a.m. The Major's examination was like that meted out to raw army recruits by a malicious sergeant-major.

Students abhorred these janitorial duties and devoted much of the week to thinking up ways of ducking them. After breakfast, a queue of complainants formed, each student with his own particular pretext, usually medical, for being exempt from cleaning chores. The problem was sorting out the genuinely sick from the malingerers. A male orderly came over from the local African hospital to help with the task and to minister to the sick. His medical supplies consisted of sticking plaster and aspirin.

'I trapped my finger in a door and cannot hold a garden tool.' Solution – sticking plaster!

'I have a pain in my head.' Aspirin!

'And I have a pain in my neck,' Billy said. 'And you're it!'

The excuses came thick and fast, most of them receiving short shrift. Billy had heard every one of them before and rarely encountered anything new or original. That is, until one particular Saturday. The excuse made his day.

'I cannot do *shamba* work or cleaning work, sir,' a student called Jehoshophat said.

'Why not?' Billy asked wearily.

'I must get my school fees from my brother who is coming on the train.'

'That's an old one, Jehoshophat. You must tell your brother to get off the train and bring your fees over to the school like everyone else.'

'He cannot do that, sir.'

'But he must.'

'It is impossible, sir. He cannot do it.'

'Why not?' Billy asked, now exasperated.

'Because he is driving the train.'

Needless to say Billy let the boy go to meet his locomotive brother. The Magadi to Nairobi goods train was to halt at an unscheduled stop so this fraternal exchange could take place. And it would involve more than money. It would present an opportunity to catch up on the immediate family, and no doubt they would swap news about relatives from the extended family. Any passengers who happened to be on the train would not be unduly put out by the delay and, who knows, if the hold-up were long enough, they might even disembark and brew up tea on their primus stoves.

Jehoshophat's excuse threw new light on the African view of time. What was the hurry? There was always tomorrow. If a train stopped in the middle of nowhere so that the driver could conduct family business, so what?

Billy had met this outlook first on the sports field when his American colleague, Buck Kramer, almost had apoplexy on finding that his students had not turned up at the appointed time of 4.45. Around five o'clock they strolled on to the field for sports practice.

'I told you guys quarter to five!' Buck exploded. 'And I expect you to be here on the dot.'

'When you say quarter to five,' Godfrey Odinga explained nonchalantly, 'for us, that means approximately five o'clock, when the sun is in a certain part of the sky.'

'If you guys want your country to be efficient,' the American yelled, 'you'd better start watching the clock not the sun in the sky.'

Billy encountered Africa time again that morning when he went to the local bank to deposit the school fees he had collected. The teller at the counter first counted the cash and then engaged him in a protracted conversation about his immediate family in Kenya and his people in the UK.

How did Billy like Kenya? Would he be staying? What were his ambitions? Could he help the teller's young brothers to find places in the school?

Meanwhile, the waiting queue grew longer and longer but no one worried or fretted. Calmness and composure were the watchwords. Life in Africa had a different rhythm.

Job Karioki reckoned that Africans learned placidity at an early age on their mother's back.

'There's none of that strict routine of four-hourly feeds and the rest,' he claimed. 'African babies sleep and waken when they feel like it and so they acquire an easy-going attitude, unlike Europeans whose lives are ruled by the clock and a strong sense of duty. How many times do Europeans begin their sentences with "I must . . ." "I have to . . ." "I ought to . . ." '

Billy did not go along with this view. He felt the attitude was the result of living and working under the tropical sun where people developed forbearance and resignation, a philosophy of *mañana*. It was the only way to stay cool.

What a contrast to people in England, however, where there would be foot-tapping and finger-drumming if there was any delay. There, so-called civilised man was always on the move, sweating, toiling, and racking his brains to find yet more laborious occupations. One thing was sure:

the African might suffer from many physical complaints but the ulcer was not one of them.

The morning ended with a 'stand-by-your-bed' routine where Billy had to accompany the eagle-eyed Blewitt on an examination of each student's personal appearance and belongings. For the boys, this inspection was vital because passing its rigorous surveillance meant release for the afternoon and a chance to go into the town to visit the market or watch a local football match.

Dormitory drill consisted of a set of petty rules. Beds had to be made up with strict conformity to army practice as defined by the Major: bed sheets to be tucked in and blankets neatly folded with rigid right-angled corners; lockers and contents to be arranged in precise order. He inspected everything and no tiny detail escaped his attention. He put on a pair of clean white gloves and ran his finger over shelves, window ledges, and the tops and backs of cupboards, hoping to find an errant speck of dust.

Lastly, the individual's personal appearance was scrutinised: his blazer, tie and straw boater. Then his face, fingernails, and teeth, which students polished and flossed with a twig, were given the once-over. The slightest speck of food on an individual's clothes and it was: 'Student here, Mr Hopkins, with filthy food all down his uniform!'

The unfortunate individual was then put on weeding duties for the afternoon.

The severest scrutiny of all was reserved for the showers and toilets. This part of the inspection was the most worrisome. Anything below Blewitt's exacting standards meant punishment for the whole dormitory since the Major was a believer in collective responsibility. He looked at everything: lavatory bowls and seats, showers, wash basins and if they were less than gleaming, it meant an afternoon of weeding and grass-cutting for all.

On the morning of Billy's duty, Blewitt inspected Livingstone House first. In the usual manner, he examined the dormitories, giving the beds, the furniture, and the students the usual going over, and grudgingly awarding them a pass mark. The students grinned from ear to ear as they saw the moment of release approaching. But the latrines had still to be checked. Accompanied by the dormitory prefect, the headmaster went into lavatory block. Five minutes later he emerged with a face as black as thunder.

'An absolute disgrace,' he bellowed. 'Washbasins filthy, floor grimy, two lavatory seats broken. Disgusting! The whole house is gated for the afternoon.'

There was a collective sigh of frustration as the students resigned themselves to an afternoon of misery.

Blewitt swept on to the other houses. Stanley House was given the same stringent treatment. They passed but with drooping colours. An award of *flying* colours was unknown. Until, that is, he reached the last house in the line.

It was Speke House and it was there that Blewitt did something no one had ever seen him do before. He congratulated the house on the high standard of cleanliness he had found in their toilet facilities, describing them as 'immaculate'. No one in the school could recall Blewitt ever awarding such an accolade before. Billy was perplexed until he found the reason later that morning.

If the Major had taken the trouble to inspect the area about a hundred yards from Speke House, he would have smelt the most terrible stench. Odinga, the dormitory prefect, had locked the toilets up for a week and made his fellow students relieve themselves in MMBA, Miles and Miles of Bloody Africa, in order to preserve the pristine condition of the ablutions block. It was one way, perhaps the only way, to beat the system, Billy reflected.

Tea was at 4.30 and dinner at 7 after which the dining hall was cleared up for the Saturday night film show. Westerns and police dramas were most popular, and exciting episodes never failed to bring forth loud gasps and peculiar hissing sounds from the audience, which signified not disapproval but a high degree of tension. What caused the greatest hilarity though was to run the film in slow motion or better still in reverse. It fell to Billy on his stint of duty to show for the umpteenth time Shakespeare's *Henry V* starring Laurence Olivier. It was one of the set books and the students had memorised the play and were able to recite the script with the actors. It could be said in truth that they knew the play backwards for running the 'Once more unto the breach, dear friends' speech both forwards and backwards invariably had them rolling in the aisles.

It was 'Lights out' at 10 p.m. and when at last Billy had seen his charges tucked up in their beds, it was with a sense of relief that he was able to return, happy but exhausted, to his own dear home.

But his responsibilities were not yet over. At one o'clock in the morning Billy was awakened by an urgent rapping on his bedroom window. It was the headmaster's servant with a message from the local hospital. There had been a road accident. Could he please send down twenty named students who were required as blood donors? Wearily, he climbed out of bed and went through the dormitories with a torch wakening the selected students to be taken down to the hospital in the waiting ambulance. Billy then returned to his own bed and went out like the proverbial light.

Chapter Thirty-Three

In early August, the Daimler arrived. It had taken over four months. Khalid Khan, the town mechanic, and Billy went in to Nairobi, in the Marimba Stores truck, to collect it from a bonded warehouse. The car was covered in dust and grease but Khalid's eyes lit up when he saw it.

'A beautiful model!' he exclaimed. 'A lot of rust but when I've finished with it, you won't know it. They don't call me Doctor Jimmy for nothing.'

Billy cleared the vehicle through customs while Jimmy checked oil and petrol.

'You understand,' the European customs officer told Billy, 'that, as a grace and favour and as a special concession for new people, this vehicle is allowed into the country without payment of excise duty provided it is for your private use only? A year from now you will be permitted to sell it if you wish, but I must warn you that if you sell it before the year is up, the vehicle will be impounded.'

Billy agreed with everything and signed on the dotted line; Jimmy started the car and they drove out along Government Road. They hadn't travelled far when Jimmy stopped.

'The engine sounds rough,' he said, listening to the

throb of the engine like a physician checking a patient's heart beat. 'It is the third plug from the end,' he announced at last. 'It's dead.' He opened the bonnet, and selecting a new plug from his toolbox, made a replacement.

'There,' he said. 'Much better.'

And it was.

In his garage in Marangu, Jimmy removed the wheels and put the car on blocks where it was to remain until the year of grace had expired. The car was Billy's investment, his hope for the future, his financial security. The big question was whether he had the patience to sit it out for so long.

Towards the end of August, Laura became ill. She and Dublin were preparing tea for the family – omelettes – when her knees buckled under her and she began to tremble violently. Earlier that day she had complained of a headache, weariness and nausea, but had turned down all offers of help and suggestions she should go to bed.

'It's nothing,' she'd insisted. 'It'll pass. I'd rather ignore it and carry on.'

The fever decreed otherwise and Billy helped her to bed and tucked her in. No matter how many blankets he piled on, she continued to shiver.

From the school office he phoned the hospital and, within the hour, Anderson was round with his black bag.

'Malaria,' he said after his examination. 'I'd stake my reputation on it, but to make sure we'll send a blood sample over to King George Hospital.'

'Is there nothing we can do while we're waiting for the results?' Billy asked.

'Keep her in bed. Meanwhile I'll prescribe a course of

chloroquine. That should do the trick. I'll be back as soon as I know something definite.'

'As you can see, doctor, my wife is pregnant – she's due in about three months. Will malaria affect the baby?'

'Shouldn't think so. The womb's in a pretty secure environment, protected by Mother Nature.'

The doctor then asked a series of questions about their recent travels and their precautions against the disease. Had they travelled in a malarial area lately? Did they sleep under nets? What prophylactic did they take?

Finally, he said, 'I find it something of a mystery because Marangu is not considered malarial at five thousand feet above sea level. Are you sure you haven't travelled out of the area?'

Billy assured him that he had been the only family member to have been outside the district, and to Nairobi at that which had an even higher altitude.

Still puzzled, the doctor left, promising to be back in a couple of days.

That night, Laura's breathing became rapid and her temperature rose to 102°. Billy desperately tried to relieve her distress by bathing her fevered brow but nothing could alleviate her tremors.

'Is Mum going to die?' Matthew asked anxiously.

'Don't be so daft,' Lucy said, giving him a push. 'Mum can't die now 'cos she's got to have the baby first.'

Cheerful, Billy thought.

He put the children to bed, making doubly sure that the mosquito nets were thoroughly tucked in. There's no malaria in this district everyone had said, but he was taking no chances. They all said prayers that Mum would recover and soon be back on her feet.

That night he consulted the books on tropical diseases. It was a mistake. As usual with medical books, it was easy to imagine the worst. In the case of malaria, he read, a dangerous form of the disease was caused by *plasmodium falciparum* which, while producing only a single bout of the disease, was exceedingly severe. And that was not the worst scenario. The cerebral form of the disease was the most to be feared since it could lead to seizure, coma, even death. As Billy lay in bed that night with Laura sleeping fitfully beside him, he cursed the day he had decided to take this job in this strange alien land where nothing seemed to have gone right. He said his own prayers that night.

Come on, God, do me a favour. Make it so that she doesn't have any of these nasty forms of the disease. As you know, I'm a fatalist and believe you were the one who got us here in the first place as part of your plan. So don't mess it up for us. Amen.

God must have heard him because a few days later Laura began to recover. Doctor Anderson called in one day with the results of the blood test. It was malaria all right but a mild form and the course of chloroquine soon took effect. Within a week Laura was sitting up, the tremors had ceased, and her temperature was almost back to normal.

In a quiet moment, Billy whispered a prayer in gratitude.

Thanks, God. I owe you one. And he wasn't sure if it was his own brain that came back with the answer or some outside agency, but in his mind he distinctly heard the words, You owe me more than one, mate.

A week after Laura's recovery they employed an ayah by the name of Euphoria. She came highly recommended, having worked for a doctor and his wife and their five children before their return to the UK. Her main duty was keeping an eye on the three kids and making sure they didn't kill themselves by falling out of the trees they loved to climb or that they didn't get hookworm by running barefoot out of doors. She also agreed to give Dublin some help by taking over some of the ironing chores. Laura had become a lady of leisure though from time to time Billy felt a pang of guilt at the idea of employing three servants. He, a working-class lad, with a retinue of servants! Who did he think he was?

A couple of weeks after Laura's illness, Billy received a note from Sir Charles asking to meet him at the club. He was still keen for Billy to take over the running of the place as losses were mounting week by week. They met, and over a drink or two in the bar Billy agreed to take a look at their books to see if anything could be done to turn the loss into a profit. Sir Charles was convinced that someone on the staff had his fingers in the till and wanted Billy to investigate. After they had downed a beer or two, he had to depart for some meeting or other and Billy was left chatting to the Tonkses who as usual were knocking it back as if intent on drinking the place dry. He noticed how they both rolled their whisky round the mouth as if chewing to extract maximum flavour from the stuff. They were extolling the virtues of Vat 69 as against Teacher's and how it tasted good in a glass of milk when Roger Bedwell, sitting nearby with Andy Towers and young Doctor Green, ogling Georgina's breasts, interrupted their discourse.

'When are you going to bring that gorgeous wife of yours to the club, Hopkins?' he said thickly, winking at his companions. 'As soon as she's had this latest kid, I hope to get to know her better.'

'The pleasure of that meeting will have to be postponed indefinitely,' Billy said equably.

'Why haven't we seen her down here?' Towers asked him drunkenly.

'I don't see how that's any of your business,' Georgina said, taking Billy's side.

'I'm afraid she's been ill recently,' he answered calmly, determined not to let their badgering get to him.

'Ill?' Vic Green frowned. 'What's been the trouble?'

'Malaria. She must have been bitten here in Marangu.'

'Not possible,' Green said. 'Not in Marangu. There are no anopheles mosquitoes here. We're too high for them.'

'Well, something carrying malaria passed it on to her.'

'You're talking through your hat, man,' Green snorted. 'I have an African health officer crawling round the district with a magnifying glass looking specifically for anopheles and he can't find a single one. Your wife must have caught it somewhere else.'

'Laura has not been out of Marangu once since we got here. Tell your man to get a bigger magnifying glass 'cos he must have missed one or two.'

'Don't talk such balderdash!' Bedwell gibbered. 'The doctor here knows best. You've only just arrived and already you're an expert on the life cycle of the mosquito? What do you know about anything, you working-class peasant?'

This touched a nerve.

'If I'm a peasant,' Billy snapped, 'you are a public-school poltroon and an upper-class twit.'

With that, he turned away and continued talking to the Tonkses.

Bedwell got down from his stool and slouched over to him.

'How dare you talk to me like that!' he spluttered, giving Billy a push that sent him sprawling on to the bar-room floor.

That was it! Billy leapt to his feet and gave him a straight left which connected with Bedwell's right eye. Now it was his turn to hit the deck.

'You blithering idiot!' Bedwell shouted. 'I've half a mind to give you a pasting.'

Billy stood his ground, both fists raised ready to give him another in the left eye, but one seemed to have done the trick. Bedwell got to his feet and, followed by his companions, departed from the club.

Uh-oh, Billy thought to himself. Another fine mess. He resumed his conversation with the Tonkses about the relative merits of different sorts of whisky but his mind wasn't on the subject. Half an hour later he too left and as he drove into the school compound, wondered what he was going to say to Laura. Getting involved in a brawl over mosquitoes . . . what nonsense! He decided to call on Bedwell and apologise, try to bury the hatchet. He knocked loudly on the veranda window and called his name.

'*Hodi*, Roger! Hello there!'

A minute later Bedwell appeared at the door in his dressing gown. He looked embarrassed to see Billy.

'Well, what is it?' he rasped.

'I've come to apologise,' Billy said holding out his hand.

'Oh, very well,' the other man replied, taking the outstretched hand. 'I suppose it *was* stupid.'

He seems in a hurry to get rid of me, Billy thought. Then he saw why. A short distance behind him stood Georgina in the shortest, flimsiest nightie he had ever seen. She looked like Monroe in *The Seven Year Itch*. No doubt she was there to give comfort to the wounded warrior, and no wonder Bedwell was in a hurry to see the back of his erstwhile assailant.

Some time later, Billy was standing at the bar of the club having a cold beer when he overheard the Nelson sisters in conversation.

'Did you get the lowdown on Georgina and her shenanigans?' one of them asked.

'I don't have all the details,' the other said, 'but I heard that Richard her husband came back early from Gilgil and when he found she wasn't at home, went straight round to Roger's place and caught them red-handed. *In flagrante delicto*, as they say. She was creeping out at four o'clock in the morning. Hardly a respectable hour for a married lady to be visiting a Don Juan in his bachelor pad! Especially as she was attired in a see-through nightie. Richard gave both him and her a black eye.'

'Serves them right. They got what they deserved,' her sister observed.

'Not really,' the other answered. 'From what I've heard, he has a bit of crumpet himself, some army officer's wife in Gilgil. But hush, here she comes.'

Georgina came into the bar wearing dark glasses and, sitting at her usual stool at the end of the bar, ordered herself a double brandy.

'Good evening, ladies,' she called to the Nelson sisters. 'Dishing the dirt, are we? Would you like me to fill you in on the juicy bits?'

'Not at all, Georgina. Richard not with you?'

'He decided to stay home. And so he should after dotting me one.'

She raised her glasses to reveal a shiner. Even that looked good on her.

'I only wish I could have returned the compliment to his little tramp in Gilgil.'

A while later she was joined by her admiring trio and it was back to the normal situation except that Bedwell now had a second black eye to match the one Billy had given him.

In the school staff-room next day, Billy was sorely tempted to hum the chorus of 'Two Lovely Black Eyes' but restrained himself.

Chapter Thirty-Four

It was towards the end of November and Billy was with 4A trying to unravel the obscure Biblical references in *Moby Dick* when Dublin knocked gently on the classroom door.

'Excuse me, sir, but *memsahib* has sent me to tell you it's time.'

'Time?' Billy said. 'Time for what?' Then the penny dropped. 'Oh, my God,' he said.

Turning to the class, he said, 'I am called away on an emergency. Go on studying the book and write me an essay explaining the real reasons why Captain Ahab was so keen to catch and kill Moby Dick.'

He fled from the room and sought out Mike in his classroom. 'I've got the call,' he said breathlessly.

Mike was quicker on the uptake than Billy had been. He looked away from the blackboard where he was writing up the solutions to a set of quadratic equations. 'OK, leave it with me. You get going to Nairobi and I'll square things with the Major.'

Billy hurried home as fast as his legs would carry him and found Laura waiting calmly with Jill. Euphoria the ayah was playing with Mark in the garden. Matthew and Lucy were at school.

'No need to panic,' Laura said. 'There's a good twenty

minutes between contractions so we should get to Nairobi in plenty of time.'

They had been planning this expedition for months. Jill and Euphoria were to look after the children. They had booked a place in the European maternity ward of the King George VI Hospital, Laura had packed a suitcase, Billy had had the car fully serviced at Jimmy's, they had a full tank of petrol and were ready for off. He had arranged to take a few days' leave from school and to spend a couple of days at the Norfolk Hotel in Nairobi to be near the hospital. They were old hands at the baby game having produced three children already, and if anyone should know the routine, they should. But this was different. For a start, it was a foreign country and the nearest European hospital was fifty miles away along a road which was ribbed like a washboard for much of its length. Billy prayed that the corrugations would not bring on the birth before they reached their destination.

Laura gave Mark a 'specially big hug, telling him that she was going away for a short time to get him a little brother or sister.

'I wanna brother,' he said, ''cos girls are big bullies. Lucy's always bossing me about.'

'I'll see what I can do,' Laura said.

The car started first time. Good old Zephyr! Good old Doctor Jimmy! They waved goodbye, and with Laura sitting in the back, Billy engaged first gear and they were off.

They made good time and despite the severe jolting along the first twenty miles of murram road, the baby held firm in the womb. Thank you, God, Billy whispered as they hit the tarmac at Athi River where they picked up speed and were soon doing sixty. They were about seventeen miles from Nairobi when the engine started to sputter.

'Oh, no,' Billy mumbled. 'Please, God, no.' His mouth turned dry and his heart pounded as he realised the accelerator wasn't doing anything. He pressed the pedal, hoping frantically that whatever had gone wrong would automatically correct itself. No use. The car rolled to a stop at the side of the road. Billy was panic-stricken as there wasn't a sign of a village or a shop. They were in the middle of nowhere and it was no use hoping for an AA or RAC patrol to come by. This was East Africa not the A34. Desperately he tried to start the engine but it did no more than produce an asthmatic cough. What a useless individual I am, he thought. I know nothing about cars or midwifery. What price an academic education now?

Stay cool, he told himself. Something will turn up. God help us if I have to deliver the baby at the back of the car.

'Can't you do anything to get the engine started?' Laura asked anxiously. 'After all, it shouldn't break down, it's just been serviced.'

Logical as usual.

'No use telling me that,' Billy whined. 'Maybe it's not *supposed* to have broken down, but the fact is it has and we're stuck.' If only he'd had an Aladdin's lamp to conjure up Jimmy to work his mechanical magic.

He got out of the car, opened up the bonnet and gazed in at the engine. A fat lot of good that was. The innards of a car were a complete mystery to him. A maze of oily pipes, wires, and a weird-looking metal object that resembled a frying pan. There was nothing he could do. Even if he'd had the know-how to identify the trouble, he wouldn't have had a notion how to fix it.

Opening up the hood of the car was the signal for a crowd of Africans to materialise from the apparently deserted countryside. They came from nowhere. Soon he had a jabbering multitude of peasants gathered round the engine offering contrary solutions.

'The engine is buggered,' one of them announced. As if Billy didn't know. 'Some enemy has put a curse on it and it will never work again until you have sacrificed a goat and been cleansed by a *mundumugu*.' Sound practical advice.

Billy told him his wife was about to give birth and this brought forth a stream of advice on the best action to take. The most intelligent suggestion came from a tall man who had remained quiet up to this point.

'The Nairobi bus will be along soon,' he said. 'You could wave it down.' And that's what they decided to do. But first they had to make provision for the car.

In one of his interminable sermons on 'Dangers in Kenya' Mike had told Billy that to leave a car unguarded anywhere on the open road was asking for trouble.

'A stranded vehicle is a sitting duck. Leave it overnight and as likely as not, you'll find it next day standing on blocks minus its wheels and any other parts which are of the remotest value.'

Billy contracted with the quiet man to stay and look after the car for twenty shillings, half now and half when he returned to collect it. The stranger leapt at the opportunity.

The Kitui–Nairobi bus came into view within a few minutes and, abandoning the car, they hitched a lift.

The top of the bus was piled high with every conceivable object. As well as fruit and vegetables, there were suitcases, baskets, bicycles, and poultry in cages. Everything but the kitchen sink one might think except that this particular bus *did* have a kitchen sink. They had seen many of these 'banana expresses', bulging with peasants taking their produce and animals to market and bearing painted slogans on their side such as THE MAGIC CARPET, THE CORONATION SCOTT, but had never before travelled in one. The eyes of the passengers followed them suspiciously as they clambered aboard. After all, white people weren't supposed to travel on African buses, and they were wedged with their suitcase in the midst of a noisy busload of babbling humanity. As Billy paid the fare, they were nearly knocked over by the smell, not of the passengers but of dried fish and livestock including goats and chickens. Billy explained their predicament to the driver and there was an immediate change of attitude: a peasant farmer offered Laura his seat; the old women stopped gabbling and nodded smilingly in their direction.

'Leave it to me, *bwana*,' the driver said. 'It is not on my route but I shall drive you directly to the *King Georgi*.'

'I don't know what the folk back at home would think if they could see our predicament,' Billy said.

'Never mind about the folk back home and what they would think,' Laura cried. 'I pray to God this baby isn't born on an African bus.'

Twenty minutes later they were there. But only just in time!

Billy paced nervously outside the delivery room, listening to the noises coming from within. The same sounds that he'd heard when Lucy had been born in Pine Grove. This time the labour was brief and the baby came with a turn of speed as if in a hurry to join the human race. Like the others he was big, weighing ten pounds, and he made sure everyone knew about his arrival for he opened his mouth and howled his protest at the indignities he had suffered in gaining entry into the world.

'He's a fine boy,' the nurse said. 'Your wife's exhausted but otherwise OK.'

'Well, Laura,' Billy said, 'you did it again. Another giant. Must be something you've inherited from your porridge-eating ancestors.'

'We only just made it this time,' she said. 'It was providential the bus came by when it did. Well, what do you think of the latest?'

'A chubby-cheeked child,' he remarked. 'Another Botticelli angel all right, but somehow he reminds me of a hamster. Maybe we should buy him a treadmill for his first toy.'

'At least it's an improvement on the first two boys who you described respectively as looking like a tomato and a prune.'

'There's one thing that will be relief to my dad in Manchester.'

'And that is?'

'This baby turned out to be white after all.'

Billy could not visit the hospital every day since he had to get back to school but Mike and Jill visited with a big bunch of flowers the next time they were in Nairobi. At the weekend, Billy took the children to see their new brother but they were not allowed into the ward. Instead they sat on the lawn outside the window and Laura held up the new baby, John, for them to see.

She recovered her strength quickly and was ready to be discharged from hospital when the baby was ten days old and, as Mike reported to the bar-flies in the club, approximately a foot longer and twenty pounds heavier.

'I swear,' Mike told them, 'he's already started a beard.'

'A tot of whisky in the little bugger's bottle should set him up,' Reggie Tonks declared.

And so young John went home. In the club it cost Billy over two hundred shillings for free drinks for the regulars propping up the bar. The baby's head was well and truly wetted.

Chapter Thirty-Five

Seeing Laura so happy after her ordeal, and his new baby son lying there in his crib so strong and healthy, filled Billy with joy. At the same time, his happiness was tinged with a certain amount of guilt when he thought back to the African children he'd seen on his visit to Job Karioki's village.

For the weeks following the driving tests, he couldn't get that picture of the African kids with the swollen bellies out of his mind. He was haunted by it and felt that somehow he had to try and do something about that terrible *kwashiorkor*. Protein was the answer, Job had said. Billy recalled again how his dad had brought a rabbit home from Smithfield Market every weekend and how Mam had turned out the most delicious rabbit pie. They had eaten the meat with great relish, scraping every last bit off the bone. If I could start a Young Rabbit Farmers' Club at the school, he thought, maybe we could get our students interested and they in turn could teach people in their home villages.

Good idea, but how would he go about getting rabbits in East Africa? He hadn't a clue where to find them or how to rear them. There was only one place to go for information of this sort. The good old Marimba Stores! There was nothing beyond them. They knew where and how to get anything.

'Yes, please, sir,' young Dalip Singh said, bowing and offering the usual cold Fanta. 'There is a man by the name of Harvey who keeps a large rabbit farm at a place called Nyeri which is about forty miles north of Nairobi. He should be able to help you.'

'That's a devil of a way to drive to buy a few rabbits,' Billy exclaimed.

'Sorry, sir,' the young assistant replied, as if he were personally responsible for the location of the farm. 'I know of no place nearer.'

'Ah, well,' Billy sighed. 'I'll have to make the journey, that's all. It's a case of "So Nyeri Yet Safari".' The pun was lost on Dalip.

Later that day, Billy phoned Harvey and made an appointment to spend a day at his farm. The following Saturday, he took the Zephyr out of the garage and got started. He decided to go alone as this was to be a business venture and he didn't want the kids along thinking they were off to buy pet rabbits.

The roads as far as Nyeri were reasonable by Kenyan standards and driving there was no problem. But the Harvey farm proved to be six miles beyond, down a rough rutted track. As he bumped and careered from side to side, Billy was reminded of Mike's story about being stopped on his last leave in England by a policeman for driving on the wrong side of the road. 'Which side of the road do they drive on in Kenya?' the constable asked. 'The better side,' Mike had answered.

After half an hour of the roller-coaster road, he came to a big gate with the sign: Bernard Harvey, Rabbit Breeder. Harvey! What an apt name for a rabbit-breeder, he thought.

Hadn't there been a movie about a rabbit called Harvey starring James Stewart? Strange how often people with appropriate names ended up in the right job. In Manchester he had seen numerous examples, like a psychologist called Ernest Braine and an estate agent called Doolittle.

He stopped the car outside a large farmhouse where Mr Harvey stood waiting. He came forward, smiling.

'Glad you managed to find it,' he said heartily, taking Billy's hand in both his.

It was all Billy could do to stop himself from laughing out loud. He had read somewhere that in time people often come to resemble their pets. The horsey set acquired equine features, blood-hound owners lugubrious expressions, with Clement Freud as the prime example; cat-lovers haughty feline faces, and so on. He had never taken any of this on board, considering it a load of codswallop. But there before him was living proof of the theory because not only did Harvey have the relevant name, he was the nearest thing to a human rabbit Billy had ever seen with his bristling moustache and prominent incisors. And Billy could have sworn he saw his nose twitch.

'My friends call me Bunny,' he chortled. 'It's their idea of a joke.'

They soon got down to business. Harvey showed Billy around his vast farm which, he said, contained around five thousand rabbits each housed in its own individual hutch.

'Rabbit meat used to be popular with English people,' he said, 'but is less so today. We sell most of ours to continental butchers in Nairobi. We are a fully commercial rabbitry. We breed them, rear them, and process them.'

'By "process" you mean "slaughter"?' Billy asked.

'Yes.' Harvey grinned, displaying his prominent incisors. 'We hatch 'em, match 'em, and dispatch 'em.'

Billy wasn't sure he'd be able to do the 'dispatching'.

As they walked along the rows of cages, he was impressed by their cleanliness because the rabbits he'd seen in England were usually knee-deep in droppings and muck. Not these. The cages were clean as a whistle.

'The floors of the hutches are perforated and made of wire mesh,' Harvey explained, 'so droppings fall through on to the trays below. We bag the droppings and sell them as manure to neighbouring farmers who tell us it's the best fertiliser they know. We even collect the urine and bottle it. Prize rose-growers swear by it.'

Billy explained his own needs, being quick to point out that he wasn't thinking of a large farm such as his but had in mind only a few animals.

'The Californian is the one for you then,' Harvey enthused. 'It's a beautiful white rabbit which looks a bit like a Siamese cat with its black smudged nose, ears and paws.'

'Why Californian?' Billy asked.

'The breed was first produced there. It's got everything. It's docile, easy to breed, and produces first-class meat. Not only that, its fur has commercial value and can be made up into a warm coat for the winter. Should suit your African students to a T.'

'How much meat on a Californian?' Billy was still thinking about *kwashiorkor*.

'A fully grown animal is about nine pounds. I would also recommend a couple of Rex rabbits which weigh a little less but produce the most beautiful fur. And if you want real weight, you could try a Flemish which can weigh twelve to fourteen pounds.'

Billy was sold. He spent the rest of the day learning how to make the ideal hutch, the best materials to use, and Harvey handed him precise instructions so that he could make the cages himself when he got back to Marangu. He also showed Billy how to hold and support a rabbit.

'Hold it firmly under its backside with your right hand,' he said, 'and whatever you do, never, ever pick it up by its ears.'

Finally he turned to the macabre subject of how to kill the beasts humanely. A stranger eavesdropping on them would have thought he was listening to Al Capone ordering a gangland killing.

Harvey said the most humane method was simply to tap the rabbit with the lightest of blows to the back of the neck. Even listening to his words went against the grain and Billy shuddered at the idea of doing it himself.

'I don't think I could ever do that.'

'You'd soon get used to it.' Harvey smiled. 'If you are going to keep rabbits for food it's got to be done, and after all it's painless. No different from what we do to chickens and other farmyard animals.'

Billy wondered how Laura and the kids at home would react if they saw him giving rabbits the chop. Probably condemn him as a murderer.

He left the farm in the late-afternoon, promising to phone back when he had built enough hutches to house the first batch of rabbits Harvey had recommended as a start-up kit.

'I'll wait for your call,' he said, 'and I shall deliver the stock to you personally. You can pay me on delivery.'

Excited if not a little worried about what he had let himself in for, Billy set off on the journey home. All the way back, he sang the popular wartime song, 'Run Rabbit, Run'.

For the next month, Twiga and Billy, with the help of Golden Boy, spent the weekends building rabbit hutches. Mike came over from next door occasionally to offer encouragement and advice.

'You must be as mad as Lewis Carroll's hatter,' he said. 'Don't forget to cover the roofs in felt. And I would recommend an enclosed compound of wire-netting for security against wild animals. I'd help but I strained my shoulder playing tennis.'

'Thanks, Mike. Remind me to offer you a piece of rabbit pie when it comes on stream. A very small piece.'

When they'd finished the hutches, Billy phoned Harvey and the following week-end he arrived with the stock. He ran an approving eye over their work and said to Twiga, '*Mzuri sana, mzee.*' (Very good, old man.)

Twiga's eyes shone with pleasure. '*Asante sana, bwana.*' (Thank you very much, sir.)

Turning to Billy, Harvey said, 'I have given you one of my best bucks and six beautiful does ready to be mated. Let them settle down for a week or two to get used to their new surroundings before you mate them. Remember always to take the doe to the buck's cage, never vice-versa, or she'll tear him to pieces.'

'Typical female.' Billy grinned. 'Doesn't like to have her boudoir disturbed.'

'I've also brought you a pair of jet-black Rex,' he said, ignoring Billy's attempt at wit. 'Also one large male Flemish weighing fourteen pounds. He's a bad-tempered bugger but I thought you might like him for Christmas dinner. Consider him a gift. Best of luck in your endeavours, and if you need help or advice, I'm only a phone-call away.'

Billy paid his bill of £18, or £2 a rabbit. They shook hands on the deal and with a wave of farewell Harvey was away.

Billy was now the proud owner of a rabbitry.

Laura, the kids and the dog came out to inspect his latest acquisition.

'I hope you know what you're doing,' she said as she surveyed the little animal kingdom.

'So do I,' he answered. '*Shauri la Mungu.*' It's in the lap of the gods.

The kids and the dog were beside themselves with excitement. Brandy began barking, his tail wagging furiously. Obviously he thought Billy had brought supper.

'Sit!' he ordered in the sternest tone, pointing an index finger and giving him a steely look. The dog got the message but not so the kids.

'Which one is mine, Dad?' Lucy squealed. 'I want these black ones,' she said, stroking their velvety fur.

'I'll take the big white one,' Matthew announced.

'And I'd like the big brown one,' Mark said.

'Simmer down, all of you,' Billy ordered. 'Let's get this straight from the start. These rabbits are *not* pets. They're here for meat, like on a farm. Don't get attached to any of them because they may not be here long.'

'Yes, Dad,' they said sadly.

'Each rabbit will have a number, not a name,' he continued 'Only the big buck will have a title which will be "Big Daddy". The rest get breed type and number which will be written on the cage. For example, California 1, California 2, Rex 1, and so on. You can help feed them but I shall be angry if I hear any of you giving them pet names.'

Chapter Thirty-Six

Billy soon fell into a routine of looking after the rabbits; feeding, watering them, cleaning out the cages and collecting the droppings which Twiga used on the vegetable garden. The Californians and the Rex seemed happy and contented and Billy enjoyed his new role as livestock farmer. Harvey had warned him that the big brown Flemish one was bad-tempered but it turned out to be worse than expected for it was viciously aggressive. Every morning, it would have had Billy's arm if he hadn't pulled away quickly. The rabbit was a bachelor and maybe that was his problem. No chance to get his oats metaphorically like the rest of the gang. He'll get his comeuppance at Christmas, Billy thought, I'll have no hesitation in having him for dinner. Serves him right for trying to mutilate me every morning.

After three weeks came the tricky business of breeding them. Billy didn't want anyone around when he brought the first doe to the buck in case of disaster. Besides, it might be embarrassing, for him, the spectators, and the rabbits themselves, when Big Daddy began doing his stuff.

Early one morning Billy crept out to the rabbitry and picked up California One, the most attractive female in the seraglio, and carried her tenderly over to Big Daddy's place. He felt like a pimp in a brothel. He hoped they were both morning types and would have no difficulty in adjusting to each other. He remembered his own first efforts on honeymoon and how shy he'd been. His two Californians, however, presented no such problem. As soon as he placed Cal One in Big Daddy's bedroom, Billy received the shock of his life. Without hesitation or preliminaries the buck leapt on to her back and went at her like a pneumatic drill. Two seconds later, he gave a little orgasmic scream and fell backwards. She too made a little squeak which sounded like a satisfied moan. Then without more ado she turned and gave her mate a couple of quick jabs on the jaw. One, two.

Billy had seen baboons in a zoo doing the most personal things to each other but he'd never seen anything like this and found himself blushing. He'd heard stories and jokes about Speedy Gonzales and his brother Slippery, but this took the biscuit. Why, the big buck hadn't even waited to be presented, and there were no preparatory investigations like sniffing around each other as dogs did. It was straight in and no messing, like a sailor who'd been at sea for a couple of years. He reached into the cage and carried Cal One back to her own apartment while Lover Boy turned to his feed tray. He needed sustenance after all that effort.

Billy had to tell someone about this. But they'll never believe me, he thought. He was right because when he described the brief encounter to Laura after breakfast, she wouldn't buy it.

'I can't accept that,' she said, pouring herself a coffee. 'Rabbits aren't like that. They're gentle creatures like Flopsy Bunny in Beatrix Potter's tales.'

'You're in for a shock when you see Big Daddy in action!'

Mike too was incredulous when Billy told him later that morning on the way to school.

'Exaggerating as usual, Hoppy,' he laughed as he stepped over a line of safari ants. 'You always lay it on with a trowel.'

But his interest had been aroused to such an extent that it bordered on that of a prurient adolescent.

'I have got to see this rabbit ribaldry for myself!'

Billy invited him to the next performance starring Big Daddy and California Two the following morning.

That evening in the club, when they were enjoying a sundowner after a game of tennis, much to Billy's chagrin, Mike took the opportunity to entertain the bar-flies with an embellished account of the goings-on at the Hopkins rabbit farm.

'He should have a big billboard outside his house,' Roger Bedwell leered. ' "Randy Rabbits For Sale. Apply Within".'

'Or what about: "Hoppy's Funny Bunny Farm: Live Performances Daily".' This from Vic Green.

Inspector Towers had to throw in his two cents' worth: 'If those rabbits were human, I'd have to arrest you for indecency and running a bordello,' he scoffed.

'All very funny,' Billy said, 'but you'll change your tune when you see the lovely white meat rolling off the assembly line after Christmas.'

'Hoppy, I can see it now,' Georgina laughed. 'What about a sign saying: "Peter Rabbit Stories. You've read the book. You've seen the movie. Now taste the stew".'

Even Billy had to laugh.

Of course Mike told Jill all about it and she had to accompany him to verify things for herself. And naturally when Laura heard about this, she too had to join in to see what was happening at the end of her garden. On the second morning, she left the four kids with the ayah and Mike brought Jill over to witness the spectacle.

In some ways, Billy felt like the proprietor of a bawdy theatre in Port Said offering live sex performances, only not with dogs or donkeys but with live rabbits. Once again, he hoped his actor and actress would not let him down.

Billy fetched Cal Two and placed her gently in Daddy's lair. The buck didn't disappoint. In two seconds flat, he was pumping away like a steam engine. Right on cue he fell backwards with his little squeal of delight and received a double sock in the mouth for his trouble. Mike was awe-struck and made a guttural noise which sounded like, 'Pwhorr'.

'That was going some,' he gasped. 'Don Juan of the rabbit world.'

Billy returned Cal Two to her chamber.

'Well, what do you think?' he asked. 'Was I exaggerating?'

'What a performance! That's what I call good theatre. I think you should sell tickets,' Mike exclaimed.

'Big Daddy obviously doesn't believe in foreplay,' Jill commented.

'He didn't even look at her,' Laura said. 'No wonder she gave him a fourpenny one.'

'A clear case of "Wham, Bam, Thank you, Ma'am",' Jill said. 'Typical man with only one thing on his mind. But did you notice the way he squealed at the end?'

'And the doe gave a little squeak too,' Mike said. 'Obviously she enjoyed it as well.'

'Sorry to disillusion you,' Billy said, 'but the experts reckon it's a squeal of pain not ecstasy.'

'That's nonsense!' Laura replied. 'How would the experts know? Only the rabbits know whether it's pain or pleasure and they can't say. If it were pain, I don't think rabbits would continue doing it, and that would be the end of them. Big Daddy was doing it with relish.'

'I agree,' Jill said. 'He was obviously enjoying himself.'

'Does it turn you on, Jill?' Mike leered lasciviously.

'Only if I were into having it with a rabbit,' she replied evenly, 'and I'm not that desperate – yet.'

'This is Big Daddy's second go this week,' Mike informed the company. 'Tell us, Billy, how often does he service the females?'

'Six times a week with a day off on the Sabbath.'

'Never on a Sunday,' Laura laughed.

'You know,' Mike said thoughtfully, 'if there *is* such a thing as reincarnation, I wouldn't mind coming back as a pedigree buck rabbit. That's the life for me. Just think: good food, lots of leisure time, six concubines at your beck and call, and Sundays off. What more could a man want?'

'You can't even manage it *once* a week, Mike, never mind six,' Jill giggled. 'And don't forget that in the rabbit world, you end up getting the chop if you can't keep it up.'

'I shall ignore those comments,' he said. 'But thanks for inviting us, Hoppy. It's one of the filthiests shows I've ever seen. Congratulations.'

A fortnight later Billy had the first indications that the matings had been successful when the does began eating voraciously and he had to keep replenishing their food dishes. This is going to cost me a fortune, he thought. And how would a poor African village keep up with the demand? They wouldn't be able to buy expensive rabbit pellets but would have to rely on leftover scraps. A week later, there was further confirmation when the does began to build nests from their bedding and from fur plucked from their breasts. Overnight, the rabbitry was transformed from a harem to a maternity ward with six pregnant mothers. He found himself worrying about false alarms and ectopic pregnancies.

Thirty days after the couplings and the blue theatre show, the results gradually manifested themselves. California One was first off. Billy was making his usual morning round when he got his first view of her progeny. In the nesting box were six healthy bunnies feeding off her. He was as excited as if he had given birth himself and ran back into the house.

'Laura, Laura! We've had sextuplets!'

Like the three bears, all the family left their porridge and came rushing out to see the mother and her new-born.

'By heavens, that was quick!' Laura observed. 'A thirty-day pregnancy! Lucky old rabbit! I had to carry mine round for nine months.'

For the next week, the does continued to deliver their offspring with conveyor-belt regularity until, by the following weekend, they had a total of twenty-eight suckling baby rabbits. The little farm had become swollen by a population explosion and Twiga and Billy were spending every spare moment feeding, watering, cleaning, and tidying up the hutches. Billy owed the Marimba Stores a month's salary for rabbit pellets already.

'At this rate,' he said to Laura, 'we're going to need more hutches, and soon. At the moment, we have thirty-eight and the number is growing because Rex Number One is due next week.'

'Remember,' she said, 'I did ask you if you knew what you were doing.'

'And you remember, at the time, I did say it was in the lap of the gods.'

On the way to school Mike cheerfully raised the spectre of a Malthusian nightmare.

'Have you worked it out, Hoppy? Let's suppose you don't sell any. Say each doe has four to five in a litter and, let us say, four litters a year. That means each doe produces at least sixteen. Multiply that by six does and you have ninety-six young bunnies.'

'That doesn't sound so bad,' Billy said. 'I can cope with that number.'

'But wait,' he chortled. 'That's not the end. If half each litter is female, that means forty-eight does each producing four. That gives us, let me see . . .' He stopped walking in order to calculate.

'Forty-eight times four, that equals one hundred and ninety-two, and each of those producing four . . .'

'OK, OK. Enough already,' Billy said, 'I get the point.'

'It means your rabbits are going to multiply by leaps and bounds into thousands.'

'I shall have to build more hutches.'

'More hutches? More hutches!' Mike hooted. 'You're going to need more bloody land! You'll take over the whole school compound and, who knows, the whole town! We could all be knee-deep in rabbits.'

'Don't exaggerate,' Billy said. 'You've forgotten I shall be culling the flock by producing meat for the market. Rabbits are fully grown when they're four months old.'

All the same, Mike had him worried when he went in to take his first class.

That night Billy dreamed about rabbits. Millions of them everywhere, and they had taken over the whole town. They had invaded the house, the kitchen, the living room, the bedrooms. The citizens of Marangu were overrun by the furry creatures and people were treading them underfoot. The classrooms were swarming and the students were trying to sweep them out but to no avail. Billy was powerless to help and Bunny Harvey, attired in Highland kilt and carrying a set of bagpipes, appeared and promised to lead them out of the town. To the tune of 'A Hundred Pipers' he marched along the main highway at the head of a vast army of rabbits. As he did so, Billy woke up in a cold sweat.

He realised what this nightmare was really about. The time was fast approaching when he would have to start the macabre business of dispatching his rabbits and he wasn't looking forward to it. Especially since, against his own express instructions, he was developing a special regard for one or two of them and deep down knew he had his favourites. Cal One and Cal Two had proved to be affectionate and caring mothers while Big Daddy's loyalty and industry had won him over. Lately, though, Big Daddy had been giving him funny looks as if he had a foreboding that something was about to happen.

Before Christmas, Harvey came over and demonstrated how to dispatch a rabbit by dealing with the big brown Flemish fellow. By the time he had finished and wrapped it up in cellophane, the meat looked like any other in the Marimba Store freezer, and they stored it in their own fridge until Christmas. Harvey promised to come over and deal with the other rabbits early in the New Year when they would be ready for market. Billy did not relish the prospect.

Chapter Thirty-Seven

Billy and Laura often thought about the folk back home and kept in touch through their weekly letters, not that the ones they received told them much. Billy's mam and dad would more willingly pay a visit to the dentist than write a letter. Mam usually did the writing and it could take her a whole morning to fill a blue airmail form. As for Duncan, one of his letters was worth more than a Penny Black. They had once tried to phone Laura's family but had given it up as a bad job; the phone system in Kenya was just not up to it. Apart from that, Billy and Laura had been so preoccupied adjusting to their new life, they'd not had time to feel homesick. Laura had been kept busy not only looking after three young children but giving birth to a fourth. Billy's job had kept him fully stretched and that, along with the work of the rabbitry, meant he too hardly had a moment to spare.

But as Christmas approached, they began to feel nostalgic and somewhat sad. No doubt they looked back on the season through rose-coloured spectacles but nevertheless there were so many things that they missed.

Around the house Laura had arranged all their Christmas cards: pictures of robins and reindeers, stage coaches and snowmen, mistletoe and stars of Bethlehem. How they brought memories of home flooding back: Midnight Mass and the 'Hallelujah Chorus', walking back through the snow all wrapped up, with the stars twinkling in a frosty sky; carollers in scarves and woolly hats singing 'Good King Wenceslas', demanding figgy pudding and getting hot mince-pies for their trouble; waking up and finding the world had been transformed overnight into a wonderland of whiteness with its promise of snowballs and tobogganing on home-made sledges. And, in their remembrance, it always snowed on Christmas Day.

Most of all the season meant visiting their families to exchange presents, with Duncan accepting his gift with a dismissive, 'Put it over there with the others,' and then solemnly offering a carefully measured glass of his twelve-year old malt. And later the gathering of the clan for a musical 'At Home' where everyone performed their party piece, the most memorable being Duncan's rendering of 'Wee Cooper o' Fife'.

Then it was across to the gathering of the Hopkins family, the gargantuan feast followed by the communal sing-song and Dad's speech, with Mam sniping at him from the sidelines.

Finally, the huge turkey dinner at their own home on Christmas Day; cracker-pulling and reading out the corny jokes; plum pudding and guessing who would get the sixpence. Then the Queen's Speech at three o'clock and the after-dinner snooze.

The mere thought of Christmas in England was enough to bring tears to their eyes. How different it was celebrating the Yuletide season in the sweltering heat of the Kenya sun! Billy found himself reciting his version of Browning's lines:

Oh, to be in England
Now that Christmas time is there!

But how could they celebrate the Nativity in equatorial Africa? The Marimba Stores did its best to create a festive spirit with its gifts and cold drinks but their efforts didn't work. An English-style Christmas was what was wanted and time-honoured customs had to be maintained no matter what. A traditional Dickensian Christmas was the aim though the nearest they got to Dickens was the showing of David Lean's *A Christmas Carol* on the club's battered Bell & Howell projector. Creating an English Christmas in the tropics was a challenge. *Memsahibs* sent forth their s*hamba* boys with sickles and machetes to comb the countryside for plants that could be used as substitutes, no matter how vaguely, for holly, mistletoe and evergreen trees. One or two expatriates had even had the foresight to bring back artificial fir trees from their last leave, along with baubles, tinsel and little fairies to decorate them. The township organised a festival of carols and readings in emulation of that from King's College, Cambridge. Laura volunteered to train the women at the teachers' college while Billy put the schoolboys through their paces. But this was Africa, not England and they had a stark reminder of the fact on the day of the festival itself.

The whole family was dressed in their finest clothes ready to set off to the college for the service. As they were about to depart, Matthew reached down to the lowest shelf of the book-case to collect his book of carols and, as he did so, heard a hissing noise from the back of the shelves. Brandy the labrador, who had been sleeping peacefully on the verandah, pricked up his ears and bounded into the room, barking furiously. Matthew looked behind the shelves to investigate and there emerged from the bottom of the case a big brown and yellow snake, its neck inflated and ready to strike.

'A snake! A snake!' he yelled. 'It's a puff adder.' Matthew had become a keen student of tropical reptilian life.

'All of you,' Billy commanded at once, 'stand up on the chairs and don't move! Now!'

They didn't need telling twice. Billy ran into the kitchen to get the big sweeping brush they kept in the pantry. He'd seen how the schoolboys had dealt with the boomslang in the classroom and followed their example by pushing the wriggling snake into the garden.

He pulled the bookcase forward to check there were no more and found to his horror that a whole nest of them had built their home in the hollow recess behind the shelves. That morning he sent a further five adders twisting and turning into the bushes.

'It's a good job they weren't spitting cobras, Dad,' Matthew said blithely, 'or we'd all be blind by now.'

Then it was time to go to the service where Laura and Billy took turns in conducting the mixed choir in a medley of English carols opening with 'See Amid The Winter's Snow'. It all went well but somehow they had never felt so far from home.

A few days before Christmas Mike and Jill threw a party for all the children of the school and domestic staff. Mike sweated in his hired Santa Claus costume, handing out gifts to all and sundry. After the tea-party they had a range of indoor games ready. Blind man's buff, hunt the thimble, pass the parcel. Their junior party-goers didn't want to know, preferring outside activities like a game of Tarzan swinging from the ropes suspended from the trees and climbing to the elaborate tree house that Twiga and

Golden Boy had built. Joshua Kadoma's son insisted on being Tarzan, Lucy was Jane, and the rest made up a menagerie of wild animals. For some of the kids, acting was hardly needed.

The party at the European Club went one better than Mike's private do because they employed a more up-market Father Christmas in the person of the District Commissioner who, in the interests of promoting good relations amongst the township brethren, had volunteered to be boiled and braised under a heavy disguise of wig, whiskers and furry red cloak. With none-too-convincing ho-ho-hos, he arrived in a tinselly government Land-Rover and distributed presents to the European members' children, at the same time terrifying the gang of little black children who observed the proceedings from their hiding places in the mulberry trees overlooking the club.

Christmas dinner at their own home, like the rest of their attempts to create an English atmosphere, consisted of fare more suitable to a bitter winter's day in Manchester than the stifling heat of East Africa. But Christmas wouldn't be Christmas without the traditional hot meal and Laura had prepared roast potatoes, Yorkshire pudding, sprouts, parsnips, and the rest. But there was no turkey. The best efforts of the Marimba Stores had failed to come up with the goods and they had to settle for rabbit pie, the meat being supplied from Billy's rabbitry. The choice did not go down well with the kids.

'I don't want any meat on mine,' Lucy whimpered.

'Neither do I,' Matthew echoed. 'I just want vegetables and some Christmas pud.'

'You've got to eat meat,' Billy said. 'Don't you want to be big and strong?'

'No,' Lucy said. 'I want to be a model when I grow up.'

'And I want to be a jockey,' Matthew said.

'What *is* going on?' Billy demanded. 'Why won't you eat some of this delicious rabbit pie?'

'I know,' young Mark piped up, 'it's because *your* friend Mr Harvey killed *our* best friend Sandy and we don't want to eat him.'

'Laura,' Billy exploded. 'I warned you about letting them give the rabbits names. I knew this would happen.' He said nothing about his own affection for Big Daddy and his favourite does.

'It's not my fault they visited your blessed rabbitry and made friends with the big brown one,' she said. 'Anyway, they'll just have to eat the potatoes and the veg.'

Early in the New Year, Billy turned his attention to the other rabbits as, in the space of a few months, they had grown miraculously and were ready for market. He thought this might be the appropriate time to bring half a dozen of the fourth-form students into the little farm to introduce them to the business. He arranged for Harvey to come and show them how to deal with dispatching and preparing the animals for sale. The Marimba Stores had already agreed to take the carcasses having, with typical acumen, identified a ready outlet in the nearby plant breeding station which employed some French and Italian staff. Billy wasn't looking forward to the awful business of slaughtering his stock but knew it had to be done.

As things turned out, the unpleasant task was done for him in a most unexpected manner. One day early in January, Billy was awakened at dawn by Twiga knocking on the bedroom window. One look at the expression on his face and Billy knew something serious had happened.

'*Bwana*,' he mumbled through his tears, '*chui!*' (Leopard.)

He said that, during the night, leopards, though Billy suspected spotted civet cats again rather than leopards, had ripped through the wire netting and wiped out half the rabbitry. All his favourites had been torn apart and their remains scattered about: Big Daddy, Cal One, Two, Three and Four – all gone! Billy's efforts had been for nothing and he hadn't the heart to carry on. They cleared up the mess as best as they could and he sold what remained to a Nairobi butcher who catered for a continental clientele.

'Do they breed well?' the butcher asked, after examining the stock.

'But of course,' Billy answered. 'They breed like Catholics.'

'Careful what you say,' the other man growled. '*I* am a Catholic.'

'So am I,' Billy replied ruefully.

Later that week he met his friend and driving instructor, Job.

'Sorry it didn't work out, Job. I had such hopes that the rabbitry would help in fighting *kwashiorkor* and relieving malnutrition.'

'*Shauri la Mungu*,' Job replied, smiling. 'It was not meant to be. As a matter of fact, it has saved me the embarrassing job of telling you my bad news. When I discussed the idea of rabbit meat as food with my family, they were not keen and had many reservations.'

'What kind of reservations?'

'First, they said they could not bring themselves to eat black or white rabbits though they raised no objections to brown.'

'Colour prejudice,' Billy murmured. He thought maybe Job had made up this excuse to soothe his feelings.

'Are you saying,' he asked, 'that Africans are reluctant to eat certain breeds?'

'Well, no, not exactly,' mumbled Job. 'In African folklore, the squirrel, the hare and the rabbit feature strongly as clever little animals who get the better of other creatures in the forest. My relatives and friends simply did not relish the idea of eating such highly regarded animals.'

'Fair enough,' Billy replied, 'though I wish I'd known that earlier.'

'Sorry,' Job said. 'But I think it best my village sticks to their traditional chickens and goats.'

Thus ended Billy's venture into rabbit-farming. Later he apologised to Laura for all the anguish his attempts had caused the family.

'At least you tried, and your heart's in the right place.' She smiled, giving him a peck on the cheek. 'Nothing's worked for us since we got here, has it? We've needed a good sense of humour to get by. I find it best to laugh and say, like Oliver Hardy, "That's another fine mess you got me into, Stanley".'

What could Billy do but scratch the top of his head and adopt his best Stan Laurel expression?

Chapter Thirty-Eight

After the failure of the rabbit venture, money was tight. Billy owed the Marimba Stores a fortune for rabbit feed and timber supplies. Apart from that, they now employed three servants: Dublin the cook, Twiga the gardener, and Euphoria the ayah, as well as paying Golden Boy half a wage. They couldn't go on the way they were. The obvious answer was to let the servants go but they hadn't the heart to give them the sack as they depended on their small wage for survival. Their dilemma was solved when Laura was offered a part-time job teaching music and English at the Women's Training College. She was attracted to the idea of working with African women, though it meant the end of their smooth domestic arrangements and the daily routine was thrown into chaos. Mornings were bedlam.

'I can't find my shoes and socks,' Lucy shouted.

'I need my PE kit today and Euphoria's not ironed it,' Matthew wailed.

'Laura, have you seen what I did with my sunglasses?' Billy cried.

'Look after your own things,' she yelled back. 'I can't keep watch for all of you. I've got to get my own stuff ready for college.'

By eight o'clock they were all rushing off in different directions, leaving the ayah in charge of the two young ones, Mark and John.

Our finances suffered because of that crazy rabbit scheme of mine, Billy thought. No use crying over spilt milk, though. All that was in the past and there was nothing they could do about it. Nevertheless every day he felt a twinge of guilt and looked around for ways to supplement his income. One night in the club he saw a small ray of hope.

Laura and Jill had finished their nine holes of golf and had taken the children and the ayahs home. Mike and Billy were recovering from a game of squash with a quick drink before going home themselves, when they met Joe Finnigan coming off the golf course.

'Just the man I wanted to see,' he said, addressing Billy. 'Do you remember telling me you wanted to move into administration? Still interested?'

Billy's heart skipped a beat. A job in admin meant higher pay and better prospects. This could be the breakthrough he'd been waiting for.

'Am I!' he exclaimed. 'Tell me where and when, and I'll be ready to start.'

'Whoa!' Joe laughed. 'Not so fast. I did say I'd let you know if ever a vacancy occurred in my office. Well, there will be one starting at Easter.'

'Tell me how to apply,' Billy said eagerly, 'and I'll get my application form in immediately.'

'You should stand a good chance as you are well qualified for the job but I should warn you that the vacancy will be advertised and open to competition.'

On the surface, Billy was calm but inside his mind was racing. He had studied public administration at university. Now perhaps here was the opportunity to use it.

'The job would involve travelling around the region, inspecting schools and checking the books and practices of district education officers,' Joe said. 'You'll need to be able to speak with people in the bush, of course. How's your Kiswahili?'

'Not so hot,' Billy replied. 'At present it's confined to kitchen Swahili, I'm afraid.'

'OK.' Joe grinned. 'I'll give you a simple test. First, tell me to come here.'

'*Kuja hapa*,' Billy said.

Joe Finnigan chuckled. 'Not strictly correct. That *is* kitchen Swahili. But very well, I'll accept it. Now tell me to go over to that door.'

Billy was stuck for a moment. Then he walked across to the door and, beckoning Joe over, said simply: '*Kuja hapa*.'

'Mark for Swahili, two on ten,' Joe laughed. 'Mark for initiative, ten on ten. Of course, if you get the job, you'll have to learn pukka Swahili for work in the bush.'

Billy rushed home to give the news to Laura.

'This job is one I have dreamed about,' he told her. 'I've always wanted to get my foot in the admin door. Not only would it mean a bigger salary, it could lead to similar work in the UK. It's one of the mysteries in Education, Laura, but demonstrably true that the further away from the classroom you get, the higher the pay. I can see myself now as Chief Education Officer of some town in England. Who knows, even Manchester!'

'Don't count your chickens,' she said. 'I should wait until you've got the job before you start spending the money.'

'I'm bound to get the job. After all, how many people are there in Kenya with degrees in public administration?'

Next day he completed the application form, citing Major Blewitt as his chief reference, and took it down to Joe Finnigan's office.

'By heavens, that was quick. You must be keen. I shall send off any applications to head office in Nairobi. The final decision will be up to them. We should know the result in about a fortnight.'

'I can hardly wait,' Billy said. 'If I get the job, I'll do my utmost to make a success of it.'

'Glad to hear it,' Finnigan said, 'but perhaps I should tell you that another member of the school staff has applied.'

'I'm intrigued. Who is it? Not Mike Sherwood, surely?'

He'd said nothing and they were close friends. No, it couldn't be Mike.

'Sorry, Billy. I'm not at liberty to tell you,' Joe said. 'I'd say only that he's not as well qualified as you are for the job. But don't worry. I'll let you know the results as soon as I know something definite.'

Billy had heard about time dragging by slowly for convicts in prison but this waiting seemed as bad. He was kept busy at school but nevertheless each day seemed like a year. Two weeks to the day, Mike and he were at the club for their usual game of tennis and afterwards wandered into the bar for the usual sundowner. Billy was hoping he might hear something and he supposed, if Mike was the other candidate, so was his friend. An hour later, Joe Finnigan walked into the bar.

They say that a prisoner in the dock can foretell a jury's verdict by studying their faces. If they avoid eye contact, it's guilty. The same applied now with Joe Finnigan. He didn't look Billy in the eye.

'I didn't get it, did I?'

'Sorry, Billy. Needless to say, if it had been up to me, you'd have been my new education officer but head office decided otherwise.'

'Who's the lucky bastard?' Mike asked.

Maybe he thinks it's himself, Billy thought.

'The job went to Roger Bedwell,' he heard Joe say.

Billy felt a stab of disappointment. He'd had such hopes for this job and was sure he was the best qualified.

But Roger Bedwell! It was a double blow.

'Surely not!' he exclaimed. 'Why, he's not even a graduate!'

'All the same, he got it. Degree or not.'

'But why in heaven's name was he the chosen one?'

'Two reasons. First he's a public-school man – it could be a case of the old boy network. The second is he's senior to you.'

'How do you make that out? I'm thirty and he's only twenty-five.'

'Seniority in the Colonial Civil Service counts from the day you arrived in the colony. He came a year before you and that makes him senior.'

'I thought the general idea was to get the best man for the job.'

'Not here, I'm afraid,' Joe said. 'Everything's done according to the book, the Code of Regulations. The only consolation I can offer is that the job does entail a lot of travelling and it might not have been right for you with a young family. I'm not sure your wife would have been keen on your being away so much.'

It didn't seem much of a consolation to Billy.

'One good thing,' Mike piped up, 'we shan't have Bedwell's ugly face around so much in future.'

'And the ladies of Marangu can rest easy and alone in their beds,' Billy added ruefully.

'Not entirely,' Joe said. 'He is still based in Marangu and will be around most week-ends.'

'No doubt Georgina will be relieved to hear that,' Mike said.

Billy was feeling utterly miserable and felt the need for another drink.

'Chui,' he called to the barman, 'a round of drinks for my friends here and a double scotch for me. *Upesi sana.*'

'*Ndiyo, bwana,*' Chui answered.

Billy was reaching in his pocket for the money when he felt a hand on his arm. It was Sir Charles.

'Here, let me get these, Hoppy. Cheers,' he said jovially when they'd got their drinks. 'Judging from your faces, you look as if you need cheering up. What's been going on?'

Billy told him briefly about the job application.

'In some ways,' Sir Charles said thoughtfully, 'it could be good news.'

'How do you make that out?' Billy asked.

'Look,' he said, turning to Mike and Joe, 'would you think it bad-mannered of me if I took Hoppy here to one side for a while? There's something I'd like to talk to him about.'

'Not at all, but it all sounds very mysterious,' Mike said.

Sir Charles and Billy withdrew to the small committee room off the main hall.

'I'll get straight down to business,' Sir Charles said. 'Earlier I came out of a committee meeting and we are deeply concerned about the parlous state of the club's finances. We have to take drastic action or we shall be forced to close down and that'd be disastrous for the town.'

'How do I come into all this, Charlie?' Billy asked. As if he didn't know.

'I think I broached the subject with you some time ago.

I am now authorised to offer you the part-time position of club manager.'

'I have a heavy teaching programme at school and I'm not sure I can find the time to take it on.'

'Look, Hoppy, I'm chairman of the governors and think I can safely say I can . . . er . . . prevail upon Major Blewitt to lighten your load. The club is an important part of life here. Town and gown have to work together and you'd be rendering a great service to the whole community. And, of course, the farming community can be of great help to the school with such things as the loan of a tractor or in supplying maize at a discount. It's a *quid pro quo* kind of society here.'

'I'd be glad to consider it, in that case. First, I'd have to take a look at your accounts.'

'Gladly. In the matter of pay, we can offer you fifty pounds a month and a hospitality allowance of twenty.'

'Hospitality allowance?'

'As manager, you would offer occasional drinks to members who have contributed to the club in some significant way. People like the captains of rugby, cricket, golf or tennis. Show appreciation of the work they do for us. That kind of thing.'

As Sir Charles was talking, Billy's mind was working overtime. Fifty pounds a month! Why, I could save most of that and remit it to my bank in Manchester. Over the tour of duty, it could amount to a tidy sum. Enough for a deposit on a house to replace the one we lost.

'Very well, Charlie,' he said. 'I'll do it on a month's trial to see what's involved. I take it you'll have a word with Major Blewitt?'

'Consider it done, Hoppy,' said Sir Charles, placing a hand on his shoulder.

* * *

'Bad news and good news,' said Billy when he got home.

'OK,' Laura said. 'What is it this time? You are not thinking of starting a mink farm or buying a shop?'

'Nothing like that. The bad news is I didn't get the administration job, but as one door closed another opened. I've accepted the job of club manager of the Marangu Country Club.'

'You know, Billy, living with you is one long ride on a roller-coaster. One minute we're up and the next we're down.'

'You've got to admit it's exciting?'

'Heart-stopping more like.'

'At last we have the opportunity to save some real money,' he said. 'Just think about it: fifty pounds a month going into our savings account. Apart from that, we have the Daimler to sell. Our Doctor Jimmy says it should be ready within a month. Then watch the shekels roll in!'

'I'll believe it when I see it.'

Sir Charles was as good as his word and Blewitt agreed to relieve Billy of teaching the junior forms so he could devote some of his energy to running the club.

The following week he went down to the club to examine the account books, such as they were. An effort had been made to write up the cash book, the ledgers and stock-lists, but no matter how hard Billy tried, he couldn't reconcile them. Whoever had tried to keep the accounts had long since given up.

Chui, the pock-marked barman, was good at his job. He knew exactly what every one of his regulars drank, as did the young assistant steward, Kitaka. From the gossip of the domestic servants in the town, Chui knew the idiosyncrasies of every club member: whether *Bwana* Tonks needed a cool beer before his straight Vat 69, or whether Mrs Tonks wanted a pink gin or a Pimm's or a Bloody Mary before her whisky.

Nevertheless, there was something about Chui that aroused Billy's doubts. Perhaps it was the way he wouldn't give a straight answer or look him in the eye. Billy called him in to go over various items but Chui obviously hadn't a notion about keeping books of accounts. Kitaka had more nous but seemed nervous of annoying his senior. Nevertheless he was able to help locate things and explain the rudimentary system they'd been operating.

'How often do you check your stock against the takings?' Billy asked.

'Once a week,' Kitaka said.

'What do you do with the bar takings?'

'I count the money and put it in the safe, *bwana*,' Chui said, interrupting.

'Who takes the money to the bank?'

'I carry the cash to the Standard Bank every Thursday,' the old man answered.

Next Billy examined their practice of ordering drinks from the brewery and found that they ordered twenty crates of beer but returned only five crates of empties.

He calculated that the profit on a bottle of beer was about equivalent to the deposit on the empty bottle. So if the bottle was lost, the profit on the sale of the beer was nil.

For a solid week Billy spent his evenings checking everything in the bar, and by the end of the period was sure of one thing. Someone was helping himself on a grand scale. The club held regular rugby and cricket matches after which there was heavy drinking by the teams. Yet there was no profit shown. He inspected the optic measures on the necks of the spirit bottles. The mysterious someone had cleverly introduced a glass marble into each of the optics, which meant the measures were giving less than the full quota. He'd once heard old Tonks complain about his whisky.

'I'm bloody sure I'm not getting a full tot,' he'd whined. 'We're being rooked by those bloody crooked measures.'

If anyone ought to know when he was being given short measure, it had to be Tonks with his finely tuned taste buds.

Billy looked at the profits from the fruit machine, the so-called one-armed bandit, into which Len Ditchfield, the cigar-smoking man in the baggy shorts, poured a fortune every night. The returns weren't right. Not unless, that is, old Ditchfield was taking out more money than he was putting in, which was doubtful because the machine had been rigged to show a profit not a loss.

'Who has the key to the fruit machine?' Billy asked.

'Only *bwana mkubwa* Gilson,' Chui mumbled.

'Have you never had the key?'

'Never, *bwana*,' Chui replied. 'Only *Bwana* Gilson has it.'

But the man looked shifty-eyed and Billy didn't believe him.

Finally he looked at sundry general expenses: soap, towels, toilet paper and the like. These were reasonable but the electricity bill was astronomical.

'Do you switch off all lights during the day?'

'Of course, *bwana*,' said Chui. 'That would be a waste of electricity.'

'What about the immersion heater?'

'I never switch it on, *bwana*. I don't know how,' Chui replied, turning ashen.

Billy had heard that it was not unknown for African servants to sell hot water cheaply to peasants who would otherwise have to heat the water on a fire with all the consequent inconvenience and expense of finding firewood. After all, getting piping hot water by means of the white man's magic simply involved pressing a switch.

By the end of the week Billy had a gut feeling that something was seriously amiss here and that to put things right would require a major shake-up of the employees. It was his job to find out who was stealing and to do something about it.

He reported his suspicions to Sir Charles.

'Leave it to me, Hoppy,' he said. Narrowing his eyes and adopting a German accent, he said ominously: 'I have vays of making them talk.'

Mike had intimated to Billy that it was not unknown for Sir Charles to adopt unorthodox methods, and Billy had wondered what these might be.

Early the following Saturday, Sir Charles summoned the whole of the club staff, the barmen, the waiters, the cleaners, everyone, and ordered them to form a line outside the bar. He went along looking each person in the eye and demanding: 'Someone has been stealing from the club. Is it you?'

His question was met with a shake of the head and a frozen stare, a blank look with nothing behind the eyes, no expression near the mouth, nothing. Each servant shielded himself behind a wall no white man could penetrate.

'Very well,' Sir Charles said when he'd finished with the last man. 'We'll try a different tack.'

He turned in the direction of the club and called out in a loud voice, '*Mumbi, kuja sasa!*' (Mumbi, come now!) whereupon there appeared a white-haired old man dressed in a monkey-skin cloak and wearing a necklace of bushbuck horns, hanging from a rusty iron chain. Large blocks of wood hung from his pierced ear-lobes which stretched down to his shoulders. Supporting himself on a twisted knobstick with a carved ivory elephant head, he hobbled on to the scene. In his other hand he carried a charcoal iron which he had heated up on the kitchen stove. The waiting line of servants cringed when they saw him for they knew only too well the traditional witch-doctor device for rooting out a thief. The hot iron would be passed lightly over the tips of their tongues. The innocent would feel no pain but the sense of guilt would dry up the guilty one's mouth and his tongue would be singed.

A little moon-faced waiter named Chupa was the first victim. He felt nothing. The same with Kitaka who was second. No reaction. The witch-doctor had reached Chui and was about to apply the iron when Chui held up both hands. The colour had drained from his cheeks. With head bowed, he stepped forward and said, 'I am the man you are looking for, *bwana*. I am the thief.'

The rest of the waiting servants sighed with relief.

'But why, Chui?' Sir Charles asked. 'Why? You have a good job and you are well paid.'

'That may be so, *bwana*, but I am still a poor man. My two sons wish to obtain wives and for this they need many goats. It is for them that I took the money.'

'Because you have been a thief, Chui,' Sir Charles told him, 'there is now a curse on you which will mean bad luck for you and your family forever unless Mumbi here lifts it from your head. You must tell all and say how you robbed the club so that we can prevent it happening again.'

Chui didn't need any prompting.

'I took the money,' he said, 'by hiding the shillings in my hair or by throwing coins into the drip bucket underneath the bar counter. I collected them up and put them in my pocket when everyone had gone home.'

'And the fruit machine?' Billy asked. 'How did you open the machine?'

'I had a second key made in the *boma*, *bwana*.'

Chui made a full confession and explained in detail how he'd helped himself to the club takings. Sir Charles instructed the witch doctor to lift the curse, which Mumbi did by a series of incantations and by touching each of Chui's shoulders seven times with his knobstick, by draping beads over his neck and mumbling more hocus-pocus.

'The curse is now lifted,' he announced at last.

Sir Charles did not sack Chui but fined him a month's wages and demoted him to the position of cleaner.

'We now have a vacancy for a chief bartender to work alongside Kitaka,' he said. 'We need somebody who's honest and can keep accounts.'

'I think I know the man you're looking for,' Billy said. 'Not only is he honest, he can do basic book-keeping and is a general handyman as well.'

That was how Golden Boy, the odd-job man, became chief bartender. It was a perfect arrangement because it allowed Billy to make a fresh start at the Club with a new system.

While it would be wrong to say there was a dramatic change in the club's fortunes, over the following month there was a gradual improvement in its overall financial position. There were several rugby and cricket fixtures played, which produced handsome profits, and Billy knew that if these could be maintained over a long period, the club would prosper.

At last, he thought, after all the mini-disasters, it looks as if I'm going to get something right.

At school Roger Bedwell was replaced by a newcomer straight out from England. Phil Lovemore came out with his new wife, June, immediately after their wedding, thinking that a tour of duty in Kenya would be a kind of prolonged honeymoon. Major Blewitt brought them round to see Billy and asked him to show them the ropes as Mike and Jill had done for the Hopkins family. Billy was to encourage them and at the same time warn them of some of the dangers they might encounter. He remembered only too well the way Mike and Jill had put the wind up them in those early days and thought it only right and proper to give the couple the same kind of reassurance he and Laura had received.

'How do you find life out here?' Phil Lovemore asked.

'We're fairly new ourselves,' Billy replied, 'but we have found that life in this part of the world is wonderful. Could be *la dolce vita* all the way if it weren't for the little snags.'

'Snags? What snags?'

'Nothing to worry about as long as you're on the alert and take precautions. Take the spiders and the scorpions, for example. You'll have no trouble if you check your boots and shoes in the morning to make sure none have made their home in there during the night.'

Phil had turned a funny colour and so had his wife.

'If you go for a walk out of doors, watch out for safari ants and also puff adders. If you are bitten by a snake, you should know how to apply a tourniquet.'

'Oh, my God,' Phil exclaimed.

'Much worse, of course, is the spitting cobra. If one happens to land its venom in your eye, be ready to wash it out with water, milk or even urine, to prevent blindness.'

'Sounds awful,' Lovemore stammered. 'At least we'll have the holidays to look forward to. We're hoping to visit the game parks.'

'Fine,' Billy said, 'but don't go swimming in any rivers or you're likely to catch bilharzia. And watch out for crocodiles which can be mistaken for drifting logs. As for hippos, they're dangerous and unpredictable. And the best way to deal with leeches is to burn them off with a cigarette. If you smoke, that is.'

'Is there more?' Phil asked, nervously. 'Or is that the lot?'

'More or less the lot,' Billy replied, 'except for the *shenzi* dogs you may see around. Whatever you do, don't stroke them because nearly all of them have rabies. Keep taking your malarial pills and I'm sure you'll be all right.'

Phil and June must have decided to continue their honeymoon indoors in bed for neither hide nor hair was seen of them for a week.

Chapter Thirty-Nine

A couple of months after the witch-doctor episode, the kids were playing in the garden and Billy and Laura were having tea on the verandah, relaxing after a long and trying day at school and college. Billy was due at the club at six o'clock to supervise the staff and to see things were running smoothly there.

Life seems to be nothing but work, work, work, he reflected. He had fallen into a mindless routine and could see it stretching off into the distant future. He needed something new and exciting to happen but didn't quite know what.

As usual they were exchanging news about the day they'd had.

'I've been training the boys' choir all afternoon,' Billy said. 'We're entering them for the Kenya Music Festival next month.'

'That's good,' said Laura. 'The training college is putting in a women's choir.'

'Great, but have you seen the pieces we're supposed to sing? Some genius back in England has decreed that we shall perform a traditional song entitled "The English Ploughboy". It goes like this: "Come all ye jolly plough-boys, And listen to me. I'll sing you a song of the soil". I ask you! Fancy requiring Kenyan schoolboys to sing rubbish like that. I often feel that we're forcing our so-called English heritage down their African throats.'

'Same with us,' Laura replied. 'We've got to sing "Come, lasses and lads", all about "away to the maypole hie". As if African women students know all about dancing round maypoles. It would be so nice if the choir were required to sing some of their own native songs for a change.'

Billy poured himself another cup of tea and was about to reply when they were interrupted by Dublin.

'There's a young boy from Jimmy's Garage outside to see you, *bwana*.'

It was Spanners, Jimmy's 'gopher', who had earned his nick-name by being on hand whenever Jimmy, with his head stuck in a car engine, yelled for a particular tool, like a surgeon calling to a theatre nurse for a scalpel.

Billy wondered if Jimmy required yet more funds for the Daimler which had been on blocks for the past year. When he had taken the car in, it had been a grotty sight to behold, having suffered the ravages of an English winter, and a Manchester one at that. There had been a thick layer of grease and dirt on the depressingly dark blue bodywork and corrosion had eaten into every nook and cranny. When Billy had seen it in the bonded warehouse he had despaired of anything being done with such a rusty old banger. Not so Jimmy. He'd been brimming with confidence and optimism from the start.

'Give me a year and you won't recognise it. We'll spray it a beautiful off-white.'

Billy had given him a solemn promise he would not ask to see the car before it was ready and Jimmy had kept it tightly under wraps. Billy's sole function was to keep him supplied with a steady flow of money for parts, paint and other accessories. At times he had felt the project was not unlike the painting of the Forth Bridge or the building of Sydney Opera House as it slowly but surely drained him of any spare funds. The only thing that kept him going was the thought of the profit he was going to make at the end. The car had cost four hundred pounds secondhand in Manchester. Shipping it as part of his personal baggage allowance had been free. Jimmy's garage bill for refurbishment was estimated at three hundred. Total cost seven hundred pounds. Billy had checked prices and was sure he could get twelve hundred from some rich farmer, giving him a profit of five hundred. He was going to make a killing. Add this to his extra income as club manager and he thought he was on the pig's back. If they played their cards right, they'd even have enough saved to buy another house if and when they returned to dear old Manchester.

Billy put his cheque book in his inside pocket and drove Spanners to the garage where he was met by a beaming Jimmy.

'OK, Doctor Jimmy,' Billy sighed. 'How much this time?'

'This time,' he grinned, 'nothing. The Daimler's finished! It's ready! For many months my team and I have worked hard on this beautiful vehicle . . .'

Billy looked over to the car. It was still under a tarpaulin sheet.

'For this great day,' Jimmy said, 'there must be a ceremony.'

The other two mechanics cupped their fists and blew an imaginary fanfare. Jimmy took hold of one corner of the sheet and, holding it firmly in his right hand, announced, 'I name this car The Masterpiece.'

With a flourish like a conjuror executing a trick, he

whipped it off in one deft motion and cried aloud, 'Abracadabra!'

Billy couldn't believe his eyes. Jimmy was right, it *was* a masterpiece. Before his eyes there stood a sparkling saloon, a millionaire's car.

'My God, Jimmy!' he exclaimed. 'I can't recognise it as the same car. How on earth did you do it?'

He laughed.

'Brains and elbow grease. Remember: I am the great Doctor Jimmy, MBSKLZ, I don't know how you say it . . .'

'It's like a new car in a showroom,' Billy said. 'Even the windscreen wipers are shining.'

'Wait, wait,' he cried. 'Look inside at the engine.'

Jimmy opened the bonnet and every engine part was gleaming, including the carburettor and the air filter. The radiator was radiant. He hadn't missed a thing. Billy examined the interior and there was that luxurious smell of polished leather.

'This car,' Jimmy said, 'is not merely a pretty face. Listen to this.'

He turned the ignition key and there followed the roar of a mighty engine which changed immediately to a gentle purr.

'Now we must take her for a spin round the town,' he said. 'You drive.'

As they rode around the town, people stopped and stared, pointing admiringly to the car as they swept by. Billy felt like a king.

He drove Jimmy back to his garage and then it was time to take the car home. Crestfallen, Jimmy and his mechanics watched Billy go. As he turned the Daimler out of the garage, they gave him a sad wave of farewell as if reluctant to release it. After all, he was taking away their creation, their baby on which they had lavished so much loving care.

'You *will* look after it, please,' Jimmy called. 'And bring it back from time to time so we may look at it once more.'

As Billy entered the school grounds, staff and servants stood open-mouthed as the dazzling Daimler swept by. There were the same gasps of astonishment from Laura and the family, and from Mike and Jill when they set eyes on his glittering automobile.

'Is it ours, Dad?' Matthew and Lucy chorused.

'It is for a little while,' Laura answered, looking sidelong at Billy, 'until Daddy sells it, that is.'

She was anxious to dispel any notion that they would be keeping this expensive toy.

'I shall take you all for a ride,' he said, 'provided you have clean clothes and no muddy shoes or sticky fingers.'

'Does that include me, Hoppy?' Mike asked.

'Especially you.'

They were all suitably impressed by the car's performance as they circled the town. Billy basked in the admiration and praise of his fellow passengers.

'It's obviously too good for someone like you,' Mike remarked. 'A rich farmer will leap at the chance of a car like this.'

'Thanks, Mike. You sound just like my dad with all that stuff about not getting ideas above my station. I have to sell it anyway to cover Jimmy's garage bill.'

The truth was it was going to break his heart to let this wonderful piece of engineering go, but he had no choice. The following week he placed an ad in the *East African Standard*.

FOR SALE: Fine Daimler Conquest Saloon de luxe. 1954. Colour White. Radio and Heater. Spot lamps. Perfect Condition. Guaranteed in every way. £1275. Write to Hopkins, P.O. Box 39, Marangu.

Two days later he had his first reply, a farmer in the Njoro area asked him to phone and make an appointment so that he could view the car. From the school office Billy made the call though it took four attempts and much vigorous winding of the phone handle to get through.

'My name is Eric Jackson and if the car's everything you say it is,' a distant voice cried, 'you've got a sale. I'll definitely buy the car at twelve hundred seventy-five pounds and I'll bring a sterling bank draft for that amount. Take the car to the Staghorn Hotel, Nakuru, next Sunday between midday and one o'clock.'

And that was it. All his planning and scheming had paid off at last. Billy's heart leapt for joy. I've cracked it! I've done it! he said to himself. After all the set-backs, he'd finally made it. All the way back from the office, he sang, 'We're in the money. We're in the money!' something he hadn't done since he'd been a young boy making the odd copper or two by lighting fires and selling firewood to his Jewish neighbours in Cheetham Hill.

Nakuru was two hundred miles away which meant a four-hour drive through Nairobi and the Great Rift Valley via Naivasha and Gilgil. Mike agreed to go with him. He would go ahead in his Fiat and Billy would follow in the Daimler, then when the transaction was complete, Mike and he would drive back with the loot. Billy wondered what it would feel like to be rich, really rich.

The night before, he checked the car over. Water, oil, tyre pressures, brake fluid. He knew full well it was unnecessary for Jimmy had just serviced it but he was leaving nothing to chance.

On the Sunday morning Mike set off at eight o'clock and half an hour later Billy took to the road. It was glorious sunny weather, as usual, and he felt somehow that today was going to be a watershed, a turning point in his life. For once, he would be ahead of the game. The drive from Marangu to Nairobi was a joy even across the corrugated murram surface and the motor sang sweetly like a well-tuned Daimler should. After Nairobi, it was tarmac all the way and at 70 m.p.h. there was only a gentle murmur from the engine. How Billy blessed Doctor Jimmy and his mechanics for their skill and devotion to the car. Half an hour more and he was passing the little village of Kikuyu. As he turned the bend, he was met with what must be one of the most spectacular, the most wondrous sights in the universe – the great Rift Valley. The world seemed to be spread at his feet. He looked down on Mount Longonot and the valleys and the panoramic landscape beyond. What great cataclysmic force in the mists of time, he wondered, had cracked open the earth's crust and created this vast crater down the length of Africa? The scene took his breath away.

The road twisted and turned down to the Naivasha Plain and he slowed down to twenty miles an hour to negotiate the hair-pin bends. Halfway down, he parked outside the little chapel which the Italian prisoners-of-war had created to commemorate their building of the road. He got out and went inside the empty church to say a little prayer. He knew that St Matthew was best for finances and St Christopher for travelling, but which one should he call on? He took a chance and directed his entreaties to Christopher, asking him to look kindly on this little enterprise so that it would be successful and there would be no pitfalls to prevent him from returning home with the money in his pocket. He remembered, though, that they had been taught at school that it was wrong to pray for money or material things and hoped that St Chris would make an exception in his case.

He continued the descent into the valley at a gentle speed but when he reached the bottom, he could see a flat, endless ribbon of road leading right up to the horizon and on to the town of Naivasha. It was time to put the Daimler through its paces. He gunned the accelerator and felt a sudden surge of power, like an aeroplane taking off, as the engine picked up speed. In seconds he was doing ninety and felt a thrill of excitement as the speedometer needle passed the hundred mark. This really was a magnificent car and a tribute to the British and German engineers who had designed and built her. Within fifteen minutes, he was on the edge of the Naivasha township. Then it happened.

With his foot still on the accelerator he felt a sudden loss of power. The pedal was dead and there was no response when he pressed it. Panic-stricken, he tried again. Nothing. Of its own volition the car had slowed down to sixty, and there was smoke issuing from the bonnet. Bewildered, he looked around for some place to stop.

Come on, Saint Christopher, he prayed. Where are you when I need you?

His prayer was answered for a few hundred yards ahead he saw a sign for a garage, 'McDougall Motors: Repairs a Speciality'. He braked ever so gently, turned in and stopped at the petrol pump. McDougall came out of his office, wiping his hands on an oily rag.

'My God!' he exclaimed. 'What happened to you? Your engine's on fire!'

'I don't know,' Billy cried in dismay. 'The accelerator's dead under my foot; there's no power.'

His mouth had gone dry and he found difficulty in getting the words out.

'Open the bonnet!' McDougall commanded.

He did so. Clouds of smoke billowed from the engine.

'The bloody thing's a goner,' McDougall yelled. 'We'd better push it away from the petrol pumps. Engage neutral and come and push. I'll guide the car into the garage.'

Inside the building, he took a closer look.

'I'll have to wait till it's cooled down,' he said, 'but I'd say that your engine is burned out.'

'You mean, ruined?' Billy couldn't take it in.

'*Kaputt*!' he said. 'Or to put it in plain English, buggered.'

In the face of this catastrophe, there was only one thing to do. Stay calm and find a cup of tea. Billy had to get a message to Mike who was well on his way to Nakuru by now. An hour later, he got through to the Staghorn Hotel and spoke to his friend who had that moment walked through the door. He was as shocked as Billy at the news and passed him over to Eric Jackson who'd been waiting with his bank draft.

'Sorry to hear about the mishap,' Jackson said. 'It's probably minor trouble with the ignition. If you manage to fix it, I'm still interested.'

By the time Mike got to Naivasha, the Daimler had cooled down and McDougall was able to assess the damage.

'I think the trouble was a fractured hose pipe. The car lost its water and the engine simply melted. It will need a complete re-bore.'

'Can you do it?' Billy asked.

'Sorry. We don't have the facilities for such a big job. You'll have to take it to Nairobi.'

On the way back to Marangu, Billy was as near to tears as he'd been as a kid when he'd found there was no Father Christmas. All his dreams had turned to ashes, literally.

'No use crying over spilt milk,' Mike said in a forlorn effort to cheer him up. 'These things happen. It was bad luck.'

'Maybe. I think I prayed to the wrong saint. Should have spoken to St Matthew, not Christopher. This wasn't about travel, it was about money.'

In Marangu, everyone offered sympathy. Laura and the kids went about with long mournful faces. In the club, the Tonkses had to have another scotch when they heard about the calamity. As for Doctor Jimmy and his team, they were as distraught as if they'd learned of the death of a close friend.

'It's not our fault,' Jimmy wailed. 'We replaced everything. Everything. Carburettor, tyres, tappets, air filter, plugs – everything! One rubber hose must have perished because of standing so long in the garage. One bloody rubber hose costing a couple of shillings.'

There was nothing for it but to arrange to have the car towed from Naivasha into Nairobi. Sid Appel's, the firm that agreed to take on the job, were no ordinary, common or garden mechanics. No, indeed. They were far grander and more prestigious. Described themselves as automotive engineers, no less.

Billy heard nothing more for a fortnight. During that time, his family and he, together with Doctor Jimmy and his team, went around as if bereaved. All their hopes had come to nought and even a letter from Sid Appel inviting Billy to attend his engineering works in Nairobi did nothing to dispel the gloom. On the contrary, it filled him with foreboding about what the engineers might report. Laura left the kids with the ayah and went to keep him company and lend moral support when they gave him the bad news.

The engineering works was a barn-like building filled with cars and vans of every size and shape and in every state of disrepair. Many had been involved in horrendous road accidents and seemed beyond hope while others were in the process of being rebuilt or reassembled. In one quiet corner of the building stood the Daimler gathering dust.

Sid Appel ushered them into his office away from the drilling and the hammering, where he offered them seats in front of his desk.

'Well, what's the prognosis?' Billy asked nervously. 'Can it be fixed?'

'Oh, yes, it can be fixed all right.'

'I suppose it will require many spare parts?'

'That's putting it mildly,' said the engineer, grimacing as if in pain. 'First, do you have a pen and a piece of paper? A very large piece of paper?'

'I do,' Billy said, holding out his clipboard, pen at the ready.

'Good. These are the spares you need.'

He reeled off the list of parts he wanted in order to restore the Daimler to life. The list may as well have been in Greek or Persian for all Billy understood of it.

'Six piston cylinders, twelve piston rings (two thou' oversize), six conrods, six gudgeon pins, camshaft followers, valve rocker arms . . .'

The list went on and on until he had filled three foolscap sheets. What on earth were rocker arms and gudgeon pins?

'I should warn you,' Appel said, 'that hardly any of these spares are available in Kenya. You will have to get a friend or an agent in the UK to buy them. Meanwhile, the car can stay here until you come up with the parts. I'd be surprised, however, if you're successful.'

When they came away from this meeting, Billy's head was spinning. Where and how in God's name was he to get hold of these spares? Who in Manchester could help? Laura's father? Duncan was a very busy man and the task would probably be beyond him. Billy's own father or his brother Les? Neither of them would have a clue how to go about it. As he drove back to Marangu he gradually whittled the possibilities down until only one name remained. Titch!

That evening, he wrote a long letter reminding his friend of how they had been close for many years and how Billy had always admired him. Titch had always been a hero in his eyes because of his intelligence, his good looks, and his reliability. In the PS, he added his request as a 'by the way', enclosing a cheque so that Titch could make a start in collecting all the bits and pieces required.

A fortnight later, Billy had his reply telling him how Titch had always considered him a twerp who never thought things through. However, he'd made inquiries at the Daimler agent, Drabble & Allen on Wilmslow Road in Manchester, and they were able to supply about fifty per cent of the list but to get the rest he'd have to scour the country, so it would take some time to assemble the things.

And that was how Billy had to leave it though Laura did suggest that it might be best to cut his losses, write the car off and sell it for scrap metal. Billy couldn't do that because to him the car was like an old friend. He thought of it mouldering in that big garage in Nairobi and felt he had a personal responsibility to see it got back on the road where it belonged.

Chapter Forty

After the fiasco with the Daimler, Billy was down in the dumps with a touch of Winston Churchill's Black Dog. Nothing seemed to have gone right. First a wild animal had wiped out most of his rabbitry, and then the sale of the car on which he had pinned so many hopes had ended in disaster. There seemed nothing to look forward to. Whichever way he turned, things went wrong. He felt like Charlie Chaplin in *Modern Times*. No matter how he tried, things didn't work out.

Then, out of the blue, he had a letter from Geoff Moulton, the bluff character who had been appointed to a headship at the coast.

> Dear Billy,
>
> You may remember I spoke to you about the possibility of coming down here to help me out with accounts, which I must confess have never been my strong point. If you would like to visit with your family during the holidays, I can offer you the use of a house belonging to one of my teachers who will be away for a few weeks. If you are free, I can offer you travelling expenses as I don't see why the school shouldn't pay for 'a financial consultant'.

Let me know in good time and I can meet your train at Mombasa railway station.

Best wishes to you and all my old colleagues,

Geoff Moulton.

His accounting skills, thanks to Duncan's thorough training, had certainly served Billy in good stead. Accountancy seemed to be one of those subjects, like mathematics, which filled many people with trepidation, as if a shutter came down in their heads at the very mention of the word.

He replied right away, saying that they'd be glad to visit and, if he could be of service in helping to sort out the school books, he should be happy to do so. It offered his family a free holiday in a millionaire's playground.

'That's the one thing I miss most,' Laura remarked. 'The sea. It's said it's not possible to live anywhere in Britain and be more than fifty miles from the sea.'

'That comes from being an island people,' Billy added. 'Here we're about two hundred miles from the coast and I suppose we feel it.'

For the next few weeks there was great excitement as they prepared for the trip.

'Shall we need buckets and spades?' Lucy asked. 'And is there a tower like at Blackpool?'

'Not quite,' they answered.

'Donkeys and Blackpool rock?'

'None.'

'What about the pleasure beach?' Matthew inquired.

'Sorry,' they replied. 'And there's no Golden Mile either, but there's the Indian Ocean and miles and miles of silver sand.'

Billy said nothing about the giant jellyfish and the Portuguese men-o'-war.

It was arranged that Laura and the two young ones, Mark and John, would go by overnight train from Athi River to Mombasa while Billy would follow the next day in the car with Matthew and Lucy. When Sir Charles and Lady Gilson heard about their plans, they asked if Laura would chaperone their two teenage daughters who would be travelling on the same train to stay with an aunt at Malindi. No problem, they said. The more points I can earn with Sir Charles, Billy thought, the better my career prospects.

On the appointed day, Laura and Billy plus the four children drove the twenty-five miles to the country station at Athi River, not far from the Kenya Meat Commission. Lady Gilson arrived a little later with her two daughters in a spanking new Ford Consul (the coffee crop that year had been particularly good) and parked next to them right up against the platform.

They piled out with their luggage and waited for the train which was due at 7 p.m. as dusk was descending. Billy looked around the deserted platform for a porter to help with the baggage but there was none. Precisely on time, the giant locomotive rolled into the station, and coaches bearing the words EAST AFRICAN RAILWAYS stopped right in front of them.

Laura went aboard first, holding Mark by the hand and carrying baby John in her arms.

'Come on, kids, hurry!' Billy called. 'Help put the luggage on to the train.'

He picked up the big suitcase and carried it into the reserved compartment followed by the two younger children each carrying a hold-all containing the things Laura would need on the journey. He hoisted the large case up on to the luggage rack and pushed the hold-alls under the seats where they would be readily available. The two Gilson girls were on board by this time with their own luggage and were settling into their seats.

'Don't hang about, kids,' Billy warned. 'Say goodbye to Mum and let's go.'

He gave Laura a quick kiss on the cheek and said, 'See you tomorrow in Mombasa. Have a nice journey!'

He turned to go but found to his horror that the train was already moving and picking up speed!

'Oh, my God!' he yelled. 'We're on our way to Mombasa!'

He looked back out of the window and saw a panic-stricken Lady Gilson waving frantically. There was nothing anyone could do as the train carried them further and further away from Athi River.

Billy rushed down the corridor to find the conductor. The middle-aged Asian man was checking tickets in one of the compartments at the front.

'You must stop the train,' Billy cried. 'At once!'

'Why must I? What is wrong?' the conductor said uncomprehendingly.

'The train set off before I could get off with my children. For God's sake, hurry, man or we'll never get back to Athi River.'

The conductor spluttered, jerking both arms spasmodically.

'But you cannot stop the train like that. It is an offence. Where is your ticket?' he burst forth.

Billy was beside himself with anxiety. 'There's no time to argue, man! Stop the train and let us off! Now!'

'It is most irregular,' the guard protested. 'This is a most serious affair. You will be fined heavily or you could go to prison! I must have your name and address.'

Billy gave his particulars and he entered them, oh, so slowly and laboriously, into his notebook after which he reluctantly reached up to the communication cord and pulled. Judging by the way he was trembling it was the first time he'd ever done it.

The huge train came to a juddering halt in the middle of the African bush just beyond the Kenya Meat Commission.

The conductor opened a door with his special key and ushered them out into the night.

'You must never board a train without a ticket,' he ranted. 'Now, please, get off my train!'

They were high above the track and so Billy clambered off first in order to lift Matthew and Lucy down while Laura and the Gilson girls gazed anxiously from their compartment window. The bush and scrub all around them were brightly illuminated by the lights of the train which hissed and snorted like a great monster angry at being stopped and impatient to be on its way. The conductor slammed the door shut behind them, the train moved off, and they were left alone in the middle of the dark continent. They could see the lights of cars on the road far off to their right but ahead was nothing but blackness.

'Didn't Mr Blewitt say there were lions around here, Dad?' Matthew asked nervously. Trust him to remember.

'I'm not sure,' Billy stalled.

'He said that lions were attracted by the smell of the meat from the Meat Commission,' his son persisted.

'I don't remember,' Billy lied.

He took their hands and pushed on towards Athi River. He was scared out of his wits but had to put on a brave face for the sake of the kids.

'Let's pretend we're having a game of Tarzan and the Apes,' he suggested.

'Bags being Tarzan,' Matthew said, perking up.

'And I'm Jane,' Lucy said.

'Right,' Billy said, 'that leaves me as Pongo, the friendly gorilla.'

It was a gruelling journey back. They scrambled through thick bush, thorn and brambles, and sloshed through mud and pools of water. After a few hundred yards, they thought they heard rustling in the undergrowth.

'Everybody freeze. Don't move a muscle,' Billy whispered, expecting at any moment to be pounced on by a hungry lion. 'Maybe it's the baddies, the wicked white hunters, trying to catch us.'

They remained perfectly still, hardly daring to breathe, and whatever it was they had heard passed on.

'They've gone,' Matthew said.

They stumbled on through the thorn bush, their arms and legs scratched to pieces, their feet soaked through.

'Jane is tired, Dad. Would Pongo the gorilla carry her now?'

Billy hoisted her on to his shoulder and, taking a firm grip on Matthew's hand, fought a way through the thick undergrowth until, sweet relief, they burst into a clearing on the edge of Athi River. A few hundred yards more and they tottered, bone-weary and caked in mud, into the deserted railway station.

It was good to see that the car was still there, exactly where he'd left it, right up against the platform. He'd left the keys in the ignition and so they'd soon be on their way.

'Come on, kids, cheer up,' he said, 'I'll have you home in a jiffy.'

It was not to be. Lady Gilson had locked his car and taken the keys. Understandably. For when she saw what had happened, it had seemed the right thing to do. Now Billy was left with the problem of how to get back to Marangu. It was nine o'clock, late for a little place like Athi River, but there was nothing for it but to stagger the couple of miles into the village where there was sure to be a garage of some kind.

'My legs are wobbly,' Matthew said. 'Can't we sit down for a rest?'

'Come on, Tarzan, not long now,' Billy said. 'Almost there.'

They limped along the main street till they reached the petrol station where they found a Sikh mechanic whom they begged to come and help.

'No problem, *sahib*,' he said, producing an enormous bunch of keys. 'You're not the first customer to lose his keys. Let's go.'

He drove them in his pick-up truck back to the station and soon had the car door open. He started the engine by shorting two wires and they were back in business. With a Sikh like that, Billy thought, who needs the RAC?

After their adventures the children were exhausted when they set off on the journey back to Marangu but they had to go to the club first to find out what had been happening. Bedraggled and muddy, they staggered into the bar where they found Lady Gilson sitting on a high stool nursing a brandy and soda.

'What in God's name happened?' she exclaimed. 'How did you get off the train? I've sent Sir Charles haring across in the Bentley to catch it at Konza, the next station! Heaven knows what he'll do when he finds you're not on it!'

Nearly all Billy's dealings with Sir Charles seemed to have gone wrong somehow. There was nothing he could do, however. Sir Charles would find out they were not on the train and would no doubt come back to the club in the end.

'Have a whisky, Hoppy!' Old Tonks called from the other side of the bar. 'You look as if you've been dragged through the *bundu*.'

'Thanks,' he said, 'but some other time. Now I have to get these children back home to bed. We have an early start for Mombasa tomorrow.'

Next morning, they were up bright and early despite the harrowing adventures of the night before. They had packed their trunk and, with a full tank of petrol, were ready for an early start on the long journey to the coast. As Billy made his final checks, the kids waited impatiently in the back of the car with Brandy and it was hard to say who was the more excited, them or the dog. Dublin and Twiga came to help load the car and wave them off. Both servants were in a happy mood for they too were due for a break. When they'd finished cleaning up and securing the property, they planned to make full use of the holiday by visiting their home villages. The house and the compound surrounding them would be almost deserted for three weeks because Mike and Jill were taking their children on holiday to Tanganyika for their first view of Kilimanjaro. Makau, who had a girlfriend in Marangu, had opted to stay around to keep a weather eye on things.

'Make sure you lock everything, Dublin, especially the windows,' Billy said as he turned the ignition key. 'And don't forget to stand the legs of the beds in tins of water to keep the safari ants at bay. And leave the keys with Makau.'

'Don't worry, *bwana*. I'll see to it.'

Billy glanced at his watch as they left. It was 6 a.m. Within an hour, they reached the main Mombasa highway and for the first part of the journey passed through mud and wattle villages, Ulu, Konza, Sultan Hamud, where the roadside were lined with smiling Africans hawking their fruit and vegetables. Sometimes they tried to stop cars by standing in the middle of the road holding up their mangoes and bananas and only moving out of the way at the last second.

In a swirl of red dust they left the other villages behind, Simba, Kiboko, Kibwezi, until they reached the edge of the Tsavo National Park at Mtito Andei. This was Africa at its rawest, not merely because of the wild animals but also because of the washboard road that rattled and pitched the car around, covering everything in a layer of red dust and gravel. Billy found himself struggling to keep control as the steering wheel shuddered in his grasp, and whenever a 'banana express' bus belching black smoke appeared on the horizon, he acted on the notion that discretion is the better part of valour by pulling over to let the juggernaut through. Invariably overladen and piled high with everything from bicycles to livestock, and with their shock absorbers and suspension long since gone, they roared along the road diagonally like monster crabs.

A few miles further on, they passed a derelict building which bore the name 'Maneaters' Motel'.

'Why is it called Maneaters'?' Matthew asked.

'This is the place where two lions ate the men building the railway line many years ago.'

'How many men, Dad?' Matthew wanted to know the macabre details.

'I believe there were nearly thirty Indian labourers and a couple of Europeans.'

'Have the lions gone now, Dad?' Lucy asked fearfully.

Billy laughed. 'Oh, yes, they've been gone a long time now.'

They had only two hold-ups along the route through the Tsavo Park. The first was when a rhino chose the vegetation by the roadside to do its grazing and no one in the three-car line up was willing to take the chance of overtaking it in case it suddenly decided to charge.

The other was when they reached Voi, the place of the elephants, and a large herd claimed right of way by monopolising the highway. There was no alternative but to wait until the road was clear. Billy kept the engine running in case they needed a quick getaway.

It was then that Matthew announced, 'Dad, I need to do a wee.'

'And so do I,' Lucy piped up.

'Oh, for God's sake,' Billy exclaimed. 'What a time to pick! Well, you can't. We're in the middle of Tsavo! There are wild elephants about! You'll have to wait.'

'I can't, Dad. I'm dying,' Matthew wailed.

'Too bad. Cross your legs 'cos you can't get out of the car.'

'I'm going to wet my pants.'

'Better a son with wet pants than one squashed by an elephant. You should have gone when we were back there in Mtito Andei.'

'Didn't need to then,' Lucy whined.

'Well, you'll have to wait till we reach Mariakani.'

'How far, Dad?' Matthew asked.

'About twenty-five miles.'

'I can't wait that long, Dad,' Lucy moaned.

'You've no choice.'

The elephants ambled off into the bush to look for better pasture and Billy was about to engage gear and move off when he noticed that the needle of the temperature gauge had moved into the red and steam was coming from under the bonnet.

'Oh, hell!' he cursed. 'Not again! This is getting monotonous. Surely not another split hose like the Daimler!'

Looking warily around for any other wild beasts in the vicinity, he got out of the car, opened the bonnet and unscrewed the radiator cap. A cloud of steam hissed out nearly scalding him. At least it wasn't a fractured hose. It's all this standing about in the hot sun, he thought. We'll have to wait until the engine has cooled down before I pour cold water in. Wait a minute . . . Cold water. I don't have any!

When he'd packed the car the day before, he'd planned so carefully and was sure he'd covered everything but the one item he'd overlooked meant they were now stuck in the middle of Tsavo. What to do? They could wait for a passing motorist but these were few and far between and there was no guarantee anyone would stop as there had been one or two robberies along that road.

They waited inside the car for a while and then the idea struck him.

'Still want to pee, kids?'

'Oh, yes, Dad. Plea-ea-se!' they chorused.

'Is there a bottle of milk in the cool box?'

'Yes, Dad.'

'Pass it to me.'

He got out of the car and slowly poured the milk into the bubbling radiator.

'Now you can each do a wee in the empty milk bottle.'

They got out on each side of the car. Even now, they were concerned about modesty and wouldn't do it in each other's presence. Billy added their wee to the radiator, and for good measure his own.

Brandy also felt the need to join them and Billy had to hold him on the leash in case he took it into his head to start a scrap with an inquisitive baboon or rhino. Unfortunately Billy couldn't catch the dog's urine to make use of it. He glanced nervously about, expecting a mad bull elephant to come tearing out of the bush at any moment. A rare event but one never knew.

Slowly and warily, they resumed their journey. The engine remained cool. An hour later they coasted into the little town of Mariakani where they stopped for petrol. Billy opened the radiator to replenish the coolant with fresh water and his nostrils were treated to the delicious smell of something resembling roasted coffee coming from the radiator. God works in strange ways, he thought.

'Mariakani sounds like the word "American",' Matthew observed. 'Why's it called Mariakani, Dad?'

These kids of mine, he said to himself, think I know everything. Little do they realise that what I don't know, I make up.

'Mariakani,' he said, 'is the name of an American calico fabric which some American missionary brought to this place when they were first building the railway.'

'Sounds dead boring, Dad,' Lucy said.

'I think the real story is too naughty for your young ears.'

'Come on, Dad,' they said in unison, 'you've got to tell us now.'

Billy had his doubts about the tale even though it had been Sir Charles himself who had told it.

'Early in this century,' he said, 'a lady missionary from the United States arrived in the country and was on her way to take up duties up-country, in a place like Marangu. As the train was going through the district where we are now, she was horrified to see the native women walking about stark naked.'

'You mean, like the women we just passed?' Matthew said.

'Exactly like them.'

'This woman was so upset, she got off the train and bought hundreds of yards of calico at the *duka* so that the women could cover themselves up. She got back on the train and went on her journey. Four years later when she had finished her tour of duty, she was on her way back to Mombasa, and as she passed through the village she looked again at the same people from the window of the train. What do you think she found?'

'Don't know, Dad,' Lucy said.

'All the women were still as naked as ever but now they were wearing the calico cloth on their head as hats. From that time on, the village was called Mariakani after the poor American lady.'

'Is it true, Dad?' Matthew asked.

'I don't understand it,' Lucy said. 'What's wrong with putting the stuff on their heads?'

'I'll tell you later,' said Matthew, aged nine.

After Mariakani, they reached the outskirts of Mombasa and thrilled at the sight of the first palm trees. There was something inexpressibly exciting about the atmosphere of the place. Perhaps it was the hustle and bustle of the polyglot population of Africans, Europeans, Indians, Swahilis and Arabs. Maybe it was the distinctive smell of peppers, spices and coffee blended together. Or was it the frangipani, the dried fish, the tang of the sea, or simply the smell of Africa? And the heat that enveloped them was of a kind they had never met before; it was nothing like the gentle heat of an English summer or even that of a Mediterranean heat wave. This heat was fierce and unrelenting and had them in a sticky sweat from the moment it embraced them.

It wasn't long before Billy found the coastal route out to the school and was soon driving along a beautiful tarmac road which ran alongside the blue Indian Ocean and miles and miles of deserted silver sand. It was 5.30 when they finally drove into the school compound; it had been a long drive and they had been on the road over eleven hours. Laura and the two young children were already there, sitting cool and refreshed, having tea with the Moultons on the verandah. Joyfully the others joined them. A little later they walked over to the house which was to be theirs for the next three weeks. It was the start of the holiday of a lifetime.

Next morning Geoff took Billy to his office to take a look at the school finances. Geoff had become neurotic about his account books since the last headmaster, Percy Allsop, had been sacked for misappropriation of funds. He hadn't stolen cash but had used government money for the wrong purposes. Geoff described graphically how late one night, and by the light of a full moon, Percy Allsop had organised a group of African clerks to carry the ledgers on their heads out to Mtwapa Creek where they had ceremoniously dumped them.

'I am a headmaster,' said Geoff, throwing the ledgers down on his desk, 'not a bloody accountant. The trouble is, the government gives us a cheque for the total grant, we collect thousands of shillings in school fees and have to account for every penny. It's all there in the safe, every last cent. I've been afraid to spend anything in case I get it wrong.'

Billy checked the accounts and could see immediately that Geoff had been having a struggle for he had given up the ghost four months back and abandoned any further efforts. He could see too that he himself was going to have to earn this holiday.

'Let's go into Mombasa,' Billy said, 'and buy a new set of books. We'll start from scratch.'

That was how he came to spend the mornings of their stay rewriting the school account books.

But not the afternoons.

After a leisurely lunch of mango, pawpaw, avocado and freshly caught fish, everyone took long naps and then it was down to the beach with all the family, including the dog, and the Moultons to bask in the clear azure waters of the Indian Ocean and ride the breakers at Shanzu beach. They had to be constantly on the alert, though, for some of the dangers that were to be found in that part of the world, like the undertow which could drag a person out to sea, and the possibility, though remote, of sharks. Occasionally they saw jelly-fish and Portuguese men-o'-war floating on the surface but were careful to avoid them. After swimming they sat on the sand in the sun, listening to the breezes rattling the palm fronds, watching the sand crabs and betting on which one would be the last to scurry back into the sea. Afterwards they retired to the hotel bar and nothing, but nothing, had ever tasted so wonderful as those cold drinks, Fanta for the children and lager for the adults, after swallowing so much salt water. The bar itself was right next to the beach and so close to the sea that spume from the waves sprayed on to the windows.

Soon the whole family had developed golden tans in the wind and tropical sun; Billy had never seen them looking so healthy. They went into Mombasa, toured the bazaars and haggled with an Arab over a rug, and explored the ninth-century Fort Jesus which had once been visited by Vasco da Gama.

To complete the picture, Laura and Billy celebrated their ninth wedding anniversary with a candlelit dinner on the terrace of the Nyali Beach Hotel to the sound of a tinkling piano, and against a background of waving palms and a tropical moon.

It was a holiday they never wanted to end. But of course it did. After three weeks it was time to go back. Laura took the slow train with the young ones and Billy drove the rest of the family. The road back followed the railway line closely and for most of the way he kept level with the train until they reached Athi River around 6 p.m. From there it was a mere forty minutes' drive home.

It was turning dark when they finally pulled up outside the house. Their own servants were still on holiday and so it was Mike's houseboy Makau who came over with the house keys.

'Welcome home, *bwana*,' he said with a big smile. 'I hope you had a good holiday at Mombasa. Here, everyone's still away. I don't expect *bwana* Sherwood and *memsahib* home until next week.'

'*Asanta sana, Makau*.' (Thank you very much, Makau.)

Laura heaved a sigh of relief as they stepped out of the car.

'Gosh, it's great to be home,' she sighed. 'After that hectic journey, it'll be so good to get inside and relax with a cup of tea. Though Dublin's not back, I reckon I can still remember how to make a pot.'

'Tea will go down well, Laura.'

Billy inserted the key into the lock and opened the door to the kitchen. They were not prepared for the sight which met their eyes.

'Oh, my God!' Billy exclaimed. 'We've been invaded. There must be billions of 'em. Correction – trillions of 'em.'

The kitchen was one black mass of safari ants. They were everywhere. Lines of them ran along the walls, over the cooker, across the fridge. The floor was a thick black carpet of writhing insects, like a lake of molten tar. The lounge was the same. The *siafu* ran along the ceiling, down the curtains, across the chairs and over the settee. In all their experiences in Africa, they had never seen a sight like this.

'Quick,' Billy said to Makau who was standing by. 'Bring your garden hose and connect it. It's the only way we'll get rid of them. Somewhere under the house is the queen, we'll have to get the Works Department to find her tomorrow. Meanwhile, let's get to work.'

Turning to Lucy, he said, 'Take Mark and John into the spare bedroom and stay in there until we call you.'

Lucy sensed the urgency. 'Yes, Dad.' No need to warn her about what ants could do.

'Laura, Matthew!' Billy cried. 'Fetch buckets of water! There's no time to lose.'

For two hours they worked, frantically hosing down the floors, the walls, the curtains, the furniture – as if the place was on fire – leaving everything soaking wet. At last, the battle was over and the safari ants were defeated and swept out of doors.

Laura picked up a toad on the veranda. The creature was a helpless, squirming ball of ants devouring it from outside in. She held it under the cold water tap and painstakingly picked off the carnivorous insects one by one until the toad was clear after which she released it into the garden far away from the *siafu*.

'That was like something out of H.G. Wells's science fiction,' she said. 'I thought we were losing the war at one point. Oh, Billy, I'm so relieved to see them gone.'

'And so am I,' he said. 'Now what were you saying earlier about a cup of tea?'

'May we come out now?' a little voice inquired plaintively. It was Lucy with the two young ones who had stayed out of the way.

'Yes, you can come out now. The ants have gone.'

'Dad, what are ants for?' she asked. 'Why did God make them?'

'I wish I knew,' he said with a rueful smile.

As the family sat drinking tea on the dripping wet furniture, Laura remarked, 'It's been a funny old time lately.'

'You mean, the battle with the ants?'

'Not just that. We've had the best holiday of our lives sandwiched between two nightmares, starting with the Athi River mix-up and finishing with the war of the worlds.'

After tea, they were busy mopping up when Makau came over with their mail which he had been collecting during their absence. There were the usual circulars, and a couple of letters postmarked Manchester which at that moment seemed very far away. There was one official-looking letter from Nairobi, addressed to Billy.

'Hullo, what's this?' he said, tearing it open.

It was from the East African Railways and Harbours Administration and it read:

Dear Sir,
It has been reported to us by one of our conductors that you did illegally board the Nairobi–Mombasa train without a ticket and it was necessary for the train to operate the emergency brake and make an unscheduled stop between Athi River and Konza. This is a most serious offence and, while we do not intend to take action on this occasion, we must give you due warning that if this occurs again, you will be prosecuted and may be fined or sent to prison.
I remain, sir,
Your obedient servant,
On behalf of the EARH Administration,
Mital G. Shah, Senior Security Officer

After all that had happened to them, they had no alternative but to put down the mops and brushes and laugh till the tears rolled down their cheeks.

Chapter Forty-One

When Billy returned to school after the holiday he found Sir Charles Gilson had honoured his promises by pulling a few strings to win him additional free periods, mainly from junior classes, so that he could devote more time to managing the country club.

The honorarium attached to the job was generous and a great boost to their family savings. Every month Billy sent £50 winging its way to their bank account in Manchester.

It sounded good but the salary had to be earned and Billy worked hard for it. Managing the club involved being present every evening to see to the smooth running of the place. He was usually first to arrive and last to leave.

As soon as school finished in the afternoon, he rushed home to snatch a quick meal before making a bee line for the club. Most evenings he managed to fit in a game of tennis or squash followed by a quick shower and change of clothes before supervising the staff and the evening activities. The first task was to check the bar stock to make sure it was sufficient to meet demand. Once or twice members had been up in arms when their favourite cigarettes had not been available which meant sending Kitaka out to the local *dukas* for emergency supplies.

Billy learned to anticipate the needs of particular sporting fixtures. Rugby matches meant not only raucous shouting, bawdy jokes and noisy horseplay, but the need for immense quantities of Tusker lager to slake the thirst of big beefy players. Cricket celebrations, on the other hand, were more sedate and associated with genteel behaviour and a demand for spirits, especially gin and whisky.

In his role as manager, he was expected to play the part of mine host and to be convivial at all times to all comers. After all, he had been given a special 'entertainment' allowance to cover this. He found he was drinking more than he had ever done in his life. What's more, he was developing a taste for it.

Being the focal point for the region, the club always had some 'shindig' taking place, especially at weekends when there might be Scottish dancing, a fancy dress competition, tombola, a beetle drive or film show. Occasionally the more adventurous types would organise a scavenger hunt when members would throw their car keys into the ring and drive off with somebody else's spouse to seek out a variety of miscellaneous articles, like an alarm clock, a pair of long johns, a thimble and a pot of Gentleman's Relish. At least, that was the pretext. Some took the event seriously and were soon back with the required items and such couples would be awarded prizes for their tenacity. On the other hand, a number of other competitors were slow to return and few, if any, of this dilatory group succeeded in locating any of the specified objects. It must be said, though, it couldn't have been for want of trying because, judging by their dishevelled appearance when they got back, they'd obviously put a great deal of effort into the search.

Throughout these activities, Golden Boy was true to his name. Not only did he prove to be an intelligent and indefatigable worker, his honesty was exemplary. One day, he turned up at Billy's house, looking guilty, with a big bag of money in his hand.

'What's all this about, Golden Boy? Why are you here?' Billy asked.

'I have done a bad thing, *bwana*. I know that servants of the club are not allowed to play the fruit machine but I put a shilling in the slot. I was hoping I might win five shillings but when I pulled the arm, I won the jackpot. There are over two thousand shillings here, *bwana*, I have not touched any of it. Please forgive me and let me keep my job.'

'Of course, you may keep your job, Golden Boy. Tell me, was it your own shilling you put in?'

'Oh, yes, *bwana*. It was my own shilling.'

'In that case, there's no harm done. We shall put the money back and no one will be any the wiser. Here's ten shillings for you since you played with your own money but you must not tell anyone about this or we'll both be in trouble.'

Billy's efforts gradually began to pay off. As the money rolled in, the club started to prosper. So much so that Sir Charles negotiated a loan with the Standard Bank to prepare a programme of improvements. It wasn't long before the place took on a smart new look. A roof was installed on the squash court, the outside of the building was cleaned and repainted, and the bar refurbished. Sir Charles was all smiles and in the bar Billy was fêted and slapped on the back. He was a big success in the club. Not so at home.

'We never see you nowadays,' Laura complained bitterly. 'The children scarcely know whether they have a father any more, they're wondering who that strange man is they see at breakfast.'

'It's not as bad as that, Laura.'

'It's worse, Billy. Every spare moment you're out at the damned club! Night after night, I'm left here listening to the grotty programmes on the Kenya Broadcasting Service.'

'Why don't you come down to the club with me then? You can leave the kids with the ayah.'

'As you well know, I am not one of your socialite wives, a club-goer. The occasional visit for a dance or social activity is enough for me. You should be the same.'

'If I'm to run the club successfully, Laura, I have to be there. There are a thousand things I have to attend to.'

'Like what?'

'I have to welcome new members, counter-sign chits for cash, give receipts when members pay me their subs, see to the bar stock. I'm run off my feet. Besides, I'm not out every night. I'm here on Mondays when the club is quiet.'

'Oh, yes, you're here on Mondays – but you spend all your time in that damned office of yours.'

'Can't be helped. I have to write up the accounts and send out bills. Monday night is the only chance I get.'

'And another thing, I've noticed you're drinking more. If you're not careful, you'll become a lush like Reggie Tonks. As far as I can see, it's one long binge at that club.'

'Nonsense! I can control my drinking. Don't forget, we're saving almost fifty pounds a month from this "one long binge", as you call it.'

'It's not worth fifty pounds a month if our marriage ends up on the rocks.'

'What do you mean "on the rocks"? Our marriage is as solid as the Bank of England.'

Laura began to weep quietly.

'Your behaviour, Billy, is rocking its foundation. Money isn't that important.'

He was deeply disturbed to see her so upset. He hadn't been aware that things were sliding downhill.

'OK, Laura, I'll try to cut down on my drinking.'

'At least stop drinking spirits and stick to one or two beers.'

'I promise you it's beer only from now on, but I don't see how I can avoid being present at the club if I'm to be its manager. Try to see the broader picture. We're saving money which one day will help buy us a home in England.'

Laura's words about his drinking had hit home and Billy did his utmost to cut back but it wasn't easy as it meant turning down all the offers of drinks he received every night.

'Don't be so bloody miserable, Hopkins,' someone would call across the bar. 'Have a whisky. Or are you too good to share a drink with us now? You're supposed to be the bloody manager after all.'

He slowed down his rate of consumption by joining in the darts corner games of three-o-one where the preferred drink was lager rather than shorts. A stranger visiting the bar for the first time could have been forgiven for mistaking the darts players for Japanese Sumo wrestlers. This worried Billy who wondered how long it would take for him to develop a beer-barrel belly like the rest of them.

The weeks and months slipped by, and by dint of nightly practice Billy became one of the best darts players in the club though he managed to avoid the physical shape associated with the game. He had responded to Laura's protests by being home every night by ten, leaving Golden

Boy and Kitaka to close up. One night, however, was different.

It was a Friday and there was the usual crowd drinking at the bar – farmers and their wives, a few civil servants, the Tonkses, and Georgina with her two Lotharios, Inspector Towers and Dr Green. Towards ten o'clock, Billy was preparing to leave when the club phone rang. It was the local police station with an emergency call for the Police Inspector. There had been a bad road accident involving a bus and an army lorry outside Marangu and the services of both Towers and the doctor were required urgently.

'Bloody road accidents!' Towers cursed. 'Alway happens on a Friday night when I'm trying to relax. Sorry, Georgina. Duty calls and I've got to go. Don't know when I'll be back. These things always take a long time. You wouldn't believe the paperwork involved.'

'Same goes for me, Georgina,' Vic Green said. 'It's all hands to the pump, I'm afraid.'

The two men drove away and Georgina was left sitting alone at the bar. Billy was about to say goodnight when she called him across.

'Sorry to trouble you, Hoppy, but I've been left stranded. Could I trouble you for a lift home?'

Georgina had a flat in the training college grounds about seven miles out of town and taking her home would present no difficulty though it would make him half an hour late. Laura would have no objections, surely, since it was helping a lady in distress. Besides, he owed Georgina for her part in his driving test success.

'Be glad to help, I was about to leave anyway.'

'I'll finish my drink,' she said, 'and then I'm ready to go.'

It was 10.20 when they pulled up outside her flat.

'Thanks a lot, Hoppy. You've saved my life.'

'Glad to be of service,' he replied. 'That's what club managers are for.'

'A drink before you go?'

He glanced at his watch.

'OK, but I'd better make it a quick one.'

'Quickies are my speciality,' she said, grinning lasciviously.

'Well, in that case . . .' Billy grinned back.

His relationship with Georgina was strictly platonic. Coming from the same part of England, they shared the same sense of humour and joked and flirted with each other from time to time. But that was as far as it went. Georgina looked on him more as an elder brother than a potential lover.

She poured him a small whisky and soda, and a brandy and ginger for herself.

'Cheers,' she said. They clinked their glasses together and knocked back their drinks in one go.

'Now I really must be off,' said Billy. 'I promised Laura I'd be home and she'll be thinking of divorcing me if I'm not back soon.'

'Goodnight, Hoppy, and thanks again,' said Georgina, pecking him on the cheek.

'Any time.'

He walked out to his car, started the engine, engaged reverse gear, and started to back up. Then, disaster! He found he had reversed into a ditch right outside Georgina's bedroom window. He engaged first gear and revved the engine, trying to move forward. In vain. The wheels simply spun round noisily, sinking deeper and deeper into the mud. He got out and tried pushing. No use. He was stuck.

His predicament didn't bear thinking about. Tomorrow morning everyone would recognise his car outside Georgina's flat and then he was as good as dead. The *boma* would buzz with gossip and Georgina's name and his own would be lower than the ooze in which his back wheels were embedded.

What to do? Georgina could appeal to one of her colleagues for help but they were a strait-laced bunch and wouldn't take kindly to being disturbed late at night in order to rescue one of her 'philanderers'. Phone for help? Georgina didn't have a telephone! Not that it mattered for the people who might have come to his aid, Mike for example, didn't have phones either. He thought of his friend and saviour, Doctor Jimmy, but he too lived in a phoneless house on the edge of the town.

Billy had no choice. There was only one thing left to do. Though it was getting late, he had to walk the eight miles to Jimmy's. It was 1.30 when he reached the house and knocked on his door. Jimmy grumbled at being woken from a deep slumber, but when Billy reminded him of the Daimler fiasco and his part in it, saw sense and changed hurriedly into his overalls. In his breakdown truck they were back at the scene within twenty minutes. As he attached a towing chain to the car, the night air was rent by the racket of revving engines and shouted instructions. The lights of several adjoining flats were switched on and there was much curtain twitching but Billy doubted if his identity had been revealed. Fifteen minutes later he was on his way home.

It was with a great sense of relief that he reached his own drive. It had been a close call. It was 2.30 and he felt done in. But there was more to come.

Laura was waiting up for him. One look at her and he knew she was profoundly upset.

'Where in God's name have you been?' she wept. 'I've been worried out of my mind. I thought there'd been an accident. And you've been drinking whisky, after you promised. I can smell it on your breath.'

He tried to explain what had happened but at the mention of Georgina's name, she hit the roof.

'That's it!' she said. 'I've had enough. This work at the club is destroying our family *and* our marriage. Tomorrow I'm going to write to my father and tell him I'm coming home with the children. I can't stand any more of this life.'

Billy tried to reason with her but her mind was made up.

'Let's get to bed,' he said. 'We can talk about it tomorrow when things have calmed down.'

They retired to bed. Or rather Laura went into their bedroom and locked the door behind her. Billy spent the night in the easy chair in his office.

Next morning, in the cold light of day, he explained more fully what had happened. She had calmed down but Billy was still in the soup.

'Billy,' she said, 'you once spoke about taking the broader view of things. Well, I think that if you go on visiting the club and drinking the way you do, our marriage is over.'

'You can't mean that?'

'I certainly do. I'm prepared to see things through to the end of this tour and then I think we should consider going back to England for good. There are so many things I miss.'

'Like the rain and the fog and the smog,' he said. 'And the penny-pinching. Don't forget the penny-pinching.'

'I remember them all only too well, Billy. Just as we were getting on our feet we decided to up sticks and come here. As for the weather, I'm getting tired of relentless blue skies and tropical sun every day. Some mornings, I look out of the window and say to myself, "Oh, no, not another bloody sunny day!" How I long for a good old Manchester drizzle . . .'

They talked, Laura and he, for a couple of hours. She felt that he should spend more time at home whereas he believed that he was justified in staying out while working as club manager. After all, he thought, he was salting away a tidy sum every month towards a family home. At the end of their *tête-à-tête*, they hadn't settled anything and they were still estranged. Billy set up a single bed for himself in his office and it looked as if that was to be a permanent arrangement from then on. He promised, though, to cut back on his drinking once again and his time at the club but knew it wasn't going to be easy if he were to carry on as manager. Nevertheless he agreed to see Sir Charles with a view to reducing his number of nights at the club to three or four a week. Furthermore, he would suggest he be allowed to go home on most working nights at a reasonable hour.

On this note they ended their discussion, with Billy still very much in the dog-box.

Chapter Forty-Two

In February 1960, Billy received the letter he had been waiting for. It was from Titch.

Dear Hoppy,
Well, at last I've done it! I've assembled all the parts on that huge list you sent to me to put your Daimler back on the road. The agents, Drabble & Allen, managed half and for the rest I've had to scour the auto magazines and Daimler Clubs. I have them all in a large leather hold-all and they weigh a ton! In other words, they're heavy and so is your bill. Now you've got the problem of shipping them out to East Africa and I'm told that it could take as long as four months by sea. What would you like me to do? And I don't want a rude answer to that question.
I wait for your answer and your cheque for the balance,
Your long-suffering friend,
Titch.

Four months! Billy thought. That's far too long. If I could get the parts flown out, it would be quicker but expensive. Also dodgy. If they were lost in transit, that would be the end of the dream.

Laura and he were still at odds and he was still banished to his bed in the office. If he could pull off the Daimler deal, it would bring in a lot of cash and go some way to making up for all the botch-ups he'd made in his various enterprises. It would be best if he went to collect the parts himself but the fare to England might put the kibosh on such a wild idea. No use standing around wringing his hands. The only way round the dilemma was to find out for sure. He had heard in the club about an organisation called Friends of East Africa which sometimes arranged cheap charter flights for relatives to come out to Kenya to visit their loved ones for short excursions, some lasting only ten days. No harm in giving them a try.

Next day he rang their Nairobi number and asked about fares for the coming Easter break. He was in luck. There had been a last-minute cancellation and they could offer him a return ticket for the give-away price of one hundred pounds. The normal price was almost three times that.

He took it.

It only remained to square things with Laura.

'This could mean a major breakthrough in our finances,' he told her.

' "It seems that I have heard that song before",' she sang. 'Surely you'd be throwing good money after bad? Why not write the Daimler off for scrap? It's given us nothing but trouble.'

'Never say die,' said Billy. 'I feel it in my bones this time. It's going to pay off, you'll see. Maybe not as much as I originally planned but I can't let all that money I've laid out simply slip down the drain. Think of the poor old Daimler, sitting forlorn in the corner of Sid Appel's garage.'

Laura relented.

'I suppose if it's only for ten days. You spend so little time at home anyway, I don't think I or the kids will even notice you've gone.'

'Thanks,' he said. She had to have her little dig, he thought. 'It's for the good of the family.'

She was humming 'That Song Before' again.

Mike agreed to drive him to the airport and the servants came out to wave goodbye.

'What would you like me to bring you from England?' Billy asked.

'A warm cardigan, please,' said Euphoria, 'for the cold nights.'

'A suit of clothes,' said Twiga, 'so that I may be smart when I go back to my village.'

'A dress for my wife, *bwana*,' Dublin said, 'so that on Sundays she can go to church with her head held high.'

'And for me,' Laura said, 'just bring yourself back in one piece. Maybe one or two surprises for the kids. Oh, and while you're at it, don't forget the Daimler parts.'

'Leave it to me,' he said.

Chapter Forty-Three

The flight back to London was different from the flight out in 1958. For a start, the old Argonaut had been replaced by the Comet, an altogether different experience; it was faster, smoother, and there were only three stops: Khartoum, Rome, London.

After a pleasant twelve-hour journey, they touched down at Heathrow and, even though it was late-March when the worst of winter was supposed to be over, London was shrouded in a dismal grey mist. As Billy descended the aeroplane steps, he felt as if he were walking into a deep-freeze. His light tropical dress didn't help matters either for he'd clean forgotten how cold English weather could be.

He was soon through the customs formalities as he had brought so little luggage with him; his thoughts were concentrated on taking things back, not bringing things in. Apart from his clothes, the only item of any value that he carried was a thank-you gift for Titch, an oil painting by an up-and-coming African artist. He caught the airport bus to Victoria terminal and sat, mesmerised, as they sped at a breakneck rate through the crazy, madcap traffic flowing in and out of Heathrow. At Victoria, he had to stand awhile to adjust, gawping at the cars and taxis that whizzed at suicidal speed round London's sunless streets. He gazed open-mouthed like a peasant on his first visit to the big city, and felt like an alien from outer space. It was so different from the place he'd left two years earlier. The people too had changed. There had been a revolution in hair styles and fashions, especially for the men. Gone were the pinstripes and bowler hats and it was on with the Carnaby Street gear. London was swinging and there was prosperity and a touch of magic in the air.

He took the tube to Euston and was intrigued by the diversity of the people who came and went as he sat there. Billy marvelled at God's ingenuity in effecting endless variations in the human face. Equally intriguing were the advertisements for lingerie, slimming pills, and ways to keep fit. 'Eat this! Wear this! Drink that! Indulge yourself. You've earned it!' the ads screamed at him.

At the station he went into W.H. Smith's and was overwhelmed by the plethora of newspapers and magazines on the stands. His eye was drawn like a magnet to the array of girlie magazines on the top shelf. He could not recall their being displayed so blatantly when he had left. He bought a copy of the *Daily Telegraph* and rejoiced in the fact that it was today's edition and not last week's. A notice in the shop told him about the forthcoming obscenity trial involving *Lady Chatterley's Lover* which Penguin undertook to put on sale if the case went in their favour.

He boarded his train and sat enthralled by the loveliness of the English countryside with its rolling hills and lush meadows, the winding roads lined with lilac trees, the furrowed fields with their neat hedges, new-born lambs frisking by their mothers, and grave matronly cows. Paradise, he thought, and what a contrast to the brown

Kenyan landscape he had become accustomed to in the previous two years. It was so good to be back and how he wished that Laura and the children could be by his side to see it. This was where they truly belonged, he thought, their own, their native land. He was surprised to discover that he had developed such a romantic notion of England but then, he reflected, it's only when a person's been abroad that he becomes truly patriotic and learns to appreciate the beauties of his own country.

He turned to his newspaper and read of national and world events: an old man had starved to death in his Peckham flat and it had been a week before any of his neighbours had noticed his absence; a school in Sheffield had been set on fire by a gang of hooligans who had afterwards stoned the firemen who responded to the emergency call; the hanging age was to stay at eighteen; best bitter beer was to go up by a penny a pint; workers at a leather firm in Lancashire had come out on strike when management cut their morning tea break by five minutes; Brigitte Bardot, the French film actress, was out of danger after taking a large dose of sleeping tablets and cutting her wrists; in Cape Town, Harold Macmillan had spoken about a 'wind of change' blowing through the African continent; in the Transvaal, sixty-three people had been shot dead in riots in a place called Sharpeville.

Billy's romantic notion of home had extended even to Gardenia Court. While far away it had been hallowed by memory. Now, in reality, he saw it for what it was: a squalid heap of malodorous dwelling places into which the authorities with their optimistic slum clearance programmes had dumped so many families. Still, it was great to be back in the bosom of his family once more after such a long absence.

Mam and Dad gave him a rapturous welcome when he knocked on the door. Dad took his hand in a vice-like grip and Mam hugged him so hard he thought she'd never let him go.

'You look so well,' they said. 'You're as brown as a nut.'

'And you talk so posh,' Dad said suspiciously.

'Leave the lad alone,' Mam said. 'Let him catch his breath. Have you had any food, son?'

'Food?' said Billy. 'What's that?'

'Enough talking,' she exclaimed. 'Let me get the lad some grub. First I'll make a brew.'

She went into the kitchen and filled the kettle.

'Mam,' he said, 'that's a miracle. An absolute miracle!'

'What, filling the kettle?'

'No, turning on a tap and getting clean water.'

'Don't you have water where you are?'

'We do, but we have to boil and filter it, sometimes twice. And up country, the women have to walk for miles with buckets on their heads.'

Mam soon had a large plate of chips, egg and peas set out before him, and he knew he was home.

After the meal, he lit up a cigarette and they talked late into the night, catching up on everybody's news. It was all so normal and yet so strange after all he had been through and all the things he'd seen. His eldest brother Sam had recently had another son; Les and his wife Annette were also expecting, his two sisters and their husbands were doing well, and the grandchildren were into their teens. Young Oliver had even started to go dancing at Billy's old haunt, Harrigan's Dancing Academy.

In his turn Billy described their encounters with Kenyan wild life, their holiday in Mombasa, gave details about his own kids, and how well they were doing at school, how they spent much of their time in the sunshine playing games of Tarzan and the Apes. He told them the latest about Laura: how she was enjoying her teaching at the training college. And he gave an account of his part-time job as manager of the country club, though he said nothing about the amount of time he spent there or about his drinking.

'Told you he'd join the toffs one day,' Dad observed. 'Next thing you know, he'll be taking up bloody golf.'

'Well, you have gone up in the world,' Mam said, 'running one of them posh clubs. I'd love to see you telling all them there rich people what to do.'

'Why don't you both come back with me,' he said, 'and see for yourself? You have a new grandson you've never seen. And, by the way, Dad, he turned out to be white. Why not come for a visit? You could help me carry some of the engine parts.'

'What, us go to Africa!' Mam said. 'That'll be the day. Why, I've never been to London, and as for going abroad, for me that means a holiday in the Isle of Man.'

'I've never heard such a daft idea,' Dad said. 'You won't find me going to Africa, no fear. I don't hold with all this here globe-trotting. I believe everyone should stop in their own country and not go interfering with one another. That way, there'd be more peace in the world.'

'Lots of grandparents come out to visit, Dad,' Billy said, suddenly warming to the idea. He didn't know any grandparents who had, but he was never a great stickler for accuracy when presenting an argument.

'I'm sure they do,' Mam said. 'But I can't see us going to a foreign country. I don't know about Dad but I'd be terrified to fly in an aeroplane.'

'OK, Mam. It was just an idea.'

Early next morning, Les and Annette called round. They shook hands warmly, embraced, and Billy congratulated them on their expected baby.

Les said, 'Anything you can do, I can do . . .'

'. . . better,' Billy finished it off for him. 'But you've got a long way to go before you catch us up 'cos we now have four.'

'Laura must find it hard going,' Annette said, 'especially with her teaching as well. I don't know how she does it.'

'She manages quite well because she has a nanny to help out. Not only that, we have a gardener and a cook as well,' he added, flashing Les a smile.

It was like waving a red rag before his socialist brother and Billy knew it. Taunting him had been his favourite hobby as kids in Collyhurst.

'The Great White Hunter!' Les sneered. 'How much do you pay these slaves of yours?'

'About two to three pounds a month, with accommodation and rations.'

'Exploitation of the workers!' he exclaimed. 'How can they live on that?'

'They live well because their life styles and needs are different from ours. For them, work means they have food, clothing and a roof over their heads. Without a job, they'd have nothing and would go hungry.'

'Exactly what Scrooge used to say. One day the masses will rise up and seize power,' Les declaimed. 'It'll be, "Power to the People!" '

'I may be Scrooge, Les, but you sound like one of those soap box orators on Hyde Park corner.'

It was no use arguing with Les about politics. For him, things were cut and dried, black and white with no shades of grey in between. No need for him to think, he'd only to follow the party line.

In the afternoon Billy went to see Titch. They embraced like two members of the Mafia and were soon chewing the fat over all that had happened since last they met. Titch was still unmarried, still living with his parents, and now teaching in a tough secondary modern in Moss Side.

'It's like entering the lions' den when you go into the classroom,' he said. 'As the comedian says, "If they like you, they let you live." '

Billy told him about Marangu School and the characters he worked with. Titch was a good listener.

'The African students are a joy to teach and voracious for learning. They resent holidays and time off which they consider a waste of precious time. Ask a question and you have the whole class straining to answer; teach a lesson and you have thirty listeners hanging on to every word; give out prep and next morning you have thirty sets of homework handed in on time. For the African, education is not only a privilege but a passport to a better job and a way of paying back their families who've made such great sacrifices. The only discipline problem is keeping their enthusiasm within manageable limits.'

'I'd love a job there, Hoppy,' chuckled Titch, 'but I don't fancy encounters with snakes, lions, and creepy-crawlies.'

'Even if you did, Titch, you may be too late. The good life there is coming to an end. Things are hotting up politically, especially after Macmillan's "wind of change" speech. Independence, what they call *uhuru*, can't be all that far away.'

As with all good friends from way back, conversation flowed easily. They turned their attention to the Daimler spare parts.

'I don't think I'll ever be able to thank you enough,' Billy said. He gave Titch the oil painting. 'Maybe this will be worth a fortune one day.'

'If it's a lost Leonardo,' Titch laughed, 'it'll about cover it.'

He brought out the bag of car spares and Billy was taken aback when he saw how bulky they were.

'I'll never manage these on my own. How about coming back to Kenya with me as a tourist? You can carry half in as hand luggage.'

'I'd love to, Hoppy, but I've got a job to go to after the holidays.'

'I'll have to persuade someone or my journey here has been in vain.'

Later that day Billy caught a bus to his eldest sister Flo's house where once again he was given the red carpet treatment, with tea and special Eccles cakes. He thought they might have another long family confab about their various experiences since last they'd met. Did anyone want to ask him about Africa? he wondered. About the wild animals, the snakes, the insects, the Mau Mau? Apparently not.

'We know all about them,' they said, 'we've seen them on a fantastic programme called *On Safari* with Armand and Michaela Denis. You ought to try to see it before you go back, Billy.'

Throughout their little chat the television had sat in the corner. Mute, in honour of his visit, he thought, until they told him that programmes didn't begin until just before five o'clock and now it was time to switch on.

'I hope you don't mind,' Barry, Flo's husband, said. 'Only we've been following this programme for the last few weeks. The kids here are hooked on it.'

As soon as the set had warmed up the whole family recited together, 'It's Friday, it's five-to-five . . . it's . . . CRACKERJACK!' And they spent the next hour watching Eamonn Andrews hand out armfuls of prizes to lucky contestants.

Maybe when the programme's finished, Billy thought, they'll bombard me with questions. But after the credits had rolled there was another programme even more pressing, *The Adventures of Robin Hood* starring Richard Greene, a not-to-be-missed episode, apparently.

He sat with the family for some time before taking his leave at the next commercial break.

'I'll be off now, Flo, Barry,' he called. 'I promised I'd visit Polly and family next.'

'Right, Billy,' they called, getting up and going to the door with him. 'Great to see you again. You will come back and visit us before you go back to Kenya, won't you? When *are* you going back, by the way?'

He could see they were anxious to return to their viewing and so he left.

It was the same at his sister Polly's. They were viewing *What's My Line?* and nothing was allowed to get between them and the irascible Gilbert Harding. For so many people here in England, Billy thought, the glowing fireside as the focus of the home has been replaced by the glowing box in the corner. When they'd left for Kenya, television had been popular, now it had come to dominate family life. For some the flickering shadows in the goggle box had become reality. Real live flesh-and-blood creatures like me are not only unimportant, they're irrelevant, he thought.

* * *

Not everyone was like that, though. A few nights later Billy met up with his old mates and they organised a booze-up in the Sawyer's Arms. How good it was to meet up with his buddies after his experiences with snobs like Major Blewitt, Roger Bedwell and the rest of the colonial set. It was as if he'd never been away. Oscar was still trying to emulate his hero Oscar Wilde with his quips and epigrams.

'Who says travel broadens the mind?' he drawled. 'Some of the narrowest men in the world are sea captains.'

'Is that true?' Titch asked.

'I never know how much of what I say is true,' Oscar replied loftily.

Some things never change, Billy thought. Though that wasn't strictly accurate, he discovered. For a start, Nobby, the profligate bachelor, had been hooked by a girl called Prudence, one of his libidinous ladies, and was no longer able to entertain the company with his bawdy stories, while Olly too had acquired a wife, Cordelia. Billy joined in the general banter but whenever he tried to say something about education or the political ferment in Kenya, they made theatrical yawns and swung imaginary lamps. They didn't want to hear about it, and besides, what could he tell them? The Kenya Conference had recently taken place in London and they'd seen it all on BBC's Panorama.

The main topic of conversation was the coming Olympic Games to be held in Rome in August.

'I don't know why we bother entering any of our athletes,' Olly said. 'A complete waste of time. The Russians and Americans simply show us how mediocre we have become.'

'Quite agree,' Nobby said. 'The only thing Britain is good at is losing. We're so accustomed to it, we should be awarded gold medals for taking it on the chin so bravely.'

'You sound almost ashamed of your country,' Billy said. 'What's happened to British pride and the Dunkirk spirit?'

'Sank without trace around 1945,' Olly answered. 'Even the Germans can teach us a lesson. We're a fourth-rate power now.'

Billy's hackles rose. 'It so happens that many people in the Commonwealth abroad believe that Britain is still Great.'

'That's because they don't live here,' Nobby said.

During the evening, the two ladies paired off to pursue their own conversation, mainly about the latest Carnaby Street fashions and recent 'in' diets.

Prudence said, 'As for that diet involving thistle extract three times a day with dandelion tea twice . . . I think I'd rather be fat.'

'Quite agree,' said Cordelia. 'Some doctor on the box said the other night that the trouble in this country is that too many people are on fad diets. I'm sure he's right. Why, even my twelve-year-old sister came home from school the other day asking, "Am I slim enough, Mum?" '

'It's gone too far. But if you want to be waif-like,' Prudence laughed, 'you should eat, or to be more precise not eat, like people in the Third World.'

'That's all very well,' Cordelia replied, 'but whenever I see those poor starving peasants on telly, I can't help but weep. I mean, I'd love to be that skinny too but not with all those flies, and diseases and things.'

The final blow came as they were leaving the pub. Billy's old friend Oscar, the most sociable bloke he knew, glanced at the television that was on in the bar.

Turning to Titch, he cried in dismay, 'Have you seen

what we've missed by being at this booze-up? We've missed a Congreve play!'

'Oh, I don't know,' Titch replied loyally. 'I'd rather be having a drink and a chin-wag with Hoppy and the gang than watching some boring old play.'

For Billy, Oscar's exclamation was the last straw. He knew then that the whole country, including some of his friends, had become a nation of telly-addicts obsessed by the idiot box.

'It's not the same here any more,' he remarked sadly to Titch on the way home. 'Things have changed so much, I feel out of touch, like an outsider.'

'I don't think things have changed *that* much,' Titch replied slowly. 'But maybe *you* have.'

Later that evening when Billy was alone in his room, he pondered Titch's words. Had he really changed during his two years' absence abroad? Since he had come back, he'd felt like a stranger in his own land. Surely England couldn't have changed that much? Nevertheless it seemed to him that the country had become somehow more selfish and materialistic than he remembered it, with a distinctly 'I'm All Right, Jack' and a 'Keeping-up-with-the-Jones's' outlook. When he recalled the poverty and frugality he had seen in Marangu, he was taken aback by the monumental waste he now saw all round him. England had become a throwaway society where things were simply discarded as soon as a minor problem appeared. Socks got a hole? No need to darn them, buy another pair. Cigarette burn on the easy chair? Dump it and get a new one.

And people seemed overly preoccupied with trivia like the latest fad diet or fashion in clothes while the popular press pretended to be scandalised at the excesses of celebrities in sport and entertainment, with all the sordid details and pictures dutifully reported. The chief topic of conversation on bus and train was last night's offering on the box, such as a game show and how some railway clerk or lowly shop assistant had nearly won a fortune. Billy was aware that in some subtle way Africa had changed his perspective and his priorities for he had learned to differentiate between the trivial and the important. Over there, the problems facing people were the major questions of survival, like where the next meal was coming from or where to obtain water that wouldn't give them cholera. Maybe Marangu was a one-horse town but he had come to love his job there, which was demanding and fulfilling. After only a couple of days in England, he found himself wanting to get back to Africa because he was missing not only his own little family but also the people back in Kenya and the country itself.

He waited until the weekend before calling on Laura's family as he wanted to be sure that everyone would be there. He wondered if they too would be infected with Tellyitis but there was no need for concern. Their set had been confined to the drawing room and did not command a central position so that it was possible to carry out normal conversation without the constant blather in the background.

Duncan and Louise were overjoyed to see him and fired a hundred questions, wanting to know all the details of life in Africa. Most important of all, was their daughter truly happy out there?

'Laura loves it,' he fibbed.

Was she keeping up with her music?

'We don't have a piano at home but she practises at the training college where she's teaching music and art.'

Seeing Duncan and Louise like this in Laura's home caused Billy to have deep feelings of guilt and conflict. Being there talking to them reminded him of how he'd had to fight to win her hand in marriage, overcome the opposition first of Duncan and then his own father. And in those early days, he'd had such hopes of creating a happy prosperous home for her and the children. Instead, he'd taken them off to Africa and, having got them there, neglected them by devoting too much time to the country club. What's more, he knew he was on a slippery slope so far as his drinking went and there was a real danger he could become, in his own mother's phrase, 'a bit too fond of the bevy'. He vowed to turn over a new leaf when he got back. His only fear was that it might be too late and Laura had already written him off as a bad job. Of one thing he was certain and that was that England was where she was truly happy and where she and the children rightfully belonged. While he had many misgivings about life in Britain, it was still their home. If she wanted to come back for good, so be it. Laura's happiness and that of the children was paramount.

The questions from Duncan and Louise continued to come at him thick and fast. Were the children all right? Was their schooling up to scratch? And what about the latest addition to the family? Was he strong and healthy? What were they doing to avoid the tropical diseases they'd read about? What about the insects, the snakes, the wild animals?

Billy answered them as fully and diplomatically as he could.

When he told Duncan how invaluable his training in accountancy had proved to be, his father-in-law slapped his knee and glowed with delight.

'I knew it would pay dividends in the end. I hope you remembered all the Inland Revenue tips I passed on.'

In turn, they gave him the latest news of their own family. Hughie, now married, was a qualified doctor and working in a general practice in Sheffield. Katie was an SRN and had recently taken up a post at a big hospital in Staffordshire. Furthermore, she had become engaged to a young doctor there. Billy reacted to this piece of news with surprise. Young Katie who only yesterday had been running their errands! When had she grown up?

'Notice all the medical connections,' Louise observed. 'You can guess whose influence that might be,' she said, smiling pointedly at her husband.

'Nothing to do with me,' Duncan said, shrugging his shoulders.

Hamish and Jennie were still living in Edinburgh and were now the proud parents of three daughters.

Louise said, 'They're proud of their children. Jennie says they're all precocious and sensitive little girls, real chatterboxes.'

'That really means they're little know-alls and big cry-babies,' Duncan snorted. 'What's more they're little prima donnas who are always answering back.'

'And Hamish?' Billy asked.

'Cheese-paring as ever,' Louise chuckled. 'Jennie tells me he saves on soap by sticking the bits together, stands bottles of ketchup upside down to get the last drop out, steams stamps off envelopes if they haven't been franked, and best of all buys yesterday's bread cheaply. Says it's perfectly OK for toast.'

'In my day,' Duncan said, 'that was known as thrift.'

'I ken the days when I lived with my family in

Kirkintilloch . . .' old Auntie began, ready to dip into her bottomless store of anecdotes.

'I'm sure Billy doesna have time to listen to you and your long-winded tales,' Gran'ma said, cutting her off.

It was good to know that here at least some things were the same.

Duncan finally changed the subject and turned to more serious business. Kenya! With their hourly news bulletins on radio and television, Billy had the impression that people in England were better informed about the political future in Kenya than those who actually lived there. Perhaps that was because people living on the spot couldn't always see the wood for the trees.

'According to what we hear on the BBC,' Duncan said, 'things are changing rapidly on the African continent. Independence has already been granted to Ghana with Nigeria and Tanganyika waiting in the wings. Kenya can't be too far down the line. What will you do then?'

'We'll cross that bridge when we come to it, Duncan.'

Chapter Forty-Four

After visiting friends and relatives, Billy turned his attention to buying presents for his family and people back in Kenya. For his own children he had bought a selection of comics and sweets not available in Kenya, and for Laura an eternity ring he couldn't really afford. He hoped it might unlock the door of the dog-box to which he had been banished. As for the servants, they'd never have forgiven him if he'd forgotten his promise. His brother Les had told him that good bargains were to be had at Isaacson's, the auctioneers in Salford, and so the following Tuesday morning, Billy found himself standing with a crowd of eager buyers at their salesroom off Chapel Street. He had to wait around for most of the day until the lady auctioneer had disposed of furniture, bric-à-brac, and a host of other odds and ends. Judging by the interest and the lively bidding, though, it looked as if there would be keen competition for the clothing. He was wrong. The first item was a job lot of shoes in every shape and size.

'What am I bid for this fine collection of men's shoes?' the auctioneer bawled.

'Ten pounds, Sadie,' a man at the front drawled. Obviously a dealer.

'But there are forty pairs of shoes here, all new,' she screamed. 'That's only five bob a pair.'

No one else seemed interested and the shoes were knocked down to the owner of the sleepy voice.

Quietly Billy observed the proceedings for half an hour until at last Sadie's strident voice screeched, 'What am I bid for these beautiful ladies' dresses?'

This was what he had been waiting for. Who would bid first? There was silence.

'You *are* a miserable lot,' she shrieked. 'Come on, anything. There's a whole rack of fifty dresses here. Who will bid me a tenner? That's two shillings a dress. I'm giving them away.'

There were no takers, not even the bored man, which surprised Billy. Perhaps the people of Salford had become spoiled by the affluent society. He thought of the poor servants back in Marangu. How happy and grateful they would be if he could only get these dresses back to them. This was too good a bargain to throw away. He raised his hand.

'Sold to the young man at the back,' Sadie yelled quickly, and banged down her hammer.

The rest of the clothing went just as rapidly and at the end of the morning Billy found himself the owner not only of fifty dresses but also twenty cardigans, all in the same mixture of red, purple and yellow, and ten men's suits still in their original wrapping. All at knock-down prices. Wait until the servants back in Kenya see my booty, he thought. He could hardly wait to see their faces. After the fiasco with the rabbits and his disastrous attempts to help the African poor, these items of clothing would go some way to make up for his blunders.

He came away mighty pleased with his morning's work.

He found a small packing firm on Regent Road and arranged for his purchases to be collected and shipped by air freight to a bonded warehouse in Nairobi.

The day after the auction, he helped Mam to do her weekly shopping at the local Co-op, which, wonder of wonders, had gone over to self-service. They had reached the checkout and were behind a couple of people in the queue where the first lady with her young son had enough food on board to feed an army of Irish navvies. In contrast, the lady immediately in front had loaded her basket to overflowing with a wide selection of cat and dog food. He wondered what Job Karioki's village back in Kenya would have made of it if they could have viewed the scene.

The lady with the boy paid at the till and turned to her son who was howling the place down because she had bought him the wrong sort of chocolate.

'I didn't want a Mars Bar,' the kid whined.

'Would you like a packet of Spangles, instead?' she coaxed.

'No,' he sulked, stamping his foot.

'No, what?'

'No, I wouldn't!' the lad snapped.

Billy's mam paid her own bill and as he was packing her groceries into her shopping bag, she hit him with a bombshell. She'd always been one for picking her moment.

'Dad and me have talked it over and I've decided I wouldn't mind going back with you.'

At first, he didn't understand. Going back with him? Where to? Had she forgotten something and wanted to go back into the store? Home with the shopping? What?

'Going back where, Mam?'

'Back to Africa with you.'

You could have knocked Billy down with a feather. It was almost like her declaring, 'I wouldn't mind playing centre-forward for Manchester United' or 'I fancy riding a horse in the Grand National'. It was so unlike her, so out of character.

'What in God's name made you change your mind?'

'You put the idea in my head and I thought to myself, it's time I saw something of the world besides the wash-house and the kitchen sink before I'm pushing up daisies. And you did say that lots of grandparents make the trip nowadays. But it's not been easy making this decision, I can tell you. You know what a funniosity your father is. He went mad when I said I was thinking of going. What about me? he kept asking. How will I manage? I thought we'd have come to blows in the end. I've waited on him hand and foot for the last fifty years, he can bloody well look after himself for a fortnight.'

'I'm glad you're coming, Mam, but how did you manage it at the finish?'

'It was your brother Les who pulled it off. He said I'd never been anywhere in my life and this would be my only chance. Promised he'd look in on Dad and make sure he was all right. So, it's on. I'm coming with you, and I'll help to carry them there spare parts.'

'I'll help with the fare,' Billy said, thinking, She's right. She's never been anywhere and I can't let our Les get all the credit.

'You'll do no such thing,' Mam retorted. 'I've always paid my own way.'

Billy phoned the Friends of East Africa office in London and was lucky enough to find Mam a seat on the same flight as his. Once Mam had made up her mind, there was no stopping her. She arranged with her GP for smallpox and yellow fever shots, started a course of Paludrin tablets, bought herself a new outfit, had her hair done, and was raring to go. The only thing she worried about was coming back alone from London to Manchester. Les stepped in again and volunteered to meet her plane at Heathrow and escort her back. A strange man was Les, belligerent in argument and benevolent in action.

The following week they were packed and ready for off. Mam's suitcase was filled with her clothes and Billy's presents for Laura and the kids, and weighed a little less than the regulation twenty kilos. Billy's weighed even less even though it contained his clothes and a few of the lighter mechanical items. He knew that suitcases were always weighed and as long as they conformed to the standard allowance, there would be no problem getting them through. The bulk of the engine parts, however, were stowed in one large leather hold-all and he was counting on that going through as unweighed hand luggage.

Dad saw them off in a taxi and Billy had a feeling he might be having second thoughts about letting his wife go off to visit, as he put it, 'the African jungle'. He looked sad as he waved them goodbye but then Billy thought, He'll be back in the boozer tonight, playing crib with his cronies. He'll live on tripe and cow-heel stew for the next two weeks, and love it.

'I do hope he'll be all right, and doesn't burn the place down,' Mam said.

'It's only a fortnight. He'll manage, and it'll make him appreciate you all the more when you get back.'

The train journey to London was uneventful mainly because they both dozed most of the way. At Euston, Billy hailed a taxi to take them to Victoria Terminal.

'We are living it up,' Mam said. 'All these taxis! The only time I ride in one usually is to a wedding or a funeral.'

'Nothing but the best for my mam. She's an international traveller now,' he replied.

As they drove across London, Mam was thrilled by the sights and the sounds.

'I never knew there were so many people in the world.'

He could see, though, that she was getting nervous as they drew nearer to Victoria.

'People are flying all over the world every day, Mam. No need to worry.'

'If there's no need to worry,' she said, 'why do they call these places "terminals"?'

To get his luggage past the check-in desk at Victoria, Billy planned his campaign with military precision. They sat behind a potted plant and he observed the procedure closely. It was as he'd expected. Suitcases were weighed and sent through on the conveyor belt; hand luggage was not.

'You go first, Mam,' he said, putting her case on the weighing machine.

The suitcase went through, her hand luggage was tagged and she was given a boarding pass. They returned to their place behind the plant. Billy waited for a while until the queue had gone down and then went forward with his own suitcase and the hold-all containing the car parts. He stood upright before the desk, doing his utmost to make the hand-luggage look lightweight though in reality it felt like a ton. The pretty BOAC clerk smiled brightly, weighed his suitcase, labelled it and sent it through. He waited for the tag for his hold-all but it didn't come. Still smiling brightly, the young lady glanced down at his hand luggage and said, 'Could you put that on the scales too, please, sir?'

Uh-oh, he thought. Just my luck. He did as ordered. The hand of the weighing machine whizzed round the dial.

Disaster.

'Dear me,' she exclaimed. 'I'm afraid you can't take that on board as hand luggage, sir. You must send it air freight. The section that deals with that is on the other side of the hall.'

'How much does that cost?' Billy stammered. 'And how long does it take?'

'I'd estimate around three to four hundred pounds and it should be with you in about three to four weeks, depending on pressure of demand.'

There was no way he could find that amount of money nor wait that length of time because when the parts did arrive in Nairobi, he would be hit for import duty as well. Had he come all this way, made all this effort, to be pipped at the post?

He went back to where Mam sat waiting, removed the tag from her hand luggage and slipped it into his pocket. Walking past the check-in desk, he waved to the smiling assistant and headed in the direction of the freight section. As soon as he reached the revolving doors, he moved quickly and ducked outside to the waiting buses.

'Which is the next one to Heathrow?' he asked a uniformed driver who was leaning on a coach. He jerked his thumb to the single-decker bus. Billy went aboard, attached the tag to his luggage and placed it on a seat.

'Be back in a jiffy,' he said to the man, showing him his ticket. 'I'll just go and get my old mother.'

He went back into the building through the revolving door and as he passed the pretty lady, gave her a thumbs-up sign to indicate that he'd sent his hold-all by freight.

Mam and he then got on the coach together and were on their way. So far, so good.

The next hurdle was Heathrow Security.

'I'll take it from here,' Mam said. 'Remember, I'm here to help.'

'Are you sure, Mam? It's heavy.'

'Of course I'm sure. I've carried heavier things than this in my time.'

She picked up the bag and placed it down on the metal counter with a loud thump. Soon a young security officer came along all business-like and requested her to open the bag which she did, unzipping it and giving the man a broad smile.

The young officer took one look and turned pale.

'In heaven's name, what are these?' he exclaimed, taking out an object not unlike a hand grenade.

'Eeh, I don't know. No use asking me,' Mam said. 'My son here is taking them to repair his motor car in Africa.'

Standing by her side, Billy confirmed the truth of her statement.

'Could you wait here for a few moments,' the officer said nervously, 'while I call my superior?'

The game's up, Billy thought. I'm for it now. End of story.

After a twenty-minute wait, the senior officer came. In a whispered conversation, his junior explained the situation to his boss who approached them and rummaged through their luggage.

'What are these?' he asked, holding up the 'grenades'.

'Piston cylinders, and those are piston rings.'

He took Billy through the whole inventory: conrods, gudgeon pins, camshaft followers, valve rocker arms, and the rest. In the end he seemed satisfied that they were indeed car parts and not a terrorist arsenal. They were allowed to board the aircraft though Billy afterwards swore the plane had difficulty lifting off the ground.

The captain announced their take-off and Mam took out her rosary beads and began saying her prayers quietly. As the plane picked up speed along the runway, the beads slipped ever faster though her nimble fingers. Once they were aloft, she relaxed and began to enjoy the flight, especially when they brought round the food trays.

'This I could get used to,' she said. 'I don't know whether to go for the turkey breasts or the smoked salmon.'

They flew over Rome and the captain pointed out St Peter's below. 'Wait till I tell the other women in the Catholic Mothers' Union,' she said.

Khartoum was next and the same little man, or at least his twin brother, in the large turban came on board to decontaminate everybody with his token squirt of DDT. A few hours later, after a good night's sleep, they landed at Nairobi airport. Immigration formalities gave them no problem as their papers were in order. They collected their suitcases from the carousel, loaded their luggage on to a trolley and chose the green channel through customs. As they passed along the corridor, a tall European official greeted them with: 'Welcome to Kenya. Nothing to declare? Perfumes, spirits, tobacco?'

'Nothing,' Billy answered.

'What about pornography?'

'Eeh, I don't think so,' Mam said. 'I don't even own a pornograph.'

They'd done it! Carried a Daimler engine seven thousand miles in their hand luggage! Perhaps they'd earned an entry in the *Guinness Book of Records*.

They walked into the bright Kenyan sunshine where

Laura and the children were waiting to greet them. It was an emotional meeting and there were lots of hugs and lots of tears. It looked too as if Billy was out of the dog-box even if it were only temporary. Maybe the eternity ring would get him out on a permanent basis.

They piled their luggage into the car and Laura drove off. Before they could go to Marangu, they had one important place to visit. Sid Appel's garage.

The Daimler was still there, gathering dust at the back of the garage, and while his family waited outside in the car, Billy delivered his precious cargo.

Sid Appel welcomed him with a big smile.

'I never thought you'd manage it,' he said. 'It was Mission Impossible.'

He checked through the items and his smile became ever broader as he ticked them off.

'Now we have the spares we should have the car back on the road in about ten days,' he said. 'You've done well. Did you have much trouble getting them?'

'Piece of cake.' Billy grinned and tipped him a wink

On the drive to Marangu, Mam was as excited as a little girl. As the Ford Zephyr sang smoothly on the tarmac road, large herds of zebra, wildebeest and giraffe grazed tamely in the near distance.

'It's a zoo, that's what it is,' she exclaimed. 'One great big wonderful zoo. Reminds me of Belle Vue.'

They passed a group of Masai Moran, spears and shields in hand.

'Look, look!' she called. 'Look at all those savages. It's like we see at the pictures, I keep expecting to see that Johnny Weissmuller feller to come swinging out of the trees.'

It was market-day in Athi River and as they approached

the town, they overtook streams of Kikuyu men, knobkerries in hand, their women trudging behind them bowed under donkey-loads of bananas.

'Don't the men ever carry anything?' Mam asked. 'Why are they walking in front instead of helping their wives?'

'They go on ahead,' Billy answered, 'because they have to keep their hands free in case they have to fight off snakes or wild animals. At least, that's what they claim.'

'Huh, a likely story!' she said. 'And why do the men have shoes and the women don't?'

'Your guess is as good as mine.'

They reached home and the servants came out to help unpack the car. Billy introduced them all. Mam shook hands with each of them in turn: Euphoria, Dublin and Twiga.

'I used to be a servant once in a big house in Macclesfield,' she said. 'The woman I worked for was a real bitch. I hope my son is treating you well.'

'Oh, yes, madam,' Dublin said. 'The *bwana* is kind.'

'You let me know if he's not,' Mam said. 'I'll soon put him in his place.'

A little later Mike and Jill Sherwood came over to be introduced, and they spent the rest of the afternoon taking things easy on the verandah with Dublin serving tea and cucumber sandwiches. With the crusts cut off, of course.

'No wonder you like it out here,' Mam said, turning to Billy. 'You're living the life of Reilly, what with the sunshine and servants at your beck and call.'

'When you've been here for a few years,' Laura said, 'you get fed up with sunshine every day. Apart from the rainy seasons, we've got only two kinds of weather. Hot and very hot. What I wouldn't give for a drop of Scotch mist.'

'Isn't that some kind of tipple the Tonkses drink?' Billy joked.

'How was your trip out here, Mrs Hopkins?' Jill asked, changing the subject..

'I loved it in the aeroplane, once I got used to it. You soon forget that you're thousands of feet up with nothing holding you up but fresh air.'

'I know you've only just arrived,' Mike said, 'but what do you think of Kenya from what you've seen so far?'

'Well, on the car ride from the airport, I saw the countryside. The grass is brown and the trees have great big flowers but no leaves. The blacks do all the walking, many of them in their bare feet, while the whites ride about in posh motor cars. And it's the women who carry everything. It used to be the same in England when I was a young woman in service.'

'You've been here only five minutes,' Mike laughed, 'and already you've got the measure of the place.'

Later that evening, Billy went down to the club to check on things. It was the same old crowd: the Tonkses propping up the bar, Georgina and her admirers, the rest of the hangers-on, and Sir Charles with Lady Gilson.

'Am I glad to see you back!' he exclaimed. 'I've kept things going during your absence but we've got behind and there's a lot needs seeing to.'

Billy made a survey of everything: a check on bar stock levels, a quick look at the bank statements and account books, subscriptions and new memberships. Things had got behind and he could see he was going to have to burn the midnight oil to bring matters up to date.

* * *

Laura had converted his office into a spare bedroom for Mam and on her first night in Africa, she slept like a log. She did not wake until the grey light of early morning, when they sent in Dublin with a cup of tea. Two minutes later, there was a scream from the room and everyone rushed in to see what was up.

'My God,' Mam said. 'That came as a shock. I was in a deep sleep having a dream when suddenly I opened my eyes and found a cannibal shaking me by the shoulder and grinning horribly. "*Chai, memsahib*," he said.'

They all laughed. 'You've already met Dublin, Mam. He's brought you an early-morning cuppa.'

The days passed by quickly and during the day Billy was kept busy at school while every night he was out at the club till ten o'clock dealing with the backlog.

Laura and Jill took Mam on a few visits to places of interest in the region, like Leopard's Lair, a local beauty spot, to Wamunyu where she bought carvings for the family in England, and on a day's shopping in Nairobi where she purchased a white cap for Dad.

'Wait till he walks into his pub wearing that!' she exclaimed.

'That's a scene I should love to witness,' Billy said. 'He might even start a trend in his local.'

'There are some lovely shops there,' Mam reported. 'And those Asians! So polite, they can't do enough for you. I wish we had shops like that in Manchester.'

In Marangu, she was revelling in life in the tropics. While Laura and Billy were out at work, she played with her two youngest grandchildren, Mark and John, in the garden. In the afternoons, she instructed the servants in domestic and culinary skills: how to iron, how to bake bread, and how to cook a wide variety of dishes. She had been awarded the honorary title of *Mama ya busara.* (Wise Mother.)

'She has taught me so many things,' Dublin proclaimed, 'that one day I shall apply for a job in the District Commissioner's residence or in a big hotel in Nairobi. Yesterday she showed me how to cook "trash".'

'Trash?' Billy said. 'Why even I know how to cook that. My wife says it's my *spécialité*. How do *you* cook this "trash"?'

'You put meat, potatoes, onions in a large dish and cover it with a crust of pastry.'

'Ah you mean "tater-ash".'

'That's what I said.'

Apart from household skills, Mam told them of many other things, about the *bwana* and his early upbringing, about life in England and her own life story.

One afternoon, Billy came home from school to find her surrounded by half the domestic staffs of the compound. They were listening with rapt interest to her tales of her early life: her extreme poverty and how she'd been evicted from her home, the cruel treatment in the workhouse, and her experiences as a servant at the turn of the century.

'Your mother is indeed a wise old lady,' Dublin declared. 'She has silver hair and knows many things. If she were African, she would be chief story-teller of my village and the people would attend to her words. My father, who has three wives, would make her his senior wife and put her in charge of his household.'

'I shall tell my mother these things and she will be highly honoured,' Billy said.

'There are many things I do not understand about the English,' Dublin continued. 'They do not listen to the advice of their elders and they neglect their old parents by putting them in special homes for the aged.'

'They may not have room in their own homes for their parents,' Billy said, defending his fellow countrymen.

'One day,' Dublin said, 'I would like to visit England for your mother tells us that if a man is ill or cannot find work, he can go to the post office, sign his name and they will give him lots of shillings. She has also said that the government will pay large sums for each child born. My father has sired twenty-two children. In England he could sit at home drinking *pombe* and smoking *murangi*. One day, when freedom comes to our country, we shall have the same.'

But that was mere pipe-dreaming. A week after their conversation, Billy was able to give the servants some good news and not mere fantasy but things they could feel and touch. The bonded warehouse in Nairobi had reported that the parcels of clothing bought at the Salford auction had arrived. As Billy couldn't get into Nairobi, he arranged for an agent to clear them through customs. Next day, the agent phoned with a few queries.

'Customs want to be assured that the items are for your personal use and not for sale.'

'But of course. They are gifts for my relatives and friends.'

'They wish to know why you need fifty dresses, twenty cardigans and ten suits?'

'I have many relatives and many friends,' Billy replied.

Two days later the packages were collected on his behalf by the Marimba Stores truck. Billy invited all the servants on the compound to come over and with all due ceremony presented the gifts to the workers. He felt good inside, like Father Christmas, as he made the announcement, 'These are my gifts to you from England. Choose what you wish to take for your families.'

All excited at the prospect, they opened up the crates.

The ladies rummaged through the dresses first and held them against their bodies for size. There seemed to be something wrong. The dresses were either very long or very short.

Jill who had been helping to unpack now said, 'These frocks were made for either three-foot pygmy women from Namibia or seven-foot Amazonian women from South America.'

'We shall get the tailors to alter them,' Dublin said tactfully. 'They should get one dress from each pair.'

'Maybe we'll have better luck with the cardigans,' Billy said, opening up the second package.

Euphoria tried one on. The left arm was twice as long as the right.

'And these were 'specially made for circus freaks,' Laura proclaimed.

'Not to worry,' Euphoria said. 'They too can be altered.'

Billy could see that the Marangu tailors were going to be kept hard at it for some time to come.

'Is there any point in looking at the men's suits?' he said. 'They're sure to be as bad as the rest.'

'Please, *bwana*,' said Twiga. 'Let us see what you have bought.'

He cut open the strings and uncovered the package. There was a gasp from the crowd. All twelve suits were luminescent lime green. Oh, my God, Billy thought, these are the worst of the lot. No wonder the people at the Salford auction were slow to bid.

But how wrong Billy was about the suits! The gasp was not one of horror but of approbation. The assembled crowd broke into spontaneous applause. So he'd got something right after all.

'These are the best suits I have ever seen,' Twiga said

warmly. 'All the men on the compound will be proud to wear them.'

The zoot suits were a great success and the envy of the town. Furthermore they were strongly approved of by the traffic police for the wearers could easily be seen in the dark. Billy only wished he'd bought more of them.

Sid Appel, the auto engineer, was as good as his word and ten days after he had received the spares, he contacted Billy to tell him the car was ready. Mike and he went in to collect it and Billy settled the account of two hundred and fifty pounds. The Daimler was gleaming and looked as beautiful as ever. He drove the car back nervously to Marangu, expecting that at any moment the engine would catch on fire, but the motor ran like silk all the way. His friend Doctor Jimmy gave it the final once-over, paying special attention to the hoses, all of which had been replaced. Billy placed the same ad as before in the *East African Standard* but this time raising the price by a hundred pounds. The response came quickly. A farmer in Kiambu offered to buy it at the price offered. Mike and he went into the same routine for delivery and this time the whole deal went smoothly. Billy paid all his bills, including the government loan, Jimmy's outstanding account, covered his air fare to Britain, and gave Mike a case of wine for his help. At the end of these transactions, he had made a hundred pounds profit. A fearful lot of hassle for such a small return. But for the man from Cheetham Hill, a profit was a profit.

The fortnight of Mam's visit went by quickly. Two days before she was due to go back, she took Billy to one side.

'A word,' she said. 'I've a bone to pick with you.'

He felt his hair stand on end. That last phrase sent a

frisson of fear along his spine. It meant serious stuff. The invitation to take part in the bone-picking exercise had long been associated with trouble, like the time when, as a youngster, he'd pinched a penny out of her purse or the occasion in adolescence when he'd stayed out all night and she'd put the fear of God into him with that simple statement, 'I've a bone to pick with you.' It was equivalent to a judge donning his black cap.

What on earth could it be? What had he done wrong? He didn't like the sound of this at all. His discomfort must have been apparent because his mam said, 'You can wipe that sulky expression off your face for a start or you'll be struck like that one day. Now, I've been watching you,' she went on menacingly, 'and you're spending too much time at that club of yours. And another thing – you're drinking too much. What's got into you, you daft bugger?'

'I'm in charge and I've got to be there,' Billy muttered. He became that adolescent again making his excuses and trying to justify himself.

'Nonsense!' she said. 'You're just like your father, too fond of the bevy.'

'They're paying me good money and I'm trying to save for our return to England.'

'Stop kidding yourself, our Billy. You're neglecting Laura and the children and you've got her so's she's ready to leave you and come back to England without you. You've bought her an eternity ring but you have to do more than give her a piece of metal, you've got to start spending more time at home. Stop being such a daft ha'porth and see some sense. You're not too old for me to give you the back of my hand,' said Mam, raising her arm.

'I'll try to do better,' he protested.

'Trying's not good enough. The road to hell is paved with good intentions. You see that you do do better. You've got a lovely family and you're risking the lot by spending every night at that damn club of yours. Restrict your visits to, say, one or two nights and if they don't like it down there, tell them to lump it.'

No matter that he was thirty-three years old, no matter he had all those degrees and was a teacher, when his mam spoke, Billy listened. He wouldn't have put it past her to give him a clout across the chops.

Next day Billy went to see Sir Charles and put the suggestion to him. To Billy's surprise, he was amenable to the idea.

'Now that the club is up and running,' he said, 'I think you can safely reduce the number of your visits to two or three a week. Why not get Golden Boy to visit you at home with a daily report?'

Laura was pleased to hear of the new arrangement.

'Welcome back to the family,' she said, hugging him tightly. 'And thanks for the eternity ring.'

It was a sad parting when Mam finally had to go. Half the servants on the compound turned out to wave goodbye. At the airport, there were tears all round as she went through the boarding gate. At the last minute, she turned and said to him, 'Remember what I told you, our Billy. Your family comes first, last and always. You just think on. But apart from that,' she added kissing him on the cheek, 'you'll do.'

Then she was gone.

You'll do, Billy thought. That was the highest accolade his mam could bestow, like being made a Knight of the Garter by the Queen.

Chapter Forty-Five

In June 1960, after 80 years of Belgian rule, the independence of the Congo was proclaimed and Macmillan's 'wind of change' became a force-nine gale. Civil war broke out in the province of Katanga and there followed an orgy of murder and mayhem. In early 1961, it was announced in Elisabethville that Patrice Lumumba, the Congo's Premier, had been massacred by villagers after escaping from custody.

The effects were felt in Kenya when thousands of fleeing Belgians, homeless and panic-stricken, sought refuge in Nairobi. They brought with them their cars and what few possessions they could salvage from the uprising. Most frightening of all, they brought stories of looting, raping and killing by Congolese mobs. If it could happen in the Congo, people said, it could happen to us here in Kenya.

In the European clubs, the possibility of revolt became the main topic of conversation and apocryphal tales of servants plotting to overthrow their *bwanas* were passed around, each group of gossips trying to outdo the other.

'My cook has assured me that nobody will rape the *memsahibs*, as happened in the Congo because the rebels there were drugged to the eyeballs.'

'My houseboy tells me that the African politicians are

selling lottery tickets at three bob a time for farms in the White Highlands.'

'I don't understand?' said her companion.

'It's like a game of tombola and when all the farms are taken from the white man after *uhuru*, the holders of the lucky numbers will win a nice mixed farm with its wheat and livestock. All for three shillings.'

'You mean, they believe that if they hold these tickets, they have a good chance of winning a farm?'

'Of course. They raffled off everything in the cities in the Congo. One Belgian air hostess was raffled a dozen times. They sold tickets for every house, motor-car and white woman in Leopoldville.'

Georgina told Vic Green that her *shamba* boy had told her not to worry because, as she had been a good *memsahib*, he would allow her to live in the garden shed after *uhuru*, he wouldn't boot her out, and she could cook for him. 'I must say I'm grateful to him,' she said.

'My overseer,' said Sir Charles Gilson, 'claims that some of my workers believe that after the white men are chucked out of the country, every African will take the *bwana*'s land, his women, and be given a wireless and a motor car.'

'That's nothing,' said another farmer. 'I am reliably informed that the talk in the market is that, not only shall we lose our land, our wives and our cars, but the *dukas* will be looted and the goods divided up among the people. There'll be plenty of shillings for everybody, no one will have to work and there'll be free *pombe*.'

'I don't think *we* shall fetch a high price,' Jill remarked to Laura. 'Africans think we European women are a sickly-looking lot and much too scrawny. What's more, we're considered pretty useless 'cos we can't carry heavy buckets on our heads.'

* * *

In the country at large, demands for the release of Jomo Kenyatta became more and more vociferous. Talk of revolution and rebellion was in the air. Even the boy delivering vegetables greeted customers at the door with his index finger raised and the slogan, '*Uhuru na Umoja*.' Freedom and Unity!

Things were becoming sticky and when people heard that the Governor of the Colony, Sir Patrick Renison, was to address the nation on radio they crowded round their little wireless sets hoping he'd relieve the tension by freeing Kenyatta. No such luck.

In ringing Churchillian tones, Renison declared that Kenyatta was 'the leader to darkness and death' and would never be released while he was governor.

There followed an outbreak of riots and demonstrations throughout the country in shops, factories, schools and colleges. Domestic staff refused to work and *memsahibs* had to dirty their hands, some of them for the first time. In Nairobi, shops were looted and the mobs threw bottles at the police who came to deal with the situation.

As he drove through Marangu market one Saturday morning, Billy's car was stoned by a group of youths. The rear window was broken and the children sitting on the back seat were showered with glass. There were no serious injuries but the family was severely shaken.

'Time to book our air tickets,' Laura announced.

At Marangu School, Henry Blewitt called an emergency staff meeting.

'It is time,' he said, 'to discuss the security arrangements for the compound. The Mau Mau may be a thing of the past but now we have the possibility of an uprising by the

Land Freedom Army and the Kenya African National Union. I have drawn up contingency plans in case of attack.'

'There is no evidence of danger from the LFA,' Joshua Kadoma protested. 'As for KANU, we are a peace-loving organisation and only want what is due to us. I think you are tilting at windmills.'

'If, as you suggest, we are attacked,' Job Karioki said, 'the best contingency plan will be to say our prayers.'

'Maybe so,' Blewitt said, 'but I prefer to rely on more practical defence measures. It's better to be safe than sorry, so this is my plan. My house will be used as a redoubt as I am the only one with a gun and I shall try to stem the first wave of attackers.'

What was going on? Billy asked himself. He hadn't bargained for any of this and no one had mentioned it when he had signed his contract at the Colonial Office in London back in 1958.

'Since Mr Nuttall's house is last on the compound,' Blewitt continued, 'it will be used as a hospital. My Wolseley and Mr Hopkins's Zephyr will be used as ambulances while Mr Sherwood's Fiat will be employed as back-up in case the others are destroyed by enemy action. It is vital, of course, that we are able to maintain radio contact with the police and army HQ.'

Billy didn't like the sound of any of this. It was a relief to hear Joshua Kadoma protest once again that Blewitt was talking through his hat.

'This is not the Congo. We are more civilised and I can assure you that the *bwanas* in this country need not fear that their precious *memsahibs* will be raped.'

'Don't worry about Blewitt,' Mike whispered to Billy. 'He likes to play at soldiers and can be relied on to make a mountain out of a mole-hill. Leave it to him and a protest soon becomes an armed insurrection.'

At home, Billy reported to Laura, 'Our car is to be used as an ambulance when we are attacked by KANU or the Land Freedom Army.'

'Let's hope nobody's car is used as a hearse,' she said.

'It's no joke, Laura. This could be serious.'

'Who's joking?' she replied.

Unrest amongst students in the colony manifested itself in school strikes which spread like a forest fire. Marangu was no exception for the day after the staff meeting the schoolboys walked out. There was no violence or noisy demonstration. When the staff turned up for work one Monday morning, there was nobody there to teach. During the night the students had simply packed their bags and left. The cooks and kitchen staff must have been in on it as they too had done a bunk. Joshua Kadoma, the local KANU representative, had been on duty that night and claimed that he'd had no inkling of it, which was difficult to believe because a hundred and fifty boys could hardly have walked out without someone seeing or hearing something. The dormitories were bare and deserted. The only things left behind were the hated straw boaters, their crowns punched through and flung on the beds. Billy strongly suspected Kadoma was somehow behind it because the smooth way the whole school had departed implied pre-planning and organisation.

'Schoolboys cannot go on strike,' Blewitt spluttered. 'They are not like workers, withholding their labour to achieve higher pay or better conditions. They are the ones who are suffering, not us. We teachers are the workers;

they are the raw materials. In teaching them we are processing that raw material.'

'Perhaps they no longer wish to be processed,' Billy said.

'That's not the way the students see it,' Kadoma explained calmly. 'They are making their protest and without the raw materials, as you call them, we are out of a job.'

Journalists from the *East African Standard* came to the school to investigate.

'Tell them nothing,' Blewitt commanded.

'Why have the students walked out?' the press asked.

'Don't know,' the teachers answered.

Next morning the headline in the *Standard* read 'School Walks Out Mysteriously'.

Later that day, a deputation of senior students reported in order to present, as was usual in labour disputes, a list of demands. Blewitt called another staff meeting so that they could hear what the students had to say. The school's dirty linen was to be washed in public. Godfrey Odinga, the Luo, was head spokesman but Blewitt had to have the first word.

'This is not the way public schoolboys should behave,' he bristled.

'That is the first point we wish to make,' Odinga said, interrupting him. 'We object to being treated as English public schoolboys. That is why we have spoiled our straw hats. We are not English schoolboys, we are Africans, and this is not Eton, it is Marangu.'

'I am only too aware that this is not Eton,' Blewitt replied testily. 'But I have tried to run the school on the lines of an English public school, in order to produce Christian gentlemen.'

'And that is what makes us cross,' Odinga said. 'We do not want to be English gentlemen. We do not want to learn Latin or Greek, or sing the "Eton Boating Song" at morning assembly. We refuse to salute the Union Jack and will no longer do the work of women, weeding the *shamba*. These things are not good for our country. Most of all, we were angry when you said we were the red KANU army.'

Blewitt looked puzzled when he heard this as did the rest of the staff.

'We have never said that you are the red KANU army,' he protested.

'One morning at assembly you said we looked like the red KANU army,' Odinga insisted.

'You mean, Fred Karno's Army?' Mike said, hardly able to hide his laughter.

'That is what I said,' the student said.

The rest of the discussion was devoted to the many other grievances the students had been nursing for years.

Moses Kanyuki, a Kikuyu, now spoke up. 'The food you serve us is a disgrace and fit only for pigs. It is stale and the cooks tell us it is full of weevils.'

'The maize comes straight from the Unga warehouse,' Blewitt stated.

'That is why it is stale; it has been in the warehouse too long. What is more, the porridge is served from buckets that you would use for animals.'

Mike gave Billy a surreptitious nudge. 'Told you so,' he whispered.

The list of grievances was long and at the end Blewitt looked shell-shocked. His cherished notions and authority had been challenged and he had no alternative but to agree to their demands. Billy had to admit a certain satisfaction in seeing Blewitt eat chunks of humble pie.

On the surface, the strike was about food, uniforms and school routine but Billy felt that these were symptoms of a deeper frustration at having to rely on the grace and favour of the *wazungu* for everything: their education and welfare, their laws, their government, even national independence.

In the end, the long period of civil disobedience in the country paid off. In August 1961, the 'Burning Spear of Kenya', seventy-one-year-old Kenyatta, was finally released after nine years in exile when a police plane flew to Maralal in the Rift Valley to bring him, his wife and their four daughters home. Parliamentary elections followed.

To his surprise, Billy discovered that he had been appointed as Returning Officer for the district of Njoro about two hundred miles away in the Rift Valley, one of the many polling stations set up throughout the country. It meant he would be away from home on three consecutive long weekends but, he reflected, as a Government Education Officer it came with the territory.

Chapter Forty-Six

Billy booked himself into the Staghorn Hotel in Nakuru and travelled out to look at the little town where the elections were to be held. Njoro was a small, up-country farming district and he was told to make arrangements for 20,000 electors to cast their votes in three separate elections. The actual polling was to take place in a large barn belonging to the Kenya Farmers' Union. There were two main political parties: the first was the Kenya Africa National Union (KANU) – Kenyatta's party which was greatly in the majority and included the main tribes, Kikuyu, Luo and Kamba; the other party was the Kenya African Democratic Union (KADU) which was made up of the minority tribes, the Masai, the Nandi, and the Kipsighis, all of whom feared the land-hungry Kikuyu.

Each party had chosen a pictorial symbol as its special symbol which was to appear next to the candidate's name on the ballot paper. KANU had a cockerel (*Jogoo*) while poor old KADU had a hand (*Mkono*). It hardly seemed worthwhile holding an election as the result was a foregone conclusion since Kenyatta was worshipped throughout the country and was expected to romp home.

To make sure there was no cheating, each voter had been issued with a voting card (*kipande*) and Billy had been given strict orders that no one was to be allowed to vote without one. To make doubly sure that the more zealous citizens did not vote more than once, electors were obliged to dip a finger in a bottle of indelible crimson ink. The right index finger for the House of Representatives election, the left index for the Senate, and the thumb for the Presidential.

It looked straightforward and as he had twelve election officers at his disposal, Billy looked forward to running a smooth operation. After all, he thought, do I not have a degree in public administration? Though that had, of course, been all theory while this was the real thing.

When the big day came round, he gathered his team of officers together for last-minute instructions and to answer any queries they might have.

'We shall have thousands of people passing through the polling station,' he told them, 'and so the most important thing is to keep the voters flowing, no matter what. I shall sit at the long table on the raised platform with a Kikuyu chief on one side and a Kipsighi on the other. If there are any problems, don't waste time arguing. Send people up to us immediately and we'll try to deal with the situation.'

'Most of the voters are illiterate,' Dr Guthrie from the Njoro Plant Breeding Station said. 'We'll have to register the vote for them. How do we maintain secrecy?'

Billy had given this much consideration and thought he knew the answer.

'As voters come through the door,' he said, 'we shall ask them if they know how to read. *Wajua kusoma?* If the answer is yes, the literates can record their vote secretly in the usual way. If the answer is no, the illiterates will have their vote taken orally and recorded by you. Simply ask them quietly which party they favour. Say "Which do you want, the Cock or the Hand?" In Swahili, "*Wataka nini Jogoo au Mkono*?" Keep your voice down to a whisper so as to maintain secrecy.'

'What about names?' Roy McPherson from Egerton Agricultural College asked. 'Are the voters' registers up to date?'

'As far as I know they are,' Billy replied, 'but the voting card is a double check that they have registered, and so it's "No card, no vote". One last point: don't forget that both KANU and KADU each have an observer present in the station and they will be watching us like hawks to see there's fair play. Now, best of luck to you all. Let's go get 'em.'

At eight o'clock, one of the officers opened up the main doors of the barn with a great show of ceremony. They could hardly believe the sight that met their eyes. The queue which had been building up since six that morning was now six deep and stretched off into the distance, at least three miles away. Many in the crowd had raised their umbrellas against the hot sun even at that early hour of the day.

'It's as bad as pre-sales hysteria outside Harrods,' Guthrie remarked.

Throughout the district, election time was hailed as a major event and for many peasants the most exciting event in their lives, the first time they had been allowed to cast their vote. Walking barefoot over rough terrain, they came pouring down from the hills in their thousands. When the barn doors opened, the crowd responded with cheering and shrill caterwauling. For many of them, it was party time.

The voters jostled their way in. Billy's organisation was immediately put to the test.

The indelible ink proved to be a curse. Voters stuck the correct finger into the bottle all right but without exception removed surplus fluid by flicking their fingers and spraying liberal quantities of crimson ink across documents and officers' faces until, by the end of the day, they looked like advanced cases of smallpox.

The 'problem cases' sent up to the high table proved to be a challenge for Billy and the chiefs. One such was a disfigured leper who lacked not only nostrils and lips, so that his teeth appeared to be fixed in a ferocious snarl, but also fingers. How could he dip a finger, the officer asked, if he didn't have any? Billy solved the dilemma by dabbing a small quantity of ink on the place where his finger would have been had he had one.

Within minutes of opening up, the station reverberated with the squawks of 'JOGOO!' and even the occasional 'Cock-a-doodle-doo!' as the illiterate voters vocalised their support for Kenyatta with pride and enthusiasm; the rooster noises continued unabated throughout the elections, prompting the Kikuyu chief by Billy's side to remark, 'It sounds like a large and busy hen-battery.'

So much for the secret ballot, Billy thought.

One would-be voter had a stock answer for all questions asked.

Jina lako nani? (What is your name?)

Sijui. (I don't know)

Wajua kusoma? (Do you know how to read?)

Sijui. Perhaps he had never tried and so was unsure as to whether he had this particular skill.

Wataka nini? Jogoo au Mkono? (Which do you choose? Cock or Hand?)

Sijui.

Billy asked the Kikuyu chief what they should do about this man.

'*Sijui*,' the chief said with a grin.

A more intractable case was the frail old man who, dressed in a long army greatcoat which trailed along the ground, appeared before the top table having been rejected by the system for having no voting card despite the fact he had queued for most of the day in the hot sun. Woe betide Billy and his officers had they let him vote because their every move was scrupulously monitored by the party observers seated on a bench opposite.

The position was explained carefully to the old man by the Kikuyu chief who told him to come back with his card and he would be allowed to register his vote. As they could get no response other than '*Mimi mzee*' ('I am an old man'), they had no alternative but to send him off back to his village. Several hours later he reappeared, still wearing his greatcoat, still mumbling '*Mimi mzee*', and still without his card, having waited the rest of the day in the line outside.

It was the Kikuyu chief who found the solution. He sent for a bottle of ink and, having dipped the old man's finger in it, sent him happily on his way, index finger held proudly aloft. The chief explained: 'In this case, the form was more important than the substance for when the headmen of the village gather round the cook-fires tonight, all the talk will be of this election. The elders will prove they have voted with the evidence of a finger and this old man, without an ink-stained finger, would have been put to shame. Now he can hold his head – and his finger! – up with pride.'

Children trying to vote were a problem. Birth certificates were unknown and ages had to be estimated, a skill at which both chiefs were adept. Scores of young girls who had obtained voting cards turned up to vote. They might well have succeeded had it not been for the vigilance of the KADU representative who objected at every turn as he saw his party's chances slipping down the plughole. Determining age, however, was not easy because some young African ladies arrived complete with baby (often borrowed for the purpose) on the back, scarf round the head, and basket on top. With these accoutrements removed, there stood a young girl of thirteen or fourteen. How to prove it was the problem. It was resolved by asking them to bring back a responsible adult who would vouch as to their age. Most didn't come back but one case was different. Three young girls aged no more than thirteen returned with their common husband who was about sixty-five years of age! He would not vouch though that they were of voting age since he was not, as he put it, 'entirely sure' since he had 'bought' them only three weeks previously.

The prize for effort had to go to the KADU observer who, on seeing (and hearing!) that things were not going well for his party, resorted to a cunning plan. One that caused Billy and the officers endless trouble.

Several hundred electors who were having their oral vote recorded in the usual vociferous way, objected strongly that they were being cheated and that their choices were not being recorded truthfully. 'A European plot,' they screeched.

Several women ran out of the polling station with their ballot papers to show the crowd outside how they were being deceived. Billy and his team were baffled. The answer came from the *askari* on duty outside.

The KADU representative had taken out a blackboard and, armed with this basic visual aid, was working his way along the crowd haranguing them as he went.

'Most of you have young children at school,' he proclaimed. 'Now if they get a sum wrong, what does the teacher do? Why, he puts an "X" next to the sum that is wrong. An "X" like this means a thing is wrong, that it's bad and you don't want it. So when you go inside be sure to put an "X" next to the name you think is wrong, next to the thing that is bad. Remember, an "X" means bad.'

It took Billy and his men a long time to restore public confidence.

On the afternoon of the second day there occurred an event which caused a great stir in the town. Inside the station things were proceeding normally when there was a flurry of activity outside with the banging of car doors, screaming ululating women and the sound of footsteps on the cinder path. The *askari* stuck his face round the door. 'Clear the station! Clear the station! The *Mzee* is here!' he bawled.

Not the old man again, Billy thought. But this wasn't any old man. This was *the* old man, Kenyatta himself.

They ordered everybody out and a few minutes later the entourage swept in. Kenyatta looked bigger and burlier than Billy had imagined, and judging by the frequent flicks of his fly whisk he was hot and tired. He gave Billy a limp handshake and sat down heavily at a bench, relishing the cool shade of the barn. His aides, dressed in dark pinstripe suits, scuttled behind him, also enjoying a few minutes' respite from the heat.

'Mr Kenyatta is going to freshen up, and then he'll be on his way,' one of them said.

'It is a great honour,' the Kikuyu chief said. 'If only we'd known he was coming we could have cleaned out the cloakroom.'

'Maybe we would,' the Kipsighi chief rejoined, 'and maybe we wouldn't.'

After a while, the toilet flushed and Jomo Kenyatta, the Father of the Nation, emerged from the primitive bathroom. Once again, he shook Billy's hand, wished him luck, took a deep breath and went out to join his joyous worshipping followers. No doubt, Billy reflected, there would be a brass plaque put up in the toilet one day to commemorate the event with a legend like, KILROY AND KENYATTA WERE HERE.

At the end of the elections, the ballot boxes were taken away under armed guard and deposited in the local police station from where they were shipped to Nairobi for counting.

It was with a great sense of relief that a whacked-out and red-spotted Billy drove home to Marangu.

'Well, how did it all go in Njoro?' Mike asked when they met in the staff-room on the first morning back.

'The same old story, Mike. We British believe our customs and practices are the best in the world so it's only right and proper that we foist them on to other people. It's a form of cultural aggression, making them adopt our ways. We do it in the things we teach, in literature, music, history and the rest. Now we're doing the same in politics. We'll only grant independence if they adopt a parliamentary democracy of the Westminster type with universal suffrage, secret ballots, and all the rest of the ballyhoo. But who's to say it's right for Africa? Maybe the notion of one man, one vote is alien to their culture.'

'And look how long that notion lasts,' Mike chuckled. 'It's a case of "One Man, One Vote, Once", and as soon as the colonialists have gone, it's back to the good old days of the all-powerful leader ruling the roost with a title like

"Saviour of the Nation" or "Life President" or some such.'

'Despite my moaning,' Billy said, 'a wonderful thing happened to me in Njoro.'

'And that was?'

'I shook hands with Jomo Kenyatta.'

'For God's sake, Hoppy, better not tell Sir Charles. He'll never forgive you.'

'But do you realise,' Billy continued, 'that this right hand of mine has now shaken the hand not only of the Great Mzee but also that of Sir John Barbirolli as well?'

'Maybe you should have a plaster cast made and mounted in a glass case,' Mike said.

Chapter Forty-Seven

Soon after the elections, the results became known and, as expected, Kenyatta and his KANU party were returned in a landslide victory. Kenya was now ruled by its own people for the first time. After that, things changed rapidly. Patrick Renison was replaced by Malcolm MacDonald, admired in Kenya as the 'colonial whizz kid', and it was rumoured that he was putting in a sixteen-hour day to speed things along. Meanwhile Renison was consigned to the equivalent of Outer Mongolia when he was made Adviser to Lord Hailsham on Sport and Physical Education.

It became decision-time for the expatriates working in the government services. A letter from the Colonial Office in London explained the options open. They could stay and help the newly independent country to find its feet or they could take early retirement and return to the UK.

Mike and Jill arranged a coffee morning for the school's expatriate staff to air their views and weigh up the pros and cons.

The Blewitts were all for going home.

'I'm due for normal retirement anyway,' the Major said. 'Daphne and I have our eye on a lovely place in Cornwall and that's where we're headed. The strike took a lot out of me and I think my idea of creating an Eton in Africa is no longer viable. We've made up our minds, we're off. The pension's good and the lump sum generous. We're taking the "golden handshake".'

Horace Nuttall was of the same opinion. He said, 'I gathered from remarks made at the time of the school strike that classical languages are not wanted and so I'm *persona non grata*. I shall be applying for a post in a public school in the south of England.'

The Lovemores who had not been in the colony long decided they'd had enough and were returning to the UK.

'Too many things here to put the wind up us,' said Phil Lovemore, glancing at Billy. 'We want a safe place where there aren't so many dangers. We want quiet, bilharzia-free lakes where we can go rowing without being sucked over waterfalls or attacked by crocodiles and hippos; green meadows where we can go for a walk without leopards and lions scaring the living daylights out of us. A place without scorpions, snakes, rabid dogs, mosquitoes, *tsetse* or *tumbu* flies.'

'Where on earth did you get such wild ideas?' Billy asked.

Jill and Mike were staying.

'We've come to love life in the tropics,' Mike said. 'The idea of returning to foggy old England doesn't appeal to us, and the package offered to those staying on is too good to pass up. Besides, where would I get a job in the UK? I've been away too long.'

'I agree with everything Mike says,' Jill added. 'We think our daughters are healthier and happier here, and the standard of education is good.'

'What about you, Hoppy? What's the Hopkins family going to do?' Mike asked.

They all turned to look at Laura and Billy.

'The jury's still out in our house,' Billy said. 'We're still talking it over.

'What's it to be, Laura?' he asked when they were alone. 'Mike has a good point when he says the incentives for staying on are attractive. Higher pay, better chance of promotion, excellent pension at the end. What do you think?'

'In my parents' generation it was the duty of the wife to move wherever the husband's job took him,' Laura said slowly. 'But it's not the same for me. We've done a four-year stint and I think it's time to go home.'

'OK, Laura. I'll go along with whatever you want to do, but I should remind you that I was in England only a couple of years ago and saw trends there I didn't like the look of. The country's become materialistic and selfish. It's a case of "I'm all right, Jack" and "What's in it for me?" '

'Perhaps that'll change. Didn't John F. Kennedy say, "Don't ask what your country can do for you; ask what you can do for your country"? That could apply equally well to Britain.'

'A pipe-dream,' Billy replied. 'And there's the ubiquitous television. People in England seemed obsessed with it. In nearly every home it's on all day even when no one is watching, like background wallpaper.'

'There's always the "off" switch,' she said. 'Apart from all that you've said, I want to go back. There's so much about home that I yearn for. First my own dear family, then all the other things we associate with England.'

'For example?'

'Oh, the Hallé Orchestra, Whitsuntide walks, Marmite, Pancake Tuesday, the Cup Final, Wimbledon.'

'But those things were never an important part of our lives.'

'Doesn't matter; they were there and part of our culture.'

'And what about the weather?' Billy grinned, thinking this was the clincher. 'Have you forgotten the rain and the fog?'

'Look, Billy, I'll take England, warts and all. I know people moan about the British weather but how I miss the four seasons! I love the snow and the frozen ponds in winter, the woods carpeted with bluebells in the spring, the song of the robin and the blackbird, even the smells of England.'

'You sound quite poetic.'

'I've had a lot of time to think about it, Billy, and I don't think there's a place in the world as beautiful or one where I'd rather live than dear, muddy, foggy Old England.'

'Say no more,' he said. 'I'm convinced. 'We're going.'

'But what about you, Billy, and those faraway places with the strange-sounding names? You've always suffered from divine discontent. As soon as you settle in one place, you pine for another.'

'Maybe that was true when I was a carefree young bachelor. Not any more. Now I have a family to think of. Time to settle down with pipe and slippers.'

The remaining few weeks in Marangu were spent in a round of farewell parties as one expatriate after another left for Blighty.

'Mark my words,' Sir Charles announced at one of these sessions, 'most of you will rue the day that you left this country. Probably when you get a taste of an English winter. For us farmers there is no choice, we have to stay.'

Billy and Laura were busy those last few days making final arrangements: paying bills, selling the car, and packing and shipping their crates. They had the problem of Brandy the dog and what to do with him but at the last moment Mike and Jill agreed to take him, much to their relief.

Their servants were sad to see them go. Billy gave each of them three months' salary and all the household possessions they were not taking with them. Twiga took all the garden tools and half of Billy's clothes; Euphoria many of Laura's dresses plus their double bed which they had bought 'specially in Nairobi; Dublin took the rest of Billy's clothes, the kitchen equipment, settee and lots of odds and ends.

'Please, *bwana*,' he said, 'could you write a letter for each of us to say that you have given us these things? Otherwise, the *askaris* will arrest us and accuse us of stealing them.'

Was this to be the new *uhuru?* Billy wondered. Guilty unless you can prove otherwise.

It was a sorrowful occasion when they said their last goodbyes to Mike and Jill, promising to stay in touch. There were tears in everyone's eyes as they shook hands and embraced affectionately.

'Remember what Livingstone said about the African bug,' Mike said. 'Once it bites, you will never get Africa out of your system. You'll be back one day, Hoppy,' he added, more in hope than belief, as Billy and his family boarded the government Land-Rover which was to take them to the airport.

At the Nairobi terminal they learned that there was to be a two-hour delay before their flight and, after checking in their suitcases, took the opportunity to relax in the airport lounge and catch up on a little shut-eye as they had been awake since the crack of dawn. As they dozed, Billy reflected on all that had happened in the previous four years. He felt a deep sadness and his eyes misted over as he thought about the many people they had met and were now leaving behind for good: servants, friends, and colleagues. As for his students, he wondered what value his teaching had been to them. Had he nurtured a genuine love and appreciation of English language and literature? Or had he been guilty of monumental conceit in believing that he'd had the right to foist his own country's culture on another people? It was a question to which he would never know the answer.

He was awakened from these melancholy thoughts by an announcement from the loudspeakers.

BOAC ANNOUNCE THE DEPARTURE OF THEIR FLIGHT 2364 TO LONDON HEATHROW. NOW BOARDING AT GATE 3. PLEASE HAVE YOUR BOARDING CARDS READY.

'That's us,' Billy said, gathering up their things. 'Come on, folks. Let's make tracks. Time to go home.'

High Hopes

Billy Hopkins

'Off to some la-di-dah college,' said Dad. 'You'll pick up bad ways from them toffs down there. I've read all about their goings-on in the Manchester Evening News.'

It's September 1945 and Billy Hopkins is off to London to train as a teacher. Despite his dad's warning, Billy survives two years in the Big City, and returns to take up his first teaching job in Manchester – on £300 a year! The catch is his first class, Senior Four, who bitterly resent the raising of the school leaving age, and are all set to take it out on their teacher – luckily the kid from Collyhurst has some tricks up his sleeve. And Billy's about to fall in love with the beautiful Laura. But is she, as his dad says, 'too good for the likes of us'?

Nostalgic, funny and romantic, HIGH HOPES vividly evokes northern life after the Second World War, and will keep you laughing till the very last page.

'A cracking yarn' *Warrington Guardian*

'How wonderful to have a book like this. A book that . . . pulls the reader back to that different world' *Manchester Evening News*

0 7472 6604 2

headline

Kate's Story

Billy Hopkins

'Dad, it's the happiest day of my life,' Kate said. 'I wish time would stand still and it could be today forever.'

It's June 1897, and Kate is celebrating her eleventh birthday on the day of Queen Victoria's Diamond Jubilee. But Kate's joy is shortlived for tragedy strikes and, before long, her family is evicted from their home in Ancoats, Manchester. With no wages coming in, a mother unable to cope, and the threat of her siblings being split up, Kate has to grow up fast.

Through the ensuing journey of hope and heartache Kate learns to fight against the odds with determination. An indomitable spirit and bright sense of humour help her to survive the hardships of the workhouse and the sorrows and losses suffered during the Great War. But will they be enough to eventually bring her the happiness she lost as a child?

Nostalgic and poignant, *Kate's Story* is a truly heart-warming read, rich in Billy Hopkins' trademarks of warmth, laughter and triumph over adversity.

'I have just finished *Kate's Story* amidst tears and laughter . . . I will treasure this book for the rest of my life' Mrs Edna Wright, Manchester

'*Kate's Story* is excellent . . . A truly magnificent book' Dr Gus Plaut, Essex

'This is to tell you how much I enjoyed reading *Kate's Story* – a lovely mixture of humour and pathos' Dr John Spence, West Midlands

0 7472 6852 5

headline

madaboutbooks.com

Also by Billy Hopkins

Our Kid
High Hopes
Kate's Story